ENDLESS TIME

ENDLESS TIME

Frances Burke

RANDOM HOUSE
AUSTRALIA

Random House Australia
an imprint of
Random Century Australia Pty Ltd
20 Alfred Street, Milsons Point NSW 2061

Sydney Melbourne London
Auckland Johannesburg
and agencies throughout the world

First published in Australia in 1992
Copyright © Frances Burke 1992

All rights reserved. No part of this publication
may be reproduced, stored in a retrieval system,
or transmitted in any form or by any means,
electronic, mechanical, photocopying, recording
or otherwise, without the prior written permission
of the Publisher.

National Library of Australia
Cataloguing-in-Publication Data

   Burke, Frances, 1937–
   Endless time.

   ISBN 0 09 182642 X.
A823.3

Typeset by Midland Typesetters, Victoria
Printed by Australian Print Group, Victoria
Production by Vantage Graphics, Sydney

This book is dedicated to all the people who have ever loved and feared to lose their love and most especially Trisha Sunholm, a great friend, a gifted critic and an unfailing supporter.

PREFACE

Devon 1806

SHE STOOD BY the window, holding herself stiffly against the surge of shock and pain. Her eyes did not focus on the printed words she held in her hand, words of hate gouged into the paper with a furious quill, lines etched in poison distilled by a diseased mind. Instead, she gazed unseeingly across the rose garden, shimmering in the heat given off by baking bricks, and wished she could recall the past minute and destroy the note before she ever opened it. But she could not.

'May you cry out in grief and pain and long vainly for release – may evil be your companion and your torment – death waits to embrace you. Be warned.'

For as long as she lived she would not be able to erase those words from her memory. She would know that someone within the close circle of her family and friends, a person who looked at her with a false mask of love, wanted her dead.

Antony's voice rose up the stairwell, calling to her. She crumpled the note and thrust it into her skirt pocket, schooling her face to hide her distress. He must not know. Nothing could be permitted to spoil this idyllic hour spent together with their child. It was the time she most cherished, and today was especially important to her.

'In here, in the nursery.' She ran to the door and opened it.

Antony bounded up the stairs and took her eagerly into his arms, looking down at the neat brown head that barely reached his shoulder.

'You are blooming today, my Jenny. I could pin you on my coat and wear you like a rose.'

His voice was deep and filled with love. It reverberated in the small room.

The two-year-old Chloe looked up from her position on the rug and crowed delightedly. 'Papa! Look! Bocks.'

Smiling, he drew Jenny with him across to the hearth and went down on his knees beside the child. Having admired the blocks and kissed the sweet face of the owner he rose and turned again to his wife, saying with mock severity, 'What is this piece of news that will not wait? I have exercised my mind over it since you teased me at breakfast, and I can be patient no longer.'

She looked at him, drawing her hand down the lean cheek, admiring the strong line of jaw, wishing to keep this moment perfect and enshrined in her heart.

Finally she said, 'We are to have another child in the spring, Antony. Perhaps this time it will be an heir for you.'

He stood silent for a moment. His eyes glistened. 'Boy or girl, it matters not. My beautiful Jenny, my lady sweet. No words can describe my happiness.'

In response, she laid her head on his shoulder and he led her to the couch where they sat in harmony, silently savouring the moment. She was glad she had waited to tell him. Their time together was so precious, and especially this daily hour spent in the nursery. The estate took him from her during most of the daylight hours, but she did not grudge him his enjoyment of the land. Born to position, his heart was in this particular corner of the Devon countryside, and she knew he longed for a son to inherit the great Marchmont holdings, and a name as proud as any in England.

Their hour passed all too quickly. Antony removed Chloe from his lap and kissed his wife once more.

'I must leave you now. It is time for Chloe's sleep and I have a dozen errands away from here.'

Reluctantly Jenny let him go, unaccountably sad to see him disappear down the curving stair. She watched him emerge from the tower door into the sunlight, look up to the window and raise a hand, before walking briskly off towards the stables. When tears filled her eyes she dashed them away and busied herself with her child's needs, enjoying the small services she could do in place of the nursemaid, and singing to cover the feeling that her wonderful day had in some way become shadowed. The letter in her pocket had begun to do its poisonous work.

The dog had been restless all morning, moving up and down the stairs from room to room, sometimes going to a window to stand on hind legs with nose pressed to the glass, staring out. Twice Jenny had left her baby and gone to look through the same windows. It was unsettling to see Feathers behaving in such an uncharacteristic way. The spaniel had more sense than many of his breed, and did not fuss over nothing.

But there was nothing to be seen. The east window of the nursery, set up in the tower because Jenny loved its curved walls and deep window embrasures, looked over a shrubbery and down a flagged path to the main carriageway. Nothing stirred under the leaden sky. Not even a gardener was in sight. When the dog moved to the southern window Jenny followed, putting a hand on the domed head and saying softly, 'What is it Feathers? What do you feel?' It was obvious from the tremors under her fingers that the animal was upset.

Yet nothing moved in the painted landscape. It looked as still and two-dimensional as a page in a *Book of Hours*. No leaves stirred, no lizards ran across the stone balustrade below. The Manor slept like Beauty's castle in a dreaming world. It seemed to Jenny that she, Chloe and the spaniel were the only living things, the only reality in that space of time.

She shivered, and stroked the dog's long silky ear, trying to wipe out her own eerie fantasy. Telling Feathers to lie quietly she promised him a walk later in the cool of the evening. She went back to Chloe and sat down on the rug to show her once more how to build her little coloured blocks into a tower.

Her mind followed her husband out riding through his fields of dried grass to talk with his tenant farmers, all thoroughly tired of this hot summer, and all speaking in the most doom-laden terms. As if Antony could possibly control the weather, she thought, indignant for his sake. He had laughed when telling her that even the animals hung their heads and looked sullen when he went by. How weary he must be of complaints.

Chloe squealed as the blocks tumbled down again, claiming her mother's attention. Jenny smiled and held up her hands in mock horror. A wave of love swept over her as she felt the chubby fingers tugging at her skirt. Was there ever a child so plump and fair as hers? Or one so loving? At two years still clumsy on her feet, Chloe gave promise of future grace and beauty, in her mother's eyes at least.

Jenny herself possessed a certain wren-like charm, but had long ago decided that her claims to beauty were best exchanged for other attributes – an interest in others, a certain skill with paints and brushes, and housewifely abilities. Antony clearly saw more. It seemed that he appreciated a pale skin lightly dusted with freckles, or so he often said. Her brown eyes reminded him of a pet doe he had loved as a child, and her long neck was made to be adorned with pearls. It was a mystery to her, but in Antony's eyes these qualities managed to outweigh her lack of presence, and the limp that resulted from a long-ago fall from a horse.

He, on the other hand, was the epitome of a maiden's dream. She chuckled at the thought of his face if she were ever to put this thought into words. But he truly was quite the most handsome man she had laid eyes on, even amongst London's finest. She felt like a dwarf beside him, and his muscular frame reminded her of a boxer she had once seen at a country fair, stripped to the waist and ready to take on any man who dared. Swarthy as a gypsy, lithe and fit as a hunting animal, yet he had an innate gentleness that called to her own nature.

She had loved him from the first moment she saw him dismount in her own village street to interpose himself between a furious drayman's whip and the broken-down horses struggling to move an impossible load. Without heat, he had made clear his objections then dealt with the matter, and ended by arriving at the rectory gate leading two very unlikely additions to his stables.

She had loved him then, totally, and as she thought, hopelessly, for the fashionable world of Lord Antony Marchmont lay far distant from her own. It was her father's death that brought about their meeting. On hearing of his sister's widowed state, the Earl of Roth insisted that she and her children should move from Yorkshire and make their home with him. He sent his only son, Antony, with the proposal, and to act as escort on the journey down to Devon. It had been a time of surprises.

Her Papa's death had not grieved Jenny too much. He had not been a loving father, although she had enjoyed working as his assistant, visiting the needy, helping where she could. Her life was even and slow-paced, a life of service save for her painting. Her mother's high connections made the neighbourhood wary, and that fact, together with her twisted ankle and lack of expectations had, she believed, made her ineligible for marriage. It was hardly to be expected that she would tumble into love with her own cousin, nor that he should return her affection.

Recalling just how he had reciprocated, she blushed and laughed, and looked down to see Chloe's brown eyes, so like her own, smiling up at her.

'Bocks, Mama. Now.' She tugged impatiently at her mother's gown.
'Yes, darling. Of course. We shall build the pretty blocks up again.'

While mother and child played together the afternoon moved on. At intervals the dog got up and resumed his pacing, now made more irritating by accompanying whines of distress. Jenny offered to let him out, but he didn't seem to want to go. He made her nervous. Several times she went to the window, then to the door, looking out down the stairs, but without seeing anything to disturb her. The poisonous note in her pocket seemed to weigh her down, destroying her peace of mind.

She had put Chloe down to sleep, and now she wanted to regain that peace in the pleasure of sorting through the box of books newly arrived from London. She was an avid reader and especially looked forward to a new volume of poems recommended by a friend. Titled *Hours of Idleness*, they were the first works of a certain young Lord Byron, and they had considerably impressed her literary-minded correspondent. But it was not possible to concentrate with Feathers misbehaving like this.

'What is the matter with you today, boy?' The dog looked at her and whimpered softly. With a sigh, she opened the door and pushed him out. 'You are too restless. Go and chase rabbits for an hour.' She went back to the books.

While she had been dealing with her recalcitrant pet she had failed to hear the door close downstairs, and the sound of a bolt being drawn into place. There was now no exit from the tower rooms into the manor itself. The outer door still remained open. A shadow moved in and out from the shrubbery, very busy, very silent. There was no one to hear the splash of lamp oil from the overturned jugs, no one to smell the fumes rising from a rope of sheets trailing across the stone passageway and up the first few turns of the stairs.

The butler, Bates, rested off-duty in his pantry, his swollen legs propped up on a stool. The heat did not agree with him. Mrs Bates, too, had her feet up for a half-hour on the couch in the housekeeper's room. Elsewhere, the maids and menservants took advantage of their freedom in different ways, none of them in the direction of the nursery wing where a kind but vigilant young mistress might sight them.

Other members of the household had taken refuge from the stupefying heat either in their bedchambers or down by the lake, under the somewhat dubious impression that there was always a breeze over water. Even the horses in the stable nodded. Only Feathers padded warily down the spiral stairs, his claws tapping on stone as he avoided the strips of offensively pungent cloth affecting his sense of smell.

The shadow drew back behind the door, and as the dog passed by, stepped out and struck him down. Throwing aside the club, the shadow grasped the unconscious animal by the collar and dragged him into the shrubbery, leaving him hidden under rhododendron branches still in full and glorious bloom.

By the time Jenny had soothed her child to sleep the business was done. The tinder had been struck, the burning spill thrown into the pool of oil, the outer door slammed and locked against a fountain of fire that erupted through the base of the tower. The shadow watched and waited.

Soon smoke foamed under the door and through the open window on the stairs, followed by bursts of cinders from burnt cloth and timber. Flames roared up the well with the runaway force of fire in a soot-filled chimney. The walls seemed to pulse with heat. Burning ash dropped through the air, setting alight parched bushes below.

The shadow ran.

Two miles away Antony Marchmont turned his horse toward home.

Ashbourne Manor, while recognised as one of the notable houses of Devon, could not compare with the principal seat of the most noble Earl of Roth, a somewhat draughty castle in Wales. In fact, Lord Edward, under his various titles, held no less than six country homes, as well as Rothmoor House in London. The newly restored Ashbourne Manor, however, remained his favourite, with its parklands famous for stands of hundred-year-old oaks, and rhododendron terraces running down to a valley where a stream-fed lake lay covered in lilies and water hyacinth. Protected by rising hills to the north, with money and attention lavished upon it, it was a Palladian gem, reknowned through the southern counties and beloved by the family who owned it.

Antony, as heir to the Rothmoor title and estates, had chosen to make this his permanent residence when he married. His aging father retired into the west wing to nurse his arthritic limbs and bask in the love of his recently widowed sister, Lady Evelyn, and his new daughter-in-law, who was also his niece. The coming of Chloe had been a slight disappointment, but the vine was fruitful.

Antony decided to give a party in celebration of his wife's twenty-third birthday. Other members of the family would travel from London and stay at Ashbourne, and friends and neighbours would join them, happy to share the sunny fortunes of such a respected household.

Antony was still a mile distant when the shrubbery beneath the west tower exploded and bloomed in a ball of light. Flames reached up over the stones like some new, virulently active creeper, and a veil of heat caused the stones to shiver and dance like a desert mirage.

He dug spurs deep into his horse's belly, and man and animal seemed to take to the air, speeding towards the distant spectacle.

Jenny's first warning came when she smelled smoke, acrid and unmistakable. She put aside her books and limped to the door. A rustling sound, like mice in paper, made her pause. Then she flung the door wide.

A blast of hot air hit her with the force of a gale. A choking black streamer spiralled up the stairway, enveloping her, surging into her lungs. She coughed, struggling for clean air. Tears streaming from her eyes, she clawed at the entrance, blinded and disoriented. Her groping fingers found the handle and she slammed the thick panelling shut. Leaning against the door she strove for control. Gradually her breathing eased. Panic skirted around the edges of her mind. She forced it back. She had to find a way of escape for herself and Chloe.

There were only two entries to the tower, one in the outer wall, and one leading into the east wing of the house. Dear God! She was cut off from both.

The windows? One glance showed the fire there, too. Heated air, smoke so thin that it was transparent, floated beyond the glass, and even while she watched several panes cracked and flew inwards, scattering deadly diamonds all over the chair where she had been sitting just minutes ago.

Now, for the first time she heard the voice of the fire, a crisp crackling punctuated with sounds of exploding bushes and glass shattering. Chloe started to scream.

'Don't, baby. Mother is here. You are safe.' Jenny clutched the child frantically to her chest, her concentration destroyed by Chloe's fear. What in God's name was she to do? Where could she go?

The roof. If she could carry Chloe up there and somehow find a way out onto the leads, perhaps they could cling there long enough for someone to find them and bring them down.

But first there was the stairwell to be faced.

Feathers! He was out there. Her faithful dog must have gone down into the inferno, pushed by herself! She could not rush out and search for him. There was no way down those stairs. No, Chloe needed her. She was the important one now.

Taking a jug of water from the stand she saturated a small blanket and wrapped it around her child, now crying wildly and flinging her small fists about. Crooning soothingly through the wet mask she formed from a napkin tied about her mouth and nose, Jenny wasted no more time. She picked up Chloe and opened the door.

Heat. Unimaginable heat, searing skin and hair, making a mockery of the mask, stabbing and tearing at her lungs. She staggered back a step, then, eyes tightly closed, felt her way along the burning stone to the upward flight of steps. Her feet scorching in their thin-soled slippers, she forced herself up, step by step, a whimper of pain escaping her whenever her arm came into contact with the wall. Elbows blistered and bleeding, instantly dried into crusts of blood. Twice she fell on her bare arms, protecting Chloe, her cries lost in the terrible cacophony that pursued her from below, growing ever closer.

The exploding timbers that fed the fire were like cannon shot echoing through the tower. The red glare of hellfire beat against her closed eyelids. She was blinded, deafened, her throat closed and parched, her feet two baking lumps of meat.

She longed to give up. The struggle was too much. She could not go another step. Then she felt the shivering bundle in her arms and willed herself on. Her heartbeat drummed in her ears, louder even than the fire. When she forced her eyelids apart the tower walls swung in dizzying arcs about her. She swayed with each pace she took, her strength almost done. But something other than willpower had taken over. The loving bond with her husband and child gave her the thrust she needed. With each step she soundlessly repeated her litany of 'Antony, Chloe, Antony, Chloe', drawing on the spiritual underpinnings of her life, forcing herself to move . . . move . . .

She rounded the last bend breathing rapidly but a little more easily. There was fresh air here. Tearing off the mask she turned eagerly to the light. It was not a window. The builders of the tower had made a small opening for air under the roof, leaving it unglazed. A dog might have squeezed through, but not a grown woman, however small.

Frantically her eyes searched the groined arches of the roof. It was a perfect lid on a pepperpot. There was no way out. With a mewling wail no louder than a kitten's, she slid to the floor, grazing her burning face against the wall.

It was Chloe's screaming that brought her back to sanity. Chloe. There must be a way to save her. She dragged herself to her protesting feet and stood on tip-toe to peer through the air vent.

Below her a group of men and women formed a chain with pitchers and pails leading up from the lake. More men were busy lashing together lengths of ladder to prop against the wall, but clearly they would never reach her eyrie.

Then she saw Antony, running as if all the furies pursued him, to fall upon the door with an axe. The bright blade swung in the sunlight, arcing wide, and she imagined she heard its impact on the timber. Her heart contracted. Antony, her dear love. She knew she was looking on him for the last time. Even if he gained entry he never could pass through the fire below.

But acceptance came hard. She cried out to him, and as if he heard he raised his head, the axe halted in mid-swing.

'Antony.'

His face reflected her agony of mind.

'I love you Antony,' she croaked, knowing he would hear with his heart, as he always did.

His arms reached up hopelessly, longingly. Her own heart heard him calling to her. Then he returned to the attack on the door, working like a madman. Jenny sank back onto the floor and clutched her baby, waiting.

Moments later she knew her time had run out. A massive eruption from below brought her to her feet, the whole tower rumbling in shock. The fire gave a mighty bellow and surged higher, seeking her, racing closer by the minute. The floor began to smoke and she remembered that it was made of boards, like the floors below. That explained the terrible noise – the other floors giving way. Hers would be next.

She fled to the opening again, trying to hold Chloe clear of the heated wall as she peered below. They knew. The human chain had stopped working. Men and women stood with faces upturned, static, helpless. There was nothing to be done. Although the outer door had finally given under Antony's onslaught, wicked tongues of flame licked out, defying any attempt to enter. He was struggling madly in the grip of several men.

Inside the tower, the fire fed on the increased oxygen. Renewed, it stampeded up the stairwell. Jenny could feel it licking at her back. Without hesitation she tore the blanket from Chloe and pushed her through the opening, leaning far forward to hold her on the brink. Her husband looked up and ceased to struggle. Their eyes met in a last farewell. As Antony shook himself free of his captors, Jenny opened her arms and let Chloe fall.

She saw him catch her. She heard her own name carried up on the draught of superheated air.

'Jennnyyyyy . . .'

The floor moved.

Pain, incredible mind-searing pain spiked through her body as flames rushed up the back of her gown. Her hair burst into a blazing corona. But it was not as fierce as the realisation that she had been cheated. All the glorious promise of life had been a fraud. Love itself was a fraud, a brief moment of paradise, then gone. All, all gone. Her cry of disillusion rose and was shattered in the incandescent blast of bursting stone and timber.

The tower wavered and fell in upon itself, carrying her body down into the heart of the fire.

CHAPTER 1

Today

OUTSIDE, LONDON THROBBED at its usual frenetic tempo. Traffic, lights, music, people, all whirled by in the wild race to nowhere in particular.

Inside, the crowded gallery was totally Mayfair. Although the room had a narrow frontage the walls swept back nearly eighty feet and the roof curved far above, its clever domed effect extended by illumination that was both subtle and dramatic. Spotlights hung from pendulous metal webs, highlighting the paintings which seemed to be placed in sporadic clumps like bright fungus springing from their pale-olive suede background. The whole setup had been the inspiration of Theodore Sampson himself. His technique had become justly famous, and no doubt accounted in part for the huge commercial success of his gallery.

Tonight was a special occasion, very special. No one in living memory could recall one similar. Tonight Theo had moved the main spotlight away from his own immaculately coiffed head and on to one of his staff, the rather stiff-looking girl he had firmly attached to his arm as he cruised the gallery.

Karen Courtney was not enjoying the limelight, and couldn't help showing the fact. She hung back, a vessel in tow rather than cruising under her own steam. Her willowy frame overshadowed Theo, who, in the opinion of one waspish critic, could have slipped through a closed door sideways.

Karen felt more than usually gawky. Her dark hair hung forward, hiding her cheeks, her wide mouth had become set in a permanent grin, and her lovely amber eyes behind their large protective lenses looked hunted.

Theo Sampson's young-old face beamed at her. 'What you need is a couple of glasses of champagne, Karen. Then you'll start to enjoy yourself. After all, my dear girl, this whole show is in your honour.' His smile switched off, then on again. 'Do make an effort, dear.'

'I'm sorry, Mr Sampson. It's difficult for me, this overnight celebrity business. The country mouse syndrome, you know.' She spoke through gritted teeth, but widened her own smile.

'Call me Theo, dear, now you are definitely senior ranking – if you stay with us that is. I do hope sudden fame has not decided you to set up as a full-time artist. Very risky, dear, especially these days.'

He knew darned well she had no intention of leaving, Karen thought. She had two good reasons for staying – loyalty and money – but Theo Sampson never could resist a prick with his little needle, even while playing the benefactor. Still, she respected him as an art dealer, she liked him as a person, and he had done her a huge favour by insisting she give a one-woman showing in his own gallery. It was rare for each work to be taken down and replaced by those of a single artist, and a complete unknown, at that. He had even arranged for the critics to come – and go away again without saying much. Oh, well. Tomorrow's papers would tell her the worst.

'Miss Courtney, I can't tell you how much I admire your work . . .'

'Miss Courtney, tell me, where do you get your inspiration? . . .'

'Karen, I'd like you to meet John Betheld, Chairman of the Betheld Corporation, and a connoisseur of new fresh work, such as your own.'

'How do you do, Mr Betheld. I'm so pleased to – '

'Oh, Madame Rothness! How delightful to see you here this evening! Allow me to present our latest discovery, Miss Courtney . . .'

And so it went on. Karen felt like a top being whipped and spun from point to point, scarcely at rest long enough to complete a sentence or to take in what was said to her. Never at ease in crowds, she could feel herself cringing each time her boss opened his mouth, knowing she was about to become the subject of scrutiny and discussion.

Rescue came unexpectedly. The latest man who had taken her hand in greeting, someone whose face was just another set of features among so many, did not release his hold. Instead he detached her from Theo's arm and drew her aside into a blessed bit of shadow, saying over his shoulder, 'Your little celebrity looks as though she could do with a breather, Theo. You run along and charm a few more duchesses and I'll revive Miss Courtney.'

Karen sank back into a corner couch, dropped her bag on the floor and rested her head against the cushion, eyes closed. She was vaguely aware that her knight errant had disappeared as swiftly as he had popped up. However, he came back almost immediately with a full champagne glass.

'Thank you. I'm grateful. But no more champagne, please.'

'It's Perrier water. Best thing in an overheated room filled with windbags. Drink up.'

As he leaned towards her his sleeve caught on one of Theo's projecting metal webs. The glass tipped and the Perrier water poured on the carpet at Karen's feet.

'Oh, Lord! I'm sorry . . .'

Her smile was the first genuine one of the evening. 'Don't worry. You missed me.'

'I'll get you another glass. Don't go away.'

She watched him hurry off to waylay another waiter, and grinned to herself. He made her think of a large, amiable bear shuffling along without any great purpose. Yet he got what he wanted, she noted, quickly and without fuss.

Demurely she accepted the fresh drink, drained the glass, then handed it back to him. 'Your prescription worked. But you are scarcely complimentary to Theo's guests.'

He flung up the hand holding the glass, fortunately now empty, and gestured towards the nearest frame. 'I'm no expert on art, but to listen to this lot you'd think they'd guided Picasso's first steps and done the preliminary sketches for the ceiling of the Sistine Chapel.'

Karen laughed. 'They're not as bad as that. Some even love the work they collect and appreciate what the artists are trying to portray. They're not all looking for capital gain. I'm surprised that you are here, if you have no interest in art.'

'I didn't say that. I like some of it. In fact, I quite like a lot of yours.' He bent forward to peer at the nearest painting, a slightly surreal portrait of a woman whose dark hair and eyes dominated the canvas so that the rest of her features and the background remained indeterminate. It was Karen's most recent piece and she had mixed feelings about it. In fact, she had only added it to the exhibition at the last minute, strictly on loan.

'That's hardly representative, I'm afraid,' she said hastily, getting to her feet. 'In fact, I'm not even sure that it's finished.'

'Oh, I think it's finished, all right,' he said, his eyes on the picture as he spoke. 'In fact, it's one of the most compelling modern portraits I've come across. Is she a sorceress?'

'Morgan Le Fay, or somesuch? I don't think so. I call her "Bella Donna".'

He turned to her, interested. ' "Bella Donna", eh? Deadly Nightshade. Yes, it's apt. It's also very good.'

Unused to compliments with a ring of verity, Karen felt a warm blush of pleasure. This turned to a gasping laugh as the man moved too quickly and caught his toe against the chair leg, losing his balance. Karen's arm shot out to catch his, steadying him.

'Thanks. Your reflexes are pretty good, too. Do you lift weights in your spare time?'

Karen shrugged. 'Self-defence classes. Some people need a little more backup than others.' Her expression discouraged further questioning. But she really looked at him as an individual for the first time.

He scarcely fitted in with the sophisticated crowd here tonight. She passed over his clothes. No fashion plate herself, she was simply aware of a casual shabbiness, a sort of 'take me as I am' air about them. His hair, as black as her own, reminded her of a dog's pelt, a shaggy hound of indeterminate breed. It drooped over his forehead and curved back from his cheeks, hiding his ears. He looked thirtyish, with rather heavy Semitic features, a wide thin mouth, and dark liquid eyes, somewhat baggy underneath.

Most noticeable of all was the aura of cheerfulness that radiated from him. Like a rock heated by hours of desert sunshine he gave off warmth to anyone within reach. She had felt immediately drawn to him, and now she could see why.

He bore her survey with a smile. 'Sorry about all the gymnastics. It happens a lot to me.'

'You were born with two left feet?'

'Nope. Just can't seem to see over my nose.'

She smiled back at him, and as if with unspoken agreement, they sat down together on the couch. Karen thought he was quite a reasonable looking man, and liked his joking attitude towards his appearance.

'Tell me something about yourself, Miss Courtney.'

'Why? Are you a reporter after copy?'

He looked thoughtfully at her wary expression. 'Would you mind if I was? A piece on an upwardly mobile young painter might be just the thing for the art and lit section of my favourite rag.'

Her eyes narrowed, then she relaxed. 'You almost had me convinced. However, Theo expressly forbade the press tonight, excepting the critics, of course. And he seems to know you.' When he merely shrugged, she went on, 'I don't know that I like your choice of words. "Upwardly mobile" doesn't sound a bit like me.'

'What, no ambition?'

'Of course I'm ambitious. But my work has always been very private to me. This is the first time I've exhibited. I also have the judgment to know that I'm not yet in the Picasso/Da Vinci league.'

He nodded. 'Sure. You have to be realistic. Although, if Theo's prepared to back you, I'd say you're just about ready to fly. What's your ultimate aim?'

Karen felt backed into a corner. What had begun as a pleasant conversation was beginning to feel like interrogation.

'Let's not talk about me all the time. I'd like to hear about your work. What do you do when you're not masquerading as a reporter?'

'And falling over couches? I'm a health worker of sorts. Nine to five, six days a week. It keeps me busy.' His smiling eyes probed gently. 'You're avoiding my question.'

'And you're very persistent.'

'I'm sorry. It's simply that I like to talk about other people's aims in life. I have a few myself, and it seems to make them come alive when I talk about them. They take on an edge. I get enthused all over again. Don't you ever do that?'

She shook her head, making her dark curtain of hair swing. Damn him for his friendly curiosity. He wasn't really a threat, she knew that. Still her feeling of agitation wouldn't go. It was getting stronger.

'Curious. I guarantee you do have an aim buried in there somewhere, all the same. Don't you want to set the world on fire with your painting, for instance?'

Karen erupted. 'Okay. I'll tell you. I have a very definite aim – independence!' The word came out like a juggernaut, powered by emotion. 'I don't ever want to be ruled by someone else. I want to be my own person.' Her voice, normally pleasantly low and husky, had taken on depth and intensity. The amber eyes hidden behind spectacles turned to a glowing pale gold like a cat's, with enlarged irises. 'No one will be able to take from me and mine. We will be safe.'

He whistled softly and expressively.

Embarrassed at the way she had revealed herself she scrambled up, not looking at him. 'I'd better go back now. Theo will expect me to circulate.'

'You're not enjoying this, are you?'

'I'm under an obligation.' Leaving the shadowed anonymity of the corner she stepped into the light, flinching at the sight of Theo heading toward her with a self-important looking dowager in tow and attendant satellites all ready to hem her in.

'Be off with you, Tom Levy. You've had our star to yourself for quite long enough.' Theo sounded genial, but he clearly meant what he said.

Tom bowed, and almost toppled over again as he tripped over Karen's bag and righted himself just in time. The satellites sniggered as he retrieved it and handed it to her. She scarcely noticed. Already the group had closed around her, absorbing her like an amoeba, making her a part of them. The bombardment of words began, and as Tom drifted away she forgot him.

Later, in a rare quiet moment, she found herself alone in a corner. Taking a long breath she turned her back to the room, pretending to be a visitor viewing the nearest work. It was a vivid full-length portrait in reds and blues, the light falling on the genderless face and body in geometric patterns, giving the subject a harlequin air, a kind of otherworldly restlessness. It seemed on the point of leaping from the canvas. There was a vitality about the work that captured the attention. Karen nodded. This one pleased her.

She moved to a smaller picture beside it, a series of smudges in plums and greys which, when viewed from a distance, became a particularly opulent cat engaged in cleaning a hind leg. This painting expressed a feeling of harem-like decadence, with the animal's total self-absorption, its leisurely stretching and abandonment to the stroking of its own tongue.

'This I find indecent. I wonder if anyone realises that the sitter is a particularly macho tomcat named Dali?'

Karen swung around. 'Billie!' She flung her arms about the little woman who had spoken. 'What are you doing here? How did you find out? Why didn't you call and let me know you were coming? How are you?'

A muffled croak emerged from the area of her chest.

'If you will let me out before I suffocate I'll be glad to fill in a questionnaire.'

Laughing, Karen released her. 'Sorry, Billie. I guess I got carried away.'

Wilhelmina Carnot tugged at her silk jacket, adjusted her collar and surveyed her niece critically. There was little likeness between the two. At fifty-seven years, and weighing no more than one hundred pounds wringing wet, Billie could give many a younger woman pointers. From her short, stylishly cut pink hair to her pale snakeskin pumps she radiated presence – a useful quality for the proprietress of an employment agency.

'Karen, I long ago despaired of you acquiring any sartorial sense, but . . . dull purple, against your hair and skin!'

Karen shook her head impatiently. The offending hair had begun to tangle about her shoulders like a slightly frayed curtain.

'What does that matter? I'll never be a beauty. So you go on providing the chic and the business brain of the family, and I'll stick with painting. Now, will you answer my question?'

'Which one, my dear? Oh, very well. I learned about your showing quite by accident from the young woman who occupies the hovel next door to yours – a blonde who could definitely use a camomile rinse.'

'But – '

'I flew across to celebrate your birthday, child. You are twenty-three tomorrow. Have you forgotten? *En plus*, Paris has been sultry for weeks, and I need a little vacation. Simone is all too inclined to forget our partnership when she has an interesting affair in hand. She can very well climb out of bed and take my place this weekend.' The complacent air which accompanied this speech forced an unwilling snort of amusement from Karen.

'Oh, Billie. She's not like that. Poor Simone, so happily married for twenty years.'

Billie shrugged. 'What has that to do with anything?' She looked about her. 'Is there nowhere to sit in this draughty room? I wish to give you your gift, child, but I cannot converse in such a crowd. They are all so noisy, and so tall – like a herd of giraffes with their heads together.'

'There's a couch somewhere. But Billie, I can't talk to you here. They'll find me any minute and drag me out to listen to their opinions of my work. I'll have to go. I owe it to Theo for his kindness.' She paused. 'He was so very persistent. Can you think of a reason why he would insist on giving me this showing, and with very little in it for him until I become well known?'

Her aunt's eyes flicked across the room to rest on Theodore Sampson's narrow but stylishly covered shoulders, then came back to Karen.

'No doubt he wishes to be known as the discoverer of a new talent. After all, it is the aim of every gallery owner, is it not?' And then without changing her tone she asked, 'Have you seen Adele lately?'

The question flicked a raw place in Karen's heart.

'You know Humphrey only lets me have her twice a month, and last time she had a terrible cold, poor little pet.' Billie sniffed. 'One would think that any man would hasten to hand over a sick child, especially such a man as Humphrey Doran.'

'Adele has a full-time nurse,' said Karen shortly, her calm tone belied by the despair in her eyes.

Billie looked disapproving, then dove into her purse and produced a daintily-wrapped parcel, thrusting it into Karen's hand.

'Here. Open it quickly, then. I want to see your face.'

It was a tiny parcel, and Karen undid the ribbon with some curiosity. Billie presented her with the oddest gifts. When she remembered to give anything at all, it could be a black pearl from a sultan's hoard, or just as easily a better form of mousetrap. One never knew.

No one watching could have known that Theodore Sampson's exquisitely arranged gallery had shuddered and heaved in a force measuring point eight on the Richter Scale. The tremor started as a pulse in Karen's brain, spreading and vibrating along the nerves, juddering through her body to explode in a full-blown seismic shock. Her nerveless fingers opened and let the parcel drop.

Billie caught it before it hit the floor. '*Mon Dieu*! That is no way to treat a treasure such as – ' She stopped, seeing her niece's glazed expression. 'What is it, child? You have the look of one who sees a phantom.'

Karen blinked, and the gallery walls settled back into place. She took a deep breath and let it out again, slowly. 'Give it to me, please, Billie.'

The exquisite frame fitted into her palm. It was a miniature about the size of a matchbox, showing a gentleman in a high collar and cravat, his dark locks artfully wind-blown, his square-chinned face quite unbelievably handsome, although arrogant, too. The green-grey eyes were vividly alive. In fact, the intensity of that painted gaze unnerved her to the point where she had to close her fingers to hide her reaction.

She said waveringly, 'I rather think I *have* seen a ghost. I know that face. I've seen it . . . him, before.'

'It is possible. A man who could afford to commission a very good miniature could well have had a full-length likeness done by someone like Lawrence, to perpetuate the family line. It was the equivalent of a portrait photograph for the times. Perhaps you have seen him in the National Portrait Gallery.'

Karen let her chatter on. But she knew by the look on Billie's face that she had given herself away. Her fingers tightened on the miniature as though she wanted to crush it.

She laughed shakily. 'It's all right, Billie. I'm not going all fey on you. Of course I've seen a similar portrait sometime in the past, and the miniature reminded me of it. I might even have seen a living person who looks like this. It's very beautiful.' She opened her fingers. The frame, wrought silver vine leaves around a square piece of ivory, had cut into her hand, almost drawing blood.

Billie shrugged. 'If you would rather have something else . . .'

'No!' Karen clutched the miniature to her, her attitude both possessive and protective. 'It's a wonderful gift. Where did you get it?' She couldn't take her eyes from it.

Billie's uneasiness was evident in her abrupt speech. 'I saw it in a small shop in Islington. I bought it because it pleased me.'

'What shop? Was it an art dealer, a jeweller, an antique store?'

'How should I recall? It was months ago. Really, Karen . . .'

'Think, Billie! What other sorts of things did you see there?'

A hand came out of nowhere and plucked the miniature from her grasp. 'My word, this is a nice piece. Where did you find it?'

Karen lunged at Theo, practically tearing her treasure from him. 'It's a birthday gift from my aunt. I was just trying to find out where it came from.'

Theo, who had looked as if he might take offence, brightened. 'Your birthday, too? Why didn't you tell me? This calls for a toast.' He raised his voice. 'Everyone.'

'No, Theo! I – '

'Everyone, take notice. This is an occasion for a double celebration. Our latest artistic luminary is also celebrating her birthday. Please, take up your glasses and join me in wishing her great happiness for the coming year. And then, dear friends, having captured your attention, I have a few words I should like you to hear on the subject of Miss Courtney's promising career.'

Karen, once more in Theo's inexorable grip, twisted about frantically to call back to Billie, 'Come and visit me tomorrow, please Billie! I've got to talk to you. Is twelve o'clock all right?'

'I will be there.' Billie lowered her tone to a mutter, so that only a passing waiter heard her add, 'Be sure that I will be there to discover more of this mystery I have made.' Becoming more French by the minute, she sniffed at the proffered glass of champagne, clearly classified it as inferior, and promptly left.

Karen thought she had herself well in hand. The shock of seeing the miniature, and its curious effect on her had lessened as she gave her attention to others, and her naturally solemn expression had the advantage of hiding her thoughts admirably. She answered questions as well as she could, parried impertinences and longed for the evening to end.

Due to Theo's insistence, his staff worked in a smoke-free environment – for the good of the valuable works on the walls, not human lungs. Of course, he could hardly apply the rule tonight, not without giving offence to certain clients. Karen had an unreasoning fear of fire, although she usually managed to conceal her reaction when matches and lighters flared. Tonight she closed her eyes whenever a flame was briefly lit, and endured the discomfort of smoke breathed upon her, as no doubt others endured in the cause of sociability.

However, she was totally unprepared for the accident. It happened so easily: a man imbibing champagne too heavily and waving his cigarette too close to Theo's cherished grey silk draperies, fortunately in the foyer, not the main gallery – and suddenly a whoosh of flame went up to the ceiling.

Standing six feet away, Karen was transfixed with terror. Her surroundings melted away and she stood alone, facing her annihilation. The sheeting flame reflected in her eyes and burned into her brain. Something screamed at her to run, yet her shivering body would not respond. For an aeon she stood and swayed on the spot, suffering a torture usually reserved for nightmares. She couldn't move, couldn't cry out.

Then as abruptly as it hit, the paralysis passed. Gulping huge breaths, Karen finally released the scream that had hovered, trapped in her throat. Arms outstretched she bored through the knot of people between her and the doorway and fled into the street.

Emerging beneath the canopy and gilded lettering that announced with quiet dignity this was Sampsons of Bond Street, she plunged blindly into the traffic. Amid the melee of horns and shouts and squealing brakes she sped, blind to danger. Rebounding from the side of a stationary taxi, she reached the opposite pavement and kept on running and running, until she had left the lit main streets and entered an area of back alleys, some covered over like railway tunnels, all paved in uneven stones. Her breath came in sobbing pants and her hair clung to her neck like strings of dampened straw. She staggered when her heel caught in a grate and tore the shoe from her foot, then ran on unevenly.

A shadow loomed in front of her and she swerved, avoiding the hands that clutched at her, not hearing the beery voice demanding where the 'ell she thought she was going. Oblivious to the real world about her, she ran from the pursuers in her mind. Even they were vague. She just knew they were there and that they represented total horror to her. She had to escape.

Alleys opened into roads, and she tore across a park, avoiding the lamplit walks and gouging holes in the soft soil of a flower bed. Somewhere she lost the other shoe. Her feet had become lumps of pain, and fire burned in her chest. Yet still she ran.

Now she was in a square, with a railed garden and gates that had been locked against her. She shook the gates and leaned against them, gasping, then turned aside looking for another way. More railings, and a set of stairs leading downward. She staggered, rather than ran, to the top of a basement area. A well of darkness lay at the bottom. Hesitating for the first time, she tripped and fell, landing halfway down in a heap.

There they found her, bruised and drained of everything – energy, emotion, will. Totally on automatic, she let two fellow staff members lift her into a taxi and take her to the nearest casualty ward. She didn't care about the scene she had created at the gallery, nor its possible repercussions. She didn't know or care that she looked like the victim of an assault, with her dress and stockings torn from the fall, and her feet covered in blood. The person that was Karen Courtney had gone into hiding, deep within, too far to be recalled.

Karen spent the night in hospital under observation, and discharged herself early next morning. She worried that Dali might not have found himself any supper, despite his splendid record as a ratter.

She also worried that she might miss Billie, who would have to return to Paris on an afternoon flight. But her overwhelming concern was for her daughter.

Very few people knew about her brief and disastrous marriage to Humphrey Doran. She'd have liked to bury all memory of the event herself, but for its outcome, her little three-year-old daughter. Billie knew, and the lawyer who was battling to retrieve Adele from her father's clutches. This afternoon Karen had visiting rights to her child, and she was determined that nothing would spoil their time together. If he could, Humphrey would deny her even this cruelly abbreviated pleasure, but she didn't believe he'd risk defying the court ruling.

Her handbag and keys had been brought in by Theo, who had also left a little note signifying his sorrow at her plight, and just mentioning that the fire had been brought under control before it reached the main gallery. She could, however, detect an undertone of pique mixed with curiosity.

She needed to avoid Theo for the next day or so – play sick, perhaps. The money she'd set aside for the court case, still several weeks ahead thanks to Humphrey's manoeuvrings, had left her short; but there would be enough for her to pursue the matter of the miniature. She couldn't have explained what drove her. Perhaps it was a need to cover over and forget the suffering every time she held her child in her arms knowing she'd soon have to part with her again.

How much she hated Humphrey for his sadistic enjoyment of the game he played with her; but even worse was the way he used Adele as his pawn. Somehow she'd get her away from him. However long it took and whatever the cost, she'd meet the price. Meanwhile, there was the quest of the miniature to keep her busy. She'd start when the longed-for afternoon was over, as soon as she had to give Adele back.

She had thought about the miniature last night, lying awake with the pain of her cuts and bruises, listening to patients wheezing and mumbling in nearby beds, the padded footsteps of staff, the whine of lifts and the clanking of trolleys that were an inevitable part of the hospital mosaic.

The miniature had stayed in her purse, in a bedside locker. She didn't need to study it any further. The painted features came to mind clearly and distinctly, and so very familiar. Where? Where had she seen him? This problem now occupied her to the exclusion of everything else, even the terrifying recurrence of her fire phobia.

A part of her mind, a very small part, reminded her that she hadn't had an attack like that in years. She should be concerned about it, and the fact that she might easily have killed herself in her headlong flight. Closing off that small nagging voice had been easy. The fact was, she had too much else to think about. If her brain wasn't to go into overload she must set her priorities and deal with them one by one.

Letting herself into the third-floor attic that her aunt designated a hovel, but where Karen had created a remarkably comfortable haven at little cost, she heard Dali at the kitchen window making himself unpleasant. She let him in, and appeased him with a breakfast of kippers. Refreshed by a shower, and dressed in her favourite painting gear she put on a Hayden concerto tape, made coffee and settled into her own particular form of therapy.

Billie rang the bell promptly at twelve. 'Happy birthday, *cherie*. *Mon Dieu*! What happened to your face?'

Karen closed the door and steered her towards a huge, puffy lounge chair that took up a good quarter of the floor space. The rest of the room had a spartan quality to it, its main feature being makeshift shelves on bricks housing dozens of books. They overflowed onto the floor, stood in columns in the corners, peeped from beneath a coffee table and the one other chair. With a modern standard lamp squeezed in behind the door, the room was full.

Pushing her aunt gently down into the lounge, Karen said, 'It's a long story, and it's only a bruise. I'm going to grill you, Billie, so prepare yourself. Coffee or red wine?' She headed for the kitchen.

Billie called after her, 'If you have acquired anything from me it is your palate. I will have wine, please. Also, the grilling will not be necessary. I have recalled the name of the shop where I purchased the miniature. Are you not pleased?'

'Very pleased.' Karen came back with the wine and handed her a glass. 'Come and see what I've been doing.'

She led the way to the next room, her so called studio, where most of the sloping roof consisted of skylight. Apart from her workbench and easel the room was bare of everything but the light itself – a wonderful light that reflected and bounced off each wall, causing Billie to wince. All the same, she missed very little.

'Why are you limping, child?'

'That's also part of the story. I'll tell you later. What do you think?' She stepped up to her easel and peered at the new work, then stepped back again, making room for Billie.

There was silence for a time.

'It is he. The miniature. The same eyes, moving, following... alive.' Billie spoke in a strained voice. 'It was not my imagination, then. You really are affected by him. This is something I do not understand.'

'That makes two of us. Come on, Billie. I could do with some wine myself before plunging into all this.'

Karen picked up the miniature from the bench and accompanied Billie back to the living room. Her hand stayed steady as she poured more wine and took a seat opposite her aunt.

'Sometimes I wish I smoked.' Karen took a deep breath. 'Of course it's nowhere near finished. I only started it this morning, yet you had no difficulty in recognising the subject. I didn't need the miniature to copy. I know him too well. But I don't know *how* I know him. Until last night I didn't know that I knew him. Can you follow that?'

'Barely. You are saying that the miniature nudged your memory of this man. You do realise that he is not of this time? He is a Regency rake, a member of the *beau monde* in the years when Napoleon Bonaparte threatened to take over the western world. He must have died at least one hundred and forty years ago.' Her glance flickered over the stacks of books. 'With your immense library of history, I have no doubt you are far better informed on the period than I could ever be.'

Karen fingered the miniature, broodingly, then looked up. 'He's not someone I've met, someone who simply looks like him. That's what makes it all so difficult. That's why I must find the person who sold you the miniature and try to discover its background, its provenance, as they say. Billie, you've got to help me.' She paused awkwardly. 'I don't ask you for much, do I?'

Billie held out a thin veined hand, and with just a slight hesitation Karen placed the miniature in it, saying with sudden passion, 'I almost wish I'd never seen the thing.'

Billie studied the arrogant male face, addressing it as if the man himself stood there. 'Yes, you know what you want and you take it. I have seen your type before.' She took a card from her purse and handed it to Karen. 'Here is the address. You can go there this afternoon. Now, you will tell me what has been happening that you are bruised and limping, *hein?*' Placing the miniature on the table between them she groped in her bag, her eyes never moving from Karen's face.

Karen flopped back in the chair, the baggy cushions sagging under her slight weight. She looked at the ceiling, where the paint had flaked, and smiled briefly at the thought that this was the first visit when Billie had failed to criticise the decor and the standard of her niece's housekeeping.

'Okay. Here it is. Last night I had a kind of hysterical fit and made a fool of myself. I ran out on Theo, and apparently got halfway across London before they caught up with me and took me to hospital. I bruised myself when I fell down some steps. The cut feet were a result of losing my shoes. I don't know where I went. I just ran.'

'Do you know why you ran?'

'Oh, yes.' Karen looked at Billie, in the act of lighting a cigarette.

As the flame leapt and lengthened into a brilliant shaft something shifted in Karen's mind.

She was on her feet instantly, trembling. 'Put it out! Put it out!' Her voice cracked and finished in a sob as Billie hastily dropped the lighter in her bag, throwing the unlit cigarette aside and grasping her by the arms.

'Is that what happened last night? Was it fire?'

When Karen could only nod, she pressed her into her chair and stood back, waiting.

'Dammit! I thought I'd gotten over all that.' Karen thumped the chair arm with a fist, hard.

'Over what? Tell me about it, cherie.'

Karen sighed deeply. 'When I was a kid I had this constant nightmare, week in, week out. It was always the same – a holocaust, flames everywhere – and no way out. I kept trying to escape. There was something precious at stake. I was so afraid, not just for myself, but someone else – I don't know who.' Her voice caught in her throat. She swallowed. 'I always woke up just as the fire touched me and my flesh began to burn.' She looked down at her hands, spread stiffly in her lap. 'My hands came up in blisters, but they went almost immediately. God, I was terrified!'

Billie's eyes widened, but she said nothing.

Karen looked up at her. 'I hid all this, naturally. I didn't want to be labelled a freak or attention-seeker. Things were hard enough as it was. Very few people have guessed. By the time I was fifteen, just about when you took me over, it disappeared altogether. Well, almost.' Her lips twisted in what might have been a smile. 'I recall once letting a friend talk me into seeing that film, the one where the people were trapped in a burning skyscraper. I treated it as a test.'

'What happened?'

'I made a spectacle of myself in the theatre. The friend never asked me out again.'

Billie had paled. 'That is a terrible story. How you must have suffered. Perhaps I was at fault when I agreed . . . Child, do you recall anything about your parents?'

'No. Nothing. Just that they died in a car smash. I was thrown from the car and saved. My memory was the only part of me damaged.'

Billie said in an odd tone, 'It is time you knew the facts.' She got up and went to take a cigarette from her bag, then threw it down again. Keeping her eyes averted she began to pace up and down before the couch, clearly having some difficulty in choosing her words. Then in a harsh voice she gave Karen 'the facts'.

Fact one was the lie fed to a five-year-old child, out of her mind with horror after seeing her parents burned to death in a caravan fire. The car crash was a fiction, invented to fill the gap in Karen's memory. It was hoped that this deliberate detachment would help her recovery. Surely it was better for her not to remember? Did Karen not agree?

Without waiting for a reply, Billie continued in that strange bleak monotone, divesting the horrible story of all emotional colour.

She told how Karen had been placed in the care of the state, in a children's home in Wales, her memories overlaid by a lie. No one had suspected the nightmares to come. It was not anyone's fault. They had all done their best.

Karen was surprised at the apologetic tone underlying the narrative. In all the time she had known Billie, she'd never bothered to explain her actions to anyone. She did what she did because it was her will, and nobody else's concern.

But Karen was not interested in allocating blame. She had no feelings of vindictiveness towards the men and women who had decided her fate when she was too young to have any say. What hurt was Billie's indifference. She wondered, not for the first time, what Billie was really like at the core. There were so many layers to her, so many promising avenues of personality which, when opened up, proved to be blind alleys.

Karen, the child, had waited and dreamed for years of a fairy-godmother aunt appearing from nowhere to carry her off in loving arms. She'd put herself to sleep at night with that picture in her mind, sure that one day she'd be restored to the kind of life she'd known with her parents.

Naturally, hope faded in time, and as she grew up she put aside fantasy. It was synonymous with fraud, and she wanted none of it. Reality was working hard for the fostering families she lived with, treated kindly sometimes, often indifferently, but always with an eye to her usefulness. She had never again felt part of a family unit.

'Did you ever really care about me, Billie?'

Billie shrugged. 'I came back for you, ten years later. Does that mean nothing?'

With a sigh, Karen gave it up. There was no burrowing beneath Billie's perfect seamless façade. 'I was a handful by then,' she remarked. 'I wanted to go my own road. What a pity Humphrey had to cross it.'

'It was a mistake to marry him. You discovered it soon enough.' Billie picked up the framed snapshot standing on the table. 'What of your *bebe*? You did not answer me last night.'

Karen got up and took the photograph from her, smiling at the sweet, scarcely formed features ringed in blonde curls. It was her only picture of Adele, and already it was out of date. Her throat closed with familiar pain. She put the picture back in its place, saying briefly, 'I will see her this afternoon. We both need some coffee. Stay there, Billie.'

When she returned with a laden tray she seemed to have recovered her poise. She saw that Billie, too, had repaired her make-up and was her old self, outwardly at least.

'Revival time. Dig in, Billie.'

'Must you use such expressions, *cherie*?'

Karen managed a grin. 'You're recovering, Billie dear.'

The two of them sat and demolished toast and coffee without futher discussion. It was a period of truce, time for regrouping and balancing their new knowledge of one another. Eventually Billie set down her cup and made the first move.

'We will not go over the past again, agreed? But there is one thing. This fear of fire, it has come back again. Last night – '

'I was already off balance, and therefore vulnerable. Then the accident took me by surprise. It was a compilation of events, that's all, Billie.' Karen's voice held a shrug.

But Billie would not be put off. 'The miniature. That is what upset you. It was a mistake.'

They both looked at the painted face lying on the table. It returned the look with perfect confidence, perfect assurance.

'It's just a trigger, Billie. Something else could have done it as easily, I expect.'

Billie shook her head. 'No. He means something to you. You have said so. When will you go to the shop? Today?'

Karen nodded. 'It will be good to have something to occupy me after I've taken Adele back.' She smiled painfully. 'Do you know, I forgot the critics! I should be out buying the papers now, searching feverishly for the words that will damn me or bring me to public notice. How could I have forgotten?'

'Pah! Critics! What do they know? I will come with you to speak to this dealer.'

'No. You must go back to your business. You can't be spared. I'll do this on my own.' It was her own quest, and she wanted to follow it alone. It wasn't as though Billie really cared. To her the miniature was a curiosity, no more.

Billie picked up her handbag. 'You are right. I shall take the two-thirty flight and be at my desk early. But mind that you contact me about the outcome. I will not be kept in the dark about my own gifts.' She pecked Karen's cheek, and brushing off an offer to find her a taxi, departed in her usual brisk style.

Karen stood at the window watching the bird-like figure on the footpath, finding herself a taxi without any trouble, and sailing away out of her life again as smoothly as she always had done. Billie did everything gracefully, including her betrayals.

The miniature was warm in her hand. She brought it up to eye level so that the light struck those amazing grey-green living eyes.

'I forgive you, Billie,' she whispered. 'I have the feeling that this gift of yours is going to make up for everything you've ever done, and then some.'

CHAPTER 2

T HE HOUSE HAD an unwelcoming face. Its narrow windows looked down with an air of hauteur designed to keep out the hoi polloi, which no doubt had been the aim of the Victorian merchant who had built it to the prevailing High Gothic trend. Its ugly brown bricks were immaculately tuck pointed, its brass doorknob rubbed thin with polishing. The garden, overshadowed by grim yews, was weedless and uninspiring.

Karen wondered how she could have stood it, even for two months. The place should have told her something about Humphrey when she first saw it.

It had always been his home, willed to him by his widowed mother, who, having taken one look at his prospective bride, promptly succumbed to her ailing heart. Karen couldn't blame her. A nineteen-year-old frowning rebel from the wrong sort of family, or worse, no family at all. An awkward girl who did not know how to dress or entertain, and couldn't have cared less. The idea was an absurdity.

Three weeks of marriage showed her how much worse than absurd it was. Humphrey the strong, devoted older man who would be her father, mother, child and lover all in one, had never existed. His façade, like that of his respectable household, was a sham. She'd married a despotic satyr who would have chained her in a cell if he'd thought he could get away with it.

She left him. Too proud to ask Billie for help, she took a job in a hamburger outlet and stayed afloat, just. He found her when an interfering landlady had her forcibly removed to hospital, halfway through labour. Adele was two hours old when the battle for her began. It had continued ever since.

Karen mounted the sweep of stone steps and banged the doorknocker defiantly.

In the self-consciously leather and wainscot study she faced him, hating his air of superiority. Don't give me your white-pointer shark smile, she thought. Just let's get it over with and let me out of this mausoleum.

'You're looking well, Karen.'

'So are you. How is the stockbroking world?'

'Couldn't be better. Can I offer you a drink?' He half-turned towards an elaborate cocktail cabinet fitted in one corner of the room. He was a big man, broad and tall. His heavy features were not unhandsome, except for a pair of pale blue eyes lined in reddish-blond lashes. His hair and moustache were the same colour, although his temples had distinguished silver streaks that Karen suspected him of deliberately adding. The most predominant feature of all, however, were those teeth, pointed and sloping back a little.

A drink, with him! Karen shook her head. 'No thank you. I'd like to take Adele now, please. We only have this afternoon.'

The predatory smile widened. He really did look like a monster of the sea. She shivered and held his look, firmly.

'As to that, I'm sorry, but she won't be able to go out today. She's been ill, you know.'

'I don't know anything of the sort!' Karen exploded. 'My baby is sick and you don't have the decency to let me know! Where is she? I must see her.'

'She's not here.' His words cut her off in her flight to the staircase. Slowly she turned and came back into the room. She knew the blood had drained from her face, and she felt a bit faint; but nothing would make her show weakness in front of this man.

'Where, then?'

He waved vaguely. 'In the country, getting some fresh air. She's quite all right now. Just a case of infantile German measles.'

Karen thought she might choke on the anger that gripped her, filling her throat like gravel. She swallowed, and waited a moment.

'You're enjoying this, aren't you? Why couldn't you give me a call before I came? I suppose you wanted the pleasure of telling me in person. The same old sadistic Humphrey.'

His satisfaction surrounded him like a haze. She could almost see it. The bastard! German measles could have complications; and besides, she would have wanted to nurse Adele herself and comfort her when she was hot and sore and needed cuddling. She needed to see her child.

Her voice came out ragged, despite her effort at control. 'When can I see her? It's been nearly a month. As if you didn't know.'

He shrugged. 'I can scarcely be blamed when a sudden crisis in the Amsterdam market called me away. You know I don't like to leave Adele and her nurse alone in this big house. Naturally they went to my sister. There was no time to inform you.'

Her eyes burned, hot with unshed tears. 'You did it deliberately. You keep flouting the court order – '

'And getting away with it,' he admitted. 'I can go on doing it, too, until you're driven half out of your mind. I shall enjoy doing it.' He strolled over to the cabinet and poured himself a large scotch, standing with his back to her and sipping with every evidence of enjoyment.

She didn't know what she might have said, if the sound of stumbling footsteps on the stairs hadn't come just then. She whirled around. A childish voice called to her, 'Mama!'

As she reached the door, Humphrey's hands clamped on her shoulders, restraining her. She fought him madly.

'Let me go! She's here. Adele, darling. It's Mama.'

She saw the beloved face above the curved rail of the stair, brown eyes alight with pleasure, the little lips curved in a joyful smile. Her hair had grown, she noted, and it was darker. Her baby was changing, and she wasn't there to see it happening.

Adele put out her arms, but she was held back by a woman in nurse's uniform, a starched-up affair whose prim manner was no substitute for a mother's love, thought Karen, herself pinned hopelessly by Humphrey's great red-haired hands.

'Mama!' Adele's voice wavered.

Humphrey overrode it easily. 'Take her upstairs at once, Miss Turner. We must keep to doctor's orders.'

Karen watched as her baby was removed, still calling for her. Tears coursed down her cheeks, and her body shook in Humphrey's grasp.

'Come, Karen. There's no need for such histrionics.'

She knew a moment of absolute berserker rage. If she'd been free, with a weapon handy, she'd have used it. Then the moment passed and she slumped, holding on to the doorjamb for support as his hands dropped away. She couldn't beat him without help. The only avenue was a legal one.

She turned and faced him. 'You won't win, Humphrey. The hearing coming up will be very different from the first one, when I was sick and run down and you used every dirty trick to make me sound like an unfit mother for Adele. I'm wiser and stronger, and I have good friends and advisers . . . and money. Enough to fight you on even terms and win.'

He met her challenge contemptuously. 'You'll never win, a little scrubber like you! You're not fit to run a pie stall, let alone a decent home and family. No wonder I threw you out.' His face showed nothing but distaste, and she realised that he actually meant it. He'd convinced himself she'd been found lacking and discarded by him, not the other way about.

'I can't talk to you. We'll meet in the courtroom.' She left the study and walked with dignity across the hall and down the steps. She didn't look back. Not until she'd rounded the corner at the end of the street did she let herself fall against the nearest wall and release the pent-up Niagara of tears.

CHAPTER 3

THE SHOP WAS shut. Karen couldn't believe it. She stared at the neat card on the door telling her she had to fill in forty minutes before she would be allowed entry.

Peering through the dusty glass she wondered whether Billie had made some mistake. Surely such a jumble store could never stock valuables like her miniature. Or was the effect deliberate? did the proprietor cultivate a look of carelessly mixed junk and objets d'art to lure the novices, the folk who thought they could still find a bargain under the unsuspecting nose of the expert?

She straightened up, wincing at a reminder from her cut feet that she had walked a long way from the bus stop to this rather mean little street. Such an unlikely milieu for her sophisticated aunt. What had brought her there?

Pondering this curiosity she retraced her steps to a small grassed area with a seat under a solitary tree, and brought out the sandwich she'd meant to share with Adele. The sun sat high overhead, but there was no heat in it. Bricks and asphalt gave off a dank chill, and she could smell the river nearby. Karen endured.

Her head ached, and so did her puffy eyes, reminding her that she hadn't thought for a whole ten minutes about how much she hated Humphrey. What a fool she'd been to trust him, and what a mockery he made of the court's ruling on access. She'd been right to press ahead for a new hearing. He had no intention of letting her see Adele, let alone take her out for a few hours. How much he had enjoyed lying to her, and knowing she knew he lied. Every small indication of her suffering had been savoured. And how eagerly he'd looked for signs of breakdown, waited for her to grovel and beg for her child. Hell would freeze over first! At least she'd denied him that satisfaction.

She checked her watch and pulled herself to her feet. Time to put aside Humphrey and get on with her quest. A few minutes later she'd arrived back at the shop, cold, and hungry, since she hadn't been able to ignore the plea in the eyes of a passing mongrel. The door stood open and she went in.

Dickens, she thought, standing in the dust and dimness, afraid to brush against precarious piles of books, china and assorted bric-a-brac. Toby jug, she added silently, seeing the squat figure rise from behind a desk piled with papers to peer at her through the gloom.

'Mr Josephs?'

He nodded. His half-spectacles slid down the bulb of his nose and he pushed them up and peered harder. Karen wondered why he didn't help himself by putting in a few high-powered globes. There were surely enough lamps lying about.

'Yes?'

'I wonder if you could help me. A lady recently purchased a miniature from this shop and I'd like to know where it came from.' She produced the tissue-wrapped parcel and began to undo it. 'What can you tell me about this, Mr Josephs?'

The painted face glowed even in that murky little shop. Caught again in its magic spell, Karen stared into the eyes and wondered, for the fiftieth time, why they were familiar. She looked up to see the shopkeeper jerk back, as if he'd been offered a cockroach. His spectacles shot down his nose to rest on two fat and hairy cheeks.

'I do not deal in miniatures. Good day to you.'

His gutteral East European accent struck unpleasantly on her already strained nerves. 'I don't believe you. You didn't even look closely at it.' She thrust the miniature at him, but he ignored it and scuttled around the desk to her side. He moved amazingly quickly when he wanted to, and she was surprised to discover that someone so short and fat could project quite an aura of menace.

'The shop is closed for the day, young lady. I suggest you try to peddle your little toy somewhere else.'

Karen stood her ground. 'I'm not selling anything, and I'm not being dismissed until I get the information I came for. This is the right address. It's written here on this card. Here. See?'

He glanced at the card. He could hardly help it as it, too, was thrust in his face. With a thumb he pushed back his spectacles and took the piece of pasteboard from her.

'Mlle Wilhelmina Carnot. She gave this to you?'

'She's my aunt. The miniature was a birthday gift from her.'

'She told you that it came from my shop?' He sounded so incredulous that for one moment Karen's certainty wavered.

'She didn't want to tell me,' she said slowly, remembering Billie's original reluctance. 'But then it became obvious that there was a connection . . .' She stopped.

'What connection? I do not like this. Your aunt had no business giving you this item. It had been agreed that she would never let the goods out of her possession until she had left the country.'

Silence fell. Karen all at once realised what a pregnant pause was. The answers tumbled into place. 'Good grief. Was Billie smuggling hot items for you, Mr Josephs? I can't believe it.' She then added hastily, 'Not that it matters to me. Look, I have a very particular reason for wanting to know who the man is, the sitter for this portrait. If I promise not to reveal where I got it – not even to tell anyone I have it, if I can get away with that – couldn't you please tell me who owned the miniature last?'

Had her pleading tone made a difference? She couldn't tell. The man's expression, such as it was, hadn't altered, but she felt the little eyes above his spectacles had a distinctly unfriendly look. She waited, making no attempt to hide her anxiety. If the miniature had been stolen, why on earth should he risk telling her the name of the true owner? What possible inducement could she offer?

A broad smile split his face, turning him into a Mr Pickwick. His whole body began to shake with mirth.

'Ho! I have been insulted. You take me for a fence, is that it? Ha! That is good. I should tell your aunt that she is the associate of criminals. She will like that.'

Immensely relieved, Karen giggled with him. 'I'm sorry. But that's how it sounded to me – taking goods out of the country and not disposing of them here.'

'My dear young woman, I simply act as a go-between for people who have no wish to advertise to the world that they are financially embarrassed. They come to me to dispose of their smaller, more portable family treasures. I have several discreet outlets on the Continent. The arrangement works well.'

'But, Billie . . . My aunt . . .'

'Is my friend of many years. She came to me one time when she needed money and I agreed to use her as a courier; and she continues to do it to oblige me.' He poked a thick finger at the miniature, a jewel shining in the litter of his desk top. 'If you take this to its original owner my reputation will be spoilt, you understand. Discretion is my business, all of my business.'

Karen thought rapidly. 'I could say I bought it in Paris – or that it was bought there as a gift for me and brought to England. Oh, please! You don't know how much this matters to me.'

'And how do you explain your knowledge of its ownership?'

'I'll make up a story. I'll say I went to Sothebys where they recognised the artist's style and looked up his works. I'll say that they know an expert in this artist, who recognised the sitter's family name – something like that. I could have had the silversmith's work traced from the frame, and – '

'Enough! I am convinced.' He shot back behind his desk and rummaged in a drawer, bringing out a ledger worthy of Scrooge's counting house. It slammed down on the pile of papers, raising a dust cloud. 'You are a veritable niece of your aunt. She, too, can talk her way through any situation.' He ran his finger down a page in the ledger. 'Here is the address – Ashbourne Manor, Ashbourne St Mary, via Uplyme, Devon. Mr Arnold Barton.'

Karen copied the details into her notebook and picked up the miniature, carefully rewrapping it in its tissue.

'Thank you, Mr Josephs. I'm so very grateful to you.'

'Ha. I did not give you anything, you wrung it out of me.' He chuckled all the way to the door, ushering her into the lane. 'Give my regards to Mlle Carnot, and tell her she is not to do it again.'

Smiling and waving Karen hurried off, her sore feet forgotten in her anxiety to be on her way to Devon and the answer to her quest. She hadn't thought beyond the discovery of the man's identity. How this would help her, what it would prove, remained a mystery. But she felt increasingly driven to find him and know him. He might be long dead, but he had an importance in her life, and she couldn't relax until she'd discovered what it was.

Her plans for an immediate departure had to be revised. The flat appeared to be under siege when she arrived home, although in fact most of the disturbance emanated from Theodore Sampson, who was trying to rouse interest in the possibility that Karen lay dead, or at the very least in a dead faint, behind her locked front door. Her neighbours seemed unimpressed by his impersonation of a rescue squad. In particular, Lola, from next door, who worked a late night shift and was not at her best until six in the evening, had taken umbrage at the disturbance.

'If you don't shut up I'll . . . I'll set Dali on you,' she shrilled from the stair landing. Hair on end, in a blowzy wrapper, she looked and sounded the complete harridan.

Theo turned from his impassioned plea to old Mr Dobbs to phone for the police to break in, and retorted, 'You can tell Dali, whoever he is, that I'll have him up on an assault charge if he lays a finger on me.'

An interested spectator, a youngish man in jeans and sneakers, noticed Karen on the doorstep. 'Hello. I'm Smith from the *Telegraph*. Do you know the missing woman?'

'What missing woman?'

'A Miss Karen Courtney. I came to get some copy on her since she seems to have made an impression on our art critic, but it looks like I might have an even better story. Do you know anything about her disappearance? I hear she spent last night in hospital – '

'Sorry. I haven't got time. I haven't disappeared, either. Mr Sampson, what are you doing here? And for heaven's sake, why are you spreading this ridiculous rumour that I've gone missing, or died, or something?'

'Karen! Thank God! I've been half out of my mind.'

She let him grasp her arm and lead her to her door, then unlocked it and managed to get them both inside before the enterprising Mr Smith could join them.

Theo Sampson was not himself. Ruffled tail feathers hung figuratively in the air. 'How could you leave the hospital like that without telling anyone? When I tried the flat at lunchtime you'd gone, no one knew where. I thought you might have had another attack like last night's. For all I knew you could have been at the bottom of the river!'

'It never occurred to me that you would worry. I'm sorry. My aunt was here this morning and then I had to go out. I should have telephoned you. I meant to, to thank you for helping me last night. I . . . I'm ashamed that I embarrassed you in front of your guests.' She met his look, not defiantly, but with a certain bravado. If he chose to take offence there was nothing she could do. She would not excuse herself. Her fears and phobias were her own affair.

Oddly enough, he seemed to understand. 'I shouldn't worry about that. But you gave me a fine scare dear, and I'll only forgive you if you make me a coffee, black and strong.' He strolled after her to the kitchen, lolling against the bench while he watched her work. His slim shoulders were today encased in dark green suede, and the pipe stem chequered trousers tucked into soft pointed boots, clearly making some kind of statement. *Outré*, and a dismal failure at his age, thought Karen, smiling to herself.

Mistaking the smile for approval, Theo preened for a moment, then said, 'Did you bother at all to look at the papers? Have you seen what they are saying about your show?'

When she shook her head he looked disappointed. 'They like you, for the most part. Quite a little pat on the back, considering the way they stress your youth and "future possibilities". You should be pleased, dear.'

'I am, for your sake as well as my own. Why did you do it, Mr . . . Theo? Why take a chance on a complete unknown and boost me up into the limelight?'

He accepted the coffee and stirred it thoughtfully for a full half minute. 'Didn't Billie tell you?'

'Billie? I didn't know you knew one another.'

He shrugged. 'We go back many years. It was Billie who suggested that I look at your work with a view to a show. I'm very glad she did. It's done us both good.'

Karen didn't know how she controlled her voice. 'How very kind of Billie,' she said, with creditable coolness, considering how she felt. 'There's no end to her interfer . . . interest in my affairs.'

'You sound miffed, dear. Don't be ungrateful, now. Everyone needs a leg up in the world sometimes, and I might never have known what a gifted painter I had on my own staff. Now, about an interview . . .'

Karen set her coffee mug down on the bench with a snap. 'Don't bother, thank you. I'm going out of town for a day or two. You did say that I could have the week off.'

'Yes, I did. But – '

'Besides, it will give the Mr Smiths of the newspaper world time to dream up a really good disappearance story.' Her smile glittered. 'Do forgive me, Theo, but I must pack an overnight bag. I have a train to catch. Please take your time finishing your coffee.'

Outfaced for once by a determination as smooth as his own, Theo drank up and left.

Having arranged for Lola to care for Dali, an hour later Karen boarded the train for Axminster, both keyed up and ready to fall down with exhaustion. Last night's episode and the morning's activities had all been a bit much, and she slept for most of the journey, deeply and dreamlessly, tucked into the corner of the carriage, the precious miniature in her handbag under her arm.

She took the local bus to Ashbourne St Mary, planning to find a room for the night. Even her enthusiasm fell short of storming a private home at this hour. Bumping along beside her reflection, a grimy ghost in the darkened window, she studied the leaflet she had picked up at the railway bookstall.

It mentioned, briefly, the house known as Ashbourne Manor, an estate recorded since Elizabethan times, and set in a vale to the north of Uplyme. Its current owner had apparently chosen privacy with dignity, or in other words, it was not open to the paying public. Karen would have to bluff her way in.

Having booked into The Bull, she unpacked her torch and told herself she would just take a short walk and get the lie of the land – in the direction of Ashbourne Manor.

The sun had dropped behind a bank of huge purple cloud. There would be a storm before morning. Karen heard several people in the bar voice this opinion as she set out. The village of Ashbourne St Mary had retained its quaintness, to a degree, although several modern shops had found their way into the main square; and council had been careful with its development planning. There was still a village atmosphere, aided consciously by the residents and shopkeepers. Karen liked the place.

At the southern end of the town in a little square of its own sat the ecclesiastical sector – an Anglican church complete with Norman tower, rectory, church hall, and a row of almshouses which might have been there for centuries. Struck by the light gilding its slates, Karen paused, then pushed open the lych gate and walked up the path to the church. She had no warning. One moment she stood in the doorway of an empty building, and the next she stepped into another world.

Light! Rich golden-white light pouring through the narrow windows in a flood that spilled over benches and aisles, bathing the congregation in visual benediction. Masses of flowers loaded the air with scent, summer field flowers, daisies, the splash of poppies, peonies, roses. But above all, there was music. A choir of young voices rose and dipped then rose again to soar among the rafters, weaving a pattern of angelic sound that touched the heart and brought tears to Karen's eyes.

Standing at the head of the aisle, she looked about her with blurred vision – seeing faces but not features, aware of rich textured gowns, coats and uniforms of an earlier era, but with outlines that were unclear. At the altar stood a priestly figure robed in white, and kneeling before him two vague forms, one wrapped in gauzy veils that trapped the light.

What was happening? Where had all this come from? The moment quivered on the air like a moth suspended in mid-dance, then it had gone. She blinked, her eyes cleared, and the church was empty of all but shadows.

Stumbling with haste, she fled. Outside the defeated day had painted a few last streaks of colour across the sky. Stars had appeared in the east but were rapidly being swallowed into the maw of approaching storm clouds. It was almost like watching a battle between good and evil, with the forces of darkness gaining ground by the second. Both hands pressed to her thumping heart, Karen hurried away from the church yard. Whatever the reasons for her sudden aberration, she was still determined to see the manor before going back.

Fifteen minutes' brisk walk down the road and she had her wish. Two stone posts marked the place where gates had once stood. The drive was a black tunnel between giant oaks, its surface pitted and broken. Karen plunged in. Her torch showed the way, although it was pitifully thin armour against the palpable darkness. It pressed in on her, as if trying to push her away. She struggled on, her determination fuelled by disgust at her own weakness. What was there to fear? She had suffered a brief hallucination, that was all, probably induced by stress and lack of food. And only children were frightened of the dark.

The house rose up at the end of the tunnel, a silhouette rimmed against the western horizon. No lights showed. It presented a closed and hostile face. Karen stopped. She strained to paint in the outline, to build a picture in her mind of how it really was. Then as if in perfect timing the clouds parted like curtains on a stage setting, and moonlight flooded through. At the same instant there was a drum roll of thunder in the distance.

Spotlight centre stage, said Karen to herself, almost in the expectation of three witches materialising complete with cauldron against the dramatic backdrop. She wanted to deny her strong feeling of impending tragedy. It's all pure theatre, she whispered. You can practically smell the greasepaint. Somehow she wasn't convinced. The atmosphere of doom had a texture and reality more tangible than any mock-up.

Without any reason she felt the first tremor of panic. She wished she hadn't come. The house frightened her. The expected warm brick façade of Tudor times had gone. In its place stood an example of the best Palladian style, white pillared portico curving gracefully out to a fan of steps, and a wide, stone-flagged terrace running the length of each wing, with graceful balustrades balancing the delicate matching roofline. Its classic beauty repelled her. She couldn't rid herself of the feeling that she was observed, that the place had an almost malign intelligence of its own. Fantastic! Yet the notion had taken root in her mind and her flesh crept at the thought of all those blank windows watching, guessing at her next move. She wanted to run and hide.

Trembling, she stood and dealt with her fears, as she'd always done – as she'd had to since childhood.

Lightning flashed behind the house, and thunder rolled, this time much closer. Karen's nerve almost broke.

'Why? What is it? What's wrong?' She screamed the words aloud, spinning about to look behind her at the tunnel of darkness, knowing the thing she feared lurked somewhere else. It was the house. It was waiting for her.

Filled with a sudden overwhelming anger, she began to run, anxious to meet her fear head on. She'd dropped her torch, but she didn't stop to look for it. Clouds scudded across the moon and the light began to fade. By the time she reached the steps to the long stone gallery darkness had descended once more. Pools of blackness lay before her and behind. Blindly, she felt her way along the balustrade, all her instincts telling her she was headed in the wrong direction. The answer she sought, the end to a search that filled her with black terror, lay waiting just a few steps onward.

At the end of the gallery she paused. Right on cue, lightning flashed once more, one brief jagged flare that was more than enough. It showed what lay ahead – a tower, or the ruin of a tower, attached like a rotting stump to a healthy mouth – a place of decay, of death and destruction.

Shock held her paralysed. She stood balanced on the edge of time, seeing, feeling, hearing the past roll over her. Visions of terror and despair filled her mind. Phantom figures beckoned, a childish voice screamed in her ears, backed by the crackle of flames and the lurid dancing light of fire on stone. She breathed scorching air into her lungs and smelled her own flesh burning. In a dream she knew the final rending of her spirit from her body and a sense of utter, total loss.

Rain came lancing across the terrace, driving into gaps between the stones and pouring over the edge in a continuous sheet. For brief instants the lightning turned the world to platinum, the flashing laser beams too dazzling to watch. Thunder reverberated between the towers.

Like a part of the balustrade Karen stood fixed, oblivious to the theatrical display going on around her. She was looking at another reality far away in time. The present could not touch her.

The storm rolled on inland, much of its energy spent. At last Karen seemed to waken to the present. Drenched and shivering she moved, blindly, drifting down the steps and across the gravel, through the mouth of the oak-tunnel drive.

Here was total blackness, except for a tiny pinpoint of light ahead. She began to walk towards the light. Soon it separated into headlamps coming towards her at speed. The motor was a powerful one. It surged through the night, its lights twin blades tearing aside the darkness as it came. With sightless gaze she walked into the glaring pathway.

The driver tried. Wheels locked and screaming, the big Daimler went into a skid on the wet surface. Light beams spun at crazy angles through the trees. A wing tore away, gouging deep into the bole of an oak. The rear end swung in an arc, carrying the momentum of a ton of metal with it. She saw it coming in slow motion, inexorable as a locomotive on track, slamming her high into the air.

Hot metal hissed on the wet gravel. There was a smell of burnt rubber and engine oil spilling over. The driver sat in shock, staring at the place where his windscreen used to be, staring at the bundle lying in the roadway just touched by one light. The bundle did not move.

Karen's broken body arrived at the county hospital with just the barest spark of life in it, and that was flickering, on the point of going out. When Billie came several hours later, she found her niece alive, but in coma. Her bruised form lay quietly breathing with the help of support systems. Her spirit had gone elsewhere.

CHAPTER 4

3 December: Monday

THE ROOM WAS small and cosy and dimly lit, the curtains drawn over windows closed against the din of a London street. There was little furniture. A desk with an empty chair behind it, a bulky adjustable lounge seat, another chair a few feet away, occupied by a figure in silhouette against the lamp. The contrived neutrality had a restful effect. The only spot of colour was provided by a painting on the wall above the desk. Its magnetic qualities sucked in and swallowed the viewer, forcing him into another dimension of rifts and cloud canyons, of light beyond the normal spectrum – a place of peace immediately recognisable yet curiously foreign.

The lamp had been angled away from this disturbing picture. The two people occupying the room concentrated on each other.

Tom Levy usually felt keyed up at this point with a new patient. He'd grown used to the fact, and not only masked it, but made sure his technique and attitudes remained unaffected. The thought of stepping into the unknown labyrinth of another person's mind never failed to fill him with a certain awe. He never knew quite what to expect.

Valerie Winterhouse had shown promise of being more than a simple case of nervous debilitation, although she didn't quite fit into any other of the classifications of neurosis so freely used by professionals and public alike. She puzzled him. Something in her reached out to him. He very much wanted to help her.

For Tom, psychological counselling was more than a profession and livelihood. It had become a commitment to others, one he had made seven years ago upon graduation. He knew his life would be devoted to helping people understand themselves and their potential; and with insight into their needs he would take a stronger grasp on his own.

In the soft glow of his desk lamp he studied the woman lying totally relaxed in the lay-back chair. Lines of strain had smoothed from her face, leaving it luminous and peaceful. Her rather large shapely hands lay in her lap, heavy with precious rings. Diamond ear studs glistened in the fall of soft blonde hair. A surprising streak of pure white ran from each temple, hinting at a good ten years more than the face showed. Her lips were parted and her jaw relaxed. She breathed lightly and slowly. She was a long way under.

'Valerie, do you hear me? If you hear my voice, raise one finger.'

He waited. Slowly the index finger of her right hand quivered and lifted very slightly.

'Thank you. You may lower the finger.'

Again he waited while she complied. She was a good subject for hypnosis. The intelligent, nervy ones always were. He hoped with all his heart that he could help her.

Other, more conventional methods had been ruled out from the start. Valerie had undergone several years of analysis in the States – it was a part of the lifestyle – and in her own words she had now 'had it up to here'. The end result seemed to have been a frightening slide into anger and depression as she refused to accept the help offered.

He didn't think she'd been honest with him. The amount of self-knowledge that must have come out of those years could not be denied, unless there was some overriding need to cancel it out. At least this way, with the hypnotic technique she'd never permitted anyone else to try, he might be able to by-pass her ever-vigilant ego and get to the real Valerie. God knew, she needed help of some kind.

'Valerie, you know that everything I say to you is true. You can trust me implicitly. You are in safe hands. Just let yourself go, relax totally. I am going to count down from twenty, and as I count I want you to see yourself walking down a flight of stone steps into a beautiful garden. It's warm and sunny, and as you move downward you find yourself enveloped in the sights and sounds and smells of the garden. It's your garden, your sanctuary. When I have counted to zero you will be standing on the grass amongst the flowers. You will be totally at peace, relaxed. Deeply relaxed. I'm going to start counting.'

His voice, always deep toned, had taken on the soothing quality of a father quieting a fractious child. It flowed evenly and richly, enveloping the woman in a stream that carried her down through the layers of her mind to the deep pool of the subconscious. There he came to her as a friend, a confessor.

'Valerie, why are you unhappy? What's happening in your life that upsets you?'

Her breath rose and fell evenly, but a slight frown ridged the smoothness of her forehead. When she spoke it was barely above a whisper.

'Why does everybody hate me? I've never done anything to harm anyone.'

'Why do you feel that everyone hates you?' He watched the trembling eyelids that indicated agitation.

'They always have. It began when I was little. My mother hated me. She never wanted a child. She even died to get away from me. All my husbands hated me, too.'

Tom didn't smile at the childish assertions. They came from a deep emotional level, and for Valerie they were truths.

He waited a moment, then said, 'Hatred can be made up of many other emotions. You can't hate someone if you don't have a strong connection with him or her. You say your husbands hated you. Did you love them?'

'I despised them. They were weak. They married me for what I had, not what I am. Yes, in the end I hated them all.'

'Why do you think you are wanted only for your possessions? Think back. Was there no one in your life at any time who loved you for yourself – not a school friend?'

He'd hit a nerve there. But the pain he saw in her was scarcely the remembrance of friendship.

'I don't want to talk about that!'

'Very well. Tell me then, Valerie – do you love yourself?'

'No!' The loosened fingers tightened in her lap. Her long nails gouged the skin unmercifully. 'I hate myself! I'm a failure. Everything I touch goes wrong, no matter how hard I try.'

'Why are you a failure?'

'Because nothing I've done in my whole lifetime has been important or worthwhile. I'm a parasite.'

'You are being very hard on yourself. Everyone has a spark of goodness, or divinity, if you like. In what way are you a parasite?'

'I live off the wealth accumulated by my father. I've never done a solitary thing I didn't want to do. Whatever was offered, I've always thought, what's in it for me? And if it didn't please me,

I didn't do it. That's total selfishness, isn't it? Well, isn't it?' Her voice began to rise, and he quieted her with soothing phrases, waiting until her fingers unknotted and she could breathe calmly.

'Why did you come to London? Were you running away?'

'What's the use of running? You can't escape yourself. I know. I've tried until I felt I'd go crazy. Maybe I am crazy. I hear voices and see people that aren't there. Weird pictures come into my mind of places that couldn't possibly exist. They're hounding me to a point where I can't go to bed sober and I can't face the world in the morning without a slug to get me going. I'm losing control over my own mind!'

'Listen to me, Valerie. You are not crazy. You're tired and confused and frightened. Sometimes this makes you feel you're out of control, but you're not crazy.' He could feel the anger pouring out of her in great waves, laced with fear. No wonder she felt out of control. Her lack of self-esteem fuelled both emotions, stoking her up until she had such a head of steam she feared either a complete blow-up or derailment. Either way she was headed for disaster.

He saw her movements of distress. Her breathing rate had increased and she plucked at the neck of her dress.

'Tell me what's worrying you, Valerie?'

'It's like my dream. I can't get any air. I'm smothering.' Her hands went up to her face and she seemed to claw at something covering her mouth and nose. 'Help me!' Her body arched away from the chair. Blood rushed to her face. A thick congested scream tore from her throat.

Tom's hands were on hers, holding gently but firmly. His voice was louder, stronger, but still calm and smooth, swamping her fears with layers of reassurance, removing her from whatever path she wandered.

He felt her begin to relax. He was getting through. When she'd totally succumbed to the spell he wove, he released her and sat back again, still maintaining the flow that connected them on this deep level. She breathed evenly now, her colour returning to normal. She half-smiled at something she saw. Hopefully, she'd returned to the garden he'd conjured for her.

He began to search her memory, taking her back to the days of early womanhood, through high school and its traumas, back to the pony-worshipping days of childhood, all the time searching for clues to her own self-hatred.

Her reaction to a stay in hospital at an early age looked promising, but eventually turned into a red herring. Philosophical about the lack of success in that area, he began suggesting to Valerie that she was growing older now and returning to her real, present age. As they progressed through the upward stages a small part of his mind went off duty. He looked at the clock, calculating the likelihood of leaving on time to meet Phil for a drink. He was looking forward to seeing him again and hearing what direction his work had taken over the past two years. Valerie had done enough this session. He thought she'd progressed in that she'd given him her trust, and next time he could probe a little deeper.

A choked cry brought him back to total concentration. His patient's hands were at her throat again in a protective gesture, and her face had changed immeasurably. He was looking at a different woman. The features had lengthened and darkened in some way, taking on a gypsyish cast. He had a queer feeling that beneath the closed lids her eyes were no longer blue, but dark, and wickedly knowing. Worst of all, he felt that for her he was no longer there. Valerie had gone off to a place where he couldn't follow and help her.

'Valerie, where are you? Tell me what's happening to you.' She didn't hear. He tried to regain control in every way he knew, gently authoritative, questioning, calming. Nothing he said reached her. With a shock he realised that her closed eyes had every appearance of looking straight through him at something only she could see. Such was the intensity she promoted he even glanced over his shoulder to check.

Hoarse with effort, he finally stopped speaking. There was silence in the shadowed room. He heard the faint sounds of traffic, muffled by double-glazing and curtains, and the clock of his desk ticked away the seconds monotonously. The atmosphere that had seemed warm and sheltering took on a claustrophobic feeling as he waited for what would happen.

She sat up. Her right arm came forward, pointing dramatically, and she spoke in a ringing voice he'd never heard before.

'A curse on ye all for a pack of scurvy knaves and whoresons. Ye were mim enough when ye'd crawl here begging your boons. Oh, aye. Then ye'd tug y'r locks and bend nose to knee, and I was good Mistress Anne. Now ye've taken into y'r thick heads that I've laid a curse on the cattle or the crops, or some such, and ye've forgot the brews that saved y'r children in t'plague two years gone. Who braved our mad lord in t'castle and brought him back to his senses afore ye were all whipped to death by his order, eh? Ye've short enough memory, by the Trinity I swear it!'

Tom's jaw dropped. Who was this woman? If it was Valerie playing a part, then she must be the greatest actress alive. Somehow she'd made herself smaller, thinner, the flesh of her cheeks hollow with the look that is worn only by the perennially hungry people of the world.

She swore a huge and lurid oath and turned on someone visible only to her. 'You, Tam Tipper. Where would your May be this day but for the herbs I gather by waxing moon and brew by the wane? Aye, black magic ye name it. But y'r wife is alive for't, not an angel looking down from heaven on ye and the five babes.'

She seemed to listen, then a scornful smile curved the full mouth. 'So say ye? Then go to't if ye dare. But beware the next storm that catches ye in t'fields.' Her eyes swept the room disdainfully. 'Go, all ye cowardly curs. A pox on the lot o'ye. Let come what may.' She made the motion of throwing a cloak about her shoulders and subsided into the chair.

Before Tom's starting eyes her features softened and plumped out. The thin body took on softer contours and diamonds glinted on hands that had lost their roughened look and now curved gracefully once more in Valerie's lap.

In a voice that had lost some of its smoothness he called to her, and she responded to his request. Quickly he brought her up to the shallowest level and awakened her. He ran a finger around a suddenly tight and dampened collar.

'How do you feel?'

She yawned and stretched and looked a little surprised. 'Fine. Just fine. Did I go under?'

Tom abandoned the idea of drinks and went straight home, taking the tape of the last session with him. He spent the evening with his feet on the fender, the curtains of the shabby room drawn against the night, his tape deck on one side and a stack of reference books on the other.

Habbakuk sat on the hearth and stared at him hypnotically. When his repeated subconscious suggestions about food failed to get results he finally sprang upon Tom's knee and sank two sets of claws into his flesh. Tom yelled and threw him off.

'Damned feline! What's got into you?'

The cat opened his yellow eyes until they almost spilled out onto the rug. Tom grinned ruefully, rubbing his knees.

'Okay. I guess it's my own fault. Sorry fellow. What'll it be, sardines or liver?' He went into the less-than-spotless kitchen nook and searched through a cupboard full of cans, all, as it happened, labelled 'liver'. Habbakuk watched with the concentration of a lion scenting blood.

When the cat had licked the bowl clean he returned to the hearth to groom himself, leaving Tom to his tin of baked beans, and a further tussle with the problem of Valerie Winterhouse.

So far he'd come up with nothing useful. Valerie hadn't struck him as severely neurotic. Worry and unhappiness lay at the bottom of her symptoms. She had admitted to feeling anxious and in low spirits, but that didn't justify an immediate diagnosis of either anxiety or reactive depression; and the notorious inadequacies of the systems for classifying psychopathology made him wary of putting anyone into any category at all.

Cases of multiple personality, commonly associated by psychiatrists with a diagnosis of schizophrenia, didn't seem to fit the case. Valerie had not appeared to split off from reality, not in the sense that the truly psychotic personality does.

He rummaged through his extensive library, nibbled his fingernails and drank too much coffee, finally falling into bed in the early hours no wiser than when he had started his research.

His next day, which included two free clinics in the suburbs of East London, and a whip around to the Children's Hospital, left him little time for further investigation. However, he had squeezed in a quick phone call to Phil Thornton and arranged dinner that night. He looked forward to renewing their once-close ties, since Phil was both friend and colleague.

Phil rang the doorbell of the flat promptly at seven, and in seconds he and Tom were hugging and thumping each other's backs like long lost brothers.

'Phil! Great to see you, Yank. You look like a million dollars. How's Carla?'

'She's fine. Sends you her love and wishes she didn't have to go north to visit some of her mother's Scottish relatives. I'm on the loose for a week, boy. Let's do the town together.' Phil's cheeky grin split his face wide, crinkling the sea-blue eyes. He might have been eighteen, not thirty-three. His appearance was as stylish as Tom's was scruffy, in a soft mole-brown doeskin jacket over a cream sweater, and pants and moccasins straight off Rodeo Drive.

He put his hand on Tom's shoulder and pushed him playfully. 'There's a definite improvement. No reek of tobacco.'

'I've given it up.' Pride rang in Tom's voice. 'It's done wonders for my nose. For instance, I can smell the smoked salmon in the parcel you just laid on that table.'

Phil grinned, then let out a yell. 'Hey, scat! Leave it alone you thieving animal.' He threw himself forward as Habbakuk leapt and landed high on top of the nearest bookshelf, a pink strip of extremely expensive hors d'oevre dangling from his jaws.

'Habbakuk, you wretch!' Tom shook his fist at him, but had trouble trying not to laugh at his friend's face.

Phil danced. 'Do you know how much that stuff costs? Just let me get my hands on the brindle bastard . . .'

'Give it up, Phil. You'll never do it. Besides, there's plenty left.'

Phil shuddered ostentatiously and handed the remains to Tom. 'I don't seem to fancy it any more, thanks. Why the hell "Habbakuk"? Of all the stupid names for a cat!'

'Phil, Phil. Don't you know your Old Testament? Habbakuk was a well-known prophet of doom.' Tom picked at the salmon as he led the way to two comfortably saggy couches set either side of a gas fire. 'Help yourself to a whisky, and sit down.' He disappeared into the nook to light the gas under a huge pot.

The room was large and shabbily comfortable, with its walls of overflowing bookshelves, the desk and typewriter set in a bay window (very beautifully leaded), the lovely old rosewood cabinet with bevelled glass doors displaying crystal drinkware, the faded Persian rug underfoot. It was a room for contemplation with shoes off, both metaphorically and in fact.

When Tom returned he found his friend had poured himself a large tot of whisky, put Prokofiev's 'Romeo and Juliet' on the CD and sunk into the depths of the best-looking chair, almost without trace.

'Feel better now?' said Tom, with false sympathy. He got his own drink, took the other chair and settled himself, still nibbling on the salmon.

The music finished and Phil roused. 'Mmmmh. I still don't get it . . . the cat's name.'

'Well, it's like this. You know what an optimist at heart I am.

I want to make the most of this world while it's still in one piece, and I think humankind can make it as long as there are enough of us around spreading goodwill on the job, so to speak. Habbakuk does not agree. He was born with his mouth turned down. He gets up each day believing it will rain and the mouse population will have died out overnight. I could never let him near my depressed patients.' He licked salty fingers and got up to pour himself a drink, tripping over the rug and just saving himself.

Phil laughed. 'You haven't changed. You're still the most pessimistic optimist I've come across . . . and the clumsiest. How's Cherry?'

'Happily redecorating the castle in mock Tudor with overtones of the Crusades. God help Harry's bank balance.' He tossed the whisky down in two gulps. 'Mind you, I don't think he'll ever notice. Too busy wondering how to spend the money as it rolls in.' He didn't sound envious. He'd never wanted the lifestyle that his ex-wife had taken to.

'Hmmm. Cherry really fell on her feet with him, considering her first misalliance with a cat-loving, lapsed Jewish do-gooder who can't even match his socks when he crawls out of bed in the morning.' He reached out and topped his glass with a liberal hand. 'Do they really live in a castle?'

Tom refilled his own and sat down again. 'Harry's all right. Just a mite too conscious of his progress up the social ladder. To answer your question, they've built a monumental mansion out past Richmond and named it Grosvenor Castle; and since I find it beyond description – ' He broke off with a laugh. 'Have you heard of "The Peacock Party?" You know –

> A party's proposed – at grand Perceval Mansion
> (Late Renaissance, Art Deco, Baroque Imitation,
> Rococo, Gold Grapes, Picture Palace collation!)

Well, that's Cherry's new place.'

'Sounds pretty upmarket.'

'Oh, it's all that and a bit more. Does lasagne and tossed salad suit you?'

Phil nodded happily. 'I'm mellow enough even to face your cooking.'

They bantered their way through the meal, eating at a small table before the fire, and mellowing further under the influence of a particularly good *pinot noir* brought by Phil. They spent the next hour bridging the gap separating their two years' graduate work together in Berkeley, and the present day. Tom had come home to set up a practice which left him little time for more than an occasional letter or phone call, but he still felt close to Phil.

Finally, after plates and remnants had been dumped in the sink, Tom drew a curtain on the mess and the two men settled down for serious discussion, with the wine close at hand.

Having already indicated a wish to talk over a case, Tom found Phil eager and waiting.

'My client has given me carte blanche in the matter. She's scared enough, and far enough down the line to let me try anything that might help her. That doesn't mean she's told me everything, of course. Some of the material that's come up must have done so during her years of analysis, but she's not admitting anything. Apparently I'm to do it all without any prompting from her – a sort of testing of my abilities, I suppose, even while she's sinking.'

Phil shrugged. 'It's not unusual. We all hesitate to trust completely. It seems to be an inbuilt phenomenon of the human animal.'

'Maybe. At any rate, I want you to listen to this tape, and then give me your opinion.'

Phil closed his eyes against a remorseless feline stare from the hearth, and listened as Tom's voice took his patient through the preliminary stages until she was answering his questions about her childhood. He started to bring her out, and her voice changed. Phil was electrified. He popped up in the chair, rigid with intensity. When Tom stopped the tape at the end, his friend appeared to be thinking furiously. Tom left him to it.

Within a few minutes Phil snapped out of his concentrated space. 'Can I hear it again, please? Just the last part, the change.'

Tom complied.

'Of course you know what you have here?' Phil's eyes flared in his head and his lean body had tensed, a thoroughbred ready to leave the starting gate.

'If I knew I wouldn't be asking you.'

'Surely you've heard of Bridie Murphy, the Bloxham tapes . . .'

'Hey, now, listen. You're not going to dig up that old stuff.'

'Not old, new. You're behind the times, my friend. The New Age studies are based on this one intrinsic belief, reincarnation of the soul. Tom, your patient has just gone through a classic past-life regression, and you were the one privileged to hear it!'

Tom couldn't speak. When he could, he spluttered. 'Absolute nonsense! Where's your trained mind gone? Wandering off amongst the daisies? I never heard such rubbish!'

Phil just smiled. 'Cool it, Tom. You did ask me for my opinion. If you're not prepared to listen, let's drop the subject. Tell me something about this client. What's her background?'

Tom cleared his throat and turned away to rewind the tape. He didn't look at Phil.

'She's forty-two, American, as you can hear, born in the blue-grass country, Kentucky, but lived most of her adult life on the west coast and following the European circuit. At present, living in London in her own apartment. Inherited wealth from father, a racehorse breeder – married three times, divorced three times. No children.'

'Come on, Tom. You're stalling.'

Tom faced him, his lopsided grin back in place. 'You're right, damn you. This one's getting to me, and I don't know why. She's all the things I most despise – idle, rich, spoiled, selfish – and she's also obsessional and terrified.'

'How terrified?'

'She's on the run, from everything that used to matter to her – friends, the social whirl. She'd skulking in that Mayfair flat, scarcely daring to put her nose out by day, and walking the streets at night because she can't bear to sleep. She's slowly killing herself.'

Phil frowned, picked up his glass and went to stand near the fire, contriving to edge Habbakuk out of his warm spot. He went with an outraged hiss.

'You'd better tell me all, friend.'

Tom had sunk right down against the cushions, his arms crossed over his chest, his chin buried in his collar as he concentrated.

'She's developed this obsession with a painting, one she saw in a Bond Street gallery window just before it went into an exhibition. It seems that, when she tried to buy it she'd been drinking heavily, and understandably, the gallery personnel were reluctant to do business with her. She admits this quite freely. By the way, alcohol is a problem, but I've found no evidence of hard drugs.'

Phil had turned away to lean on the mantelshelf, eyes closed, yet Tom knew he was attentive.

'Unbeknown to either of us, we both attended the opening night of the exhibition. It was the first by an unknown artist, and the work's magnificent. I got there early and became a trifle obsessed myself.'

'You bought something?'

'I bought the painting my client coveted.'

'Shit! What happened?'

'I suppose I was lucky I'd already left when she discovered she'd missed out. Her taxi had been involved in an accident, making her late. She created a scene, the gallery people tried to persuade her to buy something else, and she hit someone with her handbag. You don't do that sort of thing at Theodore Sampson's place. When she found they weren't going to give her my name and address she threatened them with everything from legal proceedings to arson, and was quietly removed. Apparently, next morning she came back and bribed someone for the information, and she turned up on my doorstep an hour later.'

'Did you sell her the painting?'

'Nope. She'd bullied her way past Sally into my rooms, and I wasn't too pleased with her manner. Besides, I want that painting myself.' He smiled reminiscently. 'You should have seen Sally's face when I turned down an offer of fifteen thousand pounds.'

Tom about-faced, staring at his friend. 'For a work by an unknown! You were mad not to take it.'

'You haven't seen the painting. Don't interrupt. The best bit of the story has to come. She went away and waited until I'd gone out and Sally had popped into the toilet, then calmly walked into my office, stood on a chair and pinched the thing off the wall. I came back for my briefcase and caught her hightailing it down the corridor with my painting under her arm. I brought her down with my best rugby tackle and saved it at the cost of a bruised knee.'

'What about a bruised woman? Tom, I don't see you tackling a female, whatever the provocation.' He held up his hand hurriedly. 'I know. I know. I haven't seen the painting. But I intend to. It's got magical properties.' He took a deep breath. 'So what's the end of this story? How come you took this obsessed female as a patient? I'd have thought there wasn't the slightest chance in the world of you building up a trusting relationship after all that.'

Tom shrugged. 'You don't turn away someone who's sitting in your chair looking like death but trying desperately to hold herself together.' He grinned unexpectedly. 'Especially not if you've just knocked her flying all over the corridor.'

'What you mean is you recognised another lame dog and promptly picked it up. You'll never change. I guess it's why I like you in spite of your mule-headedness.'

'Nor will you change, pal. I know you're only biding your time 'til you spring your wacky theories back on me. We might as well get it over with, so fire away.'

Phil looked doubtfully over the rim of his glass. 'Are you sure you want to? It's a poor lookout if you can't keep an open mind.'

'Try me.' Tom had carefully screened all comment from his voice. He still sat with arms crossed, which hardly augured well for his attitude of mind. However, he fixed his dark eyes on Phil, practically compelling him to begin.

'Here goes then.' Phil emptied his glass and put it down on the shelf. 'As you know, for the past eighteen months I've been working in a laboratory outside of Los Angeles. The project was pretty hush-hush, being within the military jurisdiction. I can't say much, except that it had a connection with a lot of New Age stuff. They're taking it pretty seriously these days, Tom. Even the Russians are seeking methods of using ESP projection and other elements of parapsychology in a military application.'

Tom nodded. That was the sort of fill-in news item that appeared whenever the papers ran short of grisly discoveries or pandemic disasters of some kind.

Phil continued. 'My research included the study of groups and individuals who practice esoteric techniques of mind expansion and changing states of consciousness – without the use of drugs, I may add. It got me in, Tom. There was so much which couldn't be explained by any of the known natural laws. Finally, I had to use one of the oldest methods of testing, the empirical method.' He paused, impressively.

'Go on.'

'I discovered the truth – that the old promise of everlasting life is exactly that. Death is just a doorway into another plane of existence, and we pass through it many times.'

The two men stared at each other. Then Tom uncrossed his arms and sat up.

'Religious humbug. Have you joined some kind of crazy Californian sect?'

'It has nothing to do with religion. I wish you'd rid your mind of all the prejudices you're carrying. Historically, almost every human culture has held such a belief, from the Neanderthals, who buried their dead folded in a foetal position, suggesting the belief that the dead would be born again, to the current Hindu faith. Survival after death was the central theme of the Egyptian religion. Reincarnation was taught in the early doctrine of the Christian church, did you know? As for your own Judaism, you must have learned the tradition of the kabbala in which reincarnation features. The modern Hasidic sect follows this.'

Tom sprang up. He'd gone from red to white complexion. Even as he recognised that his anger was out of all proportion to the offence, he shouted, 'Enough! I don't need you to teach me what I learned in the cradle – and later learned to despise.'

'Okay. But think of this. Something that has been believed by so many in all times and all places has at least a strong possibility of being the truth. It's just as logical as the idea that the whole of humanity has been suffering from mass delusion.'

Tom shook his head. He made an obvious effort to be calm. 'Look, this started out as a friendly consultation between colleagues. What happened? Suddenly we're caught up in this weird argument about the afterlife. It has nothing to do with my client's case.'

'So much for the open mind.' Phil took up his glass and seemed disappointed to find it empty.

'All right. You mentioned the empirical method, personal experience. Just tell me what in hell you mean by that.'

Phil's irrepressibly cheerful face grew solemn, but his eyes still had a mischievous gleam.

'I had myself regressed, Tom. I actually went back and relived a part of my life as a fifteenth-century Spanish nun.' He calmly reached for the bottle and poured himself another drink.

CHAPTER 5

London 1810

Sounds nibbled at the edge of her consciousness, voices that muttered just below the threshold of understanding. It irritated her that she couldn't make out what was being said. She had an absurd desire to lift her weighted eyelids and accuse the speakers of deliberately concealing something from her. Who were they, and why wouldn't they speak up? And what on earth was wrong with her eyes that she couldn't seem to open them?

Gathering her will she made a huge effort to move the stiffened muscles. Useless! Her lids must be glued together in some way. She tried to call out and nothing happened. The word 'paralysis' flashed across her mind, trailing a comet's tail of cold terror, spurring her on to greater effort. By the time she was ready to admit defeat, sweat beads clung to her hairline and her vocal chords felt irreparably strained; and still she hadn't moved.

Frustrated beyond bearing, she lay in the grip of whatever forces held her inert, tears oozing from the corners of her eyes and slipping down her cheeks. She'd never before felt so helpless.

Someone spoke nearby. 'Ah! My lord. Quickly. Your lady is emerging from her swoon.'

Startled, and no longer focused on herself, Karen opened her eyes quite easily and looked into a man's face. All she noticed were another pair of eyes – green as new young leaves, yet with a subtle grey shadowing beneath, and at present icy as an alpine stream. They glowed with a strange brilliance, as if they had lamps behind them. Very peculiar.

The watcher narrowed and concentrated his gaze, as if trying to penetrate the bones of her skull to seek the mind beneath. Then he turned away and in a voice husky with drink or strain said, 'She has been bled sufficiently, I think, Horbury. Bind up her arm, if you please.'

Still bemused, Karen was hardly aware of the servile mutter in the background, although she did look down at a touch, surprised to find a tight knot of cord biting into the flesh of her upper arm, and a streak of blood running from it.

I must have hurt myself, she thought. It's not painful. Nothing major, then. She felt quite wafty. It really had been exhausting, that last tremendous effort to bring back conscious control of her body.

The room blazed with light, but it was a light that moved and shifted. It bothered her. Briefly she closed her eyes to rest them.

Another voice, a woman's, scratched at her mind. It was an intrusive sound, the whine of a particularly large and persistent mosquito.

'Oh, my dear Caroline, such a relief! We thought ... we feared ... I declare, I really cannot be expected to withstand such frights in my delicate state of health. I fear I am like to faint. Antony, I beg you will give me your arm to my bedchamber. Now that I am reassured dear Caroline is recovered I must rest. You do see that I must rest?'

Karen frowned. What a silly voice, so affected and insincere. Surely no one spoke that way deliberately. And who on earth was Caroline? Perhaps someone else had been injured. Was she in a hospital ward with other patients?

'You are as healthy as an ox, Oriel. I must decline to believe that you require my support for the length of one short corridor. But by all means rest. There is little you can achieve here.' The husky voice held contempt and Karen wasn't surprised to hear a door closed with a decided bang. Whining Voice had evidently departed in dudgeon.

Still battling inertia she opened her eyes again and this time focused beyond her immediate self. Yes, she was in a bed, although much wider than the usual hospital couch; and even the most exclusive private medical clinic did not provide satin and lace quilted coverlets with gauzy bed hangings to match. Highly insanitary, she'd have thought.

Her gaze flicked to the side, avoiding the blood-filled bowl and razor, to the man binding up her arm. She stared. Were her eyes tricking her? Or had she been taken ill in the middle of a costume ball? How else could she explain the figure in a brown velvet coat and breeches, and a grubby wig sitting askew above a round good-humoured face?

'Who are you?' Her voiced came out quite unlike her own. It sounded distinctly odd in her ears. But the stranger beamed.

'Well now, my lady. We are heartily glad to see you back in your senses. Of course you know me – Dr Henry Horbury. Have I not attended your ladyship since childhood?' He deftly bound up her arm and released the tourniquet. You have given us a fine fright, if I may say so. So deep a swoon and for such a length of time . . . In my experience this can lead to highly dangerous consequences, most particularly when brought about by severe shock – '

'Enough, Horbury. You will not wish to upset her ladyship with tales of what might have been.' The harsh tone did nothing to mitigate the words, and the doctor jumped as if pricked.

'Of course not, your lordship. Nothing was further from my intention, I do assure your lordship – '

'Well,' the other broke in impatiently. 'Have done, man. I wish to be private with her ladyship. Take yourself off to the library and wait there until I come. You will take a glass of madeira before you go?'

'Certainly, certainly. Your lordship is most gracious.' The doctor grasped his bag and his still-bloody instruments, and all but backed out of the room in a display of obsequiousness that left Karen gaping.

Speechless, she looked across at the man who could treat another so ungraciously. However, his back was turned to speak with someone hidden by his bulk. Then he moved aside. A lovely pale face showed just beyond range of the quivering light. It hung there almost as if disembodied, its owner trembling between the two worlds of the flesh and the spirit.

Karen stared, then realised the woman was real. She had wrapped herself in some dark, gauzy fabric that caused her body to merge into the background, leaving the dramatically beautiful features to make their impact. Tendrils of fine dark hair escaped the veiling to fall across her cheek, enhancing the impression of mystery. Even her eyes seemed to hide beneath lids too heavy to support their own weight. The exaggerated fringe of lashes was almost too much. It put Karen in mind of a description she'd read, an eulogy to the eye of the lovely Mumtaz Mahal, the empress whose fabulous tomb still drew millions to gaze and marvel at such a tribute to lasting love.

The small spurt of amusement soon died. She could hear whispering, and the name Sybilla mentioned. She shook her head. She had her own name for this woman – Bella Donna, Beautiful Lady, the deadly nightshade – and the subject of her recent, rather disturbing painting. She shivered and tried to sit up. Something was very wrong here. Who were these people? Where was this place?

Now that her sight had adjusted to candle and firelight, she could take in the peculiarity of the room itself, so heavily and ornately furnished, so stuffy – so old-fashioned. Quite definitely not a hospital ward. But, who these days had bedrooms with great marble mantelshelves surmounted by mirrors and gilt? Who hung floor to ceiling velvet drapes, swagged their beds in yards of stuff, and filled every corner and lined each wall with bow-fronted chests, blindingly polished and carved and inlaid to the point of frenzy? Who but a slightly crazed millionaire did these things, then hired medics in fancy dress and ordered people about as if they were nerveless robots?

Using the bed hangings as a rope she managed to drag herself into a half-sitting position against the pillows. Thrusting down the cowardly notion that to sit quiet was safer, she cleared her throat tentatively. 'Excuse me.'

The man swung around and came to the foot of the bed. He leaned both arms on the coverlet, stretching it tightly across her feet, and stared into her face. 'Well, Caroline?'

Karen's heart slammed right into her ribs, flattening and rebounding. Thought and reason died as she absorbed the impact. Incredible! Impossible! She shook her head as if to deny what her eyes told her. But reality stood there, his weight pinning her legs to the mattress: the miniature, the haunting painted features of her gift portrait had taken on flesh, and he looked a good deal less than welcoming. No longer two-dimensional, the gentleman had acquired a powerful personality, seeming to fill the room and press down on her bruised senses. Those amazing light-filled eyes now bored into hers, questioning, probing.

Again she cleared her throat.

The heavy brows came together. 'Your pardon, madam?'

'I . . . you . . . that is . . .' Confound the man. It was damned near impossible to break that gaze.

Feeling like a mesmerised rabbit she used her pride as a weapon. It rushed in, sweeping away every other emotion but anger at her helpless confusion.

'Look here, I don't know who you are or where I am, or . . . or how you did it, but I know it's a trick of some sort. Dreams don't feel like this, not even the worst nightmares have the texture... the... the reality of this situation. But I'll tell you, whatever you're playing at, I'm not going on with the game any further. If you will kindly move back and let me up I'll be leaving, and you can count yourselves lucky if I don't call the police.' Her voice rose towards the end of this valiant speech, but its impact was somehow deadened by the room, swallowed up and lost in the quantities of stuffy hangings.

It crossed her mind that this might be an elaborate plot of Humphrey's devising. But surely not even he would go to such lengths to torment her. Did he have some scheme to drive her to the brink of insanity, thus undermining her case before the court? She wouldn't put it past him. No. Such a plot required imagination. Straightout standover tactics were more his style, like a couple of thugs paid to visit her flat and smash up her furniture. The idea had occurred and been dismissed within a few seconds.

The man's frown had darkened and he leaned uncomfortably close, searching her face.

'What is this strange speech? Has your mind been affected, after all? I hope to God...' He straightened abruptly, the brief concern erased from his voice as he continued harshly, 'Is this more of your trickery? What do you try to gain from such a performance – my sympathy? If so, you are wide in your aim, my heart. I long ago learned there is no softness in you, but you dearly love to play upon the weaknesses of others.'

'My heart!' The endearment slid off her like the tip of an icicle. This man hated her. It was no trick. He really had somehow mistaken her for another woman, a woman who must have done a dreadful thing to be the cause of such bitterness. Caroline. That was her name.

He stood back, seeming to relinquish his mental hold on her, and Karen blinked. As if a curtain had dropped between her and the rest of the room, she found herself suddenly detached from them all. She felt a rush of strength through her body. Muscles that a moment earlier had felt like wet string sprang to attention, lifting her bolt upright. Her mind wiped clear of confusion, she spoke with a new authority.

'Listen to me. I am not the person you think. I'm not this Caroline woman. My name is Karen... Karen Courtney. I need your help. I don't understand what's happened or how I got into this situation, but I refuse to simply sit and wait for it to sort itself out. There's got to be a reasonable explanation. And since I'm certainly not an invalid, I intend to get up and start doing something about it.' Thrusting aside the opulent bed quilt she scuttled rather than slid across the expanse of mattress, hampered by what seemed to be yards of nightgown.

Her feet had barely touched the floor when she felt herself swinging down into a black spiral of unconsciousness. Faintly in the distance she heard a voice calling to her. Her mind groped towards that voice, and she clutched fiercely at the bedpost, willing herself to stay upright, fighting the tidal drag upon her senses.

'Caroline! Are you trying to do yourself an injury? You have just been bled. Sybilla, where is her ladyship's maid?'

Karen felt herself lifted onto the bed, was aware of his warm breath on her face as he pulled a pillow beneath her neck and drew up the coverlet. She hid behind closed lids, giving her lagging senses time to catch up. A chill had crept over her, but it had nothing to do with her physical weakness. It was more like a foreknowledge that she was not going to be able to deal with matters, after all. The ordinary methods were not going to work.

'Caroline, give me your attention, if you please.'

It was a command, and even as she registered this, she had looked up in obedience. His face had changed alarmingly. Never reassuring, even when posed for portraiture, it now had quite a menacing cast. She was annoyed with herself for wanting to shrink back into the pillows.

'You will oblige me by not moving from your bed until Dr Horbury gives his permission. The injury you received could easily lead to a concussion of the brain and we must take the greatest care of you.' The indifferent tone belied his words, and she was in no danger of overestimating his professed concern. Why had she ever thought those grey-green eyes so dazzling? Now that she thought about it, they owed more to the frigid glaze of an Arctic sky. Penguins could catch cold just standing alongside the man! He was pure autocrat, concerned only that his will should be done.

She tried to whip up the spark of rebellion into a warming anger, to thaw the actual chill that had begun to spread throughout her body. Fear was a part of it, the feeling of having control slip through her hands. She had entered a looking-glass world where anything might happen. Water could run uphill, the sun might set in the east – paintings come vividly to life. More frightening than all was the fact that no one else saw it. Or if they did, they had no intention of acknowledging it, let alone giving an explanation.

She'd forgotten the beautiful woman in the background, but now she glided forward in a swirl of dark draperies to lay a hand on Karen's arm. Her smile seemed to say, don't worry, some of us are friendly. However, when she spoke it was to the man standing behind her.

'Antony, your guests will begin to arrive in but a short space of time. Would it please you if I were to act as your hostess for the dinner? Clearly Caroline is in no position to do so.'

'That is exceedingly kind of you, Sybilla. I confess, the thought of greeting thirty hungry and expectant people with the news that their meal has been cancelled does not recommend itself to me, although they will doubtless feel obligated to leave – under the circumstances.'

'We cannot permit that. Your reputation would be quite out the window.' When she smiled, her eyes slanted in an oriental manner. Quite bewitching, thought Karen, wondering how on earth she had managed to choose this particular face as a subject for her painting. Intrigued, she listened to the half-teasing, half-serious tone as the lovely voice went on.

'I shall say that I am deputising for your lady who, regretting a sudden indisposition, begs that her guests will remain and enjoy the hospitality of her home.' Patting Karen's arm she leaned over and said with sincerity, 'Rest now, sweet cousin. You have suffered a severe shock. And be assured, between us, Antony and I will administer your responsibilities. We may discuss other matters more comfortably in the morning. Sleep well.'

She brushed Karen's forehead with her lips, leaving behind a wisp of some exotic scent, then departed in a rustle of silk. Antony followed, holding the door for her and pausing to direct a last admonitory glance at Karen.

Totally swamped in the current of her fear and bewilderment, Karen slumped down in the bed. Reassurances were all very well, but what did she care about the concerns of play-acting strangers? The important thing was for her to get out of here, and judging by the brief encounter, the only way she'd do this was to play dumb, and wait for them all to go. Accordingly she again closed her eyes and willed herself to relax, listening for the sound of the closing door.

When it came, she peeked cautiously, only to see her tormentor standing almost at her elbow, smiling grimly at her confusion.

'Did you expect to cozen me so easily? Have I not had endless experience of your tricks and ploys, my heart? Too long to be anything but suspicious of your slightest movement. No, Caroline. In this matter you will obey me implicitly. You will not place foot to floor for the next twelve hours, or believe me you will regret it.' He beckoned to someone standing in the doorway, and Karen was freshly humiliated to realise that his contemptuous words had been overheard, not by the mystery woman, but another, tall and narrow in cap and apron, with the uncompromising demeanour of a wardress.

'Roberts will attend your needs. 'Tis unfortunate that your own maid is also indisposed this evening. Yet I venture to say you will find this woman efficient and loyal, to me.'

She knew her face must mirror her feelings, for he smiled unpleasantly before turning away and finally leaving the room.

So much for her escape plans. She watched her jailer move about, tidying away the medical debris, mending the fire and in turn watching her charge from the corner of her eye. There would be no slipping past her.

Still pretending compliance, Karen sipped the hot milk offered, and permitted her pillows to be straightened. Then she closed her eyes and set herself to think hard about a way out of this mess.

She knew nothing more until wakening in the chill of a watery dawn.

She was parched. Her tongue stuck to her palate and her lips felt and tasted like old clag paste. She moved her aching head on the pillow, seeking a cool spot, and felt sticky tendrils of hair catching about her neck. She remembered what had happened.

Hallucination! She'd somehow ingested some drug – LSD? crack? – and gone on an horrific trip. That had to be the explanation. It accounted for so much, including the way she felt now, like the newspaper wrapping from last night's fish and chips. So, when she opened her eyes it would all be over.

Light filtered through square-paned windows, a moody, ungenerous light from a surly sky. Someone had drawn back the curtains to reveal the naked limbs of a frostbitten tree. The room bore no resemblance to her own attic flat. Cold and airless, stale with the ashes of a near-dead fire, it was the room of her hallucination –

the room where she'd encountered her miniature in the flesh, the man named Antony.

Alienation gripped her. Don't panic! Relax. Hold on for a minute. She squeezed her eyes shut, then opened them again, cautiously. Nothing had changed. A domed clock on the mantelshelf tinkled like a music box, and a bird in a hanging cage trilled a reply. Hooves clattered and iron wheels rumbled below the windows. Silence came down like a blanket, thick and smothering. Karen raised her hands to her face – and screamed.

They were not her hands. These dainty, beringed fingers belonged to someone else. Where were her familiar, longer, somewhat hardened hands, the square cut nails, the one knuckle knobby from holding a brush?

In total panic she tumbled from the bed, catching her feet in her nightgown as she raced to the mirror over the fire. She stared into the terrified blue eyes of a stranger.

Clutching at the marble shelf she felt a faintness rising to engulf her, passing over and gradually receding.

It isn't true. This is not happening. God, don't let it be real! She forced herself to look again. The face was enchanting, pearly skinned, dimpled, classic nose, rosebud mouth, the works. Too good to be true.

She probably has a thick neck, was her jaundiced thought – a slander she was unable to verify as the lovely stranger had the added attribute of a petite figure which simply didn't allow her to see any higher in the mirror. A pocket Venus, she judged, considering her lack of inches, and the almost embarrassingly voluptuous curves her fingers traced through the folds of satin bedgown.

There was one other thing, her hair. That really put the lid on it. Karen's own hair, black, straight, fringed, could never in a million years be mistaken for a flaming halo, writhing and curling and clinging about her bare shoulders. Even in such a tousled state it shouted for notice. It had a bold attention-seeking vitality, demanding a personality equally extrovert. Certainly that wasn't Karen.

'You're not me,' she whispered through cracked lips. 'Who are you? And where is my body?'

The mirror image reflected her anguish. 'What have you done with me?' it mouthed back.

Karen whimpered and flung herself down on the hearth-rug, her new face buried in her new dainty hands.

Much later the clock tinkled its chimes and she raised her head. Her lacy sleeves had fallen back and she noticed the bruising on her right arm above the elbow. Pulling up her gown she saw another great spread of purpling stain running up her right thigh and hip, and when she prodded, she yelped with pain. What had happened to it . . . her?

Conscious of the cold biting through almost to her bones she dragged herself upright. The irony of physical discomfort taking precedence over agony of mind didn't escape her. You could trust the body to always look after itself, whosever the body might be! She pulled the bedcover off and wrapped it about her, returning to the hearth to crouch over the faint remaining warmth. She thought about what had happened to her.

Acceptance came hard. Like most of her contemporaries, she'd come across a smattering of religions other than her own, even toyed with the idea of looking into them more deeply, some time. She'd always been too preoccupied with other things. The circumstances of her life scarcely encouraged a belief in a loving creator, still less a wish for immortality of any kind. Who wanted to stay on forever in a world so rife with unhappiness?

Of course there was another side – beauty, challenge, achievement. She discounted love. If it existed it was too vulnerable to survive in the climate created by humanity. But, on balance, the pluses didn't seem to be enough. She'd never thought about why so many millions of people accepted reincarnation as a fact. Now she had to. Whatever had happened to her might not fall exactly into the category of rebirth; it was more a transference of the soul, the essence of Karen Courtney, into another human vehicle. Nothing she'd ever read or heard of could explain that. Fervently she wished she'd gone into these matters in detail. Since it was far too late now, with a certain amount of fatalism she recognised the body she now inhabited was for all purposes her own; and someone had done something to it. That being so, it might pay her to find out who and what.

Perhaps its previous owner had tried to kill herself. Not so surprising, if she was married to a tyrant, she thought resentfully. It would not be her own choice. She'd sooner fight back. The man obviously needed a lesson. Such autocratic treatment of wives went out last century. But then, this *was* last century. It had to be – the furnishings, the manner of dress and speech all fitted the period of the miniature, late Georgian or Napoleonic times.

Yet, attempted suicide didn't quite fit the circumstances. Someone who had thrown herself downstairs should surely have more damage to show than a few bruises and an aching head. Maybe it had been a simple accident. Which still didn't explain how she, Karen, had become involved. The more she puzzled and worked at the conundrum, the worse her head felt.

Outdoor sounds of hooves and wheels on cobbles probably meant she was in a town of some size, possibly still in London itself. What a relief. Or was it? There could be few similarities between a city pre-electricity, pre-major industrialisation, and a capital in the age of technology.

Something niggling at the fringes suddenly burst into the forefront of her mind. What if this Caroline person had been dead before she fell? What if she'd been murdered and thrown downstairs to give the appearance of an accident?

Familiar waves of panic rose and swelled to a crescendo, finally wiping away all control and sending her scampering to the doorway, a trapped animal desperate to escape.

He stood there waiting for her, as if he knew the exact moment when she would flout his orders.

'Return to your bed, Caroline. You may rise after you have eaten a good breakfast, and not before.'

'No! Let me past. I've got to get out of here.' She tried to dart by and was caught and held. Kicking and thrusting futilely against his strength she was born back into her prison.

'Let me out! I'm not Caroline. I'm not your wretched wife. This isn't even my time. You don't understand.'

'Hush. You are hysterical, Caro. Just lie down and I shall send for Dr Horbury.'

'No, no, no!' She bounded straight back up from the bed where he had deposited her, her shriek enough to rattle the lustres in the lamp overhead. 'Listen to me. I'm from another time, from the twentieth century. My name is Karen Courtney. I live in Acacia Road, St John's Wood, and I have an aunt named Billie, and a cat, and . . . Oh, my God! Adele! Adele!'

Desperately she tried to dodge him but his arms enveloped her, smothering her cries against his chest.

'Caro, Caro. You rave. My dear, calm yourself.' Real concern coloured his voice, proof that her anguish had reached him, but it didn't help Karen.

A sob caught in her throat as he released her suddenly limp body, carefully laying her back on the bed. She turned away from him, burying her face in the pillow and biting into it fiercely. Her hands clutched at the sheets, her nails tearing the fine lace edging as she strove to check her hysteria. The vision of her child crowded her mind to the exclusion of all else. Adele needed her. Her baby had no one but her mother – and who and where *was* she?

A shudder passed through her, leaving her calmer. She turned over and faced the man who was her enemy, and heard him sigh.

'Oh, Caro. If your mind has been affected . . . Dear Lord, you know how lunatics are treated, as witness the sufferings of our unfortunate monarch.'

She shivered responsively. Oh, yes. She knew. Poor old George III, restrained in a monstrous iron chair, tortured with hot poultices to draw off evil humours and gagged to stifle his cries – all in the name of 'modern' medicine. Who would dare go out of his mind in those times?

'I am not mad,' she said calmly, although her fingers still clutched at the sheets as if they were a kind of lifeline. 'Really, I'm not. But I have to explain to you how frightening it is for me to find myself in a stranger's body in another world so distant from my own.' Seeing his expression darken, she faltered, then continued. 'It's difficult for you to understand, I realise that . . .'

'Not difficult, impossible. Madam, you speak too much with reason. I do believe that you are not lunatic, but devious. There is some plot behind this charade of yours. If it please you to continue, then do so, but be warned that it will not benefit you. I am not to be deceived. Nor do I believe that you yourself can underestimate the dangers of such a game. Do not try me too far, madam, or I might very well be driven to have you committed to some institution for the care of diseased minds. It would buy me some peace,' he added with bitterness.

Karen was silenced. If her fears were a reality, and she had actually stepped into another era, she would have to be wary, hiding her thoughts and guarding her actions. She knew all too well that any man of his times, let alone a nobleman, as this man appeared to be, held enormous power; while a woman of whatever rank counted as little higher than a good horse.

'Well, Caroline?'

'What do you want me to do?'

Some of the lines in his face relaxed. 'If you are well enough to come downstairs, Sybilla and Lady Oriel are in the small sitting room. I am persuaded that you will wish to reassure them personally regarding your health.'

She put on an expression she hoped was suitably submissive. 'I'll come down when I have eaten. My clothes?'

'Your maid has made a remarkable recovery from her indisposition. She will bring you a tray, and later will assist you to rise.' He crossed to the fire and pulled the bell rope hanging there, then turned and said with the merest hint of irony, 'May I say that I am overcome with delight at your own swift return to your senses, my dear.'

Stung, she shot back at him, 'You have given me little choice. You've called me a liar and accused me of some kind of plotting. But as far as I can see, it would hardly be surprising if my brains were as scrambled as eggs after the fall I had.'

His slight start confirmed her suspicion. Obviously, he had not wanted her to recall the details of her 'accident'. Last night he'd shut the doctor's mouth smartly when he'd begun to talk.

'How much do you remember, Caro?'

'About what?'

He shook his head. 'Your speech is peculiar. I wonder now . . .'

She leaned back against the pillows and marshalled her thoughts. 'Look here, it's obvious that I fell heavily. I have the biggest bruises to prove it, plus a headache that'd put a wharfie to bed. What I want to know is how did it happen?'

'You tripped and fell from the head of the stairs, but fortunately, you were able to catch at the banister rail and lessen the impact considerably. Nevertheless, it was a severe fall. It might have proved fatal.'

His unemotional tone riled her. 'I might have broken my neck!'

'Yes, you might.'

'And that would have delighted you.'

'No.' He smiled, and this time with true, albeit wry humour. 'Although you may be forgiven for doubting it.' He stretched out a hand to her. 'Come, Caro. Can we not deal better than this? I am willing to bear my share of blame for the coldness between us, and would make amends. Will you not meet me? What do you say, my dear?'

She'd have given a good deal to be able to respond to that offer, so charmingly put and seemingly so honest, but she didn't dare. Having seen the hard side of this man, knowing he was capable of cutting her down with a word, and even perhaps using his strength against her, she couldn't afford to relent. Plain fear dictated her reaction, and unfortunately, this showed plainly in her face.

He withdrew at once. 'Very well. As you wish. However, I will not permit you to shame me, either publicly or within the family. You will preserve the amenities and hold yourself ready to accompany me down to the small parlour within the hour.' With the slightest of bows he left her.

Karen felt dreadful. Each new revelation passed over her with the impact of a steamroller, as did every meeting with this Antony person. All the effort of standing up to him and trying to put her own point of view had been wasted, too. He wouldn't listen. Still, in fairness, how could she expect him to believe her story? If it were not the only possible explanation she wouldn't believe it herself. Time travel! It was the stuff of science fiction, the creation of an Asimov – or more correctly, the original mind of H.G. Wells. To expect the Georgian mentality to encompass such a notion was on a par with putting a baby in the cockpit of a space shuttle.

'It does not compute,' she muttered, and giggled idiotically. She'd have to watch that. She might go really off her brain.

The door opened to admit a maidservant carrying a tray set with dainty porcelain and silver. Eyes downcast, she bobbed. 'Good morning, my lady. Will you take your breakfast now?'

'Yes, all right. Put it down there, thanks. I want to get dressed. Will you help me?'

Astonishment made the girl look up. 'Why, surely my lady. Will you wear the yellow poplin, or perhaps the new green china silk with floss trim? It arrived but yesterday and with the most charming shawl.'

She put down the tray on one of the hideous chests and went to fling open the wardrobe doors, all six of them. It was Karen's turn to be astonished. A perfect fountain of colour gushed from the openings, billows of fabric – silk, cotton voile, lace, brocade, and a dozen others she couldn't recognise. Plain, dotted, frilled, embroidered and flounced, fringed, ruffled and beribboned, all were for the enhancement of one woman, this Lady Caroline.

For one moment she stood at the mercy of her femininity, praying the clothes would fit her, then remembered, still with astonishment, she had a new body. Or rather, she occupied Lady Caroline's exquisite little form. If she hadn't been in such a fix she might have derived a good deal of amusement and pleasure from trying on such lovely clothes. As it was, she didn't give a damn what the woman wore.

'Anything. You choose.'

The maid's jaw dropped, but she obeyed Karen's impatient gesture and quickly selected a pretty jonquil-coloured gown, shaking out ruffles and minor creases caused by its folding. It seemed coat hangers were an invention yet to come.

Feeling like someone out of an *Arabian Nights* tale, Karen sat on the edge of the bed and drank her too-sweet chocolate, watching the girl's preparations. One quick glance under the domed covers on the tray, and she decided to skip the meal. Kidneys and bacon, sliced beef, ham. It had to be a refinement of torture. Or did the Lady Caroline actually like such food in the morning?

Someone brought hot water to the door in a brass can, and the maid took this and poured it into a flowered basin on a stand. With a towel over her arm she stood waiting.

Then followed an elaborate ritual of washing, drying and powdering, much to Karen's dislike. But she let the girl do her job, primarily because she felt rather weak as well as grubby. Her body covered by a sort of shift, and precious little else, she let the girl roll on a pair of patterned stockings and help her into the yellow gown. It felt rather thin for a wintry day, but she was inclined to thank capricious fortune for not landing her in an era of metal-ribbed corsets or worse. The long sleeves restricted her under the arms, the one hundred and one buttons down the back tried her patience, and her voile-covered bosom, thrust up by the high waistline, felt distinctly chilly. However, the addition of a shawl in finest cashmere did help.

'Will your ladyship wear the lemon kid slippers?'

Karen inspected the little heelless shoes being held out and nodded. The girl sounded nervous. Had Lady Caroline been such a dragon of a mistress?

'What is your name?'

'Why . . . Munstone, my lady.'

'I mean, your first name.'

'L . . . Lucy.'

Karen smiled kindly. 'Well, then, Lucy, do you think you could help me do something with this ginger bird's-nest I've suddenly acquired?'

The refractory hair was brushed smooth and drawn high on the back of the head to a cluster, then teased into ringlets to fall over forehead and ears. Karen admitted to a certain satisfaction with her final appearance, followed by irritation at its lack of appreciable effect upon her self-styled 'husband' when he came to fetch her.

His gaze moved over her with indifference. He bowed slightly and offered his arm.

For the first time she noticed the scar from a vicious cut. It ran along the outside of his left hand and wrist to disappear beneath the cuff of his shirt. The skin had puckered into a raised welt, as though stitched by a handyman rather than a doctor.

'Why do you hesitate? You have seen it before, and much more.' He turned his hand over to look at the scar. ''Tis strange how beauty's perfection cannot bear to look upon the imperfect.'

Something in his husky tone made her wish she hadn't hesitated. She placed her hand in his arm.

'Shall we go down?'

A footman threw open the door of the sitting room and she passed in. Two women sat there, one elderly, very grande dame, with her high-nosed features framed in a Valenciennes cap, and arrogance oozing from her grossly obese frame. Guessing that this must be the Lady Oriel, Karen crossed the room to greet her.

The most noticeable thing about her was the smell. Squatting in her chair by the window she reminded Karen of a gigantic, overdressed toad, and the odour of stagnant pond was quite overpowering. She hid her distaste as the woman put out a hand covered in dirty rings and briefly touched hers.

'How delightful to see you so blooming, dear Caroline. So fortunate that you sustained no permanent injury.' Eyes like grey agate gave the lie to these sentiments. The toneless whine she had heard before, last night, from the woman whose delicate nerves could not tolerate a sick room.

'Thank you. I am feeling much better.'

Antony said smoothly, 'Lady Oriel was exceedingly distressed by your condition, my dear – indeed, almost prostrate.'

Enjoying the woman's expression, she turned as the other, younger woman approached, both hands held out in greeting. This must be Sybilla.

'My dearest Caro, I cannot describe my relief! When I saw you lying at the foot of the stairs, so white and still, my heart turned in my breast.' Taking Karen's hands she held them tightly, searching her face for any mark of her shocking experience.

Karen felt warmed. At last! Someone who cared what happened to her – a friendly voice in this wilderness of double-talk and intimidation. It was a pretty elegant wilderness, all the same. Her first quick glance about the room had registered pastel colours and dainty furnishings. Someone with a delicate touch had chosen the chintz coverings, and pretty little tambour tables to set off walls of pale apple-green silk, and hangings of white and green; while the lamps, small pieces of china and sketches of country scenes all blended admirably. A ceiling-high window took her eye, its white painted shutters folded back to reveal a vista of pleasant paved courtyard with a fountain, and stone benches amongst the shrubs. In spring it would be idyllic.

She gave her attention to Sybilla, still favouring the flowing drapery mode of last night, but today revealing a love of peacock colours that could only enhance her beauty. Black eyes, black hair, the kind of matt skin most women dream of. Karen's appreciation showed.

Sybilla smiled brilliantly. 'Come and sit with me, Caro. You must take care after your experience, must she not, Antony?'

He inclined his head and pulled a chair closer to the fire, holding it as Karen seated herself. She clutched chilled fingers in her lap and felt depression settle over her. What was she doing here with this strange lot? She didn't belong, and never would. Panic pulled at her nerves, threatening her precarious stability. Yet she couldn't afford to give way. If she was ever to break out of this time trap, she had to act a part, stay calm and wait for some kind of signpost to appear.

If she could only remember what events had preceded her journey into the past, then she might learn how to reverse them. At least it would be a start. She could recall most of that momentous day, from her dreadful interview with Humphrey up until she left the Bull Inn. She'd gone for a walk before bed, but she couldn't remember just where or why. It was somewhere beyond the town . . .

Antony interrupted her thoughts to speak softly in her ear. 'Your wits are wandering, Caroline. My aunt has addressed you twice already without response.'

She hid her resentment at the minatory tone of voice. There would be no more confrontations just yet, not until she'd found a way of countering his power. Forcing a smile she begged pardon.

'I was wool-gathering, I'm afraid. What did you say, Lady Oriel?' Such a cross face, she thought, and wondered what life had done to sour the woman so badly.

Lady Oriel very deliberately took out a snuff box from her reticule and made a business of pinching a large portion between finger and thumb, then snorting it up – a process attended by all the delicacy of a walrus sniffing the wind – then followed this with a gigantic sneeze. Snuff showered down over her bosom to settle in a fine layer of dust.

Sybilla said hastily, 'Mama was enquiring as to whether you cared to proceed with our proposed shopping expedition. You will recall we had planned to visit the modiste today to discuss new gowns for our Christmas visit at Camray Castle. I myself require a new ensemble for the house party, and I venture to state that Antony will not begrudge us the loan of his barouche to transport all our new finery.' Her half-roguish look brought an answering smile from him, indicating to Karen that the cousins were on the best of terms.

Lady Oriel cut across the conversation with a shrill complaint, vowing she had not a decent rag to her back. 'Were it not for my whist party, I declare I should come with you, child. George is so skinflint I do not know how I dare to show my face abroad; and for you my dearest one, he shows not a tittle of care, his pinching ways bidding fair to ruin your chance of forming an eligible connection. I had held such high hopes for this Christmas visit,' she mourned.

Looking at Antony's cynical face, Karen thought, he's heard it all before.

Sybilla's quick disclaimer followed. Karen could appreciate the control that allowed the younger woman to refute her mother's obvious sponging without showing her in a poor light. Yet the shopping trip was clearly important enough for her to pursue the matter. When all three looked enquiringly at Karen, she had no answer for them. Certainly her new body seemed well enough for such a mild expedition, but the inherent social intricacies and expectations could bring trouble.

Antony, as usual, displayed little patience. 'Come, my dear. Surely you can say whether or not you feel able for such an outing. Naturally I would wish you and Sybilla to do me credit at all times. You may call upon me for whatever sums are necessary to see you both comfortable.'

Neither Sybilla nor her mother seemed to find any fault with this speech. Sybilla sent her cousin a warm look of thanks.

Karen seethed, wishing she could throw his patronising offer back at him. But she could put forward no valid objections to the excursion, and found herself committed to leave the house with Sybilla soon after lunch. Thank heavens she hadn't eaten any breakfast. With Antony's eye upon her, she'd have to eat something, or put up with another harangue.

Satisfied, Antony pulled the bell and instructed the answering servant to bring in Miss Chloe and her nurse.

They must have been waiting nearby for the summons. Almost at once a little girl of about six entered the room, prodded from behind by an overflowing nanny figure in a starched cap and apron. The child looked first at Antony, who silently indicated his aunt. With a sullen slowness the child moved across the carpet to curtsey before the older woman. Karen didn't blame her for her reluctance.

Dismissed with a curt nod, the girl sped to Sybilla and kissed her cheek, taking up position beside her chair. Karen noted the fondness between them. Sybilla was clearly a favourite with the family.

Interested, Karen waited for the child's reaction to herself. It was disappointing. With wooden obedience she dipped and rose, then moved back to Sybilla's side, making her allegiance clear.

'Chloe, your mama-in-law has been ill. It would be a politeness to enquire after her health,' Sybilla gently reminded.

The little lip stuck out mutinously.

Sadly accepting the signs of dislike, Karen inspected her newest relative. Was a mama-in-law a step-mother, perhaps? She thought she could see a resemblance to Antony in the firm chin and straight nose; and the eyes, too large for the small pointed face, were very like his in shape and colour. Pixie ears stuck out from the short dark cap of hair, but the child's thin body looked malnourished, although whether from lack of food or affection Karen couldn't tell.

Pain stabbed through her at the obvious reminder of her own child. Adele, too, was slight, and she knew all about the need for loving arms to run to.

She wondered why this child wanted nothing to do with her. Had the obnoxious Caroline been jealous of her husband's affections? Studying the wary-eyed face, she realised that Chloe hated being in the room. She fidgeted and darted longing glances at the door where her nanny waited patiently. At least the nurse had a kind if rather bovine face, thought Karen, but where did the child get her stimulation? Too young for a governess, at a guess; probably attended by servants, brought down for a daily quarter-hour with largely indifferent adults, as was the custom of the time – and miserably lonely most of her waking hours.

Her lips tightened as Chloe turned towards her father, the small face anxious, ready to spring to life. He was so coolly unaware. Sybilla had withdrawn into a discussion with her mother, something to do with dress patterns. So Karen smiled and beckoned.

'Chloe, would you like to come over here and tell me what you have been doing this morning?'

Chloe scowled and pretended deafness. Only Antony noticed. His frowning glance bent on the child, who immediately shrank back, looking with frightened eyes from her father to Karen.

Appalled, Karen stood up, drawing attention to herself with a gasp. 'If you will excuse me, I think I should go up and rest before lunch. I feel a little faint.' She managed to sway on her feet.

Sybilla ran to her, taking her arm. 'I shall go with you, dear.'

Nanny surged into the room and gathered up her charge, and Karen saw them go, with relief. She noticed Antony looking at her with that odd intensity of his. What had she done now? Had her effort to protect Chloe been obvious? Well, what of it? He had no business bringing such a look to any child's eyes. He was her father, for heaven's sake! You'd think he would show her some kindness. Had he perhaps disliked his first wife, and consequently, her child also? Was Chloe his child, in fact? She wished she knew more of the family set-up. It was like inching her way through a minefield. The idea of peace and quiet upstairs on her own began to appeal.

She felt Lady Oriel's basilisk stare and gave her a sweet smile in farewell. Antony accompanied her and Sybilla to the stairs, remarking that he would not be in to dinner as he had an evening engagement.

'I shall not lunch at home, so may I wish you both a pleasant shopping excursion this afternoon, ladies?' He opened the door on a book-lined room, and stepped back hurriedly, almost knocked down by a dog rushing through.

The spaniel headed straight for the stairs, and Karen, falling upon her with delighted doggy yelps. She backed off and found herself half-lying on the stair, her face being thoroughly licked.

'Hey, you're lovely, but you're ruining my dress. Get off, you great mutt.' Laughingly she fended the animal, while trying to get up.

Sybilla and Antony stood stunned. Eventually Antony pulled himself together and dragged the dog back with a hand firmly twisted in its collar. His face still expressed the blankest astonishment as, with his free hand, he helped Karen to her feet.

Karen brushed at her muddied skirt and said cheerfully, 'That was quite a welcome. What's his name?'

She couldn't miss the changed quality of the silence. Looking at Sybilla she saw amazement and something very like fear in her face. Antony's expression could not be defined.

He said slowly, 'His name is Feathers. You've known him for twelve months under circumstances of mutual animosity.'

While she tried to think of something to say, he added, 'Can you tell me what happened on this very spot a month since?' He waited, while she just looked at him.

'No? Then I shall refresh your memory. In some manner Feathers contrived to give offence and you struck him with your crop. He retaliated by biting you on the calf, a wound that required stitching, as I recall.'

Without warning he released the dog, bent and raised the hem of her gown knee high, at the same time whipping down her left stocking. His hands were hard and bruising on her calf. She looked at the marks where broken flesh had healed.

Sybilla gasped. 'Oh, dear heaven! She has lost her memory. Oh, Caro.'

But Karen was looking at Antony. His eyes bored into hers, lasers that stripped down her mind, determined to get at the truth.

'Memory loss would explain many things. It does not account for Feathers' extraordinary change in attitude. What has happened to you, Caroline?'

'I told you, I'm not Caroline. I'm Karen Courtney, and I don't belong in this century . . .'

'Stop it!' His hand flashed up, catching her jaw in a pincer grip. 'No more lies, Caroline. I want the truth from you. You were warned, and I am no longer prepared to wait for your explanation.'

Fury burned in the grey-green eyes. He was dangerous, and she couldn't satisfy him because he would never accept the truth. Karen tore his hand from her jaw and ran.

The unexpectedness of her flight gave her a lead. She was at the front door, opening it before he moved. Behind her she heard Sybilla cry out, and then a heavy thud and a curse. Risking a backward glance she saw Antony stretched full length and Feathers tugging at his coat.

She flew down the steps and across the pavement. The crescent garden opposite looked vaguely familiar, but she didn't pause in her headlong dash towards the street. There she halted briefly. The buildings looked like an elaborate stage set – for a play by Sheridan, perhaps, or even the lighter side of Dickens. An elegant sweep of pale stone terraces, a railed-in park, smart equipages going by. Was it all a big charade, after all? Was she running into the wings, about to get a glimpse behind the scenery?

The beginning of hope gave her an extra spurt of energy. Deaf to the shouts and running footsteps behind, she picked up her skirts and plunged ahead into the maze of old London.

CHAPTER 6

Running steadily, she turned east and slightly south towards the city, hoping to find familiar streets. Instead, almost immediately she entered unknown territory. Without warning, fashionable residential districts fell away into a squalid maze of lanes and courts and alleys; those paved so covered in filth that she might as well have been running in a ditch.

In the middle of the streets open kennels overflowed with the most disgusting vegetable and animal refuse, miring her skirts to the knees. She slipped and fell several times, eventually bruising her leg so badly she had to stop. She leaned against a crumbling brick wall to catch her breath, past caring how she looked. The rows of miserable tenement houses crowded in upon her, blocking out the sky. No current of air penetrated to the street, and she seemed to be breathing in a foul miasma from the stones themselves.

Now that she'd stopped running she felt the cold. It struck through her thin house slippers, numbing her feet and ankles. Her dress was no protection against the bitter air, and her teeth began to chatter of their own accord. The bits of sky she could see between the rooftops looked like swags of dirty washing hanging low and threatening. She pushed herself upright and began to move slowly on.

A woman stood in a doorway opposite, watching her. It had to be a woman – she wore a skirt, to which two young children clung, whining. Another baby sat on her hip, its face buried in her bosom, obviously suckling. Looking into the coarse-grained face under lank greasy hair, at the pipe held in broken and blackened teeth; and the whole air of degradation that hung upon the woman, Karen felt revulsion and pity run through her.

'Tipstaffs after yer, dearie?' The woman advanced on her with predatory eyes.

Karen ran.

Each street seemed to lead to a worse one. Some were busy, and she was often forced out of her way by itinerant vendors, beggars, pot menders pushing their tools in barrows, even gangs of half-starved, ricketty-looking children playing wild games of tag, or kicking the blown up entrails of a beast as a football, their little stick limbs scarcely strong enough to carry them.

After an encounter with a drunken man outside a tavern, she avoided the houses with signs above them, even preferring the stinking alleys where the contents of open privies ran down over her feet.

There was a stitch in her side, and her leg felt as though it was on fire. She sobbed as she ran, the tears making runnels in the soot that had settled on her face. She'd been wrong about everything. The world she found herself in wasn't a stage set, nor a cruel trick played upon her. It was horribly real. She hated it. And she'd never been so alone and afraid before.

Her foot met something slimy, and she slipped and fell, for the last time, landing on her hands and knees in a pool of filthy stagnant water. It was too much. The pain, her fear, the awful lost feeling, lay on her like a ton weight. She stayed where she was, an inert huddle, just another piece of refuse in the gutter.

'My dear, you are nigh frozen through! Oliver, give me your coat.'

Swaddled in a smart cutaway that provided little enough warmth, Karen found herself lifted and deposited onto the padded seat of a closed carriage. The woman followed and sat down beside her, wiping her face gently, chafing her hands and uttering small soothing sounds, interspersed with commands to her companion to place the lady's feet so, and mind that he directed the coachman straight to Park Crescent.

Karen opened weary eyes and forced herself to sit upright. There was a terrible smell in the coach, which she couldn't locate. The gentleman whose coat she wore sat opposite in his shirt sleeves, his chin buried in a cravat of enormous proportions. From the delicate yellow hue of his pantaloons, and the extravagance of his waistcoat, she knew she was in the presence of a dandy, or one who aspired to the term. Even his hair, as yellow as his thin legs, displayed the severe cut back from the face and down-drooping lock over the forehead that proclaimed him a Regency 'pink'. But his eyes were kind, and he appeared to bear no malice for the appropriation of his coat, even on so cold a day. Of course, the carriage was warm enough inside. Where was that awful smell coming from?

The lady beside her said, 'Lady Caroline, pray allow me to present

Mr Oliver Stamford. 'Tis not every gentleman who would emulate Sir Walter Raleigh with such a good grace. I am Amanda Crayle. We have met, of course, but infrequently, and I doubt you will recall my name.'

Karen blinked. The woman was even more noticeably turned out than her companion, and would be memorable for that alone. Scarlet velvet predominated, with a white fur trim, giving her the appearance of a sweet-faced, blimpish little Santa Claus. Her sleeves looked like nothing more than two strings of saveloys, caught together at intervals, and ending in a ruffle that hid the small gloved hands. Her hat resembled a red cake tin adorned with a white rabbit or two.

This extraordinary little figure leaned forward, her face falling into a dimpled pout. 'Oh, you really do not recollect our meeting. What a set-down for me.' Her smile peeped out again. 'Mama would say I was well served for my temerity.'

'Oh, no. Please. I'd never be so rude. The trouble is . . .' Karen put a hand to her aching head, and realised with horror that she was the source of the revolting odour in the carriage. She seemed to have put her hand in something indescribable that had once been alive. 'Your carriage! Your clothes! They will be filthy.'

Amanda Crayle said calmly, 'Both may easily be cleaned. Pray do not disturb yourself. Only explain to me how you come to be in such a distressing situation, Lady Caroline. I give you my word I have never been so astonished in my life as I was to see you in the gutter of Chicken Lane. How very fortuitous, to be sure, that we should chance to be returning from the Holborn dispensary at that very time.'

Karen thought quickly. While most of her seemed numbed by pain and cold, her mind worked well enough. She could clearly remember Sybilla's horrified exclamation on the staircase of Rothmoor House.

'I must have lost my memory. I was in an accident where I hit my head and I can't recall the people I should know, nor the places, nor even who I am.' Karen heard the half-truth come out quite easily. After all, she had to say something believable, and it looked as though she'd be repeating it for some time to come.

'You poor dear!'

'Demmed awkward!'

The two spoke in unison. Amanda frowned at her escort and took Karen's hand in her own.

'I am so very sorry for your situation. I will not tease you further, but tell me if you recall your name and place of residence.'

'They say I am Caroline Marchmont, of Rothmoor House. I don't know where that is. I think I must have run for miles.' She heard the resignation in her voice. If she had to stay in this strange world for the time being, she'd far sooner belong to its privileged ranks, after having glimpsed what lay behind the façade of elegant Georgian London. The misery and squalor she'd witnessed made her feel sick when she thought about it.

Oliver Stamford's slightly timid smile was clearly meant to be reassuring, and she realised how lucky she'd been to fall in with her two rescuers. A bitter wind had risen, driving rain against the windows of the carriage. She shuddered and pulled the meagre coat more tightly about her, closing her eyes against further interrogation.

Their arrival at Rothmoor House and her re-entry turned into a progress, with so many people pressing around her to exclaim and scold and question that she was deafened. It was noticeable how quickly they backed off when they detected the smell of fetid rookeries that hung about her.

The main entrance was meant to be imposing – its floor laid with chilly tessellated marble, the walls arched and pilastered with more of that cold stone. Each niche had its bust or urn, or a high-relief carved bouquet, and over all presided a great ice-crystal chandelier, its prisms clinking and swaying in the wind from the open door. Karen had already dubbed the place porridge – neutral, bland, colourless and unwelcoming. Now, in her present frame of mind it felt like the anteroom to hell – a cold and echoing bedlam.

The redoubtable Miss Crayle took immediate charge, pushing Karen through the crush, ruthlessly elbowing aside those who would stop her. One figure, however, was immovable. He turned out to be Charles Hastings, secretary to Lord Antony, and very much ruler of the household in his lordship's absence. He and Amanda faced one another – the little red turkey hen versus the stolid mastiff.

'I tell you candidly, sir, the Lady Caroline is in the most urgent need of rest. She does not require to be brow-beaten and questioned and . . . and *driven* by a horde of importunate persons.' She swept a red velvet arm in an arc, almost connecting with Lady Oriel's out-thrust jaw.

The secretary nodded. 'I am perfectly in agreement with you, ma'am.' Turning on the crowd he dismissed all the servants, barring the butler, then contrived to usher the other ladies and gentlemen, still pushing forward, in the direction of the drawing room. He did it without giving offence, which in the case of Lady Oriel constituted a remarkable feat.

Karen silently applauded. She handed Oliver Stamford's coat back to him with her thanks and accepted his stuttered good wishes for her recovery. He seemed embarrassed by his unconventional and uninvited appearance in a nobleman's home, and immediately trotted back out to the carriage.

Amanda waved to him and explained to Charles Hastings, 'He is not very comfortable in society, you know. He will be happier waiting in the carriage. I expect he will want to see the horses walked so they do not take a chill from standing.'

The secretary bowed, quietly giving orders for men to go in pursuit of Lord Antony and the other searchers, and a tray of suitable refreshments to be taken in to Lady Oriel's interrupted whist afternoon. He left Karen to Amanda's care.

As she was supported towards the stairs Karen looked back at this competent man and decided she liked what she saw. Of no more than medium height, and neither dark nor fair, but an indeterminate sandy colouring, he impressed her with his air of civil assurance and his ability to command the respect of all. In just a few hours she'd grown tired of the class demarcations she'd encountered. It was refreshing to see someone who knew who he was and respected himself without reference to his station in life.

However, when Amanda whispered in her ear, 'What a fine looking man, to be sure. Is he not a very Apollo in form?' she looked again, and wondered at the extravagant phrase.

'He seems to have a pleasant face and manner.'

Amanda stared, then laughed. 'Of course, you are wedded to Jove himself. I daresay he has spoiled your taste for men of gentler mien.'

It was Karen's turn to pause on the stair. 'You mean Lord Antony? Do you consider him handsome? I've never seen him without his brows drawn in a frown and his mouth a grim slash. Perhaps you're right. He has the graceless arrogance of power.'

'I am persuaded you are not serious! Why half the female society of the ton fell into mourning when he wed again last year. He is held to be a very proper man in every respect.'

'He's a bully,' said Karen waspishly, and saw Amanda's expression change to one of concern.

'My dear, never say such a thing. Now come, let us find your maid and have you laid down on your bed.'

Bed again! Karen had a vision of herself cowering against the pillows while her jailer brought up blisters on her with his tongue, and her whole nature rose in rebellion. She would not allow herself to be treated like that ever again. She was a modern woman, liberated in every way. Not even Humphrey at his worst had succeeded in making her cringe, and he had a quite physical way of extorting obedience. At least this Regency rogue used his tongue only. If she'd been feeling entirely herself she'd have given him a good match yesterday. Now, of course, he'd be quite furious with her for causing such an upset, with visitors in the house, too. She'd be blowed if she'd hide away in her bedroom waiting for retribution.

'I'm not going to bed. I'll take a bath and change and then I'm coming downstairs.' She raised her voice. 'Mr Hastings, would you be kind enough to tell Lord Antony when he comes in that I will meet him in the library?'

He bowed, and she fancied she had surprised him. Amanda's reaction was interesting in that she seemed torn between deploring such physical exertion after shock, and admiration for Karen's clear challenge.

'You are a woman after my own heart, Lady Caroline. I can see that I should have paid less attention to gossip and made my own judgments. You will pardon my plain speaking, but I had no notion that you were one of the new breed of female determined to challenge society's dictates and force recognition of our equality.' A decidedly martial glint had appeared in the brown eyes, and Karen realised she'd misjudged Amanda's temperament every bit as much as Amanda had hers.

She smiled with real friendliness. 'I welcome your honesty, Miss Crayle. There seems to be little enough of it about in these times. Please come with me to my room while I freshen up, I'd like to talk to you. Oh, and by the way, don't give me my title. I'd rather be Kar – Caroline.'

'You know, they think I'm mad.' Having dismissed Lucy, Karen sat squashed in the hip bath before the bedroom fire, soaping herself, while she discovered how much she liked Amanda Crayle and wanted her friendship.

'It is always the first solution to cross the commonplace mind,' Amanda observed. She had removed the terrible hat and the even worse coat, and emerged as a young woman in her mid-twenties, of normal bodily proportions, although plump, and clad in a gown of slate blue twill which actually enhanced her complexion. Dark curls, cut modishly, clustered around her cheeks, now pink and blooming from the cold. Her vitality gave her a freshness that surpassed mere prettiness, thought Karen.

'I can't blame them for thinking it. The things I've said must seem quite crazy. But it's so bloody frustrating.' She threw the bath sponge down, splashing water over the rug. Blue eyes flashed fire as she gripped her folded legs and sank her chin moodily onto her knees. 'Amanda, you're the first normal person I've struck since I arrived. Do you think . . . would you help me?'

Amanda looked at her thoughtfully. She sat so prim and neat with skirts arranged about her, Karen wondered if she'd made a mistake, after all.

'Your speech is unusual, and you talk of having "arrived". Pray tell me what you mean by that?'

Karen searched for the right words. 'Look, I've only told this story once, and the reception it got scarcely encourages me to tell it again. But I must have help. I've just got to get back to my own time. It's vital!' She looked up at Amanda's intent face. 'I'm not Caroline Marchmont. My name is Karen Courtney and I live in the twentieth century. Last night I went for a walk in the country, and woke up in a strange bed, in another woman's body. This place, these people, they're all totally foreign to me. I'm trapped in the wrong time, and I don't know how it happened, nor how to get out of it. *He* doesn't believe me. He says if I tell anyone else I'll be taken for mad and clapped up in an asylum.' Her voice cracked. 'He insists that I'm his wife, Caroline, and it's obvious that he hates her . . . me. What can I do? Just tell me where, in God's name, can I turn for help?'

She lowered her head and wept, not just for herself, but for the child she loved, and who depended on her.

Amanda let her cry for a minute, then picked up the big bath sheet and brought it to her, encouraging her to get out of the cooling water and dry herself. 'For you do not need to contract a chill to add to your troubles. My dear, I am perfectly willing to listen to your tale, and help you if it lies within my power. Now, dry your eyes and wrap yourself warmly. I shall help you to dress as we can converse more privately without the presence of your maid.'

Feeling slightly better for the release of tears, Karen stepped into the gown and shift laid out earlier by Lucy and accepted Amanda's help with buttons and laces. The stiffness in her leg had eased, and only her headache and scratched hands remained to remind her of her recent ordeal.

She looked at Amanda with affection. It helped a lot that she had taken the revelation with composure and was prepared to listen further. Life had taught Karen the foolishness of taking an almost perfect stranger into her confidence, and she could only think that Amanda's sincerity had been the key. Sybilla's kindness, while very welcome, had not led to immediate trust. Maybe it had something to do with Lady Oriel being a perfect old horror. A few maternal genes must surely have been passed along during Sybilla's conception.

'Thank you, Amanda. Let's sit by the fire and I'll try to tell you as much as I know. Lord Antony will be home at any minute and I'll have to go down and face him.'

Shrewd eyes searched her face. ''Tis clear you do not enjoy a good relationship with him. Forgive me, my dear Caroline, but rumour has it he has every right to be angered at his wife's conduct.'

'I'd gathered as much. But as I'm not his wife, it's hard to accept the censure. I find myself wanting to tell him a few home truths about his treatment of his wife. She's probably been driven to misbehaviour by his own beastly conduct.'

'Beastly! Surely, you cannot mean . . .? He has not offered you violence, Caro!'

Karen laughed, a little bitterly. 'He doesn't need to. He has a tongue like a scorpion's tail. Oh, Amanda, it's such a mess. I can see that while I occupy this body no one will believe I'm not Caroline Marchmont. It's not reasonable to expect it. But I'm honestly not her. Can't you tell from the way I speak I'm not one of you? I don't use your idiom. I don't know anybody. I can't even find my way around London, a city I've lived in all my life.'

'I believe you.'

'What?'

'I believe that what you tell me is quite possible. There are so many things for which we have no explanation – matters which reach beyond the world we know. In the planes of existence that lie beyond, who knows what natural laws might be suspended? The phenomenon of time itself could be non-existent.' She smiled at Karen's surprised face. 'I am a student of the occult science, and I am perfectly sure that there is a way to assist you in your dilemma. If I cannot do so, there will be another who can.' She raised a warning finger as the maid entered the room. 'This is not the time for discussion. If I mistake not, your husband has returned and is calling for your presence.' She raised an eyebrow and Lucy bobbed in Karen's direction.

'His Lordship awaits you in the library, my lady.'

'Thank you, Lucy. I'm coming now.' When the door had closed behind the maid she turned to Amanda. 'I hope you meant what you said, about believing me.' She searched the other woman's face, seeking reassurance. 'You're not simply humouring a crazy woman who's lost her memory?'

Amanda clasped hands with her. 'Caroline – I must continue to address you by that name – I give you my word that you may trust me. You are, however, in a difficult, perhaps even a dangerous position. Allow me to offer a modicum of advice.'

'What do you mean?'

'We must instantly slay these rumours of madness. Loss of memory is perfectly permissible, although within certain bounds, and within the confines of this house. Socially it would damn you. Should you fail to recognise one of the Royal Dukes, and your bow lack the correct degree of deference, no amount of later explanation will see you forgiven. Now, if the notion pleases, I shall undertake to instruct you in the niceties of social conduct, impart to you the names of persons of rank, and those you must be seen to recognise and treat with the proper observance. I shall take you about until you are familiar with your surroundings, and in general become your guide and mentor as you launch yourself once more into the ton.'

Karen paled. 'I couldn't! I'd fall flat on my face the first time I tried to fool anyone. I'd rather be thought mad.'

'Caroline, you have no understanding of the horrors of being locked away as a lunatic in this century. You have enemies, or rather, the Lady Caroline has enemies who would be delighted to see her removed from her present social eminence.'

When Karen would have pursued this, Amanda shook her head and drew Karen to her feet, draping a warm shawl across her shoulders and handing her a pair of mittens to hide her damaged hands.

'There is no time. You will not wish to add to Lord Antony's ire by keeping him waiting. Muster all the energies of your character, my dear, and go to beard the lion. I shall call upon you tomorrow.'

She donned the awful hat and coat that transformed her from a normal young woman into a bloated red sausage and accompanied

Karen down the stairs, farewelling her in the main hall.

Karen hesitated. A footman sprang to open the doors to her right, then closed them behind her. Antony Marchmont stood by the fire, his arm resting on the mantelshelf as he gazed into the flames. He seemed lost in thought. For an instant Karen saw him as others must, a well set-up man, tall and muscular, his profile cut sternly but beautifully. Yes, in a dark, almost saturnine way, he was good-looking, if the arrogance in every line didn't set up your hackles and make you long to bring him down to ordinary mortal level. Jove, indeed!

A gust of sleet hit the windows, rattling like a drum muffled in velvet draperies. It broke into his thoughts. He looked up at Karen, and she unconsciously braced herself.

'So, you have returned.'

'Yes. I had no other choice.' She shivered and made herself approach the fire. How did people stay warm with such unsuitable clothing in such vast rooms?

He moved aside so that she could have the full benefit of the warmth, but she was conscious of him standing close behind her. Was he furious? She couldn't blame him, if he'd been out searching for hours in deteriorating weather.

Pulling the shawl tight around her shoulders she faced him. 'I'm sorry I caused so much trouble. I hope you were not caught in the sleet.'

'Thank you. I returned before the worst of the storm.' He moved to a nearby table and poured from a decanter into a crystal glass. 'You will oblige me by drinking this. Your cheeks are too pale.'

She accepted the glass in something of a daze. Where was the biting tone, the barked order for an explanation? Raising the glass she sipped the brandy distastefully, knowing it would help bolster her courage if nothing else.

Then she set the glass down and clasped her hands together under the shawl. 'We should talk.'

'You echo my sentiments, madam. Pray be seated.'

Taking chairs on either side of the fire they faced one another in wary silence until Karen could endure it no longer.

'I was forced into it. I know it was cowardly to run, but I simply couldn't take any more unanswerable questions. My memory – '

'Yes,' he broke in. 'Your inconvenient memory loss. It explains much, but not all. This tale you tell, this fantastic farrago of coming from another time . . . It will not do, Caro.' He spoke heavily, as if more weary than enraged. 'I know your love of fantasy. I have good cause to know, have I not? Your romantic escapades are becoming a matter of public interest. But this is going too far. I have the name to consider.' He closed his eyes briefly then looked at her again, this time with the more usual hardness in his eyes. 'I want your pledge, Caroline, that you will cause no further embarrassment with your imaginings. We are, unfortunately, tied together in this life. I will never permit divorce to sully my house, and I have already warned you of the dreadful consequences to yourself should you persist in exhibiting all the symptoms of lunacy. I must have your bond of good behaviour.'

She met him stare for stare, but inwardly she flinched. There had been a threat in those last words, a note of warning that reminded her how she'd been found at the foot of a staircase, bruised from ankle to waist.

'I see. In other words, I conform to your notions of a well-behaved wife.'

'You have grasped my meaning exactly.'

'And the "or else"?'

'Your pardon?'

'If I don't conform?'

'Then I must regretfully restrict your activities, and confine you to your rooms. With your powerful understanding I have no doubt you will grasp the full import of such an embargo. You will be virtually incarcerated for the rest of your days.'

The lack of any emotion behind such words filled her with real fear. He could do it, and would do it if she thwarted him. Then she'd have no chance at all of finding a way back to her own time. Her one hope was to go out into the world and look for someone who could help. Locked away at the top of Rothmoor House she'd see no one, and she'd stay there until she rotted.

With as much dignity as she could summon she rose to her feet and moved away towards the end of the room, allowing him to see the contempt she felt but dared not put into words.

'I will obey you because I must. Your good name will never be brought into question by anything I say or do, and I shall strive to regain my memory.'

He too rose, and bowed. 'I am delighted that we are in agreement, at last. Yes, Charles?' He had heard the door open and faced it before she was aware of a sound.

Charles Hastings didn't notice her standing in the shadow of a Chinese screen. His naturally solemn expression had not altered but he said with some excitement, 'There is an urgent dispatch – ' He broke off at Antony's quick gesture.

'I shall deal with estate business after we have dined, Charles. Will you inform Bates that Lady Marchmont is ready to be served?'

Slightly flushed, Charles slipped the paper he carried into his coat breast and bowed in Karen's direction.

'May I say how happy I am to see you have suffered no ill effects from your misadventure, my lady.'

She thanked him just as stiffly, and made herself take Antony's offered arm as escort. Now she'd have to face a barrage from the obnoxious Lady Oriel, she supposed. At least she would have Sybilla to talk to.

The company assembled in the drawing room all turned to stare as they entered. She was glad to see that most of the guests had left.

'Well, cousin, you have set the cat among the pigeons this time.' A totally strange man approached with languid steps and bowed over her hand.

Karen looked from him to Antony in confusion.

Antony murmured, sarcastically, yet with deliberate clarity, 'You are not asking me to believe you have forgotten Basil Frensham, Sybilla's twin – a wastrel who waits for a dead man's shoes.'

Basil stiffened, then shrugged lightly. 'I fear I was meant to overhear those unkind words. Fair cousin, can you not bring me into favour with your husband? I have done nothing to deserve such dispraise, I assure you.'

'I will readily believe that you have done nothing to any purpose, Basil,' remarked Antony.

Observing his mincing walk, the extravagant cut of his coat and the truly blinding pattern of his waistcoat, Karen classed Basil as more fop than dandy. His thick black hair could have been cleaner, and she'd been almost overpowered by the mixed wave of body odour and scent as he bent over her hand. She could scarcely believe him to be related to the beautiful, fastidious Sybilla.

Then Lady Oriel descended upon her, a staggering figure in her virulent purple gown and equally virulent temper.

'My son is voicing the general opinion that you have managed to make a complete fool of yourself, Caroline, and upset the household quite unnecessarily. I should not be surprised to find the dinner uneatable if chef's nerves have been affected.'

'Pray, Mama, do not be pinching at poor Caro. You know she has been unwell since her accident.' Sybilla smiled at Karen, offering her a welcome conspicuously lacking from any other person in the room.

'I trust you are mistaken, my love. If there is one thing I cannot endure it is a poorly cooked dinner.' Having voiced his apprehensions, the grey-whiskered gentleman whose huge bulk teetered on the hearth, absorbing most of the heat, raised his eyeglass and stared at Karen. He looked to her like a large one-eyed walrus, and she was forced to stifle a giggle.

Lady Oriel snorted. 'George, pray be silent! And Sybilla also. If I wish to express my displeasure – '

Antony's voice cut across, clear and unequivocal. 'You will, I trust, do so in less heated terms, and in private, Aunt.' He turned to Karen with a slight smile. 'I see Bates patiently waiting to announce that you are served, my lady. Shall we go in?'

Silently, she took his arm and led the rather formal procession to the dining room. What a strange man he was. Apparently no one was permitted to criticise her but himself. She wondered whether he had cancelled his dinner engagement that night to keep an eye upon her, perhaps because he guessed she would need some support? Or had he merely decided it would look bad to absent himself under the circumstances?

As the footman deftly seated her at one end of the long polished table, she had time to absorb the atmosphere of the room. Like most of Rothmoor House it was lofty, chilly and unwelcoming. It was also as gloomy as a cavern. Branches of candles and a fire battled with the deadening influence of royal blue velvet and heavy Jacobean panelling, not to mention the surfeit of gloomy family portraits peering down their aristocratic noses at the diners. Karen's spirits sank even lower.

Then the doors opened and the courses began to arrive.

Encouraged by her father from early childhood, she had developed an interest in history, more especially his own field of modern British and European. Her carefully chosen library, housed in the makeshift brick and board shelves of her flat, included books on the Regency period, and therefore certain aspects of Georgian life came as no surprise to her. She did not wonder at the quantity and variety of dishes offered at dinner, yet she found such super-abundance nauseating and could eat little herself. As fish followed fowl, followed by roasts, ragouts and fricasse, each with several side dishes to choose from, she watched the Honourable George and his lady devour everything put before them, swilling down each mouthful with whatever wine was at hand.

They munched their way through vegetable compotes, tartlets and syllabubs, then made their selection from the pastry baskets and sugared comfits, refusing only fresh fruits from the Rothmoor succession houses down in Kent. Karen decided she'd been mistaken. Lady Oriel was more hippopotamus than toad. How could the woman possibly heave herself out of her chair when the time came to move?

Desultory conversation was the order while the serious business of dinner was in hand. However, by the time everything but fruits and nuts were removed, the talk had become general. Basil's efforts to interrogate Karen on her afternoon's escapade were foiled by Antony, who blandly turned the subject as often as it was introduced; and Lady Oriel was too somnolent to bother.

Charles Hastings sat silent and preoccupied, while Sybilla tried to make polite chat – rather difficult when the persons and events alluded to meant nothing to Karen. However, at long last the interminable dinner ended.

Catching Antony's discreet signal, she gladly prepared to depart the scene. It had been a most uncomfortable meal, and she hoped it wasn't representative of the norm, while fearing it was. As she rose, so did the gentlemen, although the Honourable George's sketchy raising of his posterior was more of a gesture. It took two footmen to haul Lady Oriel erect and hold her until she attained her balance. Her face had ballooned, and there was a more than usually malignant look in her eye. As the ladies trailed after her to the withdrawing room, Karen resigned herself to another baiting.

Deposited in the most comfortable chair, feet up on a stool, Lady Oriel took out her embroidery bag and prepared to open hostilities. In this, however, she was foiled by her undutiful daughter. Sybilla took her seat at the piano and began a noisy rendition of Handel's Fireworks Music. She played continuously for twenty minutes, and only ceased when the gentlemen appeared, along with the tea tray.

The Honourable George grumbled audibly that the port had circulated only twice. 'Unheard of! Never known such a thing!' He subsided in a chair as close as possible to the fire, continuing to mutter to himself.

'Thank you,' Karen whispered as she helped Sybilla tidy the music and lower the piano lid.

Sybilla merely smiled. 'The tea tray has come in, Caro. You will be expected to pour.'

Karen spread her skirts in the chair before the low table, confident of one expectation she could meet. The only drawback was the proximity of her 'cousin', Basil Frensham. Taking station beside her he proceeded to conduct a gossipy monologue in her ear, obviously under the impression that she enjoyed spiced anecdotes about ladies of society. His whispered tales of peccadillos varied from innuendo to outright slander, and covered a range of activities from public display of a garter to the more salacious details of sexual romps with footmen and stableboys.

She turned her shoulder to him and tried to engage his father in conversation, but with little success. Having dined and wined far too well, The Honourable George seemed on the point of falling asleep, and most likely into the fire as well, if he didn't take care.

Basil continued to murmur in her ear. 'No doubt you have heard of Lady Silerten's monstrous behaviour when she was in the straw?'

Karen set her cup down firmly. 'No, Basil, I have not. I really don't care if she did cartwheels in a hayfield. Lady Silerten's behaviour is of no interest to me, and nor are your smutty stories. Please go away.' She'd have liked to tell him to take a bath, but didn't quite have the courage. As it was, he gave her an ugly look before moving off in the direction of the decanters.

Karen's head began to feel peculiar. She felt she was slowly turning on the spot, or else the room was. Pressing her hands against her eyes she shook her head to clear it.

'You would be wise to retire early, my dear.' The cool husky voice steadied her, as no doubt it was meant to do. Antony's hand slipped under her arm, helping her to rise.

What a picture of connubial bliss, she thought, acknowledging the wishes of the company for her to sleep well, and allowing herself to be led away. If Antony intended presenting to the world a new improved angle on his marriage, he was going about it the right way. Nothing could have been more solicitous than his manner for the past few hours. But it didn't fool her. He was thinking about his precious family name. The minute she stepped out of line, she'd feel his whip.

He left her at her bedroom door, delivered into the hands of Lucy. Soon, tucked up before the fire in her nightgown she accepted the milk that the little maid had heated, then dismissed her. She wanted to think for awhile before sleeping. It had been a long day and she needed to sort out her impressions, and her options.

The main point to emerge was her need for circumspection. She must do nothing to annoy the lord and master, or at least nothing that was likely to come to his ears. Amanda looked like being a true friend. Something about her inspired confidence – almost as though she really did understand what had happened to Karen, incredible as it seemed.

Could she possibly know of someone who could help? Seers, sorcerers and psychics abounded in every generation, although, unfortunately, in this age there would have to be a distinct shortage of quantum physicists. Karen hardly knew into which area her problem fitted. But she'd proved one thing, that running away was not the answer. In this Georgian world, once you stepped out of your own milieu safety evaporated. For those without protection it was a dangerous place. Like it or not, she needed the umbrella of Lady Caroline's rank and family connections, and that meant playing the part, however distasteful it might be, until she found a way out.

As usual, she spent the last few minutes before sleep thinking about Adele. What might she be doing now? Was it night back in her child's time? Had she gone to her little bed unkissed, emotionally neglected, however well she might be in the physical sense? Humphrey's notions on child rearing came closer to the Georgian ideal, and she ached to hold her baby in her arms and give her the love she desperately needed. She had to get her away from Humphrey. She had to be there in court when the case came up, or lose, by default, any hope of regaining custody.

Her nails dug into her palms, creating a secondary pain, but they couldn't dislodge the misery of her own thoughts. Amanda was her best hope. She'd tackle her the moment she arrived.

Overcome with weariness she put down the cup, almost too sleepy to make it to the bed. Her head hit the pillow and she was out.

The fire had burned low and the room grown cold. Wind-driven sleet hissed against the windows, open just a crack because Karen had insisted. There was the sound of a key turning. Then the latch of the bedroom door lifted silently and a gap appeared. Very slowly it widened until finally a shadow slipped through, closing the door behind.

'So, my lady sleeps, as planned.' The voice was no more than a whisper, yet it held a note of satisfaction. The shadow glanced at the empty milk glass beside the bed, and smiled, then glided to the window, threw up the sash and stepped hastily back to avoid the rush of ice-laden wind. A few steps more, and Karen lay almost bare in its path, her bedclothes trailing to the floor, her hair and nightgown already touched with frost.

The shadow stood for a long time, contemplating the sleeper. There was no need for haste. It's purpose would be achieved some time while the house slept. And when the dawn came, and my lady was discovered, cold and stiff, without so much as a sheet to cover her, why, then it would be thought that her tottering mind had taken that final step, carrying her over into oblivion. And that would be the end of my fine lady. At last.

CHAPTER 7

6 December, Thursday

TOM SAT AT his office desk writing his regular six-monthly letter to his sister, Rachel. Once he actually sat down to the job, he enjoyed it.

Dear Sis,

It was great to hear all your news, and I'm really pleased that kibbutz life agrees with you so well. You tell that great ox of a husband to take good care of you and Benjamin and Naomi. I'll try and get out to see you sometime next year, but you know me, always taking on something extra because it looks interesting and a bit of a challenge.

Rosa seems to have settled into the farming routine she always wanted, and New England suits her. Her letters are few and sparse, but I get the underlying contentment. Isn't it odd that two sisters should choose similar lifestyles in such widely different areas?

You'd better let two lucky strikes out of three satisfy you. I'm pretty sure I was never meant to be a Jewish Papa so you can stop all that scheming and plotting. I won't come within a thousand miles of you if you're planning to trot out some sweet little Israeli for me.

To change the subject, last week I bought a painting. It's definitely not the sort of thing I normally take to, and yet there's a touch of Turner to it with that big whirling sky and the hint of gorges falling away into the depths. It's the work of a new young artist, a Karen Courtney. I met her at the gallery showing a few nights ago. Theo Sampson is promoting her work with unusual vigour, considering she's a relative newcomer.

There's something a bit odd about her. She looked uncomfortable being dragged about and lionised by Theo, which is probably a sign of the girl's common sense. However, I got the impression she wasn't entirely happy about her work being on public exhibition. I suppose an artist can feel possessive in that way, although I have a feeling it's more than that. She's striking looking, but does her level best to disguise the fact with awful clothes and hair. (Who am I to talk? Carla says I remind her of a 1914 Stutz Bearcat – which presumably means I'm shaggy, and out of date, and certainly not a classic.)

But, can this girl paint! I was astounded at her range, and wanted quite a few of the pieces. When I found *Beyond and Within* it struck a nerve with me. I had to have it. Strange title, and yet it seems to suit. The picture itself is beyond description, formless and yet totally meaningful, to me, at least. What meaning, exactly? I don't know yet. That's half its charm. I'll have to study the thing to work it out. I've hung it in my office. I want it near me so I can study it in odd moments during the day. Already it's making an impact on the patients. You wouldn't believe!

Carla and Phil Thornton are over visiting from the States. They're full of batty ideas about the afterlife. I'd have thought they were both far too intelligent to get caught up in that sort of thing, but you never can tell. Since our post-grad work together, I haven't seen all that much of Phil, yet I suppose he's the closest friend I've got. It's a pity, but the way he's talking these days, I'm wondering whether we're even on the same wavelength any more.

Not that I'm opposed to new discoveries. I use hypnosis as a tool in therapy. But taking someone back into a supposed previous life is just a bit too radical for me. We've all come across examples of Jung's synchronicities, and I accept the phenomenon of deja vu. I'd be a fool not to admit that there's a lot to be discovered about the human psyche. I'll even say that I had far more confidence in my diagnostic ability and 'knew' far more about psychological theory in the first years after graduation than I do now. Daily I'm astonished and humbled by the layers of mystery we uncover in the mind. However, I do deal in reality. I do not believe that we can cross the gap between our present reality and whatever existed before birth. I do not believe we have more than one existence upon this earth. I don't want to believe it. Perhaps that's a problem for me. Meanwhile, I work on with my disturbed kids who are having problems adjusting to this life. One thing at a time, say I.

Cherry drops in occasionally to see how I am. Talk about a

civilised arrangement! She and the beer baron even want me to spend a weekend down at their mansion, but I'm not that civilised. Besides, boredom can kill. There, now, I've come over all catty again. Strange, isn't it? I don't give a damn that Cherry's remarried happily. I'm glad for her, but I can't forget my own failure. Ah, well. I'm beginning to sound as though I spend too much time around Habbakuk. He and Phil are deathly enemies, by the way.

Love to you all,
Tom

PS Do you think Miss Courtney would marry me? I could be happy for the rest of my life surrounded by her paintings!

Tom sealed the letter and left it on Sally's desk for the post, then ushered in his last patient for the day.

'Sit back and make yourself comfortable, Valerie. How did you sleep last night?'

'Badly, I'm afraid. I'm just worried that we're stirring up the goblins.' Pale and tired-looking, she seemed glad to sink back into the recliner and put her feet up.

She was, as usual, impeccably turned out. Tom had the feeling that little short of a bomb blast would cause Valerie Winterhouse to appear in public less than perfectly groomed. Which was one good sign. In his experience, patients who began to neglect their appearance were well on the downward slide. It was only an indication, however. Women of her type prepared for the day automatically, as likely to appear naked in public as without make-up.

'That's what we're aiming for. A good stir in the sludge brings things up to the surface where they can be dealt with. It's painful, sure; but it's worthwhile.'

'I hope you're right.' She smiled a little, and her eyes moved straight to the painting on the wall in front of her. 'I dreamed about it, you know. I dreamed that I took a knife and carved and slashed until there was nothing of it left.'

He was amazed that her voice expressed satisfaction, rather than horror. 'I thought you were crazy about it.'

'I am. It was only a dream.' She dismissed the subject and turned to him eagerly, wanting to begin the session. Her large white hands plucked at the padded chair arms. She was not as much at ease as she would like him to believe.

Tom could not dismiss the dream, or rather, her attitude towards it, quite so easily.

'You've felt very strongly about the painting ever since you first saw it. Why do you think that is?'

'I don't know why.'

'I think you do. This is important, Valerie. Think about it for a minute.'

Her fingers drummed irritably on the chair arms, but at length she answered. 'It has a peculiar drawing power. I can hardly take my eyes off it when I'm in the same room. I don't like that.'

She wouldn't, thought Tom. Not many people were comfortable with the feeling they were not totally in control at all times. Was she so afraid of losing control that she wanted to slash the object exerting such power? He decided to let the matter rest, for the present, aware that his own horrified reaction stemmed from his feelings for the painting, and had no place in this interview.

'Okay, let's go back again to your childhood, since we've already made some discoveries there. Are you happy to do that?'

'Why not? It's a very relaxing experience since I don't remember what happens.'

'Well, we're changing that today. I want you to remember, and I'll give your subconscious that message before you regress.'

Her face altered, sharpening. For an instant he was reminded of a vixen caught up in the hunt.

'I don't think I like the sound of that. There are parts of my youth that I've managed to forget. If I have to talk about them, I will, but going through the actual experiences again . . . I'd rather not.'

'Very likely, but that isn't why you're here, is it? We all bury hurtful incidents. Often it turns out we've merely driven a splinter deep under the psychic skin to fester and worry us at a lower level. You're here to dig for splinters. You can't face your life any longer without clearing out the past and its repercussions.' He waited, letting the words sink in. If she couldn't agree to his form of surgery she must tell him now, before they began.

He had given a lot of thought to her curious behaviour in the past session. Having dismissed Phil's notion of a past-life regression, he had decided that a far more believable label was the one put forward by Jung himself – psychic projection – or in layman's terms, interference by the patient's own subconscious mind. He was certain it would not happen again. As he hadn't told Valerie about it, her conscious mind remained in ignorance of the whole startling event. There was no reason to believe in a random recurrence.

'Valerie, as you know, after each session we discuss the matters that arise. It's not too threatening, as you've discovered. But, to actually re-experience an event and have total recall is far more effective.'

'I imagine it is,' she said dryly. 'It's probably one hell of a nasty jolt.'

Tom smiled. 'Not always. It can be delightful. If something painful does arise I promise I won't allow you to become too distressed. We can move away from any hot spots and return later, if necessary. The main thing is to pinpoint these as we progress. You will probably find them cropping up in your dreams, or even as conscious memories; and instead of being frightening or confusing symbols they'll be recognisable. We can look at how they're affecting you in the present, and if necessary, clear them away.'

He waited more hopefully. She seemed to be giving his little speech quite some consideration.

'You know, I never had much of a sense of humour, especially not directed at myself, but you've really got to laugh. Here I am able to buy and sell you a hundred times over – used to people jumping when I give the order, expecting and getting the best of everything this world has to offer – and I'm sitting in a shabby little room with an equally shabby man who is telling *me* to jump or get the hell out of here and stop wasting his time. It's funny.' She looked more irritated than amused.

'I didn't say – '

'Your tone implied it. Well, that's the way it goes. I don't suppose I can blame you. You've got the upper hand.'

Tom thought about the hours he spent with desperately unhappy people, people he wanted to help get their lives back on course, and his lips tightened. Then he shrugged mentally and put aside personal reactions. Valerie was every bit as much in need as his other patients were, and he'd do his damnedest for her, whether or not she appreciated his motives.

They looked steadily at one another for a long minute. Then Tom said, 'Shall we begin? Let go all the muscles in your feet and toes. Feel them flopping, lying totally at rest. Now the muscles in your calves and shins. Feel them growing heavier and heavier . . .'

Three minutes later she'd gone down to that pleasant garden he had evoked for her. He allowed her to wander there listening to his voice guiding, reassuring, then began gently pushing her back through the years to early childhood.

He sat in the shadow thrown by his desk lamp, his face deliberately masked by that shadow, although there was no one to see it. Valerie had gone hours ago. She'd insisted she was fine, and considering the fact that she'd been the one to go through the experience and remember it in fine detail, he felt she had survived the extraordinary session in far better shape than he.

Recalling his frenzied attempts to bring her out of the regressed state, unsuccessful for far too long, the sweat came out on his forehead. He hadn't thought it would be like that again. He'd never have risked it. None of his patients ever slipped away from him as Valerie had. None of them turned into another personality before his unbelieving eyes.

He'd replayed the tape until he could repeat it word for word, but it hadn't helped. Now he switched it on again and listened. Valerie's voice had changed astonishingly. No longer educated, and marred with a burr, it was scarcely intelligible with its Old English intonations. It was the voice she'd used before, and the same gypsyish features had emerged from a subtle remoulding of her face. She, or her subconscious, or whatever, had reverted to the woman who swore and stood her ground so effectively against invisible tormentors.

This time, however, the situation had changed. Deaf to Tom's voice, she carried on a conversation with someone, a child perhaps, who was fretful and needed soothing. She questioned and probed and made movements compatible with stroking and sponging a body.

This continued for some minutes, with Tom making periodic attempts at contact. Then she straightened up to confront someone, her voice laden with repulsion.

'So then, 'tis witchcraft to brew tansy and bathe a fevered child wi' vinegar, Sir Priest? 'Tis following the Anti-Christ to hold back a life wi' prayers and the fruits of God's own earth? What would ye have me do otherwise? I am no heretic. Ye cannot affright me wi'y'r prying and tale-telling. By cock's muddy bones, I defy ye to prove aught against me!'

She appeared to listen, her head turned aside. 'Aye, ye've a care to the folk living here in t'parish. But there's no threat to their souls – not from me. I lighted my candle in t'chapel on St Anne's Mount this very day, and prayed to Our Blessed Lady for my own soul's salvation. Go pry in some steamy midden, Sir Priest, for t'smell o'brimstone does not bide here.'

A long pause ensued. Then the silence was broken by Valerie's normal voice. 'Who the hell are you? What am I? . . . What am I doing . . . Jesus! What a set-up!' she broke off again, and said more calmly, 'I thought you promised me a delightful experience, Dr Tom Levy.'

Tom pushed the rewind button. He sank down, chin on chest in his usual attitude for deep thought, and examined the personal philosophy behind the therapeutic methods he practised. He'd always believed that the course taken and its outcome should be as much the patient's responsibility as the therapist's. No one could make someone else change unless that someone, at some level within, wanted to change. Hence his tendency towards what has been labelled 'existential' therapy and away from such methods as hypnosis, which concentrates power and responsibility in the therapist. Or so it should. But in Valerie's case something happened which shouldn't have happened. Perhaps this particular form of therapy was not in the patient's best interests. Perhaps he, Tom, should decline further intervention and encourage her to approach another worker in the field.

He sighed and longed for a cigarette, but reached instead for a piece of chewing gum in his desk drawer. He'd have to make a decision soon.

When the phone rang he knew it would be Phil.

'How did it go?'

Tom didn't pretend ignorance. 'It happened again. She was on her own for nearly fifteen minutes, and it scared me silly.'

Phil whistled. 'Have you read any of the literature I left with you?'

'Some.'

'That's something, I suppose. Can I come round and we'll chew the fat a little? You know the old saying about two heads.'

He had known it was coming. Did he want to talk over the outlandish suggestions, the impossible theories, the ravings of the New Age pioneers?

'Okay. I'm willing to talk. But no evangelising, Phil?'

'Agreed. With you in twenty minutes.'

'This isn't just a new therapeutic technique, Tom. It's a method of opening up a whole new incredibly rich world of the psyche. We're now able to move away from the old interpretive emphasis. People no longer simply answer questions and let the therapist decide what the answers might mean in their particular context. This is living the answers – direct experience of trauma buried deep in the unconscious and carried forward from other lives!'

Tom tried to be reasonable. 'I've read about it, of course. I've even seen some of Joe Scranton's work on film. But, Phil, there's no system to it. Where is the documented research?'

'All around you, if you care to look. There's Helen Wambach, Morris Netherton, Ian Stevenson. Great Jehoshaphat! There's thirty years of detailed *systematic* research to follow. But if your eyes are closed you're not going to see it, are you?'

'I've already started looking, and reading. There. That's the stack of information you landed on me last night. I'm halfway through.'

'You're in good company, pal. There've been some big shifts in popular opinion on the subject, here as well as in the States. I know what's eating you. Words like reincarnation and karma have occult connotations. You think of freaky gurus, oriental hocus pocus. What I'm talking is a new and powerful tool in our discipline, something I've seen help people who couldn't otherwise be helped. Believe me, Tom, this is not another Californian crackpot philosophy grafted onto oddments of eastern culture. It's a new psychology emerging.'

'Okay. Okay. Calm down. Anything that sets you alight to this extent has got to be worth investigation. However, I still don't believe my patient is regressing to a past life. She's simply letting out unconscious inhibitions. She's play-acting. You see examples of it in every text from Freud onwards.'

'And what about that moment of confusion at the end of the tape, where Valerie is clearly re-entering her original time zone?'

'It's simply confusion, as the subconscious lets go and the ego steps back in. It's enough to confuse anyone.'

Phil stretched his long legs in front of him and settled into the recliner as though for a prolonged stay. 'Do you keep any medicinal reviver about the place? I could do with it.'

Tom reached into the cupboard and produced a half-full bottle of Haig and two tumblers. His work space was small enough for him to reach most things without moving from his worn leather chair. The patients' recliner was just as old, but sturdy too, and very inviting. Kept deliberately beige and neutral, even shabby, as Valerie had pointed out, the room had only the one bright spot, the painting. At the moment it lay hidden in the shadow behind Tom's head.

Phil lifted the glass and saluted his friend with a grin. 'I wasn't pulling your leg over that regression of my own, Tom. I know you refused to take me seriously, but one day you'll listen, I hope.' He waved away Tom's rude gesture. 'It's clear that your patient was re-enacting a life, whether real or imaginary, as a wise woman some centuries back. It didn't sound particularly traumatic this time. She wasn't afraid of that nosy priest.'

'Hmmm. She did reveal interesting character facets, however. All this conflict with other people. Most of her conversation was assertive, not to say aggressive – much like her true personality, I'd say. Of course, she disguises it when it suits her.'

'There's trouble ahead, for sure. Very likely you'll come to it in the next session. That first time – in the beginning when she started screaming. That's probably the crux of it. You know, there's no rule that says these trips back take place in sequence. Tom, I have to warn you. If this is a true regression, as I believe it is, and since you have an admittedly depressed patient undergoing past-life trauma, it could be dangerous.'

'Oh?' Tom felt uncomfortable. He *had* lost contact with his patient on two occasions, and re-established this only, it seemed, at her personal whim.

'It's dangerous, Tom, because you could come to the death experience.'

'Oh, come on, Phil. I've done some of the recommended reading on that topic and I can tell you I'm not too impressed with all these coincidentally tallying tales of floating to the ceiling and tunnels of white light, etcetera.'

'Forget it. You can take it from me you'll change your perspective if you ever watch a patient going through a difficult death experience. I don't want you to be caught up in this and not be ready for it. People have suffered prolonged agony in such circumstances. In fact, once or twice a patient has had to be revived when the therapist attempted to bring him out of the hypnotic state.'

'Scare tactics, Phil.'

'God's honest truth!'

Tom still tried to sound reasonable. 'Look here, I'm not rubbishing the technique of hypnotic regression. I'm aware that the personality has multiple layers, skins if you like, and that acting out the part of each personality is a valid method of a patient's releasing inhibitions and coming to accept that he is many persons in one. It goes with the idea of the mass unconscious. Whether or not we really reach into past experiences of life on earth has still to be proved.'

'Right. I'm not saying you have to agree with me. Just keep an open mind and remember what I said about the experience sometimes being overwhelming for the patient. You, as therapist, have a responsibility to recognise the inherent dangers, and be able to protect the patient from his own memories, or fantasies, or whatever you decide to call them. For some, the sudden exposure of a mangled nerve, a totally unsuspected nerve, is too much, too soon. Don't go in blind.'

'I won't. Phil, I appreciate what you're doing. I can see it really is important to you that I understand.'

'So much so, I'm asking you to let me sit in on your next session, with your patient's permission, of course. I wouldn't dream of interfering . . .'

'Sorry. Our talk this evening has just confirmed me in my decision. I think it's too dangerous to go on with this form of therapy. I'm ceasing hypnosis altogether, and trying another method.'

Phil sat silent for a time. Tom had the feeling he was disappointed, not just for himself, but for Tom. At length Phil said in a deceptively quiet tone, 'Sometimes a patient who has begun to regress will fall into the pattern the minute she hits the couch. You may not be able to prevent it.'

'Nonsense. I've already applied the blocks preventing her from entering the hypnotic state without my say so. I know you mean to be helpful . . .'

'But thanks, but no thanks. I get the picture. Well, I tried.' He got up and buttoned his coat against the November night air.

'No hard feelings, Phil?'

'I guess not. Keep me informed, will you? Just for old friendship's sake?'

'You can be sure of it. Good night. My love to Carla.'

Tom locked up and went home to the doubtful companionship of Habbakuk, and his even more doubtful thoughts. Dinner and a warm bath did something to soothe his restless spirit, and he decided to turn in early.

Around the time that dawn crept up on the sleeping city he began to rise from the deepest pit of unconsciousness. Hovering just below the threshold of wakening, he began to dream. Darkness swirled about him and he extended his arms to clear a pathway ahead towards the light. Gradually he became aware of a grassy track and trees overhead. The soles of his sandals slid a little, and his long robe flapped around his legs. He felt hot and scratchy, and he smelled rank.

Quite suddenly he emerged into full sunlight. The path had become a muddy village lane edged by rough stone byres with ragged thatch rooves, and a stinking kennel running by the doors. Pigs and geese wandered at will, but the scene lacked people. No faces appeared in openings as he traversed the lane. Insects buzzed about his face, a dog barked at him, but there were no children playing in the dust. Yet he felt eyes upon him. He hurried on, sandals slipping on refuse and the slimy clay edging the ditch.

Hay fields lay beyond the village, now just stubble burning under the sun, but there was another track of sorts leading to a copse. Once in its shade he stopped to rest and take stock. He had no idea where he was or why he was dressed in this rough woollen garment with a bit of cord around his waist and . . . yes, a cross hanging about his neck. He held it up and studied it. Carved with the figure of a tortured Christ it was clumsy work, and ugly too. Tom's flesh crawled. He'd always hated the masochistic aspects of religion, any religion. Certainly with his Jewish upbringing, he'd never owned a crucifix of any kind, let alone worn it on his person.

Then he noticed his hands were not his own. They were thick and gnarled, ingrained with years of dirt, and nails torn rather than cut. They looked like the hands of an ancient derelict, a piece of the human flotsam usually found washed up on park benches. He touched his cheek and felt a day's growth of his beard. His eyebrows seemed to have practically disappeared, as had his hair. There was just a rim of coarse growth circling his skull A tonsure! He was a monk, or priest of some kind.

A dream. It's just a dream. Tom squeezed his eyes shut, then opened them again. He still stood in the copse on the edge of a clearing, near another little hut. This one seemed better made than the village hovels. It had a neat garden plot to the side, and pots of herbs hanging from extended beams. The tiny window lacked glass but had a covering that looked rather like thick mica, to keep out weather and allow the passage of some light. The door stood open and beside it a rustic bench was occupied by the gypsy woman.

Tom knew he was dreaming, and knew he was building on Valerie's regression, assuming the role of her priestly foe. But some part of him believed in the role. A part of him had taken on the mediaeval mind set, feeling a surge of superstitious fear at the sight of this woman, arrogant as no woman had a right to be.

She wore a gown of washed-out blue cloth, belted at the hips, and her dark hair fell almost as far. Her eyes were, as he'd thought, dark and flashing. She was young, and the word 'comely' came to him. Yet even as he thought these things he was swept by a storm of feeling. He knew that he hated this woman with every fibre in him. He loathed and feared her. He wanted to wipe her out of existence.

The last of his detachment fell away and he was that priest, trembling with primitive emotions. Now he saw her through a red haze of mist pouring into the clearing from all sides, writhing and twisting about him in the most obscene shapes, filling his throat and nostrils until he choked. She smiled, mocking him, her dark eyes glowing with an inner fire. Her long hair rose like a cloak to float about her strangely translucent body. He took a step back as she seemed to rise above the ground and glide forward, her arms outstretched to embrace him. With a hoarse cry he turned and stumbled, then picked up his robe and fled.

CHAPTER 8

Antony Marchmont sat in the late-afternoon gloom of his library. He had not called for candles to be lit, and the fire had been allowed to die down to embers. The snowstorm that followed the night of sleet, having raged for twenty-four hours, had blown itself out. Then another two days of steady rain came to wash away all traces of the snow, leaving the world dank, grey and covered in slush. Like his mood, he thought, with some savagery. Deep in deliberation, he took no notice of the cold. However, a part of his mind was aware of the steady downpour beyond the windows, and it depressed him even further.

What was he to do about Caroline? Why in God's name had he ever crowned a brief flare of sexual attraction with the consummate idiocy of marriage? Her flamboyant beauty had lured him, as it had many others. Seeing her flirt her delightful way around a ballroom, following the curve of her mouth when she smiled that roguish smile and tilted her deep blue eyes, he'd fallen under her enchantment and, like any mooncalf, lost his head.

He had been unfaithful to Jenny's memory and he had paid for it – was still paying for it.

Perhaps he was, in part, responsible for Caro kicking over the traces. He had failed to make her happy. It was impossible, once he had seen beneath the surface tricks and posturings to her selfish core. Her beauty was a deception, masking a spiritual void which, while it might be no fault of hers, made him long to turn back time to the days of his great happiness with Jenny, his lovely, sweet, caring soul who had taken the light from his world with her when she died.

His hand tightened on the glass he held, threatening to crush it. Pain scorched through him – familiar pain – an old enemy that had been with him for years. He thought he had beaten it down. Months of work, travel, physical activity of every sort had brought him to a state bordering on exhaustion, but he had thrashed the pain into submission. Now it rarely caught him unawares. Yet, this afternoon he had opened the door to it by letting himself think back, inevitably stirring remembrances best left in the past.

He must decide about Caroline. This latest incident, this attempt to put a period to her own existence, was it the final proof of a mind hopelessly diseased? Was she indeed mad?

When the doors opened behind him he turned, ready to rend whoever dared to interrupt him. Charles Hastings came into the room bearing a branch of candles which he set down on a side table. He then moved over to the windows and drew the heavy wine-dark drapes, shutting out the miserable prospect beyond. His pleasant face expressed both deprecation and defiance, but he performed his services with assurance. When he had mended the fire he stood silently waiting to be addressed.

Antony sighed. 'Charles, you know what a risk you run.'

'I think not. The latitude you have always allowed me emboldens me to tread where others might not dare. To speak plainly, you may hoax your family and retainers into believing you a monster of harshness, but not your secretary. I know you too well.'

'Do you, indeed?' The weary voice held an undercurrent of amusement. 'Take care, my friend. One day I may forget childhood oaths of brotherhood and dismiss you out of hand.'

'I beg leave to doubt that, if for no other reason than the fact that you would never manage your affairs without my invaluable assistance. I am a very paragon of secretaries.'

'I am aware of it. You are also insufferably puffed up in your own esteem. Take a glass of madeira with me and sit down.' He gestured to the other wing chair and waited until Charles had filled his glass and seated himself with a flip of his long-tailed coat. 'What brings you here? Is there further news on the war front?'

Charles shook his head. His sandy head picked up the fireglow. His face had been thrown half in shadow, exposing his profile, thickening the long nose, sharpening the chin, adding bulk to the heavy brows. Antony looked at him with affection. That face had been a part of his youth and its owner shared with him memories that were everlasting.

'I came to bear you company. You have sat too long with your thoughts.'

Antony did not comment. He stared at the liquid in his glass.

'Lady Caroline has made a good recovery, I believe. The doctor called for his carriage more than a hour since, and welcome news has come downstairs.'

Antony looked at him. 'Charles, it will not fadge. The whole world will soon know the truth of the matter. My wife has sought to take her own life, and very nearly succeeded. I carry the burden of this tragic happening. If she had not been so unhappy she would not have taken such a step. Good God! She is a young and beautiful woman with her whole life ahead of her! What must she have suffered, what shocking misery must I have caused her!' He closed his lips on the words that threatened to come pouring out, cutting off Charles' response with a quick gesture. 'No, I have no desire to listen to your reassurances, well-meant though they may be. I must put aside my self-recrimination and come to a decision about my wife's future treatment.'

'She is not mad, Antony,' said Charles gently.

'Perhaps not. But, in view of recent events, a certain degree of affection to the brain may be assumed.' His voice took on a harsh note. 'Charles, are you aware that she has actually claimed not to be herself – that she is a woman come from another period of time? And you can still say that she has full control of her faculties?'

'I believe that of late Lady Caroline has suffered from an excessive melancholy. Her recent accident on the stairs resulted in the temporary loss of her memory and understanding. I think it possible that last night she mistakenly took too great a quantity of laudanum to help her sleep. In her stupor she opened the window wide and flung herself upon the bed, unaware that she was exposed to the elements. We have no reason to suppose that these actions were deliberately planned. You refine too much upon the matter.' He stopped, then said with a deliberate emphasis, 'I do not believe that your wife was bent upon self-destruction.'

Antony bowed his head. 'You plead an excellent case. However, I cannot risk it happening again. She must be watched.'

'Certainly. She is not well, and it may be many weeks before her mind assumes its normal tone.' He broke off as the doors opened once more and Amanda Crayle was announced. She came tripping in, all ruffles and bows and dripping with a great fringed shawl. Both men rose.

'I do apologise for disturbing you, Lord Antony, but I believe that it lies within my power to do you and your lady a service. Will you spare me a few moments of your time to discuss the matter?'

He bowed and said coolly, 'I am obliged to you for the offer, but I believe we shall do better to keep my wife's difficulties within the confines of the family. She cannot entertain callers while she is suffering from . . . delusions, and memory loss.' It cost him some effort to maintain a pleasant demeanour, and Amanda acknowledged this with a nod.

'You are in a rage because you have suffered a shock, and because your pride is injured. I comprehend perfectly. But can you not ask yourself whether the sacrifice of a modicum of privacy is not worth your wife's recovery? If she is mewed within these walls she will decline. She needs to have her mind and memory stimulated by confrontation with people and places, and events that were once familiar to her.' She smiled, dimpling her plump cheeks and turning up the corners of her wide brown eyes. She looked very persuasive.

Charles ushered her to a chair and stood looking admiringly at her.

His employer flushed to his hairline. 'Madam, I must assume that you have my wife's interests at heart – '

She interrupted without apology. 'I do, sir. I have conceived a very great liking for Lady Caroline, and I believe, as I said, that it lies within my power to help her.'

'In what way, Miss Crayle?' Charles put in swiftly.

'I have concocted a plan. 'Tis a simple measure, really. With his lordship's permission, I should take his wife under my care, socially, and instruct her in the many things she has forgotten. I can impart information on members of the ton, the ways of society, how to go on in public. Driving with her about the town I shall recall to her mind the homes of friends, the situation of such commonly known buildings as churches, libraries, theatres. We shall visit jewellers and modistes.' Again she smiled. 'A woman is far more likely to recall the establishments where she ordered her gowns and other articles of adornment. In short, sir, I shall undertake to restore the lady to the full enjoyment of her senses, including the memory she presently lacks.'

Antony stood with folded arms, thinking. His frowning stare had no effect on Amanda. She sat placidly waiting for a response.

He noted her self-possession, and the effect it, and she, had upon his secretary. Then, unwillingly, he examined Miss Crayle's accusation. Was pride at the root of his desire to keep Caroline immured within the house? The good name of his family meant much to him, yet common humanity demanded that in this case he should risk that

111

name. At all events, Caro had already smirched it with her misbehaviour. His mouth tightened. It was hard to deal with whispers and innuendos, although God knew he had proof enough. Admittedly, she had recently changed her attitude. Yet, might not her cool wariness be more a result of her failure of memory? He should not add isolation to her sufferings.

Another, even less savoury reason for his reluctance occurred to him. Was he in effect punishing Caro by keeping her restricted? He found the idea too distasteful to contemplate. He was not a vengeful man. However, there was no avoiding his dilemma. Caro undoubtedly needed help, as the assured Miss Crayle had pointed out.

'Your suggestion is well founded, but my cousin, Miss Sybilla Frensham, is equally well-positioned to assist. She could go about with my wife and tutor her, as you propose to do.'

Amanda remained unruffled. 'I suggest that you try if she will. Let her give thought to the amount of time she would need to spend with Lady Caroline, day after day. She would be forced to forgo many of her own pursuits. Also, if I may speak candidly without offence, Lady Oriel Frensham is in the habit of accompanying her daughter into society, and she is known to be quite out of sympathy with Lady Caroline. Such forced proximity with the lady would not be wise.'

Admitting the truth of this statement, he said more mildly, 'My aunt is possessed of a difficult temperament, and I grant you she has an unfortunate way of expressing her opinions.'

'Unbridled, is the word I should choose,' muttered Charles in the background.

Antony let that slip by. 'Miss Crayle, I could not permit you to make such a sacrifice for strangers. You have your own activities to pursue.'

'I do you no favours, Lord Antony. To be seen in your wife's company can only add to my own consequence. I should also be grateful for the greater freedom of movement accorded me. My mother's health is such that it precludes her going about as my own companion.' The dimples appeared along with a mischievous look. 'I have another, even less noble reason. It may have come to your notice that my disposition is of a somewhat managing nature. I like to teach. The guidance and instruction of an intelligent pupil will please me while I enjoy the companionship of her intellect.'

Caro – a woman of intellect? Antony bit his lip. However, the lady had a forthright attitude that demanded an equally forthright response, and there seemed no good reason for him to deny his wife this chance for rehabilitation.

'It shall be as you wish. Miss Crayle, you have my gratitude, along with any reasonable call upon my purse. Caroline is expensive and I would not have you out of pocket on my behalf.'

She nodded matter-of-factly and gathered together her belongings, which included reticule, muff, handkerchief and the shawl dripping fringes at least a foot long which threatened to become entangled about her, like cord around a parcel.

Charles rushed to assist her to her feet and untie the fringe. She waited with composure while he performed this service. Both men then accompanied her to the entrance hall where Bates waited with her cloak.

Antony extended his hand. 'My wife is fortunate in your friendship, and I count myself honoured by your acquaintance. You will not hesitate to advise me if you are in need of assistance?'

'You are very good. I shall not hesitate. Now, I propose to call again tomorrow to see how Lady Caroline does, although I do not think she should stir over the threshold in such inclement weather. She is still weak.'

Placing her cloak about her shoulders, Charles insisted upon escorting her to the carriage. He re-entered the house wet and shivering but with a beatific expression that amused Antony considerably.

'A charming lady, Charles, do you not agree?'

'Delightful.' Without apology, Charles drifted off to his own office beyond the library.

Clearly a stricken man, thought Antony, smiling to himself, and gave orders for his carriage to be brought around.

Bates stood ready with his hat and the caped greatcoat that would be needed on such a night. 'Will her ladyship be dining, Sir Antony?'

'No. Have a tray taken to her room when she rings.' Aware that he sounded curt, he could not bring himself to dissemble. Whatever the reason, Caro's actions were unforgivable. He could not bear to contemplate what fresh chagrin she might bring upon their marriage with her loss of memory and her known penchant for mischief-making. Amanda Crayle little knew what she had taken on. Yet he must give Caro every opportunity to recover her mind. He must protect her because she was his wife. He must play the role that he had cast for himself, and play it well, whatever the cost.

As it turned out, Dr Horbury had been mistaken. Karen's cough turned to an inflammation of the lungs, and soon she was too sick to care where she was.

Life was blanked out for a time. Later, when she learned she'd been out of action for over a month, her feelings threatened to overcome her. If time here marched in tune with future time, then her court hearing had come and gone without her. Christmas 1810 had passed while she lay in a feverish stupor. Had Christmas at home done the same? After all her struggle to get Humphrey back before a judge, had she missed her opportunity?

Numb with misery, she huddled into her pillows and cried for her child. Her arms ached to hold the little warm body. Her mind echoed like a hollow cavern with the knowledge that she might have lost Adele forever.

Slowly recovering from her grief, she lay and fretted, filling in time devising ever wilder plans which, she knew, had no real hope of success. Humphrey's downfall was first of all contingent upon her return to her own time, and she could see no hope of that at present. Tied to her bed with weakness, she couldn't even make helpful contacts. And if she could, where was she to start?

Somewhere in the back of her mind there was a vague idea that someone had offered help, but she couldn't think who it might be. After a determined struggle with the elusive memory she decided it was one of the many fantasies that had plagued her during her illness. She'd have to get on her feet as soon as possible and go searching for help, herself. There was no one else she could rely upon in this foreign world.

By the day she was pronounced convalescent she'd grown heartily tired of the over-trimmed bedroom, and even more tired of feeling like a helpless baby. Evidently visitors were discouraged, as she'd seen only the woman brought in as a nurse, Lucy the maid, and Antony, who had come each evening to enquire meticulously after her well-being, leaving after a few minutes' stilted conversation.

There had been several notes of condolence over her illness handed to Bates and brought to her by Lucy, among them some so impassioned and specific she felt embarrassed for Lady Caroline. She tore these up in disgust, reflecting that she had quite a reputation to live down.

Sybilla came, but infrequently. Karen was puzzled by her manner and eventually taxed her about it.

'Why are you stepping around me as if I'm a live bomb? Is there something I should know, Sybilla?'

'No indeed. You are fanciful, my dear.' Her smile was somehow not as reassuring as it should have been. She fidgeted.

'I know I've been pretty ill. Did I do or say something to upset you? You know I didn't mean it.'

'You have said nothing to incur censure, I assure you.'

Karen picked up on that immediately. 'But I've done something, haven't I? You may as well tell me now. I have to know sooner or later.'

'I . . . Oh, Caro, why did you do it? Why did you not confide your distress to someone? I should be glad to do anything in my power to help you, you must know that.' She twisted her fingers together in her lap, echoing the distress in her voice. Her beautiful face, schooled to its madonna-like calm, showed only a ripple of the disturbance beneath.

'For God's sake! What did I do?' Karen's anxiety showed only too clearly. She pushed weakly at the bedding, trying to sit up, and inwardly cursed. 'I hate this room. Whose rotten taste is responsible for it, I'd like to know.'

'Don't, Caro!'

'Don't what?' She glared at the other girl, then realisation hit her. 'Oh, oh. I'm supposed to have furnished in this . . . this second-rate bordello style, is that it? All right. Just put it down to my memory loss. But what else have I done recently to make you wary of me?'

When Sybilla simply shook her head, she snapped, 'Look, I'll find out if I have to question every person in this house. You'd better tell me.'

'You do not recall the events of that night after you . . . after you ran away into the streets?'

Karen frowned. 'I remember dining and going up to bed early, that's all.'

'You were found drugged and near naked in your bed, with the window wide and water everywhere. Had Charles Hastings not happened to return late and his eye been attracted by your curtains flying in the wind, you would have frozen to death.'

The silence grew. Karen felt the blood drain from her head. She lay back, fighting desperately against encroaching weakness. What had happened to the old Karen Courtney, strong enough to survive ten years as a state ward, tough enough to stand up to Humphrey's intimidating techniques?

Finally she said, 'I see. And everyone thinks I meant to kill myself.' Her scornful tone hid the fear that squeezed her heart painfully. Another near fatal incident. Another attempt to be rid of her... or her alter ego, Caroline.

Sybilla's face lit. Why did Karen have the feeling that she was not showing her honest feeling?

'You are saying that you did not mean it so? Oh, Caro, if I could only believe... But, there have been so many accidents lately, and your manner... so strange. What were we to think?'

'Most likely what you do think, that I'm mad and should be put away for my own safety.'

'Do not say such a thing! But it would be idle to deny that the thought has occurred to some.'

'Who? Lady Oriel, I've no doubt. Perhaps your father and your brother, too?'

Sybilla hung her head in answer. Antony's name hovered in the air, unmentioned by either. Moreover, Sybilla herself had failed to declare her belief in her cousin's sanity.

Karen's sudden surge of anger evaporated, leaving her empty. She closed her eyes and wished Sybilla would go away. Eventually she did, leaving 'dear Caro' to her unpalatable thoughts, not the least of which was that as her supposed ally Sybilla didn't really fill the bill. She could never understand Karen's feelings – there was no common ground. Bonds of friendship were forged through trust and empathy, and how could Sybilla begin to show either when she was clearly baffled by every word Karen spoke? No, Sybilla was too much a woman of her times to be entirely trusted.

Karen had never felt so totally alone. Her solitary life back home in the twentieth century had been her own choice. Her failed marriage had given her Adele to love, and, even while keeping private her innermost core, she had moved amongst her own kind, people who thought in the way she thought, who had the same social and cultural backdrop to their lives. Here the background was confusion and the unexpected was the norm. No wonder she felt disoriented.

Then Amanda appeared, holding out a lifeline to her new friend. She settled herself in a chair at the bedside and took Karen's thin hands in her own, infusing her with her own warmth and vitality.

'I am here to help you, my dear. I am aware of the bewilderment you must be suffering and I shall disabuse your mind of its foremost burden by informing you that you did not make an attempt to take your life. You have been very ill, and very likely in moments of weakness you have doubted yourself. Never do so. I stand your friend, and you may call upon me at any time in any manner you choose.'

Karen squeezed the hands holding her own, and couldn't prevent a tear from running down her cheek. 'Thank you. I . . . could do with a friend.'

Releasing her hold, Amanda sat back, arranging the ubiquitous shawl which had slipped from her shoulders. 'Let me tell you of the agreement I have come to with your husband.' She proceeded to review her original scheme for the regaining of her friend's memory, giving every reassurance that she would not have to face anyone until she was well-schooled.

Karen approved. Here was her chance to get out and search for information on . . . what? On time travel? It was enough to bring on an attack of defeatism, she thought. Who would even admit to having an interest in such a thing?

Amanda's soft, insistent voice drew her back from her thoughts. 'There are two other matters we should discuss, the first, and most urgent, being the danger which surrounds you in this house.'

Karen's eyes flew to her face. 'So you suspected, too. Have you any idea who my enemy is, Amanda?'

'I cannot imagine who it could be, for I do not know any member of the household well enough to guess at his or her motive for trying to destroy you.'

'What about Antony, my husband?' She drew a deep breath. 'He hates me . . . Caroline, that is. I can see it in his eyes, even when he is saying polite things to me.'

'I do not know. It is possible,' said Amanda gently. 'There is a great amount of hostility under this roof, I have felt it. Some, at least, is directed at you, and you must take every care that the ill-wisher is given no further opportunity to harm you. When you are well again, you should go out into society as much as possible. Do not stay here alone in the house, if it may be avoided. Lock your door at night, and your window. Look carefully before putting foot on the stairway. Above all, do not take food or drink that is not shared with others. You must surely have been drugged that night.'

Karen remembered her suspicion that 'Caro' had been dead before falling downstairs. Then she thought of the luncheon tray she had just sent back to the kitchen, empty.

'I am getting up today, Amanda. I'm no longer an invalid. Oh, for a good course of antibiotics! I'd have been on my feet weeks ago.'

'No doubt you are speaking of some remedy from your own time. This brings me to the second matter for thought. Do you recall my saying to you that I believed your very unusual story?'

Karen shot upright. 'So, it was *you*! You said you could help me. How could I have forgotten? You are the one person in this place to treat me as a normal human being. Amanda, why do you believe me?'

''Tis not easily explained.' Amanda took a deep breath and began. 'You must know that I come of a family long gifted with the ability to foresee future events. Some of us may sense certain things about a person merely by handling an item of jewellery that is worn frequently. My father could heal sick animals with the touch of his hand. As a child, I was taught to use my abilities in the service of others, although we tried not to speak of these matters outside our immediate circle for fear of ridicule. It would have distressed dear Mama, who is not psychically aware, and could not understand our "peculiarities".'

Karen was interested, but unimpressed. 'So, you are intuitive, clairvoyant and practice psychometry. Naturally I see that these attributes would give you an interest in esoteric matters, and therefore you would be more likely to at least examine my story with an open mind, but – '

'You lack patience, Caro. Allow me to continue. Because of my father, I have had the advantage of certain teachings. I will not go into them. Sufficient to say they have a bearing on my belief in the reincarnation of the soul sometime after it has left the body. It is a very old belief and crosses centuries and cultures.'

'I've heard of it. It's quite a hot . . . I mean, many people in my time take great interest in the theory. In fact, a good proportion of the world's population believe it implicitly, although I'm not one of them.'

Amanda looked pleased. 'Then you are familiar with the basic idea of spirit being the energising force in a body, and at its core, the soul – the intrinsic being forever connected to its creator. Our churchmen preach to us on the Day of Judgment. Well, I believe we judge ourselves. When we cross the border from this life, we return to our Source and are helped to evaluate our progress, or lack of it, during earthly existence. We decide which aspects of development need further work, and at a chosen time, the soul returns to the world of the flesh, ready to grow and learn and expand even further.'

Karen sighed and leaned back against the pillows. 'We're getting in deep here. I can see you have faith in this system of belief. However, it's not only difficult for me to accept, but I don't quite see what it has to do with my predicament.'

'I shall endeavour to explain.' Amanda folded her hands in her favourite lecture pose. 'If you can give credence to the possibility of a soul entering into a new body when it has decided to return to the earth plane, then it is no great step to the acceptance of another possibility – that a soul already in possession of a *living* body can be shocked out of that fleshly vehicle and into another – even across time.'

Karen gaped at her. 'You'll have to let me think about that for a minute. Let's see if I can put it into my own words. Your first statement, about reincarnation, I understand. Now, if I can believe in the rebirth of the essential spirit of a person, you say there should be no barrier to belief in that spirit leaving its body and being transported across time into another living body. Which means two souls occupying the same body. I can't accept that!'

'There is no reason why you should, my dear. In the specific case we are discussing, the body of Caroline Marchmont was vacant. Her spirit had fled.'

'You mean . . . she was dead – before I arrived?'

Amanda nodded. 'I believe that was the case.'

'You think she was murdered, don't you?'

'There were no marks upon your body, beyond a few bruises – nothing to show why the real Caroline's spirit had fled, or when. What could be simpler, after all, than to administer a large quantity of laudanum and fling the victim from the head of the stairs? Who would know she had not tripped and fallen, and died as a result of that fall?'

'My God!' Karen's voice was a whisper. She took a moment to control her chaotic thoughts. 'And what about my own body? What's been happening to it back in my own time? Will it still be there when I get back?'

'I see no reason to doubt it. However, you understand that I am unable to guarantee anything. I simply do not know.'

'So, I must take my chances. Amanda, I find it very hard to believe in this possession of another woman's body. What could have happened to set my own spirit roaming off across time to just happen on a vacant "vehicle", as you put it?'

Amanda gave this some thought. Then her face lit. 'While I have no knowledge of the initial impetus, I can speculate upon the reason for your soul's choice of a new residence. Possibly there is a connection of some kind. You may very well have lived before as a person of these times, and therefore feel drawn to them.'

'Never!' Karen shuddered, remember the stinking alley where Amanda had found her. If she had lived in Georgian times, the odds strongly favoured a miserable existence as one of the myriad poor, not of the favoured few at the top end of society.

Her face must have reflected her feelings, for Amanda rose and kissed her cheek, saying, 'I have tired you, and it is imperative that you regain your strength as soon as possible.' She gathered up her belongings. 'Do not forget that you have my belief and trust. I shall call upon you each day, and as soon as you feel able we shall begin our lessons. I shall be your governess, and you my young pupil. It will be amusing.'

She put on a mischievous face. 'Our reward will be a scandalously expensive descent upon the shops. Your husband did offer us the freedom of his purse. You will enjoy that, my dear.'

She had gone before Karen remembered she had not told her friend about her desperate need to return to the twentieth century as soon as possible. It was amazing that Amanda knew nothing about her, and yet was prepared to give her time and energy to Karen's cause. Karen made a promise to herself that somehow she would repay this kindness, after she'd found a way of damming the flow of words long enough to say something herself.

Reflecting on Amanda's kindness she could understand that her training as well as her inclinations had led her to use her extraordinary abilities in the service of others. Hence her involvement with the Holborn dispensary. Now she was prepared to devote her energies to Karen.

Her remaining days of convalescence flew by, crammed with Amanda's tutoring, careful but determined exercising of wasted muscles, cautious conversations with the few family visitors permitted now that she was no longer bedridden. She watched her tongue and hid her reactions to Lady Oriel and Basil of the sly eyes, the more easily because their visits were brief and conducted under the watchful supervision of Antony. However, he and she had little to say to one another, and Karen began to speculate whether he had any interests at all outside of his clubs and sporting activities.

Fashionably, although somewhat carelessly turned out, he appeared to be the epitome of the London buck, engaging in all the normal male pursuits of the times. His amusements consisted of attendance at race meetings, cockfights and boxing matches, and he made no secret of the fact that his nights were spent in gambling and drinking at one or another of his clubs. She had Sybilla's word for it that he rarely appeared at any of the balls, routs and soirees that formed the essential backbone of the London Season, although in the country he hunted and had no objection to joining shooting parties.

It seemed he had no taste for the company of women. Hardly surprising in view of his disastrous marriage, Karen thought, and again wondered what had happened to his first wife. Sybilla closed like an oyster whenever the subject was mentioned, and who else was there to ask? Amanda had never met the lady, and in any case, disliked gossip; and with Charles Hastings, for some reason she just didn't care to pry.

However, she welcomed his visits. He brought her books from Hookhams – some excruciating novels as well as informative tomes on Georgian London, at her request – and in his own quiet way did his best to entertain her. One afternoon he seemed preoccupied, and when she probed, revealed a real concern with the well-being of the nation. It appeared that matters were not going well for England economically. Costs had rocketed and people starved because Napoleon's Continental System was squeezing shut the trade routes that supplied essential goods, not to mention the country's inability to export its own manufactures.

Karen's interest rose. 'Charles, this is January 1811, isn't it?'

'Yes, the eighteenth. Why do you ask?'

'Then we are at war with the whole of Western Europe.'

He sighed. 'Indeed. Our new Regent is about to assume power at a most difficult time. One must hope that he will take a firm grasp of matters of state.' His gloomy tone was not reassuring. ''Tis but a matter of weeks since Sweden's Crown Prince bowed to Napoleon's decree and declared war upon us – the final link in the chain that will try to strangle this country.'

'I feel sure you need not worry. Prince Bernadotte is a friend to Britain. He will never enforce the blockade no matter how much French pressure is brought to bear.' Remembering, too late, that the feather-headed Caroline would have no interest in foreign affairs, she added, 'Or so I have heard from . . . from Amanda. She is very politically minded, you know.'

At the mention of Amanda, his amazed expression gave way to one of bemused fascination. He'd certainly been hit hard, thought Karen, and wondered whether Amanda felt the same way. Regardless of her open friendliness, Amanda had a depth of reserve that Karen did not like to broach, very like Charles' own in fact. She tactfully changed the subject.

Having unburdened herself to Amanda on her grief for the loss of Adele, Karen was inclined to discuss her old life with the one person willing to listen. She was disappointed when Amanda began to discourage this.

'My dear Caro, this is a difficult undertaking for you, and you must never for an instant allow yourself to become distracted from your purpose, which is to survive your extraordinary translation from your own time and launch yourself successfully into society.'

'Amanda, my purpose is to get back home to my own time. I don't give a fig for your social whirl. I'm only learning to prance and posture and talk with half a dozen plums in my mouth because I want to get among people and question them. I've somehow got to find this gap in time and squeeze back through it.'

Amanda's eyes danced. 'Is that how you see us? Dear me. Half a dozen plums!' Her mood changed and she said more gently, 'I know how you suffer, Caro. I know what your child must mean to you, and how exceedingly difficult it is for you to practise control and try to conform to a way of life so entirely foreign to your own. But you must recall the further purpose behind our scheme. We are protecting your life, and if possible, we intend to discover and expose the wicked creature who would wrench it from you.'

Karen sighed. 'We're no closer to doing that than I am to finding that time gap. It could be any one of the household, including the servants. Lucy has something on her mind. I sometimes catch her looking at me very strangely. And it was she who gave me the hot milk that night I nearly froze to death.'

Amanda dismissed the milk with a wave. 'Anyone could have

tampered with it. As for your maid "looking strange", I am scarcely surprised. My dear Caro, you are not precisely the model of a great lady, although I have no doubt you soon will be.'

'I wouldn't be too sure of that. I admit I've given people a few shocks in the past weeks, sometimes deliberately. You know, I can't believe the way servants are treated by their own kind. The hierarchy is amazing, and quite cruel. Everyone's afraid of Bates. He's at the top of the pile, and then Mrs Bates terrorises the maids. The menservants tyrannise the women and take shocking over advantage of them. I even found one of those poor half-starved little scullery maids crying in the kitchen corner last week and nursing a scalded hand. I discovered she'd been deprived of her supper and made to scrub the floor with that hand because she'd dropped a plate when she accidentally scalded herself! I soon fixed that! But it's appalling, the amount of bullying going on.'

''Tis very bad, but . . .' Amanda did a classic double-take. 'Caro, do you mean to say you actually paid a visit to your kitchens?'

'Yes I did. And it's no use telling me a lady does not do so because I know. I had a domestic riot on my hands.'

Amanda began to laugh. 'You amaze me. I wish I had been present to see such a sight. Of course you are in the right of it. The rigid structure of the servants' hall can be a cruel prison to many, and 'tis difficult to effect change without resentment. Also, I fear, many mistresses have no wish to disturb a well-run household and bring inconvenience upon themselves. I congratulate you upon your valour. Pray, tell me what eventuated.'

Karen smiled reminiscently. 'They tried to put me in my place and I threatened to sack the lot of them. They then formed a deputation under Mrs Bates to protest to Antony.'

Amanda gasped. 'What did he say? Oh, my dear, he would be furious.'

'Well, I quite thought so myself. But I was too angry to care. Surprisingly, he informed them that they were to take orders from me or get out – or words to that effect. You know how well he expresses himself.'

Amanda seemed to be struck dumb. So Karen went on. 'At any rate, things have settled, and I rather think I've earned a totally spurious reputation as an Iron Mistress. Which brings me back to my suspicions of Lucy. She behaves like a timid rabbit when she's around me.'

'Never mind your maid. We should be searching for the person who has something to gain from your death.'

The discussion ended in the usual impasse.

The day finally came when both Dr Horbury and Amanda pronounced Karen ready to re-enter society, and in some trepidation she prepared for the event.

Standing by the window she stared into the frosted garden while waiting for her bath to be readied. Her desperate urge to return to her own time had abated a little. During the first weeks of her illness she'd fretted, and in her delirium had wept for her child – whereupon the resistant Chloe had been brought to her bedside. When this proved unproductive, she'd been dosed with laudanum and kept drugged until she ceased to struggle. Strangely, she had hazy memories of Antony being with her whenever she woke from her drug-induced sleep. He seemed kinder, almost as if he cared about her misery. Strangely enough, his presence had been a comfort. Perhaps he'd sensed her loneliness and had the compassion to be there whenever she looked for him. And perhaps this was all a part of her dreams.

A period of lethargy had set in, when she no longer cared what happened to her. Finally, with the realisation that she must have missed her court appearance, and consequently forfeited her plea for custody of Adele, there came hysteria, followed by resignation. It would all have to be done again, when she got back home. Meanwhile, she must regain her health and concentrate all her energies on finding the way back.

As she dressed for Lady Wharton's soiree, allowing Lucy to minister to her in a way she'd have thought impossible not so long ago, her mind was occupied with this need. She knew it was time to press Amanda. Her intuitiveness, almost a psychic ability to read people and their motives, daily became more noticeable to Karen. Her friend seemed able to predict events and behavioural reactions, and there was nothing superficial about her. She cared about people. If anyone could find a solution to Karen's dilemma, it would be this gifted woman.

That night, stepping down from the carriage before Lady Wharton's elegant townhouse, Karen had her nerves under control. She knew she looked attractive. Her gown of green silk flattered her skin and hair, and hid the too-prominent shoulder bones with a demi-cape of ribbon lace that ended in a pretty ruff under her chin. It was not strictly in the bare mode usual for evening, but as Amanda pointed out, the Viscountess Marchmont was an acknowledged leader in fashion. All she need do was carry it off as the latest whim from Paris.

They swept in together, Karen on Antony's arm, Amanda worshipfully attended by Charles Hastings. It had been Amanda's suggestion that her charge would feel more comfortable in such a party on this difficult first occasion, and Antony agreed.

Their hostess greeted them with a fluting cry of joy, dropping a kiss in the air above Karen's cheek, while loudly decrying her long absence from the world. Curiosity gleamed in her eyes and Karen was sure she had missed no detail of her appearance. Then they passed on to make way for new arrivals.

Since this was an informal sort of occasion, Amanda whispered, they would make their way unannounced into the ballroom which had been set up as a concert hall with chairs grouped about a platform for the musicians. Potted ferns and floral arrangements on stands helped to create an effect of arbours. Karen gladly moved to one, away from the blatant stares that followed her.

Antony excused himself and dragged Charles off to speak to an acquaintance, leaving Karen strangely bereft. A string quartet fiddled with their instruments, extracting the obligatory cat yowls that preceded a performance. The room buzzed with loud talk and occasional bursts of laughter. A hundred candles sent out their heat and light, and the heavy perfumed air seemed to press down on her head. Karen briefly closed her eyes to rest them from the kaleidoscopic movement of the throng.

Her air of poise hid a longing to be back in the stuffy bedroom in Rothmoor House. She wished even more fervently that she could open her eyes to her own spare, cool room in her own flat.

Amanda pinched her arm to bring her to attention, whispering the names of the men and women approaching, wreathed in smiles, their mouths uttering pleasantries and their eyes punching holes in her mask, eager to discover what lay beneath. It was rather like Theo Sampson's opening at the gallery. Drawing on her memory of that night Karen responded, automatically using the phrases taught to her by Amanda, bowing and smiling appropriately.

Then as Lady Wharton clapped her hands and called upon her guests to be seated for the performance, she gratefully subsided into a chair beside Amanda, plying her fan to cool herself.

'That was well done, my dear. I am proud of you.'

'Thank you. But it's only the beginning.'

'Hush. Most of the evening will be taken up with the music. Madame Berelli is to sing, I believe, after the performance at the opera has finished. There will be little time for polite conversation.' Amanda smiled reassuringly, but her expression froze as an elegantly dressed man detached himself from a party of friends and crossed the room to their corner.

There was no time for warning. Karen found her hand seized and carried to a hot mouth to be kissed.

Eyes burning in a thin and smiling face, the stranger murmured, 'Treacherous Venus! Why have you not answered my notes? With all that lies between us, how can you leave me hanging in limbo with no word to give me hope?'

He pressed uncomfortably close, and Karen shrank back in her chair, repelled as much by the mixed odour of sweat and scent coming from him as the sudden awareness that this must be one of Caroline's conquests.

Now he had both her hands in his clutch and she could see people looking. At any minute Antony would notice.

Amanda delivered a painful rap to his knuckles with her fan. He hurriedly released Karen. 'Kindly take your innuendos elsewhere, Jack Thornton. They are not welcome here.'

He smiled, and Karen wished he hadn't. There was malevolence in that twist of the lips. The man meant mischief.

'Madame, I have nothing to say to you. I was addressing myself to the adorable Caroline, my Star of Love, my Incomparable . . .'

Antony appeared at Karen's side, standing close and resting a hand heavily on her shoulder. 'You mistake, Thornton. My wife is not yours in any way, and I will thank you to refrain from coupling her with yourself in any mode of speech.'

Stifled by the two men hemming her in, their antagonism as oppressive as their physical nearness, Karen felt her head swimming. Amanda said sharply, 'Stand away, both of you, if you do not wish to create a scene with a swooning girl. Lord Antony, if you must continue your argument, pray do so in another place.'

His expression was grim as he stared down at Karen. She met his look squarely. Sick as she felt, she'd be damned if she'd be browbeaten into some sort of guilty submission.

'Antony, you are absurd. Mr Thornton was merely declaiming some verse he had composed in my honour.' She made herself smile at the other man. 'Thank you for the compliment, sir, but you must take your seat now. The music is about to commence.'

Antony's eyes shifted to his adversary, their expression still unpleasant, but he said coolly enough, 'You must forgive my error. However, in future you will not approach my wife either in public or private without my permission. Do I make myself plain?'

A surge of violins drowned Thornton's reply, but Karen caught the words 'dog' and 'manger', said with contempt. However, he moved away back to his own party, and her husband took his seat behind her, his presence very much felt although he neither touched her nor spoke again.

Amanda put her lips to Karen's ear. 'Excellent! I doubted you possessed such presence of mind, my dear Caro. Do you feel well enough to remain for the performance?'

Karen nodded. This was her test night and she was determined to pass with honours. But she was furiously angry, and oddly enough, that anger was directed at the woman whose place she'd taken. She must have been a stupid spoiled bitch to humiliate her husband so, and with a low taste in men, if Thornton was anything to go by.

She made a vow that she would alter Antony's opinion of her before she left – if she left. No, make that when she left. Adele's little face darted into her mind but she was quick to close it off. Not now. Tonight she must do her part. Tomorrow, after she had demonstrated her ability to move in this artificial society, she would corner Amanda and insist that they openly discuss the problem of finding someone who could help spring this trap. The time for evasion had gone. She couldn't wait any longer.

CHAPTER 9

Antony left the following morning for a protracted tour of his estates, including a visit with his father who preferred the rural pace of life in Devon. He did not offer to take Karen, for which she was relieved. Sybilla had told her the elderly Earl of Roth suffered considerably from arthritis and rarely came to town. She also gathered he was a formidable old gentleman, who would take unkindly to the discovery that an heir to the title was highly unlikely to eventuate.

Naturally it had been Lady Oriel who had enlightened her as to the reason for Antony's remarriage – his father's order for the sake of the name. Since the whole household must know he never came to her room at night, she felt sure Lord Edward would by now be informed of that fact, and she had no wish to face his disappointed wrath.

Besides, she had more to worry about.

Amanda, cornered in her own home where Karen had come to take tea and conversation with Mrs Crayle, led her friend aside when the invalid lady retired for her pre-dinner nap.

'Come and sit in the window and we can watch the quizzes strut up and down displaying their finery. You are looking well, Caro. I believe you are fully recovered.'

'I'm as fit as I'll ever be . . .' Karen began, then halted at the look in her friend's eye. She laughed.

'Oh, very well. I should say, how kind of you to say so, dear friend. I am well, indeed, and most anxious to take counsel with you upon a matter of some urgency.'

Amanda approved the speech, and bowed to the inevitable. 'You have played your part in our bargain, and it is now my turn. I will admit to being proud of my pupil. Not one person could have doubted that you are truly Caroline Marchmont. Now, as it happens, I have been pursuing certain enquiries on your behalf, and have learned that there is a man of power, a Pierre Marnie, who worked with my father years ago. I believe he may be able to assist you.'

'Amanda! That's wonderful! Where is he? Can I see him at once?'

'Unfortunately, he lives in southern France, in Avignon.'

Karen slumped. 'Then it's hopeless. There's no way I could get there with the war going on.'

Amanda put a commiserating arm around her shoulders. 'I am so very sorry, my dear. Yet all is not lost. We may find a way of reaching this man. I have friends who maintain contact with the Continent, despite the Corsican Monster's blockade. Leave the matter in my hands, and I shall endeavour.'

After the half-hour's discussion of ways and means, followed by Karen's indulgence in an orgy of reminiscence of her little girl, she took her leave. Disappointment left her feeling hollow. Unreasonably, as she now realised, she'd counted on Amanda having a solution to her problem and the let-down was terrible.

With little heart for enjoyment, she forced herself to be companionable at the opera with Sybilla and a party of her friends that night, automatically fulfilling her own new role and carrying her end of the conversation easily enough. Amanda had taught her well, and she'd had plenty of practice.

She did feel it was a pity that none of the people claiming close acquaintance with Caroline Marchmont sparked off a desire in her for closer intimacy. They just weren't her kind. Their shallow interests left her cold, and she had nothing but contempt for the men and women who spent their days, and nights, in endless pursuit of amorous titillation. They had so much in the way of material support and opportunity, yet were too bored to make use of it.

The so-called exclusivity of the ton was as much a fake as the polite manner covering a seething pit of gossip and scandal. Many an aristocratic lady made no secret of the fact that her children had different fathers, and the hottest topic at any gathering was often the last criminal conspiracy, or act of adultery. And those too high-nosed to associate with tradesmen and others who worked for a living, lowered their standards soon enough when it suited them. Money gilded and ennobled, as it had always done and would continue to do in Karen's own time, but the blatant hypocrisy sickened her.

She could laugh at dandyism and other fads promoted often enough with tongue in cheek; yet she found it hard to reconcile the heedless waste and indebtedness with the poverty she knew existed beyond the magic privileged patch stretching between Regent's Park and St James.

A visit to the Royal Academy at Somerset House was more to her taste, although she was amazed and disappointed at the haphazard way the pictures had been hung, crowded together, frame to frame, as high as the ceiling, the feet of the subjects of full-length portraits often at level with the viewer's eyes. Pushing hordes of sightseers didn't improve her first impression.

However, her disappointment turned to a shiver of excitement when she realised the rather slovenly-looking, rough-around-the-edges man being presented by Amanda was the great Jospeh Turner himself.

Karen turned an eager face to the painter, her mind busy with dates. He'd be about thirty-six, and still acclaimed principally for his work in oils.

'How much I enjoy your work, Mr Turner. Your recent water colours of Scarborough Castle are so luminous, so glowing.'

'Thank you. As it happens I plan to spend this summer touring through the south counties in search of material for the illustrations of Mr Cooke's book on views of the southern coastline of England.'

'Ah, yes. *Plymouth with Mount Batten.*' She stopped, remembering that that work would not be finished for two years.

Fortunately, he assumed she was referring to a possible subject, and said he would bear it in mind. He then went into a monologue on his work, barely pausing to allow her any comment.

Acutely conscious of her slip, she set a guard upon her tongue, but the excitement of knowing what lay ahead for this gifted man made it hard for her. His greatest work was yet to come, ten, twenty years ahead. The people who praised him now could have no idea what was in store for them.

When he did solicit her opinion, her genuine interest and knowledgeable comments on the style of the works exhibited kept Turner at her side. He finally said approvingly, 'You may care to visit my own gallery in Queen Ann Street, Lady Marchmont.'

She glowed. 'Thank you. I should be delighted.' Her eyes moved to the man at his side, tweaking his sleeve in demand for presentation.

'My dear fellow,' Turner turned at once, drawing him forward. 'Lady Marchmont, please allow me to present my good friend Andrew Robertson, the miniaturist. You were expressing a particular interest in lithographic work, my lady. Robertson does a little of that in the architectural line, himself.'

Robertson bowed. 'Nothing that would bear comparison with your own, Joseph.' He looked admiringly at Karen. 'Lady Marchmont, I believe your husband commissioned a portrait. Yes, I am positive . . .' He broke off in confusion. 'I beg your pardon. I must have been mistaken.'

Karen smiled. 'Do not be embarrassed. You would have done a likeness of the first Lady Marchmont. I have not seen it.'

'It was a mother and child together. I also painted your husband's likeness on ivory. The settings were particularly fine, as I recall.' Red-faced over his faux pas, he soon excused himself, leaving Karen curious and determined to search out the miniature portrait of her predecessor. The unmentioned, but not forgotten, Jenny Marchmont had really begun to intrigue her.

Later, when leaving, Amanda taxed Karen with having concealed her interest in art.

Karen defended herself with vigour. 'You asked me not to speak of my previous life. I was to put it behind me and study to turn myself into a woman of fashion. Well, that's what I have done, Amanda, and still you are not pleased.' She turned away and allowed the footman to help her into her carriage.

Amanda followed, distressed. 'I have wounded you, my dear. Nothing was further from my intention. You have succeeded in your task to admiration, and I am perfectly sure no one could guess you are not what you seem. Now, I beg you will appease my curiosity. What is your interest in the world of art, and how did you acquire so much detailed knowledge? I declare, I was ready to drop with surprise when you began discussing matters of technique with Mr Turner. I have no doubt but that the use of cross-hatching is an essential, but what does it mean?'

Karen shrugged. She was still a little annoyed. 'Cross-hatching is simply a term for the series of closely spaced parallel lines used by Mr Turner in his engraving to give a uniform colour or shadow. He crosses the first set of lines at right angles with another set, to deepen the effect. As for my interest and knowledge, I am an artist myself.'

For once Amanda could find no words. She sat back against the cushion and stared.

'I supported myself working in a London gallery, but I have always painted. On the night before I . . . disappeared . . . my work went on exhibition to the public for the very first time.' She smiled wryly.

'Who knows? I might have become famous by now. I wonder whether I shall ever find out?'

'It held much meaning for you, your painting?'

'Oh, Amanda. If you only knew.'

'Then we must see what may be contrived. Since Lady Caroline displayed no such talent you cannot be seen to work in your own house. However, you could hire a studio and go there each morning. Who is to know that you are not promenading in the park?'

A few days later the two women took a hackney to the unfashionable neighbourhood of Chelsea, and viewed an attic room recently vacated by a not very successful artist who had decided to return to his father's business. They were standing in the middle of the dusty floor, discussing Karen's needs, when a young man bounded up the stairs and through the doorway, coming to an abrupt halt when he saw them.

'I beg your pardon, ladies. I believed the studio to be uninhabited.' Despite his youth, he appeared quite gnome-like, but his ugly, pock-marked face presently expressed such an odd mixture of chagrin and admiration that Karen struggled not to laugh.

'You are welcome to come in, sir. We were about to leave.' She moved forward holding out her hand. 'I am Caroline Marchmont.'

'William Etty, at your service, my lady.' He bowed awkwardly. 'Er . . . may I be so bold as to ask whether you have an interest in renting these premises?'

'I am afraid I have already done so. Did you hope to move in yourself?'

His disappointment was swiftly banished. 'By no means. That is to say, there are many such rooms available. I do not despair of finding a suitable lodging and studio.'

She looked at him with such concentration that he began to grow pink.

'William Etty. Of course!' Her eyes widened and she looked mischievous. 'Mr Etty, I shall dare to make a prophecy concerning your future.'

'Caro,' said Amanda, warningly.

But Karen didn't heed. 'Young man, you will one day be acclaimed as a Royal Academician, famed throughout the art world for your portrayal of the female form.'

'F-f-female f-form?' Now he was scarlet.

'Yes indeed. Nudes, after the style of Rubens and Titian.'

'Madam, I am a student at the Royal Academy Art School. I paint landscapes.'

'I daresay. But in your later years your female studies will be represented in every important gallery and collection in this country, and will command a higher price than the work of Constable and Lawrence. You will set a standard, Mr Etty. I congratulate you.' Taking Amanda's hand she swept out, leaving the astounded man to make what he could of her words.

Amanda's scolding went over her head. She felt exhilarated. This was the first positive result of her unfortunate body change. It had been a thrill to meet someone and know for certain what his life path would be. She had not dared to enlighten the great Turner, a public figure in a most public place, but she simply couldn't resist little Mr Etty. What a heady feeling, to confound him with promises of marvellous prospects! All the same, she did agree to be more circumspect in the future. It would never do to be talked about, at least, not as some sort of crackpot aristocratic soothsayer.

The atmosphere at Rothmoor House remained strained. Lady Oriel and the Honourable George seemed to avoid Karen's company, while Basil definitely spied. She'd caught him more than once listening to her conversations with visitors, and had seen him give money to Lucy.

Sybilla, too, seemed to have changed. Her former friendly attitude had slipped into a slightly unfriendly coolness towards her cousin, and there was a watchful look about her these days. She reminded Karen of a dog that has lost a treasured bone, casting about amongst possible foes, ready either for attack or defence. This puzzling change remained a mystery, for Sybilla kept her distance. She no longer invited Karen to join parties of friends for outings on horseback or to the shops and theatres, but whispered in corners with Lady Oriel, ignoring Karen much of the time.

She saw little of Charles, who still, in his deliberate detached way, remained a friend. With his employer absent he seemed busier than ever, although not too occupied to spend time with Amanda, a frequent visitor to the house.

The days seemed long to Karen, and the evenings longer. She couldn't spend too much time at her studio, yet would not give the remaining hours to idle chatter and peacocking in the latest ensembles. She didn't ride (although she hid this fact by stating that her recent illness had left her with a weakness of the limbs, and her medical adviser did not recommend riding); and while she enjoyed dancing (medically approved) she found the elaborate formality of Almacks wearisome, and the constant backbiting and criticism of matchmaking mamas and their silly daughters even more so.

Few of the gentlemen clamouring to escort her could be trusted to keep the line, or as she would have said, keep their paws to themselves. Those she danced with seemed evenly divided into three sectors – feeble-minded bores whose interests never rose above sport and gambling, callow and impressionable youths who had to be fought off in the conservatory, and the more dangerous predators who remembered Caroline Marchmont's reputation and acted accordingly.

Nice women avoided her, and men of wit and education assumed her to be an empty-headed flirt. She couldn't win.

Frustrated, Karen decided to redecorate. The simplified taste of the period had not been welcomed in Rothmoor House. In her opinion, no one had done anything for the place in the past thirty years. Taking the hopeful view that Antony's attitude towards the servant crisis would carry over to her spending his money, and defiant and unhappy enough not to care, she began with her hated bedroom.

Out came the ornate furniture, the hangings and swags, the rugs with their hideous patterns. She would show them what could be achieved with a minimum of fuss. The wallpaper was painted over in oyster white so that only the faintest garland pattern showed through. Woodwork, including the heavy window shutters, gleamed with fresh white paint. Draperies were replaced with white silk worked in a faint gold pattern, and rugs scattered on the polished boards – Chinese patterns in soft green, pink and gold. The great bed was stripped of its hangings and covered in apple-green silk. Whispered reports from the servants' hall held that her ladyship had gone mad indeed, exposing herself to noxious night airs.

Faded watercolours and landscapes covered in darkened varnish were banished to the attics, along with the ugly furniture and multitude of china bric-a-brac. Six oriental silk panels, discovered in an importer's warehouse and horrendously priced, now graced the walls, their delicate brushstrokes hinting at dawn over lakes and mountains, long-legged birds fishing amongst reeds, and blossom trailing along the bamboo rails of a tea-house. One Meissen shepherdess was permitted to remain on the chimneypiece to point her toe at her reflection – and that was all.

Karen returned from the studio unexpectedly early one morning.

Hearing the sound of scuffling as she entered her room, she paused. Although there was no sign of disturbance, the dressing room door stood ajar. Angry at the continued spying and scuttling about in the house, she marched over and flung back the door. Two defiant eyes stared up at her. Chloe crouched behind the firestand, her sharp little face drawn tight and, Karen suspected, teeth gritted.

'Chloe, what are you doing here?'

The child said nothing. Her eyes darted sideways, measuring the distance between Karen and the door.

'I asked you a question, Chloe. Please answer.'

'I wanted to see the pretty room.' The words came reluctantly, but with a note of recalled pleasure.

Karen took her chance. She held out her hand. 'Then come with me and look.'

For a long thirty seconds the child hestitated, then she came forward and allowed Karen to lead her into the next room. She stood at the foot of the bed and slowly turned her head, taking in everything.

'What is it you like most, Chloe?'

'The light. It's so white and light. I feel like I am standing in the middle of a white flower.' The pixie face glowed with animation. It was almost pretty.

'Ah, yes. All those old dark colours were too heavy. They absorbed the light. A bedroom should be airy and soothing to the senses.'

Chloe slid her free hand over the bedcover. 'I should like to have a pretty bed.'

'Should you, my dear? Perhaps we might do something with your room. Would you like to show me where you sleep?'

It took some cajolery, but Karen's gentle approach, plus Chloe's obvious longing to have a room like this, eventually won her over.

They scurried up the extra two flights of stairs to the nursery floor, startling a housemaid into dropping a pile of linen and creeping past Nanny asleep in her rocker in the day nursery. Chloe slept in a dark brown cavern, its oilcloth floor worn patternless, and its cupboards and timber surrounds bearing the marks of generations of kicks and thumps. The sight of the little iron cot pushed into a corner created a lump in Karen's throat. She dropped down bringing her face on a level with Chloe's.

'What is your favourite colour, pet?'

'Pink. Pink like a rose petal.'

'Then you shall have the prettiest, pinkest bedroom this side of

Harrods. Come along with me. I have pattern cards and colours to show you in my room.' She smiled conspiratorially. 'We shall creep back past Nanny on mice feet and tell no one what we are up to. It will be our secret.'

That day was the turning point. With the transformation of her night nursery under way, and Nanny necessarily let into the plot, Chloe clearly welcomed her afternoon visits to the small parlour where, to the chagrin of the other two ladies, she now attached herself to Karen. They looked at picture books bought at the Pantheon Bazaar, and studied patterns and ells of pretty muslins and velvets to be made up by a local seamstress into a new wardrobe for Chloe.

Lady Oriel's snide comments on silk purses and sow's ears made no impression. Karen had managed to convince Chloe that she was pretty, and as her confidence grew so her surly attitude melted away. Karen viewed the transformation with satisfaction, Sybilla with a noticeable frown.

'You will turn the child's head. She is paid far too much attention as it is. I dare not think what Antony will have to say when he returns to discover his daughter grown into a malapert miss.'

Karen decided that her first favourable impression of Sybilla had been an error of judgment. Chloe's allegiance had changed, and understandably Sybilla was hurt by this, but if she'd had any true affection for the child she'd have been happy to see her emerging from her moody shell.

'Antony? I imagine he will continue to look through her, as usual,' she answered, although not in Chloe's hearing. Antony's lack of fatherly interest was unpardonable. The child was lonely, and had other needs that were not even recognised, let alone fulfilled. Karen intended to approach him about at least one of these needs as soon as she could corner him.

Her opportunity soon came. One morning, a week later, she left for her studio early, unaware that Antony had arrived home at dawn. Her latest work inspired her and she wanted to finish it.

The studio had been made comfortable with a square of carpet and two braziers, one at either end of the long room. The light was excellent, pouring in through the sloping skylight directly onto her work space. She'd put in a couple of tables and chairs so that Amanda might visit with her, and for the use of her model; but apart from these she had surrounded herself with clear space, wonderful space with no pictures, ornaments or non-essentials of any kind. The walls stayed bare – no gilding, no panels, no scrolls. She felt comfortable in her eyrie and more secure than at any time since her translation from the future.

Meggy, her model, came tripping in, divesting herself of wraps and feathered bonnet, and chatting like the gaudy parakeet she resembled. Karen listened with half an ear, already immersed in her work, her fingers itching for the knife and palette.

Her lips working like a mill bobbin, Meggy took up her pose in one of the chairs. She'd been a serving maid in a nearby ale house, and Karen had found her by the simple expedient of picking her up out of the gutter where she'd been thrown by her former employer. Bruised and raging, Meggy permitted herself to be brushed down and persuaded to accompany Karen back to the studio, and thus into an altogether different line of work. Dark and voluptuous, she proved to be just what Karen needed for her experiment in semi-cubist techniques – and a welcome relief as a conversationalist. No rounded periods and clipped consonants were needed with Meggy, who spoke an argot as foreign to Karen as Esperanto, but infinitely less taxing since she was not under any compulsion to copy it.

'Shut up, Meggy. You disturb my concentration.'

Meggy grinned and obliged. A half-hour passed and Karen was about to suggest a rest break when thunderous footsteps on the stairs made her look up. The door went back with a crash that shook the building. Dust sifted down from the bare rafters and coated the still wet canvas.

Antony, the man of icy composure, charged in like a maddened bull.

Karen looked at him in astonishment, but before she could speak he forestalled her. In a voice thick with rage he lashed out.

'Bitch! Faithless, whoring strumpet! I have but to turn my back and you plunge straight into the mire.'

His driving fury was a frightening force in the room. For an instant Karen thought he might actually throw himself at her and do her an injury. Apparently Meggy thought so, too. Veteran of many bar-room brawls, she wasted no time considering the situation. Skirts hitched, she grasped the chair she'd been sitting on and lifted it high over Antony's head.

'No, Meggy!' Karen screamed.

Antony looked up and threw himself aside, but not in time to avoid the chair entirely. One leg grazed his head, knocking him against the wall where he slumped and slid to the floor, blood running from his scalp.

Meggy looked at her handiwork and spat on it. 'That for the bleater! Attack a woman, would ye? I've a mind to darken yer daylights while I'm here.'

Karen came out of her daze and went down on her knees beside the half-conscious man. 'Oh, no. You've done quite enough already. Thank you for your help, but I really am quite capable of looking after myself. Now we must revive him.'

'What for? Give 'im the chance and he'll like as not have at ye.'

'I don't think so. The first thrust of his rage is past. Besides, he's in no condition to attack anyone. Do you think you could run out and get him a brandy?' She looked up from wiping at the rather heavy flow of blood. Meggy's disgusted face made her laugh.

But the girl nodded. 'Flash o'lightning'd be the thing. I'll fetch it right enough, but 'tis a waste pouring it down the bolt o'the likes o'him.'

'All the same, I think we should. Take some money from my reticule there on the table. And, Meggy, hurry!'

Antony's colour was bad and she couldn't seem to stop the bleeding. Using a fresh paint cloth she made a pad and bound it to his temple with her handkerchief, hoping for the best.

It was while she was loosening his neckcloth to make his breathing easier that he opened his eyes and said in a shaken voice, 'I crave pardon for my behaviour. I must have been crazed.'

'I think you must. Now sit still for pity's sake and let me help you. I do not think that you are concussed. You are bleeding rather heavily, but the cut is not so deep. Well, that's a relief.'

'I have no doubt you are correct in your diagnosis. But permit me to remark that I do not share your satisfaction.' Now she heard the faint tremor of laughter in his tone.

She stood up and eyed him with growing annoyance. 'You may find it amusing, but there was nothing funny about the fright you gave us. You deserved everything you got. In fact, you might have had your skull cracked open if you hadn't been so quick.'

'Ah, yes. Your delightful companion. Where is the termagant?'

'Gone to fetch you a drink. And I'd advise you to be more polite when she gets back. Meggy's come up in a hard school. She can take care of herself.'

'As I see, and feel.' He touched the pad at his temple. 'I didn't intend to hurt you, Caro. I really cannot explain my loss of control.' His hand went out as if to take hers, then was quickly withdrawn.

She stood up, her concern now completely turned to hostility. 'Judging from experience, men don't commonly feel the need to explain. They let themselves go and then try to pick up the pieces later. And they get away with it every time.'

His face darkened with more than pain as he edged himself to his feet. She didn't help him. Picking up the overturned chair she set it with the other then sat down. After a moment's hestitation, Antony joined her. He looked at her with dislike.

'Well, Madam, what is your explanation.'

'*My* explanation!'

'You have surprised me, Caro. I believed I had your measure, that my recriminations had brought you to a new understanding. Foolishly I allowed myself to be taken in by an unfounded hope that past misbehaviour was at an end. Since the accident you have exhibited a different, I must say a more mature nature. I believed I could place my trust in you.'

The bitter emphasis on the word 'trust' brought a flush to her face. Her hands clenched in her lap, but she waited for him to finish.

'Instead, you have merely delayed until my absence freed you from constraint, then hastened to resume your former loose practices. Where is your paramour? Or are you in the expectation of receiving him? I shall remain to greet the blackguard who fouls my honour.'

Karen shook with bottled rage, but her voice remained admirably calm. 'How like you, and all the men of your time. You are so hypocritical. You all have your little *cheres amies* set up in suitable establishments, and you all visit the likes of Harriet Wilson, expecting your wives to turn a blind eye. Then at the first hint of a woman reciprocating in kind you begin to rant about that figment of the imagination, honour. It seems to me that indiscretion is a parlour game for society in general, but only men are licensed to go public.'

She paused, but he seemed too thunderstruck to reply. 'Let us be specific. You accuse me of setting up a meeting place for my lover, or perhaps a string of them. By the way, how did you know where to find me? Oh, never mind. I can guess, Sybilla or Basil, one of the two household spies.' She felt chilled. Anger was supposed to be a hot emotion, but her fury was more like an ice-cold wind blowing about her shaking body.

'Without any reason to think that I would be indulging in sexual romps, let alone proof, you burst in here and start throwing accusations about like a man insane with jealousy. Since plainly this is not the case, I can only assume that someone has been feeding you a line – I mean, making up lies about me, and your pride is pricked. Good God! Look about you. Does this look like a love-nest? There's not even a couch in the place.' She swept her arms derisively.

Antony seemed to have recovered his voice. He got up and began pacing the room, regardless of his wounded head. 'What other reason can there be for such deliberate secrecy? Why else do you inform my aunt and cousin that you are driving out with Miss Crayle or doing the grand strut in the park?'

'Because I don't want them to know what I *am* doing, of course.'

'What are you doing? What possible explanation can there be . . .?'

She walked over to the easel and turned it around to display the almost finished painting.

Antony examined it. Finally he took out his eye-glass and bent over the work, scrutinising the odd wedges of paint seemingly applied at random. Then he stepped back with a curious expression on his face. 'You try to paint?'

Despite her rage, she laughed. It was the reaction she'd expected. 'Try moving back a few feet and half-closing the eyes. Can you see what it represents?'

'No, I regret that it remains a meaningless jumble. Can that be an eye in the top left-hand corner?'

'Never mind. Probably my attempt at analytic Cubism isn't all that successful. Perhaps this will convince you.'

With an effort she reversed the large canvas leaning on the end wall, and stood back. It was a full-length portrait in the Romantic style – a girl in a plain flowing gown, rather in the manner of Lawrence's *Pinky*. The background, a mere wash of dark blue, threw up the child's exquisite complexion and enhanced the lustrous eyes. She smiled shyly out of the picture, her little slipper angled as if she was about to step forward and greet the viewer.

'Chloe!'

'It's a good likeness, I think.'

He swung around on her. 'Do you seriously expect me to believe that this is your work?'

'I don't really care what you believe. It's my private affair, and no one need know about it. You would not have known if you hadn't been too ready to listen to poisonous whispers.'

He set his teeth. 'When did the child sit for this? I am unable to credit that Nanny would bring her without protest to such a place as this.'

'I did sketches at home and worked from those.' Karen pointed to a batch of drawings in a folder on her painting table.

He riffled through them, pausing now and then to look more closely. 'Chloe posed for you? She permitted you to watch her at play, dancing? You?'

'Chloe and I have become friends,' said Karen serenely, enjoying his loss of poise.

''Tis past belief. Yet I have the evidence before me. Unless...' Suspicion loaded his voice. 'You will permit me to show this portrait to a friend, a member of the Royal Academy?'

Karen shrugged. 'Check it out if you must. Just don't keep it too long. I promised it to Chloe for her birthday next week.'

He shook his head as if to clear it. 'I had forgot. You must indeed be companions to be aware of the date. You never before marked the occasion with a gift.'

'Yes. Well. As you have noted, I've changed.' She took a shawl from a peg behind the door. 'We can wrap this around the painting to protect it. Is your carriage below?'

'I brought my curricle, it was quicker.' She curled her lip and he flushed. 'My tiger is walking the horses and I may not delay any further. Permit me to escort you home.' He looked about for her coat.

'No, thank you. I have not finished working. Bates expects me back for lunch, and that,' she consulted her watch hanging on a chain at her waist, 'that is not for another hour.'

'Caro...' He took a hasty step towards her, then stopped at the look on her face. She had made it a blank, but too much seethed behind to be quite hidden.

Stiffly he bowed. 'As you wish. I have not yet offered my apology for the unfortunate error – '

'Is that what yer calls it?' Meggy's strident voice came from the doorway. In her vivid red gown she wore for the session, hair awry and tumbing down from the haste with which she had left on her mission, she was an arresting sight. One hand rested on the doorjamb, the other clutched an open bottle. She had screwed up her face into a look of disdain as she thrust the bottle at Antony.

''Ere. I hopes it chokes yer.' She touched Karen's arm. 'Are ye well enough, lady? 'Tis a strange matter for the likes o'me to take up wi' a gentry mort, but ye were kind and I always pays me shot.' She darted a venomous look at Antony. 'What's to do wi' this petticoat squire, eh?'

'He's leaving, aren't you, Antony?'

Swallowing the implication that he was a pimp, Antony bowed ironically to both women, put down the bottle and picked up the painting. 'Good day to you, ladies. Caro, I look to see you at lunch.'

He made a good exit, but Karen followed, to see him using the stair rail as assistance on the way down, and he staggered, rather than walked.

She turned a smiling face to Meggy. 'I enjoyed that. At long last I had the chance to say what I think on a few matters. Next I think I'll tackle him on his treatment of Chloe. That child needs a kind governess.'

'Ye'll never be seeing that hedge-creeper again! There's no telling what he might do when he flies into the boughs.'

'Well, I'm afraid I must take my chances there. You see, he's my husband.' All the same, the prospect didn't really daunt her. In fact, the thought of coming clashes made her feel positively exhilarated. She grinned at the other girl. 'Come along. I want to finish this morning. Take up the pose, my girl. I believe I might do a cartoon-type thing next, something along the lines of Hogarth's social comment. I might even get it published as a broadsheet. Can't you just see Antony's face?'

Bates opened the door and bowed her inside with the news that Sir Antony would be in for lunch. Karen grimaced. She was hungry, but the atmosphere around her table would be sure to bring on indigestion.

'Do you know what bicarbonate of soda is, Bates?'

'I regret, my lady, I do not.'

'Then would you please ask Mrs Bates if there is any in the house? Cook would know.'

He bowed himself off to the back regions and Karen moved towards the stairs slowly, tugging off her tight-fitting gloves. The voices in the library were not loud, but the doors had failed to catch. Karen was halted by Charles Hastings' exclamation.

'You are wounded! They suspected you after all. It grows too dangerous, Antony.'

'Hush. My pride is more damaged than my head. 'Tis not the French you should blame for my injury, but two remarkably self-sufficient Englishwomen.' His laugh was cut off abruptly. 'I should not give way to amusement, at least not until my head is mended. Charles, you will have these documents delivered to the War Office in the usual way. I was too much in haste to see you this morning, and carried them off with me.'

'You take so many risks. If it were known what course you follow your life would not be worth a farthing dip.' Charles' voice roughened. 'A dead man can do nothing to serve his country.'

'I know, my friend. I shall not be so careless again. Now, I should change before my lady wife returns to lunch with me. I wonder whether Bates could procure me a suit of armour.'

CHAPTER 10

'Is there a strain of madness in my family, think you, Charles? Some hitherto undisclosed weakness of the brain which appears rarely, but in an acute form in adult males approaching a certain age?'

Charles looked uncertainly at his employer and friend, clearly gauging his humour. 'I have not heard of it,' he said, cautiously.

Antony's smile was tinged with bitterness. 'Nor have I, and yet I have reason to believe that my own path lies in the direction of such a morass. I must speak of it, and yet it is not fair to burden you with maudlin maunderings. My friend, you see before you a man divided against himself.'

Charles' habitually severe expression relaxed. He even managed to look sympathetic without giving offence. All the same he maintained a diplomatic silence.

'You do not answer, Charles. Very wise.' Antony sighed and walked away to gaze out of the library window onto a garden giving hints of spring. Bulbs peeped half-open in the beds and thick buds had appeared on trees and bushes. There was a feeling of awakening in the air. He pushed the windows wide and stepped through. 'Come out, Charles. Sniff the new season with me. Humour my declining wits.'

Charles joined him, and together they strolled up the pathway to the stone seat overlooked by the small parlour window. A glance showed Antony that the ladies were not about, and he sat down, hands in pockets, leaning back to gaze up into the not-quite-leafed boughs of a cherry tree.

His voice was measured and emotionless. 'I require your honest opinion on a matter of some delicacy. Do not, I beg, fob me off by reason of this delicacy. What is your opinion of my wife, Caroline?'

Charles shied like a startled horse. He actually stepped backward.

Antony said testily, 'Sit down, and do not pretend to misunderstand me. You cannot have failed to notice the difference in Caro since her accident before Christmas. It is too marked to be attributed to memory loss alone. Her whole nature has altered, or so it seems to me. What is your opinion?'

'Hrrrrum.'

'Could you not be clearer?'

Charles lifted his coat tails and sat down gingerly on the end of the seat. His words came slowly, but they had the ring of genuine feeling.

'I believe that Lady Caroline has been matured by her recent experiences. She has become a woman of both sense and sensibility. Her mind is now occupied by matters formerly of slight interest to her. She discusses political and cultural matters with ease, and her manner towards myself and other persons of lesser rank is without height. In short, she has to my mind become a great lady.'

'Hmm. You speak with fervour. And yet, I had thought you harboured no great admiration for Caro when first we wed. Nor she for you.'

'That is true. And therein lies the miracle. We are now on such terms as I might even claim to be friendship.' He looked steadily at Antony. 'This is, I collect, your own particular difficulty? You stand upon different terms?'

'Precisely.' He bit the word off. 'Our incompatibility is no secret. Within two months we had recognised that our marriage was an unqualified disaster. I do not hesitate to mention what has become a subject for common gossip. Yet, over time a change has taken place. It is not my imagination. You have just proven this.'

They sat in silence for a few minutes, so still that a small brown bird came down and hopped about their feet, foraging. It flew off like a dart when Antony spoke.

'Unlike you, Charles, I have not achieved that admirable state of intimacy with my wife. We barely speak on terms. I realise much of the fault lies with me, but I am unable to retrieve myself. I fear to trust where once I was so grievously wounded; I cannot accept such a sea-change. There are times when I feel she is not Caroline at all, but a changeling woman, and this is the basis of my dilemma. I can no longer rely upon my own judgment.'

'What is it you fear?'

Antony hestitated, then said softly, 'I sometimes see my Jenny in the way she turns her head, or speaks a phrase. I fear that I am indeed no longer rational.'

Having unburdened himself to the one person he did trust, Antony achieved some relief. He did not expect an easy solution, and Charles had not attempted to offer any; but sharing his fears had weakened them. Of course he saw Jenny in the new, gentler Caro. Feathers followed her as his new mistress, Chloe loved her, Lady Oriel continued to be as scornful and unpleasant as she'd ever been with Jenny. There was also Caro's love of art and music, both attributes shared with Jenny, and now, the liking between her and Charles.

But there the likenesses finished. His first wife had been of a self-effacing nature, always deferring to others, always happy in serving people. She had enjoyed the domestic arts, cooking, preserving, handwork of all kinds, and had interested herself endlessly in the affairs of those less fortunately situated than herself.

Caro seemed to cloak herself in an instinctive wariness. Her trust was not easily won, as he could testify. There was a self-protective mechanism working in her that seemed to expect rejection, even while she looked for understanding. He had almost used the word, affection, in place of understanding. Caro – in need of affection! Certainly none of this had been evident to him when he married her – blind idiot that he was.

Only his strong sense of duty and love for his father had sent him out into the marriage mart once more. It was Caro's misfortune, and his own, that their paths had crossed.

Deliberately he searched his mind for other instances of the difference between the two women. Some memories even made him smile. Caro and domesticity were mutually exclusive. Fine foods and wines appealed to her, but their preparation and presentation remained a mystery known only to the staff. She could not sew without pricking her finger and bleeding over the stuff she handled, and household matters frankly bored her. But her taste was impeccable, and the difference she had wrought in the gloomy chambers of Marchmont House delighted him.

Many people had commented upon the pleasantly uncluttered style, and he had accepted these compliments on Caro's behalf, and kept them to himself. He still could not bring himself to risk exposure. Was she angered by his indifference, or merely indifferent herself? Sometimes he noted a depth of sadness in her eyes when she thought herself unobserved, and he felt an urge to comfort her. But so far he had conquered that urge. It was better so – safer to avoid involvement.

This decided, he dismissed his wife from his thoughts and bent his mind to the serious and secret work engaging him more than ever as Britain grew more isolated in a world dominated by Napoleon Bonaparte.

The policy-makers in Whitehall had become increasingly anxious about the intentions of the Tsar, and the less prestigious, but strategically important, new Crown Prince of Sweden. Antony had had some dealings with Bernadotte, and respected his desire to create an independent sovereign Sweden. But clearly Napoleon expected the support of his former Marshal, and was prepared to use force to claim it. Bernadotte trod a wary path, placating, intriguing, avoiding direct confrontation. It was part of Antony's work as a secret emissary to keep British interests to the forefront of Bernadotte's mind.

He had been in Stockholm in November when Sweden was forced to declare war on Britain, and had received Bernadotte's personal assurance that this was a formality. There would be no aggression, no enforcement of the blockade against British shipping. Antony had believed him, and so far his belief had been justified. But the French were bringing pressure to bear, and soon Bernadotte would have to decide which way to go, with his former master, the ruler of Europe, or with Britain and Russia, the last strongholds against a megalomaniac aggression. The odds were not good.

Having decided to dismiss Caro, she thereupon stole into his consciousness when he was least prepared. He discovered from Charles that she was interested in history and the politics of the day, and marked this down as another instance of her latent peculiarity. It was her failure to follow the expected pattern that teased his interest and, despite his determination, kept her in his thoughts.

One night at dinner, in quixotic mood, he brought up the subject of the war, encouraging his guests to discuss a topic that would normally have waited until the ladies had retired from the table. He did not give political dinners, and was ostensibly uninterested in the state of the nation. However, this night, blandly ignoring surprised looks, he challenged his neighbour to the left, a rabid Whig and one-time Foxite, to support his oft-stated view that the war with France was a mistake.

Tim Rawleigh rose instantly to the bait. 'We ain't in a position to pay for war, that is the truth of the matter. The country is on the verge of bankruptcy, the ports at a standstill, the price of bread gone beyond the ability of the poor to pay – and to cap it all the

North American states are threatening to break the blockade and attack our ships.' He paused triumphantly.

'It does seem you have proved your point, Tim,' drawled Antony, looking pointedly at Charles, seated further down the board.

His secretary obliged. 'I say we cannot afford not to fight the Corsican. If we allow events to take their course we shall wake one morning to find ourselves vassals of France.'

'Nonsense!' blared another voice, far gone in wine. 'The self-styled Emperor is too busy enjoying his new wife and baby son to be a menace.'

A scandalised feminine titter travelled around the table and Charles hastily continued. 'He is biding his time. He waits to see what the Russian Bear will do.'

'And the Swedish Fox. You said yourself, Charles, that Bernadotte is sitting on the fence.' Karen's interjection brought a sudden silence, which Antony broke.

'I had not thought you to be so concerned with foreign policy, Caro. Tell me, do you think the Emperor will attack the Tsar? Will he be so foolhardy?'

Karen raised her chin and said steadily, 'I believe he will, within twelve months.'

A babble of talk rose, some supporting, most rejecting her reading of the situation. Amused, Antony continued to watch his wife defending her belief, admiring her ability to stick to her guns under pressure.

Tim Rawleigh argued heatedly for his, and his party's point of view, although Antony was aware that many of the longer heads amongst the Whigs were in favour of war.

'We need peace,' bellowed Tim, striving to be heard. 'The country needs social reforms and we must not squander the necessary funds on machinery for war.'

Karen's voice interposed strongly. 'Certainly we need social reforms, but they need not be dependent on more funds. If the Corn Laws were repealed you would do away with immense misery among the poor. They could afford to buy bread again.'

Rawleigh was not the only person to stare. Again it was Antony who filled the silence caused by his wife's comment. 'True, my dear. But I fear the landowners would never agree. They make a very good thing out of keeping the price of wheat raised – and parliament is full of landowners.'

'Then parliament should be changed! Do away with all the rotten boroughs and blatantly purchased seats and put in honest men who care about more than lining their own pockets.'

This caused uproar. Tim Rawleigh beat upon the table with his hand to signify approval, shouting that this was what the Whigs would do, put honest men in the House. Amanda looked approving, as did a rather startled Charles. But amongst the other guests endorsement was not so widespread. The ladies in particular seemed to resent the adoption of a topic so uninteresting to them, and murmured to one another their distaste at such sentiments publicly expressed by a woman.

Lady Bessborough, the mother of the flighty Caroline Lamb, and equally as flighty herself, expressed open discontent. 'Can we not speak of something else? Politics give me the headache.' She arched her eyebrows and smiled at Karen.

'I apologise for giving you pain, although the discussion was not initiated by me. Perhaps you would prefer to talk about the people who are affected by politics, the children who are sent half-starved into the mills to bring home the pennies for the over-priced bread. I've seen such children, my lady, and they have no head for politics, either.'

The lady shrank back, confused by Karen's wintry tone in contrast with her smile. Other female heads bent together and the murmurs grew louder. Amanda looked anxiously at her friend, then at Antony.

He interposed himself once more. 'Unfortunately, politics are a fact of life, as is war at present.' He looked at Tim Rawleigh. 'You want peace for our land, as do we all, but not at too high a price.'

Rawleigh wagged his head stubbornly, as did several supporters around the table. 'Bonaparte is invincible. Just look at his record. Wherever he appears at the head of his troops, the battle is lost to the French. We must have peace before he runs us over.'

'Demme, man, why sue for peace just when we are beginning to turn the tide in Spain?' Charles had actually raised his voice. 'Napoleon has never set foot there, and Wellington has the French on the run. I say 'tis as well our Prince now supports the Tories. The Whigs would never have brought in the necessary taxation to continue the fight!'

'Traitor!' Rawleigh banged down his glass and jumped to his feet. 'Go lick the boots of our turncoat Regent, if you will – '

'Shame, shame,' came the call from around the table.

'If only Fox had lived. He'd have put the country on its feet,' mourned someone.

'Aye.' Rawleigh's voice held a suspicion of a sob. 'There was a great man for you.' He staggered, and sat down abruptly.

'Perceval is good enough as leader. He will maintain the government and keep it stable until the Prince is confirmed in his Regency next year.' The speaker, Harry Anstruther, was another of Whig persuasion, but with the ability to give his enemy his due.

Antony smiled at him and raised his glass. 'Well, then, Harry, I give you a toast – to our new Prince Regent and his Prime Minister, Spencer Perceval.'

All but one person rose with Antony and honoured the toast, although some with a distant lack of enthusiasm. 'The Prince Regent and Spencer Perceval.'

As they took their seats, curious eyes turned to Karen, still seated at the end of the long board, her wineglass untouched. Her face had grown chalky and the blue eyes stared, giving her the look of a doll.

Antony thrust back his chair and moved swiftly to her side. 'My dear, what is it? You are unwell?'

Her lips moved but nothing emerged. She got up jerkily and excused herself, allowing him to take her arm and assist her from the room. Outside in the hall she turned to him. Her eyes had lost the opaque look of non-life. Now they searched his with an unusual intensity.

'Antony, I must say this, even though it will enrage you. You will not understand, but you must . . . you *must* believe me. A man's life is at stake. In May of next year Mr Spencer Perceval will be assassinated in Parliament – the only British Prime Minister to suffer such a fate. You may be able to prevent this. I don't know. But I had to tell you.'

Antony felt her mittened fingers trembling in his. He could not doubt her sincerity. His own feelings were mixed. Astonishment, doubt, some suspicion, and a strange sweet fascination with the workings of this woman's mind.

Jenny would have spoken out in just such a way, he thought. But Jenny had no understanding of politics and policies. And she would never have disrupted a dinner party because of some fey notion that she could see into the future.

He deliberately hardened himself against the pull of those pleading eyes. 'I do not doubt that you believe what you say, but it is not a matter I can easily accept. Where is your proof? Perceval may not even be in office in another year's time.'

He saw her intensity wilt. 'He will be, and he will die,' she said drearily. 'I can offer you no proof.'

'Then I suggest that we curtail this unprofitable conversation and return to our guests. They will be concerned.'

She looked at him, her expression unreadable, then turned away towards the stairs.

More shaken than he would ever reveal, he hesitated on the brink of calling her back. What an unfeeling cur he was. He could have shown more sympathy with her obvious shock. Whatever her twisted reasoning, she was a woman displaying empathy for someone she believed to be in danger. He recalled thinking how seldom she smiled these days. Whatever her mood, it always seemed brushed with a melancholy overlay, like a veil over a lovely ornament.

'Caro.'

When she hesitated, he crossed the space between them, holding her at the second step with a hand on her arm.

Her eyes were on a level with his, and it seemed that they grew larger, widening into huge blue pools of pain as she searched his face.

'I was too abrupt. I did not intend to hurt you.' He watched her mouth trembling with the effort of control, and cursed himself again. 'My . . . Caro!' Without thinking, he had grasped her hands and drawn her close, feeling her breath on his face as his own mouth came down to cover hers.

It was a brief kiss, piercingly sweet and hot as burning steel to his lips. His whole body flamed, as longing swept through him. Then she had jerked away from him. His hands tightened instinctively as she tried to free herself.

'Let me go!' The words were a harsh whisper.

'My dear, you must let me – '

'No!' This time she shouted, and wrenched away so hard that he let her go, rather than injure her. Immediately she whirled about and rushed up the stairs, skirts clutched high above her ankles.

About to follow, Antony was halted by Bates' deprecating cough. He glared at the butler, who bowed, and continued his stately advance to the dining room, laded with fresh wine. By then, Antony had recalled his duty to his guests. It would serve no purpose to follow Caro, he thought. She had withdrawn the very moment he had shown his disbelief. He had destroyed his chance of building confidence between them. Had he really wanted that chance, or had he deliberately chosen to kill it off? Did he still see it as a trap?

The irony of his situation struck him. Still afire with the feel and taste of a woman he believed he hated, wanting and yet not wanting to recreate the intimacy that had once inflamed him almost to the point of delirium, he had encountered total rejection. She had looked at him with loathing. She had bruised herself to escape his touch.

Still shaken by the suddenness and strength of the emotional storm, he stood waiting to regain command of himself. On the second stair he saw a small patch of lacy fabric and bent to retrieve it. Carrying it to his face he inhaled the fragrance of roses – her fragrance. With eyes closed, he pressed the scrap hard against his lips, enduring the bitter-sweet pain of loss, then slipped it inside his coat. Resuming his habitual mask, he returned to his guests, polite excuses for his wife ready on his tongue.

Karen rested her elbows on her dressing-table and covered her eyes. Her heart beat painfully against the wall of her chest, and she breathed as if she'd run ten times further than the few yards to her bedchamber. Her first impulse had been to scrub her lips clean, but as her injured pride recovered she could assess her feelings more honestly. She'd been disappointed in Antony's reaction to her news, and humiliated by his obvious disbelief. He had thought she was 'recovering' from her illness, and been shocked by her relapse. What else could she have expected?

But he had also been genuinely sorry that he'd given her pain. And his kiss had been anything but hurtful.

Cautiously, she explored her reactions to his peace offering. For that was all it had been. Taking her hands away from her face, she stared at herself in the mirror, watching her expression soften as she thought of Antony's mouth on hers, feeling again the sense of shock and familiarity as she succumbed to him just for those few seconds. Yes, she'd enjoyed being kissed by him. She had to admit it.

But she'd felt like a traitor to herself. She was Karen Courtney, not Caroline Marchmont, and she had no business entangling herself with anyone from the nineteenth century. She was going home, to her own time, to Adele – come hell or highwater!

That was why she'd torn herself from Antony's arms and fled like a virtuous maiden. And it was a good reason to stay away from the man, with his insidious charm. It would be all too easy to fall victim, without knowing whether she could trust him. She had to remember that he was a domestic tyrant, that he was uninterested in a real relationship, and that haggard good looks could hide depths of character she'd rather not explore. She wasn't about to fall into that trap.

She sat erect and picked up the hare's foot, patting powder over her face. It was time she went downstairs to face questions and exclamations, and the eternal drawing-room gossip. Oh, how tired she was of the silly social round. So far, Amanda's efforts had achieved very little, with no word from Pierre Marnie, and no other hopeful avenues offering. It was already the end of May, over six months since she'd been thrust into this world, and she was no closer to finding her way back to her rightful place. Was she doomed to exist amongst strangers as Lady Caroline Marchmont, a woman of poor repute? Would she ever see her daughter again? It seemed as though she'd reached a dead end.

She admitted in the darkness of her despair that she was lonely, living in an isolation that few could have known outside of a solitary confinement cell. Marooned in her alien dimension, she sometimes looked in the mirror and began to doubt her own existence.

That's what made Antony so dangerous. He attracted her as no man had before. She sensed a depth of feeling in him that rarely surfaced – a strong temperament held under tight rein. On that memorable day at the studio she'd recognised the challenging possibility of attraction between them. Sometimes she deliberately tried to goad him into response, through sheer devilment and a desire to break up the pattern and shatter his remoteness. But he could not be drawn. Never until tonight.

He puzzled her. She knew his surface existence of aimless pleasure camouflaged a very different mode of life. If she had correctly interpreted the conversation she had overheard between Antony and Charles, Lord Marchmont was one of those daring patriots who risked their lives for no reward other than the private satisfaction of helping their country.

At first astonished and disbelieving, she had eventually concluded that her husband was exactly the kind of man suited to such work. She'd come up against his strength of will and character often enough.

He was not a happy man and most likely he discounted the value of his life. What was there for him to regret? Chloe? She'd seen how little interest was there. His father? He never spoke of the old man in her hearing. His wife? That was her cue for derisive laughter. It had been demonstrated. Antony Marchmont was the ideal spy. And she had it in her power to destroy him.

Steps in the passage outside her door brought her to the alert, but they passed on. She hadn't forgotten the two attempts upon her life, and never relaxed her guard entirely. But the past months of freedom from attack had made it difficult to maintain a sharp edge. She'd made no headway with her investigations. Even questioning Lucy had been quite abortive. The girl was either stupidly cunning or terrified to speak.

As for Antony, she couldn't believe he was the kind of assassin to sneak by night, to drug and leave his helpless victim to a slow death in the cold. Damn him! Why couldn't she put him out of her mind?

Jenny Marchmont, her gentle predecessor. What had she been like, this unforgettable girl wife? No one ever spoke of her in this house, which was sad. Even Antony hugged her memory to him like a miser. There was no likeness of her, nor any of her own work hung in the many rooms available. She'd asked Charles, and he had simply said it was Antony's wish. Why had all traces of Jenny been swept out of her own home? Or had they? Surely Antony had a picture of her somewhere. Everyone kept a memento of a loved one. Hadn't that associate of Turner she'd met at the exhibition said something? Yes! He had been the one to paint the miniatures. Somewhere there was a likeness of Jenny and her baby.

The chimes of the little carriage clock by her bed recalled her to her duties. She stood up and automatically shook out the folds of her gown. Her appearance didn't interest her greatly. Reluctant still to go down, she thought she might look in on Chloe in her new pink bower before facing that lot in the drawing room.

Halfway along the landing, on an impulse she stopped and turned back. She retraced her steps and continued on to the entrance to Antony's apartments. No sounds penetrated here. Servants were either occupied with the aftermath of the dinner party or taking their ease. Beds had been turned down and rooms tidied for the night. No one was about.

She didn't question her impulse. She simply knew she had to have some sort of answer to at least one of her many questions, and it might very well be found in a part of the house she had never entered.

A lamp stood on a table just inside the door, its soft glow illuminating the apartment. She stepped cautiously in and looked about her at the rather spartan furnishings of a man's sitting room, if there was such a thing. She supposed it was more of a study, a place for relaxation, the smoking of a pipe before bed. It was certainly more pleasant than the chilly, darkly furnished library where Antony spent so much of his time, and which she had not liked to alter. It would have been some sort of intrusion, she felt, although hardly less reprehensible than her present sortie into his privacy.

Stifling her better feelings, she began with the desk, going swiftly through the drawers, feeling behind as well as inside. Nothing. Going on to a flat-fronted bureau she found nothing more exciting than books and papers. No concealed cupboards lay behind the two small etchings of country scenes, and the window draperies hid no secrets, merely a balcony similar to her own. She moved into the bedroom.

This was a large chamber lit by two more lamps of frosted glass set on tables either side of the chimneypiece. A fire in the grate threw more light, but it also wove a web of shifting shadows that brought her nerves close to the surface. She made herself go on.

No doubt the door opposite her led to a dressing room, which she would search last, if necessary. But the object that claimed her attention in this sombre chamber was the bed. It was vast, a mighty edifice of oak draped in bottle-green velvet hangings, and it could have comfortably accommodated Henry the Eighth and all six wives at once.

Karen had never seen such a bed. It looked Tudor in style, with its panelled boards and bunches of carved fruits bulging from each post. A set of steps led up from floor to coverlet, almost waist high. She was seized with a sudden childish urge to run up and throw herself upon the wide sea of green velvet, but she resisted. Already she'd been here too long.

Dragging her gaze away from the temptation, she made a careful search of every drawer and cupboard, learning quite a lot about Antony's tastes in apparel, in jewellery, in snuff, but nothing about the person who interested her most, Jenny. She turned back to the great bed.

If she wanted to hide something there, where would she choose? The fruits and vines twining up the bedposts positively leapt out at her. Such a profusion of scrolls and knobs and lumps to twist, so many hollows to press.

A voice behind her said, 'Try the apple on the bedpost nearest to you. The one above the grapestalk.'

Karen almost leapt out of her slippers. Whipping around she found Sybilla's face inches from her own.

Bending from her greater height, the other girl moved closer until the lovely oval face seemed to fill Karen's vision. 'I know what you are seeking. 'Tis behind the panel. Twist the apple knob and you will see.'

Karen stepped backwards and came up hard against the bed. Sybilla followed, taking her hand in a grip like pincers, forcing the smaller white fingers around the apple knob and twisting. The closest panel in the bedhead slid back and Sybilla released her.

'There. Look.'

Still shaking, Karen looked. Reposing in the small cupboard space was a pile of what looked like letters, some documents tied up in ribbon, and a small velvet case.

'Take it out. I have, many times.' When Karen didn't move Sybilla reached impatiently past her and brought out the case. She opened it and thrust it into Karen's hands. 'There she lies. The sorceress herself and her brat.'

Karen closed her eyes. This was not how she had wanted it. She had not wanted to discover Jenny in such an atmosphere of bitter triumph and hatred. For it was hatred she heard in Sybilla's voice. The familiar soft tones had a grating edge, the words were a desecration of the madonna façade. Was this the real Sybilla? Did she go about her daily life harbouring a monster of ugliness inside her, feeding it with secret visits to Antony's hiding place? The thought made Karen feel sick.

A hand came down hard on her head, bunching her curls and twisting painfully, forcing her neck to bend. 'Look at her. Behold your rival . . . and mine.'

With tears of pain blurring her sight, Karen looked down at the exquisite miniature. Andrew Robertson, the miniaturist, had recalled that it was a mother and child pose, but not that each was almost a replica of the other. Jenny, the woman, had a bird-like look, all soft brown hair and winged brows over the most expressive pair of eyes Karen could remember having seen. The girl's heart showed through these soul windows, luminous, and clear as spring water flowing over beds of brown moss.

Fascinated, Karen continued to stare for a long time, unaware that Sybilla had released her and moved aside to view her reaction.

Chloe had her mother's pointed chin and lips, so soft yet cut so fine. Baby ringlets hung over the pixie ears, and the cheeks were peaches coming into ripeness. There was no mistaking her. The seven-year-old asleep upstairs had once looked like a much-loved cherub.

Sybilla's tongue stabbed and shattered the moment. 'What a pretty sight! It turns my stomach, that sugared smile, the simpering, sly air of holiness. She was just a little brown thing with a limp. What was her secret? How did she manage to ensnare and hold him. How did she *do* it?'

Karen felt the other woman's frustration as a series of energy waves pulsing through her body. She stepped back, tightening her grip on the miniature case.

'I don't think you could understand. By all accounts Jenny was sweet and kind and loving – all the things that you are not. I think Antony loved her for her goodness.'

Sybilla threw back her head and laughed. Karen wanted to cover her ears. She wanted to run, to distance herself from the malignity that looked out at her from Sybilla's face. She didn't do either. An odd feeling had risen in her. She felt she must champion the little painted brown Jenny wren and her cherub child, just as if they were real living people – not one a memory and the other a half-forgotten appendage to a man with a broken heart.

Sybilla had stopped laughing. 'Pah! Men want more than milk and water goodness from a woman. What arts did she practise to keep him in her bed? What siren's lures did she learn, and where?'

'Come on, Sybilla. She loved him, he loved her. That's all there was to it.'

The black eyes narrowed. Then Sybilla said in a more normal voice, 'But you could not take her place. He has not come to your bedchamber in a twelvemonth. Despite your beauty he has not longed to spread your "tempest of bright hair" on the pillow before him. That is what he called it once. I listened to you both, my ear against the wall, and heard him writhe in the depths of passion for your exquisite little body. But you could not hold him. His fever was spent within a few weeks.' Her lips curved with rich satisfaction.

Karen was speechless. She couldn't have been more outraged if it had actually been she who was the object of Sybilla's eavesdropping. The added knowledge that Antony's cousin was eaten up with desire for him scarcely came as a surprise, since it had been obvious from the moment Sybilla had commented on the miniature. But the ugliness of it deprived her of words.

Sybilla was standing with closed eyes, looking inward at a picture all too clear to Karen.

'You don't love him,' she said, accusingly. 'What you're feeling is plain old lust, and I doubt that Salome herself could attract Antony. He's not interested in women.'

Sybilla ignored her, swaying on her feet, her hands moving sensuously through her own long hair, streaming it out behind her. Her movements grew more explicit as, lost in her erotic dream, she fed the hunger she had awakened.

'Sybilla!'

Her eyes snapped open. She looked at Karen in bemusement. 'He shall know such pain. Oh, there are so many delicious ways to torment a man.'

Bile rose in Karen's throat. She pressed her hand to her mouth as Sybilla snatched the box from her and returned it to its hiding place. The panel slid shut.

She turned back to Karen with her serene smile in place once more. 'I am so pleased we have reached this understanding.'

'What understanding? What are you up to, Sybilla?'

'Why, your understanding that my cousin belongs to me. I have seen it written in my future. It was promised by the houngan that night before we left Jamaica. Antony and I have a destiny to fulfil.' For an instant something evil peeped out from behind the mask to touch Karen.

She recoiled, not understanding why. A moment later she was bracing herself with a dash of common sense. 'What a lot of nonsense you talk, Sybilla. Antony is my husband, and while we may not have a deliriously joyful relationship, it's still a legal fact.'

Sybilla shrugged. 'It has been promised.'

'By a voodoo witchdoctor? I somehow think it will take more than a few spells and the Dance of the Seven Veils to capture Antony.' Did Sybilla really think she had black powers? Incredible! But her obsession could be as dangerous as it was unhealthy.

Sybilla said reasonably, 'You do not understand. I have been taught the sacred rites. My nurse was blood sister to the Obeah. I have powers you do not dream of.'

Karen gaped. Here was clear paranoia. She decided to ignore the wild claims. 'Why did you call Jenny your rival? She's been dead for four years.'

'And he has mourned her for four years. Even when he sniffed like a street cur around your ankles his heart was never engaged. She has him still bewitched.'

'Then what has changed? Why should he suddenly turn to you after all this time?'

'Because I have at last perfected the incantation. It has required my sending to the Indies for some of the sacred ingredients. I needed these to call upon my Lord, the Baron Samedi. Now, I am almost ready.'

Only her eyes gave her away, thought Karen. If you looked long enough into the hypnotic depths you could see there was something wrong, something slightly askew. She wondered whether anyone else had made this discovery. Surely the parents must know. Maybe this explained the overbearing Lady Oriel's more subdued behaviour in her daughter's company. Maybe she was afraid of her.

Aware that she was wandering dangerously from the present, Karen blinked and pulled free of that fascinating gaze. She looked down and saw that Sybilla was now holding a hairbrush. It was a heavy tortoiseshell-backed piece, meant for a man's use.

Sybilla turned the brush over and picked at the bristles. 'The spell calls for some of his hair. Body hair would be ideal, but that is too difficult for me to obtain. There are other items, also. But soon . . . very soon . . .' She began to croon to herself, hugging the brush to her, her vision fixed on some ghostly scene in her own imaginings.

Karen backed slowly away towards the door. When she was within a few feet of it she turned and ran, speeding out across the sitting room, along the corridor and down the stairs. She entered her own drawing room with heightened colour, fortunately still some time ahead of the gentlemen, and slipped back into her role as hostess.

She might despise the gossipy cliques huddled together to paw over the latest on dirt, but they did have the advantage of being relatively sane.

CHAPTER 11

7 December, Friday

Tom was profoundly stirred by his dream. The intensity with which he had lived those moments in the copse, the superstitious fear which had claimed him, could not be easily dismissed. He lay awake until dawn, his brain so alive he felt it could jump out of his skull.

Trained to think logically, he was shocked to discover that his processes could fall into such disarray. Snippets of remembered sessions with other patients mixed in with the tapes of Valerie's, along with his own dreams and fantasies. Bits of Phil's off-beat theories interspersed with whole paragraphs from the books he'd recently absorbed. When he tried to sort them into order, to establish some kind of pattern, they broke apart and danced beyond his reach.

At last he admitted defeat and scrambled through the bedside drawer for a cigarette. He smoked two consecutively before he could really appreciate the familiar relaxing response. God, it felt wonderful!

Once more in charge of his brain, he did some more marshalling, and came to the conclusion that he was not the right therapist for Valerie. He was getting far too involved. When it came to his subconscious dragging him into her fantasy land first chance it got, it was time for him to depart the scene and hand his patient on to some less empathetic type.

Perhaps he'd been wrong to try hypnotherapy, but he'd honestly thought it might help where nothing else had. Valerie knew too much about the psychotherapeutic techniques. She'd been the rounds for too long. She knew how to play the game. Possibly, she had deliberately sealed herself off from help, although he wouldn't believe that until forced to.

He pulled out his little book of contacts and began to search for someone he felt might meet her needs. There was Bill Copley – no, he'd gone to Luxembourg last year to join a clinic there. Maybe that fellow in Edinburgh . . .

Sound exploded against his left eardrum. His head hit the top of the bed. The dreadful shrilling went on and on until he realised it was the phone. Because he slept heavily he'd installed a bell that sounded like the clappers of hell. Sometimes he had regrets.

The voice on the end of the line sounded dazed. It took him a few seconds to realise that it was Valerie herself.

'Wait a minute. I can't hear what you're saying. Valerie, it's still the middle of the night and . . .'

He stopped protesting. The skin on the back of his neck crept as if a little breeze had stolen across it. He listened. 'Valerie, it's going to be all right. I'm coming. Just hold on and I'll be with you in fifteen minutes.'

He flung down the receiver, missing the phone altogether the first time and grabbed his pants. Within sixty seconds he was out in the street with one shoe on, shouting for a taxi. He put the other shoe on while urging the driver to hasten to Bellevue Gardens, Mayfair, and an extra pound in it if he made it in ten minutes.

Nine and a half minutes later he was pushing the bell on the front door of a classy modern block of apartments. The doorman, half-dressed and clutching a nice sausage and toast, seemed in two minds whether to let him in.

'I'm a doctor, called urgently to Mrs Winterhouse. Which apartment?'

The magic words swifty elevated him to the fifth floor. The main door of No. 11 stood ajar. He stepped inside and closed it on the man's inquisitive face.

Valerie lay on her stomach in the lobby, the expensive cream rug under her stained with vomit. Her breathing was so shallow he could hardly believe in it. But it was there. Tom let out his own breath with an explosive sigh.

After putting her in a coma position on her side and checking her airway, he left her and telephoned Phil. That done, he went into the bedroom and pulled a blanket from the bed to tuck around the unconscious woman. He moved automatically, not really thinking about his actions. His mind was furiously occupied with questions.

Why had Valerie chosen this particular moment to do away with herself? Then, having set things in motion, why had she apparently regretted it? Was it a ploy meant to disrupt her treatment, a cry of 'wolf' that had gone badly wrong? Was she far more disturbed than he had realised?

He looked down at the pallid face and felt a touch of panic at its emptiness. But she still breathed.

What would happen to her now? He should, of course, notify the authorities and have her removed to care, but he was reluctant to do this. It would mean the end of their sessions together for some time. He found he didn't want that, after all. Valerie's plight had touched something very deep within him. He couldn't let her down. So, why not keep this episode quiet, and go on helping her himself with the aid of Phillip Thornton MD? He supposed it depended on how badly affected she was by whatever she'd taken.

He risked leaving her again to dash into the bedroom and search for a pill container, but found nothing. There was nothing in the bathroom, either, nor in the kitchen nor sitting room – except for a half empty bottle of vodka and tumbler on the floor by the couch.

As he searched he was only half aware of the apartment layout and decor. Pastel peach predominated, a colour he loathed. All the surfaces had a suede-like texture, the chairs a mushroom softness sinking into the rugs. He had a sense of overwhelming sponginess, as though the place might very well open its pores and absorb him completely.

When the doorbell rang he shook off his fancies and went to let Phil in.

Fifteen minutes later Phil stepped back from the bed where Valerie was now tucked up, looking slightly less corpselike. Tom saw him pocket a pill container he'd taken from Valerie's dressing-gown pocket.

'She'll do. She's vomited a good deal of the drug, and the alcohol. But she was never in any real danger. Of course she'll have to be watched for some hours, but I don't think we have anything to worry about.'

Tom looked at him incredulously, then decided that the statement was normal medico tunnel-vision, narrowed down to the immediate moment.

'What had she taken? Barbiturates?'

Phil shook his head. 'They're old hat, nowadays. No, she'd ingested rather a lot of one of the benzodiazepines and washed it down with vodka. Not a great combination. But also not necessarily fatal. Her respiratory function was affected, as you saw. However, she has a strong heart, and really, it's just about impossible to kill yourself with such drugs unless you decide to drive a car under their influence.'

'So she wasn't serious?'

'Serious enough. I think she just wasn't aware of how much safer these new sedatives are.'

Tom sank down on the sofa and rested his head in his hands. Phil continued to pack away his medical gear, while watching his friend.

'What are you going to do?'

Tom raised bloodshot eyes. He felt terrible, and he'd have killed for a cigarette. 'I'm going to help her, of course. I feel as though I've let her down.'

'That's what I thought you'd say. Do *you* want any help?'

'All I can get, Phil. We could have lost a precious life tonight. I won't let it happen again.'

Phil closed his bag and stood up. 'Okay, I'll arrange for a nurse to special her for twenty-four hours. There's no need to hospitalise her and put her through all those questions. She'll sleep quietly, and by tomorrow she should be able to talk to us . . . if it's what she wants.'

'There's not much doubt of it. This episode was the classic cry for help . . . and I was just about to turn my back on her.' Tom lumbered to his feet, telling his protesting legs to shut up and get on with moving him around. It was Friday, with a full case load, and he hadn't so much as shaved. 'I'm off home to snatch some coffee before I go in to work. Did I remember to thank you, Phil?'

'My middle name is Shylock. I'll get it out of your hide one of these days, pal. Go home and do something about your horrible face or you'll frighten your clients into fits. I'll wait here until the nurse arrives.'

'There's no hope of talking to her just yet, I suppose?'

'Valerie? Not a chance. She'll sleep for hours. Off with you.' He punched his friend lightly on the shoulder and pushed him out the door.

On the front steps of Bellevue Mansions Tom stood with his face raised to the early morning sun. All around him activity swirled – buses, cars and taxis jockeying across the traffic lanes, people hurrying along the pavements. In a park opposite men trundled wheelbarrows and wielded spades, children ran and romped, their schoolbags clashing together like warriors' shields as they mock battled. Horns, tyres squealing, voices shouting, dogs barking. Somewhere, roadworks in progress. The noise was infernal. It was life. He'd never appreciated it as much as he did now he'd helped to save a part of it.

He took a huge sniff of petrol-perfumed air and hailed a bus.

Valerie rang that night.

'Tom? I don't know whether to thank you or send you a letter bomb, you damned interfering quack!'

'Phil's the quack. I'm just an interfering s.o.b. How are you feeling?'

'How do you think I feel? It's worse when you know you've done it to yourself. I think I must have gone into a fugue or something. Isn't that what they call it when you do something you don't really mean to do, and don't know it?'

'No. You can stop trying to impress me with your jargon and tell me when you're coming in to see me.'

There was silence on the line.

'Valerie?'

'I'm still here. I'm just wondering whether it's any use, Tom.' Her voice began to wobble. 'Oh, God, I'm a mess. I'm frightened. I'm cracking up, and I don't know what to do about it.' She began to sob, deep, painful sobs that tore at her throat, making her gasp for breath.

He heard movement in the background and the sobbing faded away. Another woman's voice came down the line. 'Dr Levy? This is Sister McPherson speaking. Mrs Winterhouse is a little upset and I've got her to lie down. She will be quite all right. Dr Thornton saw her only half an hour ago.'

'Right. Thank you, Sister. Please tell Mrs Winterhouse that I expect to see her in the morning at nine o'clock. If there's any problem with that would you mind giving me a call? Mrs Winterhouse has the number.'

'Certainly, doctor. Is there anything more?'

Tom said there was nothing, thanked her and put the receiver down. It was an advantage having a doctorate. Hardly anyone went beyond the assumption that he was a medical man, which opened many a door closed to those outside the profession.

There was a probability that Valerie might not come. Yet, the first move had to be hers. He should not pursue her any further. Their relationship had reached a thin spot. Like the delicate membrane stretched across the opening in a baby's head, it barely covered the pulsing life beneath. A sudden break could be disastrous.

He slept well that night, and if he had dreams he didn't remember them. He was at his desk, swivelled around contemplating his painting when Valerie came in. Phil followed thirty seconds behind her.

The three looked at one another.

Tom spoke first. 'How are you feeling, Valerie?'

'Okay, I guess.' Her eyes flicked from Tom to Phil and back. 'I suppose I should thank you. I don't like to feel a fool.'

Phil grinned. 'Join the rest of humanity. We all make idiots of ourselves sooner or later.'

Tom nodded and led Valerie to her chair. 'He's right. Valerie, how would you feel about Phil sitting in on our sessions, as an observer? Besides practising medicine, he's also an experienced psychotherapist. I've already discussed certain aspects of your case with him on a professional basis, and I think it would help us both to have another point of view.'

He thought she looked ill under the heavier-than-usual make-up. Her eyes had a smudged look and she seemed very tense. Her glance flickered restlessly around the room, finally stopping at the picture behind Tom's desk. Then he saw her start to let go, shoulders relaxing against the back of the chair, jaw muscles softening.

She said in a low voice, 'Yesterday I had the living daylights scared out of me. I thought I was going to die, on my own. So I'm not about to quibble at anything you might suggest to help me. Besides which, I'm afraid for my sanity, and to me that's the bottom line. I'll agree to anything at all.' She turned to Phil. 'You probably know all about me by now. So go ahead, sit in, observe, comment. Whatever.'

Tom trundled his chair over to the recliner and sat down facing his patient. 'You do realise that the same thing will probably happen? You will start to relive a sequence, whether real or imaginary, in which you will be under some kind of attack from others, and I won't be able to intervene.'

'I've thought about it. It's scary, but I also have a sense of things working out in some way. I'm getting closer to whatever it is that's driving me crazy.' She looked at him squarely. The grey rims about her irises seemed to thicken and grow more luminous. He felt she was trying to project an integrity formerly lacking in their relationship – that she was now in earnest. Whatever her reason, fear, remorse, perhaps more than a touch of curiosity since that last revealing episode, he sensed a new rapport with her.

They began the session.

Tom cut out everything from his awareness, to concentrate on his patient. Slowly, carefully, he took her away from the conscious world, deliberately pacing her descent. It was an effort at retaining control, but almost immediately he knew it was wasted. Valerie had gone ahead of him. Her face remoulded itself while he watched, sharpening into the gypsy features of the woman he had privately named 'The Battler'.

She sat practically rigid. Her fingers clutched at the chair's arms, digging into the leather with such ferocity that he thought she might break her nails. The tendons in her throat stood out and he knew her teeth would be clenched. He was startled when her lips parted and she spat at him, or at someone she saw in his place.

He wiped his sleeve with his handkerchief and said calmly, 'What is it, Valerie? Why are you upset?'

Her fingers ground into the leather.

Phil whispered, 'She's gone, hasn't she?'

'I'm afraid so. She's listening to someone else, not to me. It's someone she doesn't like.'

Her face worked. Different emotions flickered across it like shadows on a screen. Again Tom had the feeling that the black eyes burned behind their closed lids.

'No!' she screamed, suddenly. Her voice sounded raw and husky. 'I will not lie. Ye condemn me at your peril.' She began to pant. It was a horrible animal sound magnified in the silent room.

'Lying whoresons! Y'r Hammer is a tool of Satan. 'Tis an instrument that glorifies torture, and ye who follow it will end in hell y'rselves.'

She paused, listening again. Globules of sweat sprang up at her hairline, started to gather and trickle down her forehead.

'I deny it all, Sir Priest. Y're mad and full o'sinful lusts to think such. Ye accuse my cat of being my familiar. She is but a cat. My herbs are brewed to help folk. I have no magic potions to help me fly.'

She brought her hands up as if to deflect a blow, then doubled up in the chair, the breath knocked out of her.

'Good God!' Phil sprang to his feet, pointing. Tiny droplets of blood began oozing from her fingertips. Her arms hung down by her sides and her neck sagged. She was unconscious.

Tom already had his fingers on her pulse. He talked to her in a low encouraging murmur, trying to penetrate the barrier between them.

'She's being tortured!' Phil's eyes bugged. 'We've got to stop it!'

Tom broke off his one-sided conversation to say with asperity, 'She's in the middle of a witch trial, obviously, and if I knew how, I'd certainly bring her out of it. As it is, all we can do is wait.'

He patted Valerie's fingers dry and wiped her forehead, laying her head to one side so that she could breathe more easily. As the seconds passed without event Phil resumed his seat, or rather, perched on its edge to wait.

Finally she began to quiver, then to rock her body to and fro, moaning. Her hands shifted into her lap, pressed tight, as if they were bound together. Tom even fancied he could see welts on her wrists. Her lips looked dry and cracked, and sunken cheekbones spoke of illness.

She abruptly stiffened. Terror was a mask clamped over her face. 'No! Not again!' She dug her heels into the chair, dragging against the force that pulled her forward. 'Have you no mercy? Is God sleeping?'

Her protests died into a broken jumble of words and then to silence as she once again seemed to face her accusers. Her head came up in a parody of its former pride. Her bowed shoulders straightened.

'Look at her stand up to them,' muttered Phil. He was leaning practically on top of Tom, his former horror apparently overlaid with professional curiosity.

Tom paid no attention. 'Valerie, listen to me. You know my voice. You must listen to me and do as I say. Leave that place. Come back down the path to the beautiful garden we created. Come with me, Valerie.' His tone was urgent, yet controlled, but it still failed to pierce through into the terrifying space Valerie occupied.

She had braced herself to face what came. 'Ye judged me guilty before I came to this court. 'Tis y'r sworn duty to smell out a witch, Sir Priest, and find one ye will, where e'er ye go, because y'r mind is set on't.'

Again she listened. Then, for all her bravery, she flinched. 'So, I'm to burn. Then if I must perish 'twill be in my own way.' Her voice rose, harsh as a cracked bell. 'Before I go I lay a curse on ye, all o'ye that stand here and watch a woman brought down like a squirrel midst a pack o'mad dogs.'

An ugly smile split her lips, drawing blood from the cracks. 'I lay this curse on ye, Sir Priest. My spirit will follow ye in this life and the next, and wreak a most horrible vengeance. Ye'll not sleep nor rest for the pain acrying in y'r bones. Ye'll suffer without cease, and ye'll beg for the death that I alone can bring ye.'

She flung up her bound hands as if beseeching heaven. 'I curse the mother that bore me and taught me the ways that ha' brought me to this pass.'

Without warning she burst out of the chair, throwing the two men aside as easily as straw bundles, racing out of the room and along the corridor, heading straight for the stairs.

They followed. Tom was only two paces behind her when she leapt from the top step, her terrified scream rebounding off the walls. He flung himself forward, one hand grasping the railing, the other catching about her waist, arresting her fall. He cried out himself as his arm jerked almost from its socket. She dangled in his grasp, her knees buckled under her on the stairs. Then Phil was there to take her weight. Between them they carried her back to the office and laid her on the recliner.

They stood looking down at her, seeing the transformation take place. Her cheeks plumped out, features subtly altered and aged. Valerie had returned. Tom brought her slowly back up to consciousness.

She opened her eyes and tears ran out and down her cheeks. For a full minute she cried, unable to speak. Tom supplied her with tissues, patted her shoulder and waited gravely until she was ready.

'That was the most horrible experience of my life.' She laughed and hiccupped at the same time. 'What am I talking about? Which life? It all came back to me, you know. I remembered exactly who I was and how I came to be in such a fix.' She blew her nose violently. 'Well, there can't be much doubt now, can there? I never could have made up such a ghastly episode. I'd never want to put myself through that. What a monstrous evil those witch hunts were, and how twisted the men who took part in them in the name of a loving God.'

'Are you all right? No lasting effects?' Tom could feel the thud of his heartbeat against his chest wall as he realised how close they'd come to disaster. If Valerie had headed for a window and he'd been a split second farther behind her . . .

Phil had been doing things with a stethoscope and rolling a cuff bandage on her arm. Now he put these away and pronounced her unharmed. He looked at Tom. 'I told you you might come to the death experience and that it could be quite traumatic. This one was a lulu.'

'It certainly appeared to be a suicide attempt. What did you do, Valerie? Jump off a cliff?'

She nodded, her gaze still turned inward, viewing the horror she'd experienced. She spoke as if her throat were raw and hurting. 'I escaped while they were all still reeling from the curse and ran towards the swamp. It was night, and I was running from the flares into the dark. The path went from under me. I fell through the air and down into the bog and it sucked me under. I suffocated.'

'Extraordinary!' Phil seemed fascinated, rather than appalled, and Tom looked at him curiously.

'A dreadful experience,' he said. 'I'm sorry you had to go through that, Valerie.'

She shook her head. 'No. It was necessary. Meaning has come out of it. It's my karma to make amends in some way for that terrible curse.'

Tom groaned. 'Not you too! Valerie, listen to me.'

'No, you listen to me. All this week I've been reading up on this sort of thing. It's fascinating. And now we've got actual proof. We've simply got to face it. I mean, the natural law that says everything in this universe occurs as a result of cause and effect.'

'Exactly!' Phil started up out of his chair, his face alight. 'The law that says we are born with a basic blueprint laid out for a life, but within this pattern of destiny we do have free will. In other words, we can change our destiny, but only within the bounds of a pattern chosen before birth.'

Tom frowned at him. 'But how does that affect what happened here?'

'Well, matters not dealt with during a particular lifetime are stored away in a kind of memory file in the higher regions of our souls, to be worked on later. Strong desires, unfulfilled wishes, and above all the effects of our actions will be taken out of the file at the appropriate time and carried forward to be dealt with in a future life. These things are all a form of energy, and energy doesn't simply disappear with the death of the body.'

Valerie smiled at Tom's confused expression. She leaned forward and took his hand in her large white one. 'It's quite simple. The law says things must balance. Uncompleted or very strong relationships with people keep drawing us back to them time after time, life after life.'

'And you think that your relationship with this priest was a real one, centuries ago, and that now, in this lifetime you must make amends for having cursed him?'

Both Valerie and Phil nodded.

'I think I must be dreaming this!' He detached himself from Valerie's hold, got up, and stood before his painting, his back to the room. 'And if I accept this theory, where does it take us? What will you do in a practical sense, Valerie?'

'I don't know yet,' she said slowly. 'I don't think we have all the information we need to formulate a plan.'

Tom stared into the whirling sun and felt it grow larger and more vibrant until it seemed to fill the room. He could feel it pulsating, glowing within him. Its warmth pervaded his mind and body, drawing on his senses until he no longer knew what or where he was. He drifted in a delicious euphoric cloud, mindless and insensible. Then gradually he became aware once more. Feeling returned, and a consciousness of time and space. Utterly unwilling, he found himself back in his office facing the painting, a two-dimensional piece of art, not a magic mirror into another sphere. Slowly he turned to face the others.

They looked at him enquiringly.

'Well?' said Phil. Clearly Tom's unsettling experience had left no apparent outward mark.

He leaned forward onto the desktop to support himself. 'We go on. There's nothing else we can do. If you and Valerie are right, we shall eventually perceive a pattern to this thing.'

'I know we will.' Phil turned to Valerie. 'Do you feel okay to be alone? Would you like to spend the night with Carla and me?'

'No, thanks all the same. I've got some thinking to do, and I do it best in bed in my own place. Don't worry. You've confiscated my pills and I've thrown out all the liquor. I'll be back for the next round on Tuesday.' She grinned at Tom.

He had an uneasy feeling that she was too pleased with herself. The waters got deeper and muddier, and he was already in far beyond his depth. Maybe he should have heeded the impulse to back out before they reached this stage. But it was far too late, and Valerie had gone.

Phil picked up his discarded jacket and prepared to leave. 'That's quite a lady, Tom. When you think what she's just gone through, wouldn't you expect her to be a mess of quivering nerves? Instead, she's gone off to do some serious thinking. I believe I'll do the same . . . unless you'd like to have lunch at some pub?'

Tom shook his head. 'No thanks, Phil. I need time to myself.'

'Fair enough. I'll give you a ring in a day or two.' At the door he hung on his heel. 'Er . . . Sorry I wasn't much help to you. I think I panicked. I've never seen anything quite like that before.'

'It's okay. I don't think you could have done much. *Ciao*, friend.'

When he had the room to himself Tom deliberately turned back to the painting and fixed his eyes on the whirling sun. For ten minutes he stood immobile, waiting. Nothing at all happened except that his strained eyes began to water.

It was his habit on a Saturday to go hiking somewhere out in the country. Today he locked the office door and went home to hibernate, and try to sort out the tangled ball of yarn in his head.

CHAPTER 12

Karen sat at her desk in the small parlour, dealing with her mail. She was alone, Antony having left the house early, and the ladies keeping to their beds until the sun was well up. She enjoyed this time of day, when she planned what she would do, most likely at either the studio or the dispensary, and blithely discarded most of the invitations which arrived in a steadily increasing stream.

Caroline Marchmont might not be approved, but her blood was of the bluest, and as such conferred on her an impeccable aura of ton. As the daughter of the late Marquis of Shelton she might go anywhere, and notwithstanding Amanda's advice, now chose to go practically nowhere, if she could help it. Her 'mother' lived in the country a self-absorbed, hypochondriacal existence. Caroline Marchmont had no brothers, and her only sister having married a German Baron and gone to live in Saxony, there was no awkwardness there for Karen. She didn't have to hide from people who knew her really well, nor obey the dictates of parents who might have wanted to see her have a greater presence in society.

And obviously, Antony didn't care.

A good deal of fulfilment now came her way through personal service. Having turned against the mindless activities of the polite world, Karen had looked for occupation, something apart from her painting. Her social conscience had been stirred by her memories of that terrible day when she'd found herself unprotected and vulnerable in the back streets of a great city; and there were daily reminders of the discrepancies between her comfortable existence and that of the majority of the population. Enquiries about hospitals brought her answers that disgusted her. Not simply places to cure people, they were charitable reforming institutions, piously and constantly reminding the patients of their lowly station in life, and their obligations to God and their social betters. She wanted more than that.

Expressing her dissatisfaction to Amanda, she heard about a recent development in public health. The London authorities had set up a number of dispensaries for the poor, primarily as centres for smallpox inoculation. Amanda, herself, gave a good deal of her time to one of these centres in Holborn, and had actually been returning home from there on the day she found Karen on her knees in the gutter.

On hearing of the acute need for more than inoculation, Karen immediately volunteered. She found she enjoyed teaching the elements of hygeine and basic child care to women who had never been shown either. Their appalling lives were more of a revelation that she'd imagined, and their courage and ironic humour earned her admiration. She also enjoyed giving over her extremely generous quarterly allowance from Antony to the needy. It might be a Lady Bountiful act, but she did it in a spirit of respect and human sympathy for others more disadvantaged than herself. It was all she could do, at present.

Charles knocked at her door and came in smiling broadly. She regarded him with interest. Had Amanda at last consented to be his bride?

'Lady Caroline . . .'

'Caro, Charles.'

'Er, yes. You will want to deal with this immediately. It bears the Prince Regent's insignia.' He handed her the elaborately patterned card.

It was a message bidding Lord and Lady Marchmont to a grand summer fete to celebrate the renovation of Carlton House Palace, the Prince's greatest pride.

Karen felt a flutter of excitement. Because of her self-imposed retirement from the more snobbish events of the social calendar, she'd never met the Prince Regent; and although she'd heard he was a convivial man, ladies were excluded from the sort of revels which made him a byword with certain prim elements and provided his enemies with much ammunition. Some of the cartoons so widely circulated must have made him blench.

She also wanted to see Carlton House. It was the talk of London – its splendour and extravagance even a matter of parliamentary discussion since its restoration had overrun the future king's allowance by hundreds of thousands of pounds.

'How exciting! Charles, will Antony be at home on this date? I mean, he will not be away, on business?'

He looked up at her sharply. 'As far as I know, Lord Marchmont will be at home. Do you wish me to forward an acceptance, my lady?'

'Charles. You disappoint me. I had thought we were friends. Yet still you will not give me my name.'

He stiffened at the reproach, then smiled reluctantly. 'It is difficult to break the habit . . . Caro. I fear that protocol is ingrained in my nature, and an awareness of my place.'

Her quick ear caught the faint bitterness. She patted the couch companionably and waited until he had, with some reluctance, seated himself beside her. His large square hands moved uncomfortably on his thighs and he didn't meet her eyes.

'Tell me, Charles, what is your place? I have never understood the relationship between you and Antony, which seems so much more than that of employer and employee.'

Evidently her genuine interest acted as a key in a lock. She saw him make the decision to open a very private door to a friend and allow her in.

'My place is difficult to define, since it is usual to base one's position in life according to one's father's own place. I do not know my father. My mother was Annie Hastings, a farm girl on one of the Marchmont estates. Her parents turned her out when they found she was with child and she tramped the roads, almost starving, before being taken in by Jonas Frewin, my stepfather. They eventually wed – he was a lawyer in a small town and not unsuccessful – and although burdened with a rapidly multiplying family, Jonas charged himself with my upbringing and training at law.'

He sighed and looked down at his hands. 'I could never like him. Seeing him as a psalm-singing, patronising do-gooder, I would not accept his name. He turned the other cheek admirably by educating me as the son of a gentleman. Yet precisely because I knew gratitude was due, I withheld it. Now he is dead, and I may not thank him even if I would. No doubt he did his best for me, but gratitude, like love, cannot be bought.'

She put a hand on his, lightly, and left it there for a moment. 'Believe me, I know exactly what you mean. To the young there is nothing more galling than a sense of obligation to a person one dislikes. It's a constant chafe that can work itself into a running sore. I expect you suffered a good deal from your contemporaries, boys who knew your circumstances?'

She'd always thought his face pleasantly nondescript, but now it had taken on a satiric expression that changed him entirely.

'I had my full share of taunts, and a broken nose to prove it.'

'It adds character to your features.'

'Thank you.' He bowed slightly. His face had resumed its normal pleasant expression. 'My mother is quite beautiful. Certainly she cannot be responsible for such a protuberance of, er, character.'

'I gather your mother is still alive.'

'Living in that same little town, along with my six younger half-brothers and sisters – Jonas' revenge upon me.'

'I see. You have made yourself responsible for them, as Jonas Frewin did for you.'

'Exactly. Do you suppose he looks down from whatever heavenly cloud he occupies and laughs silently at my plight? Or is it perhaps forbidden for angels to enjoy a sense of irony? Jonas will definitely have qualified for angelhood. My mother's nightly intercessions on his behalf would buy grace for Lucifer himself.'

His relationship with his stepfather might have been unhealthy, but she detected a note of loving tolerance in his attitude towards his mother. There was fondness there. Charles was revealing himself more than he knew, and turning out to be a quite complex character. Certainly she had discovered the reason for his air of stiffness, as if on the alert for a snubbing.

'How did you come to meet Antony?'

'By leaping the wall of my school and running back to Ashbourne Manor as often as I could. I was obsessed with the notion that I could find my father in the place where I was conceived. In fact, I was sure that Lord Edward himself was the man, and Antony my own half-brother.'

'Oh, no! Surely not. How cruel.'

His hands clenched, then he deliberately relaxed them. She could see the effort he made to calm himself.

'Of course, it was a boy's dream, quite unfounded. I never did discover who my father is, and my mother's lips are sealed upon the subject. But I had managed to bring myself to Lord Edward's attention. He saw the liking between Antony and myself and invited me to make my home with them, attend the same schools and generally be a companion to his lonely son. You see, Antony had just lost his older brother in a tragic accident. His mother having died at his birth, he had no one, apart from Lord Edward.'

'It was amazingly generous of him.' Karen liked this side-light upon her father-in-law's character. It made him far more human than the description given by Sybilla.

'He is generous, like his son; and for one who occupies a great position, he is also astonishingly democratic in his outlook. Who else would do as much for a nameless nobody?'

'And so you and Antony grew up together. No wonder he trusts you so.'

Again he looked at her sharply. 'The trust is mutual. I also admire him greatly. He is everything that makes a true gentleman, a man of honour. I know I can count him my friend under all circumstances.'

'That is praise indeed.'

He hesitated, as if he wondered whether to go on. Karen almost bit her lip in anxiety. Surely, now she would learn something of her husband's background. He couldn't stop now!

'Antony is changed from the young man he was. You did not know him before the tragedy that struck at the very foundations of his life.'

'People have told me that he loved his first wife very much, and she died young in a terrible fire.'

'Jenny was almost too perfect. I never saw her in a temper. I never heard her speak an unkind word. She could be firm, but always in a pleasant manner. Because she adored Antony she was prepared to have his uncle and aunt living in her home, even when patronised so odiously by that woman. Fortunately, Antony soon had their measure and would not see his wife subjected to such treatment. They were asked to leave the Manor after he was wed, and offered a home in Lord Edward's London house. He naturally continued to support them.'

'Why naturally? Did the Honourable George have no source of income?'

'Only what derived from the Jamaican estates, which he had effectively ruined by mismanagement. That is why he brought his family home, to live off his brother's bounty. But that is an unedifying tale. I was saying that Jenny lit her husband's life. After her horrible death he seemed to abandon interest in all his old activities. His music was lost through an injury sustained in the fire. A burning beam fell upon his arm when he tried to carry out a rescue. His voice, also, was affected by the heat. So then, all that remained to him was his child, who reminded him painfully of his lost wife and was too young to try to heal the wound with her love.'

'How awful.' Karen felt her eyes fill with tears. It was so easy to picture the tragic rending of the little family. Love such as Antony and Jenny had experienced was a scarce commodity, and precious beyond price. Its loss must have crippled Antony.

'Awful, indeed. His friends and family feared for his reason. However, when the first grief passed he did recover his mind, if not his happy nature. He could never return to the Manor, yet would not have the ruined tower repaired. It still stands derelict, attached to one of the loveliest homes in southern England. Lord Edward resides there, but is forced to travel to another of his estates if Antony is to visit him.'

'How sad for the old man. I wonder why he stays on in a house of bitter memories?'

'It has many happy memories, too. His sons were born there, and Chloe. His wife, Lady Margaret, loved the Manor and would not live anywhere else. She died at Antony's birth. Then, Lord Edward's widowed sister, Jenny's mother, lived with him for a time, although she did not long survive her daughter.'

'You called it Ashbourne Manor.' Karen tested the words aloud. They sounded familiar. However, the teasing memory would not be captured.

'It is not the Earl's principal seat. Rothmoor Castle is in the west, a bleak place.'

'No wonder he prefers Devon. I think I should like to meet Lord Edward, some day.'

Charles looked uncomfortable.

She had no trouble reading his thoughts. 'I see. We have met and he dislikes me.'

'My apologies, Caroline. I do not always remember that this background information really is new to you. Amanda did assure me that your memory loss was genuine and total. I am sorry for it. 'Tis a heavy burden to bear.'

'Not as heavy as some. I am grateful to you for telling me all this, Charles.'

'I felt that you should know your adversary.'

'A dead woman? Jenny, the paragon?'

'An ordinary woman, much loved.'

Karen felt a bitter-sweet pang somewhere in the region of her midriff, but shrugged it aside. 'Thank you also for trusting me with your own private story. I appreciate what it must have cost you, and I think I know why you did it. You love Amanda, do you not?'

'Is it so obvious?' He seemed taken aback.

It amused her to reflect that all lovers seemed to believe in a mysterious cloak of invisibility that hid their private affairs from the world. She'd felt that way about Humphrey – whose mother had known immediately. Later, in a mood of bitterness, she'd mentally accused the woman of deliberately dying to escape the humiliation of such a daughter-in-law. Mama Doran should have waited around, she thought grimly. She'd have had her adored son back within a couple of months.

She brought her attention back to Charles. 'I am afraid it is no secret. Do you fear that Amanda will reject you because of your illegitimacy?'

He changed colour at her plain speech, but met it with honesty. 'No. I believe I know her character sufficiently well. She will not despise the circumstances of my birth and upbringing. But how can I ask her to share my life when I have so little to offer her? Lady . . . Caro . . . She is all that any man could wish for in a woman, but I will not drag her down to my own level.'

He looked so miserable, and she could think of nothing to comfort him. It was true. Amanda might not count the cost of wedding an obscure and impoverished gentleman without a name, but he would count it for her. Now that she thought about it, it was strange that Amanda had not yet confided in her friend. They were so close, and yet Karen had no idea of the true situation with Charles.

'Have you spoken to Amanda about this yet?'

'I have not, and I have no intention of doing so. I trust you will not betray my confidence, Caro.'

'You may safely trust me. But I do think you should speak to her. If she loves you, as I think she does, together you may be able to work something out.'

He shook his head and stood up. 'It has relieved my mind talking to you. You are a kind woman. And Antony is a blind fool.' He bowed and left her to absorb this tart compliment.

He'd given her a lot to think about. So had Sybilla, and oddly enough they had both said the same thing about Jenny, that she was an adversary. Karen recognised the truth in this. Not only was Antony still in love with his first wife, but Karen herself must be exhibiting sighs of infatuation. Two people had commented upon it. How many others were slyly noting the fact? How amusing for them – a wife falling in love with her husband. How hilarious.

The worst complication, however, was Sybilla's declared intention of annexing Antony for herself, just as if he was a piece of territory and she Napoleon with a *grande armee* at her back. Things could get quite embarrassing if she ever decided to make public claim to her cousin.

Thinking over last night's confrontation, Karen had decided it held more pathos than drama. Poor Sybilla. She had to be quite unbalanced, carrying on with voodoo spells and a complete disregard for the rights of others. Karen, herself, might not be well-versed in the traditions of karma and reincarnation, but she only had to compare Amanda's attitudes and way of life with Sybilla's to see that black magic and the practise of evil was an aberration in the scheme of things, and certainly it could never work towards the benefit of any soul. She was, however, uneasy about such powers. The mind could do strange things. Sybilla's dedication to her sinister arts might very well produce the desired effects, perhaps by way of the psychology of an intended victim.

Karen couldn't laugh away the idea that she was being insidiously worked on. Anyone who could travel through time and space and end up as she had, had better keep an open mind.

Thinking about the forces that had moulded Sybilla, she concluded the sudden abandonment of the Jamaican plantation might be a clue. Had her parents brought her to England for treatment? Perhaps her condition had deteriorated rapidly, making it impossible to hide. Yet she had seemed quite normal when Karen first met her.

If she'd thought about Basil, which she didn't if she could help it, or Lady Oriel herself, she might have seen the signs earlier. Sybilla simply hid her true nature, while the rest of her family blatantly displayed theirs. What a collection!

She puzzled over Sybilla's history for some time, but eventually abandoned speculation through lack of material. To discuss it with anyone else, except maybe Amanda, would be to brand herself as jealous and neurotic. She'd take no risks while her own reputation for soundness of mind remained suspect. So Sybilla, ostensibly serene and balanced, would simply be kept under observation.

But, what an actress! Her façade had no crack. She'd even fooled everyone into believing she cared for Chloe, although her tone last night when speaking of 'the brat' in the miniature had destroyed that illusion for Karen. Thank heaven she'd won the child's confidence herself and not left her to the dubious affections of her cousin.

Which brought her to the point she had been avoiding. Karen felt a shiver run over her. Last night Sybilla had displayed the perfect temperament for a killer. She would have little compunction in disposing of a rival, and she had the advantage of living on the spot. It took little cunning to push someone down the stairs; and what could be simpler than drugging a glass of milk and opening a window onto a storm? And – Sybilla had motive. She coveted Karen's husband. Had she decided not to wait through a protracted and socially damaging divorce? If so, what was to stop her trying her hand at murder again at any moment?

Deep in thought, Karen failed to hear the parlour door open. She jumped violently when Charles spoke.

'I beg your pardon, Caro, but I did not have your answer to His Royal Highness' invitation.'

'Oh. Ah, yes. Yes indeed. Certainly we accept what amounts to a Royal Command. It should be a most interesting event.'

Interesting it was. It was also the longest, most drawn-out affair of the season, and after nine hours Karen had had enough. She knew she would remember those hours, not only for their exhibition of the most wanton extravagance she was ever likely to witness, but as a panorama of all that Regency England represented when viewed from a position of privilege.

Down the length of Pall Mall the carriage approached Carlton House in the soft light of a June evening. The Prince's newest plaything displayed itself against the sky in all its Grecian splendour, columned, porticoed and pedimented like the work of some latter-day Phidias. A building of magnificent proportions, its interior design and decor would bring it renown as one of the finest small palaces in Europe, and one of the most short-lived. At its owner's whim it would be pulled down within a matter of a few years.

At nine o'clock exactly the horses swept through the portico with a flourish, and Antony and Karen stepped down from their carriage into the entrance lobby. Along with the expectant and unusually punctual crowd of guests, they moved through to the great hall, all green marble and yellow scagliola columns with a splendid coffered ceiling overhead. There were glimpses of heavily gilded furniture, but most of it was hidden in the crush.

'Two thousand guests have been bidden,' said Antony in Karen's ear. 'Prinny will have surpassed himself in the spending of public monies.'

'Whatever will that cost? I hear it whispered everywhere that he wildly overspends his budget.' She waved to an acquaintance and bowed acknowledgement of other greetings. It was impossible to have speech in this din unless the speaker placed his lips almost against his auditor's ear.

'The cost of this function will be in the region of one hundred and twenty thousand pounds, I am told.'

Translating that into modern terms, she was aghast. The nation at war, exports frozen (discounting the extremely lucrative smuggling trade), people starving all over the country, and its own Regent spending as if he were a Croesus.

'It's wicked,' she said, but her words were lost in the babble around them.

Joining a favoured few, they were guided by footmen into an anteroom hung for the occasion in blue satin with gold embroidered fleur-de-lis. Their invitation had stated that the fete was given to honour the Comte de Provence, the self-styled Louis XVIII of France, and it was with a thrill of expectation that Karen advanced down the room towards a small group standing in the window embrasure.

It was dominated by two enormously fat men. Louis came as a disappointment. The heavy Bourbon features did not lend themselves to majestic presence any more than they'd done for his murdered brother. But the Prince Regent, despite his corpulence, retained some of the famed beauty of countenance that had brought him the sobriquet of 'Prince Charming' in his youth. He was certainly not trying to hide his bulk in the scarlet uniform of a British field marshal. Ablaze with orders and festooned in gold braid – even the seams of his coat were embroidered – he emitted an aura of royalty. His jowls rested in the folds of his high cravat and he seemed likely to burst out of his corseted pantaloons, but Karen felt no disillusionment. He was a character, a figurehead, and with all the charm of a practiced beau he raised her from her curtsey, taking her hand and presenting her himself to the exiled king of France.

Again she dipped into the exceedingly difficult obeisance considered the due of kings, and which had cost her some effort to perfect. Louis murmured an indifferent greeting, but his host more than countered this. Waving Antony away he took Karen on his arm and proceeded to introduce her to Louis' family and entourage, all the while maintaining a running patter that was both amusing and embarrassing.

'You have been too long absent from court, Lady Caroline. Such beauty should not be hid. Our debutantes will all be cast in the shade by such a sun goddess.' He put up a hand to her flaming hair, contriving to brush her bare shoulder as he did. His heavy body pressed close.

'This ungainly fellow is my brother Cumberland. Do not, I beg, be put off by his scowl. He has the fiend's own temper and just now no means of dispersing it.'

Given no time to do more than curtsey in the direction of this forbidding Duke, Karen was hurried on to greet Lady Hertford, the Prince's current friend, a dame of haughty appearance who gave her two fingers and then ignored her. Karen had no trouble in believing the rumour that she had forcefully declined a cosier relationship, and merely wished to guide the Prince culturally and politically.

For the next ten minutes she was towed about the room clamped to the royal side, being slyly stroked, fulsomely praised and almost choked with the effort of holding back her laughter as he gave wicked sotto voce descriptions of the other guests.

Here was another complex character, not easily defined, and using his exalted position both as a weapon and an instrument of benevolence. One minute he could speak of a man with high praise for his acumen and ability, and then be dragging down another for the pettiest reasons. She saw him turn his back on George Brummel, once his closest confidant, and tell anyone who cared to listen that his morganatic wife, Maria Fitzherbert, would not be present that night as he had refused her a seat at his own table, while a place there was reserved for Lady Hertford.

He also paused to listen to a hard-luck story and thereupon commanded an equerry to immediately hasten to the home of a young cornet of his regiment laid low with fever and in debt, taking money from the household purse. A strange mixture, this prince, and quite unforgettable.

Eventually Antony reclaimed her and they were able to leave the reception and take their place in the line descending the remarkable baroque staircase to the lower ground floor.

Karen halted to marvel at a room lined with ionic pillars, its ceiling moulded and gilded and set with allegorical panels, its walls hung in silk and swagged in tasselled braid. The couches were of matching velvet, their legs clawed and marvellously carved, the doors inlaid and again dazzlingly gilded. Chandeliers fell in ropes of crystal, ending in sunbursts that dazzled the eye, and giant mirrors reflected a shopful of ornaments, busts and urns, clocks and figurines, all, inevitably, layered in gold.

'I've never seen anything so overdone. It's pure loco rococo.' She laughed, unsure whether she was stunned with amazement or sickened by so much excess.

'Reserve judgment until you have seen the conservatory,' advised Antony, clearly enjoying her response to her surroundings.

'It surely can't be any more exotic. The Prince Regent seems to have taken for his motto, "Nothing succeeds like excess".'

Antony smiled. His eyes rested on her face for one moment then travelled over her gown. 'I have not yet complimented you upon your appearance, Caro. You do me honour.'

Karen had admitted to herself as she dressed that she hoped to please him. The occasion was a very grand one and his wife's appearance would, to a degree, affect his standing. It was the way of the world, and for once she didn't rebel against standards that were not her own. Despite his seeming indifference, and her determination to hide her own feelings, she valued his praise.

'Your gown is a triumph of simplicity against this background. You are to be congratulated.' He took her hand to his lips. There was no doubting the admiration in his eyes, and something else that she did not care to analyse.

She flushed and looked away, meeting her reflection in a huge looking glass. It framed her slim white gown with its collar of lace cut low and edged in diamond drops. The lace at the hem sparkled with the same stones, as did the rose in her hair. Her shoulders rose white and sloping from the lace, bare of jewellery, as were her arms. Only the flaming copper curls gave her colour, and the vivid blue of her eyes.

She could admire this snowy beauty without feeling it was any part of her. Even after months of living in Caroline Marchmont's body she still felt like a stranger in costume. It made it hard to value any compliment; but it was doubly cruel to at last receive a genuine tribute from Antony and know it was not really meant for her.

She gave herself a mental shake. There she went, daydreaming again. It would be disastrous, as well as highly improbable, for Antony to fall in love with her. For one thing, Sybilla would go off like a nuclear bomb, and the fallout could cause a lot of damage.

Then there was her own response to be considered. As long as it had been just a dream, she could afford to let it be, but the reality would end up pulling her apart. She never gave up hope of returning one day to her own time, and Adele. It would be more than stupid to create a loving relationship that she would have to leave behind. Much better to walk a lonely way and save herself worse pain in the long run. Besides, Jenny still had his love.

Antony offered her his arm and escorted her into the conservatory.

She had seen W.H. Pyne's aquatints, but realised they were inadequate preparation for the reality. Someone had described the monolithic structure as a 'neo-perpendicular extravaganza of cast iron and translucent coloured glass'. Now she saw for herself the great web of fan-vaulting, the ornate arched colonnades hung with gothic lanterns, the floor marbled in black and white squares, presently hidden by a two-hundred-foot long table reaching from the west door through the length of the hall and the dining room beyond.

Antony's shoulders shook.

'What is it?'

'Look at the table.'

Its centrepiece was unusual, to say the least. Before the Prince's chair sat a pond with gold and silver fish, and from this basin a stream meandered the whole length of the board, bounded by mossy banks of flowers. Comments amongst the guests indicated wonder and high praise.

She met her husband's dancing eyes and laughed. 'Do you suppose we are to net our own dinner?'

'Possibly. I have ceased to wonder at Prinny's whims.'

The royal party entered to the strains of martial music, and proceeded to the head of the table. Taking his place beneath a great gilded coronet, with a gracious smile the host indicated that they all should be seated, and the banquet began.

Sixty servitors ran with tureens, plates and bowls, all of silver, and as many changes as were wanted. Soups, roasts and cold meats came with vegetables and fruits in and out of season, the best of wines and iced champagne.

Hours passed, and still they sat, sated and, in Karen's case, talked out. At the Regent's table, where she and Antony were placed, the conversation had been brilliant at times. The Prince was an accomplished musician and knowledgeable. He discoursed on the later works of Beethoven and Handel, and discussed the merits of various opera singers at present in London. Mr Sheridan's plays came under discussion, and in deference to the guest of honour, those of Voltaire.

When art took its turn Karen joined in the commentary, much to the surprise of those men and women whose interest it was to patronise such work. Lady Hertford herself unbent to discuss the rival virtues of watercolour versus oils in landscape painting. She advocated Mr Cotman's watercolour of Greta Bridge as a prime example, and Karen countered with John Constable. They enjoyed their discussion very much. It was unfortunate that Lady Hertford should comment on her efforts to persuade the Prince to have his portrait done by Mr Lawrence.

'Oh, it will be a very fine work, with His Highness in garter robes,' said Karen, and could have bitten her tongue.

Lady Hertford looked at her strangely, and began to converse with her neighbour. Karen felt annoyed at her slip, but after all little harm had come of it. She threw herself into a light-hearted conversation with the Duke of York, who was only too pleased to explain to a pretty woman just how he would have won the Battle of Trafalgar in half the time it took that fellow Nelson.

Finally, in the early hours of the morning, the Prince rose from the table and released those persons who could still stand. Many slumped quite comfortably in their chairs snoring. Some even lay on the floor.

'Would you care to see the gardens, Caro?'

She looked at Antony with gratitude. 'Fresh air and a chance to walk off this dinner! Please, lead me to it.'

Outside there had been other transformations. Karen found no vistas of trees and lawns, but covered walks with painted trellis and flowers and mirrors, and more tables set up to accommodate the guests who could not be fitted indoors.

'We might as well be at Vauxhall with all these artificial galleries and promenades.'

'But you have enjoyed the evening?'

'Oh, yes. I would not have missed such an opportunity. Do you think we might steal just one glimpse of the throne room before we leave?'

Antony laughed. 'What, you still have stomach for more splendours?'

How could she explain that she was storing up memories for the time when these would be unique to her alone? Her face clouded as she thought of the difficulties still in her path. Amanda was proving less helpful that she had believed. There had been no word from the French seer, Pierre Marnie, and now that she thought of it, her friend seemed to be avoiding the house lately. This should be looked into.

Apparently mistaking her suddenly dimmed mood for weariness, Antony soon arranged for them to take their leave, postponing the viewing of the throne room to another occasion.

They drove home in the dawn light, hearing London come awake all around them. Street criers were out in force, vending everything from milk to rabbits, and the saucepans to cook them in. A chair-mender staggered by, a wooden frame slung over his shoulder and a bundle of canes underarm. Carts rumbled in the distance, carrying produce in to the markets. A weary child stumbled out to sweep the crossing for a pedestrian. It was all so misty and theatrical. Karen, her head nodding on her shoulders, felt she was adrift in a dream world. Any minute she'd waken in her bed in St John's Wood, hearing Dali's peremptory call to be let in the window after his nightly prowl.

She felt Antony place an arm around her and lay her head on his shoulder, and she slept.

Facing the stairs to her apartments Karen gladly accepted his support. At the door of her bedchamber she turned and gave him a tired smile. She felt his mouth warm on her fingers. Amazing, how different the sensation when it was done by a man she liked.

'I shall have to make another trip into the country very soon.'

Something inside her lurched. Her fingers tightened on his. 'Oh? Will you be long away?'

'A full se'ennight, at the least.'

'What a pity. You will miss Lady Scranton's ball,' she said mechanically, hoping her face had not given away her dismay. He was going into danger once more.

'I pray you will give my excuses.' His smile lit his eyes and her own sparkled in acknowledgement. They both knew he loathed balls and attended only under duress.

'Will you be seeing your father, the Earl?' She questioned him at random, unwilling to let him go.

'Not this time, alas. I must journey . . . north.'

Sweden? Russia? It was so terribly dangerous anywhere on the Continent for an Englishman. She wakened to the fact that they were standing holding hands and not speaking. But his eyes said much, and she feared hers did too.

'Caro, may I say how greatly I have enjoyed the privilege of your company these past hours? What should have been a tedious duty, for me has become a memory to be treasured.'

Intense pleasure flooded through her. He had liked her company. And she . . . Oh, God, how much she had enjoyed his. Seated beside him for hours on end, constantly aware of the short distance between them, their fingers brushing occasionally as she reached for a wineglass, or he prepared fruit for her plate; watching him applaud the wit and beauty of other women and feeling the shaming stab of jealousy; knowing when he turned back to her by the sensation of light flooding through every cell of her body, warming, enlivening. It had been a night of magic, made all the more unreal by her fairytale surroundings. Cinderella in borrowed finery in a world far distant from her own. Cinderella with the clock about to chime midnight.

Hastily she retrieved her fingers to stifle a false yawn. 'I am weary. Pray excuse me, my lord.'

He stood so close. She felt him looking down at her but dared not meet those disturbing eyes. Then he leaned forward and opened the door. Warm perfumed air rushed out to meet them.

'Your bower awaits you, milady. But, where is your maid?'

'I will not let her wait up for me until such an hour. She has to work during the day as well.' Karen moved inside, now anxious for him to go. She glanced up and surprised an expression of shock on his face, which was swiftly hidden. Then, almost too quickly, he had made his bow and gone.

What had she said? What was so startling about letting her maid have her rest? What an enigma he was. And how dangerous to her peace of mind.

She set about the task of getting herself out of her dress without help. Too tired to do more than wash her face and pull on her nightgown, she flicked back the sheet and stood frozen.

In the middle of her bed lay a crude wax doll. Dressed in a scrap of green silk, it had big paper eyes coloured crudely in blue chalk and a clump of glued-on hairs of a coppery shade that she knew had come from her own head. But the thing that held her transfixed was the sight of a long thin ivory-handled blade thrust into the doll's breast, in roughly the position where the human heart would beat.

CHAPTER 13

8 December, Saturday

TOM MADE LUNCH for Habbakuk and himself and settled down with his textbooks in search of witches.

He began with the early Christian and Hebrew attitudes towards the devil, that he was the instigator of man's unacceptable behaviour, but that man did have some responsibility in the matter. It seemed that, prior to the Middle Ages, churchmen such as St Augustine writing in his *Confessions*, did acknowledge other outside influences. All the same, the devil was believed to be a real force working against the power of God. During baptism a form of exorcism was used to drive out the evil spirit felt to be in possession of the babe.

About the time of the sixth century a new belief crept in, that sexual misbehaviour of men was caused by women, and that 'woman is a temple built over a sewer'. Women with psychological problems, and those who consorted with monks and other 'holy' men, were accused of being in league with demons. The female sex as a whole became linked with witchcraft.

Heretics were seen as followers of the Antichrist, and therefore sexually degenerate. At trials they were accused of extraordinary practices including child sacrifice (of children born as a result of sexual orgies), the burning of infant bodies so that the ashes could be made into a paste that enabled people and objects to fly, and cannibalism. By the time the Inquisition came into being in the thirteenth century, the stage was set for an orgy of torture and murder of millions of innocent people.

As Tom read on he began to wonder whether he should have eaten lunch. Decidedly queasy at the descriptions of Black Masses and other coven rituals, he skipped over the more fanatical excesses of the flagellants, and the orgies enjoyed by Luciferans who believed that sexual activity on the face of the earth was sinful but fine when practised underground. About to take a rest from such indigestible matter his eye was caught by two words – Malleus Maleficarum.

'Witch Hammer', he muttered. Hadn't Valerie used the word 'hammer' in her accusation against the priest? He looked up the allusion and found that a book of that name had been written around 1485 by a Heinrich Institoris, which became a guideline for inquisitors and others seeking to identify witches. It advocated almost unrestrained torture, among other things, and was an indictment of the author's own mental stability.

But it did help to explain some of the excessive zeal of the witch-hunters. People lived in a fear-filled world. Witches were regarded as being responsible for sickness and disease, the loss of children and all kinds of personal tragedies. Society in the Middle Ages was victimised by plagues and famines. Life was short and hard, and the only hope lay in God's offer of eternal salvation in exchange for the hunting down and stamping out of evil. In fact, it was abnormal *not* to believe in witches and demons.

'Poor devils.' Tom was not clear whether he sympathised with the victims or their tormentors. Perhaps both. It wasn't easy to enter the medieval mind. But then, judging by the current interest in films like 'The Exorcist', demonology might not be such an outmoded interest after all.

His own attitude towards Valerie worried him. The dream in which he'd seen himself as the harrying priest of her regression showed strong reservations. Did he see her as practising the black arts on the people she ostensibly helped? Or had she merely been the victim of a man blinded by fear and prejudice, and perhaps hope of preferment?

'You are out of your tree, Tom Levy,' he said to himself. 'You're treating a dream as if it were an actual happening. It's time to take a good hard look at yourself.'

He glanced up to see Habbakuk's mesmeric yellow eyes on him, and shivered. It was easy to imagine more than animal intelligence there. No wonder that the impressionable and the superstitious had seen familiars on every hearthstone.

The following day he abandoned witchcraft for everyday mysticism, and as a result of a few enquiries, took a trip to Earls Court.

Guru Rama Satya's rooms smelled musty and sandalwoody, and the fumes of burning incense choked Tom as he pawed his way through the gloom of drawn curtains and multitudes of bead hangings to the inner sanctum, otherwise known as the Guru's sitting room. A gnome-like figure of indeterminable age, he squatted cross-legged on a cushion, his eyes rolled up so far he seemed to be looking at the inside of his turban.

Tom crouched on another cushion in front of him, trying not to cough in the thick air, and beating down a host of negative reactions.

Reedy music whined in the background somewhere, and as his vision adjusted to the gloom Tom was confronted by several pairs of slanty eyes glinting from different heights and angles. One lot even seemed to hang in the air above the guru's head. These eventually incorporated into the outline of a cat perched on a cabinet behind the holy man. Evidently he favoured familiars of his own.

Tom organised his thoughts and made his challenge. 'I want to know about karma and past lives. Can you help me?'

Slowly the turban nodded. A soft whispering voice issued from beneath. 'For the soul there is never birth nor death. Nor, having once been, does he ever cease to be. He is unborn, eternal, ever-existing, undying and primaeval. He is not slain when the body is slain.'

'Yes. Well, does that mean that the soul inhabits many different bodies in many lives?'

'As a person puts on new garments, giving up old ones, similarly the soul accepts new material bodies, giving up the old and useless ones. It is said that the soul is inconceivable, immutable and unchangeable. Knowing this you should not grieve for the body.'

That seemed fairly definite. Tom considered his next question. 'How, then, does a person escape from this eternal round of rebirth? Surely there comes a time when he's paid all his debts and earned his reward.'

The turban nodded. 'A man engaged in devotional service rids himself of both good and bad actions even in this life. Therefore strive for this yoga, which is the art of all work.'

'But . . . what is yoga?'

The turban sighed. 'Abandon all attachment to success or failure. Such evenness of mind is called yoga.'

It was Tom's turn to sigh. 'But if a man detaches himself from ambition, what is left for him?'

'I have said, the wise, engaged in devotional service, take refuge in the Lord, and free themselves from the cycle of birth and death by renouncing the fruits of action in the material world. In this way they can attain that state beyond all miseries.'

Tom was dissatisfied. In his book, life certainly wasn't all misery and therefore to be avoided; and while devotional service to the Lord was okay to a point, the world would soon stop working if everyone decided to do it at once. This guru was decidedly impractical.

As if reading his mind, the turban intoned in a stronger voice, 'One who is not disturbed in spite of the threefold miseries, who is not elated when there is happiness, and who is free from attachment, fear and anger, is called a sage of steady mind. He who is without affection either for good or evil is firmly fixed in perfect knowledge.'

'Then I doubt whether I'll be attaining that state. To be without affection for anything in the world would be like cutting myself off from humanity. It's monstrous!' Thoroughly ill at ease, Tom scrambled up off the cushion, barking his shin on something metallic that went rolling away in the gloom.

The turban hissed. As Tom felt his way back to the door he could hear the guru having the last word.

'When your intelligence has passed out of the dense forest of delusion, you will become indifferent to all that has been heard and all that is to be heard.'

Clattering downstairs and emerging into a street cloaked in misty rain Tom laughed to himself, ruefully. He hadn't even got as far as asking about karma. The old boy was too mystical to be understood.

He was disappointed. He'd hoped for much more. Surely there was someone who could explain in western terms the concepts that Phil and Valerie seemed to find so easy.

He took a bus back into the city and soothed his soul with a walk down the undeniably material world of Bond Street. Here amongst some of the richest shops in the world he'd expect to find many a person firmly attached to success, and its fruits.

A jeweller's window caught his eyes, and he stopped, fascinated by the glitter of fabulously expensive baubles. Two women stood in the shelter of an awning, admiring and coveting the display. Their voices began to annoy him, whingeing, dissatisfied, dripping with greed. He tried to turn them off. And in his ear came a reedy whisper that startled him.

'While contemplating the objects of the senses, a person develops attachment for them, and from such attachment lust develops, and from lust anger arises. From anger delusion arises, and from delusion bewilderment of memory. When memory is bewildered, intelligence is lost, and when intelligence is lost one falls down again into the material pool.'

Tom whipped around, but there was no turbanned guru nearby. There was no one at all within ten feet. He shivered, and glanced again at the two women, whose faces mirrored unintelligent lust. He began to glimpse something of the truth behind the holy man's words.

He walked on, deep in thought, until he found himself before a window displaying an exceptional artwork – the face of Karen Courtney's *Bella Donna*. He turned into Sampson's entrance.

Theo himself marched up and down in the foyer, directing the rehanging of yards of grey silk curtaining. He pounced joyfully and dragged Tom forward to give an opinion.

'What do you think, dear boy? A trifle dim, perhaps? You think a trim of gold braid on the pelmet would lift them a little – or, no, perhaps not. Much too Monte Carlo for Sampsons.' He broke off to dart forward and chide a workman swinging a ladder in imminent danger of meeting with the draperies.

When the crisis had passed and Theo was able to give him more than half an ear, Tom did a pounce of his own and propelled him into the office.

'Theo, I want a word with you. Can you give me ten minutes without rushing off to supervise the resurfacing of the dome, or something?'

'Of course. Let me give you a drink.'

Comfortably lost in the depths of grey leather chairs the two men surveyed one another. But Theo still had his mind on his premises.

'Did you hear about the fire? Disastrous! I assure you, I expected to see the whole collection go up. Quite irreplaceable! And she's so young.'

Tom sat up. 'What fire? What happened?'

'You didn't know!' Theo seemed put out, but decided to overlook such a philistine lack of interest in his important world. 'It must have been after you left. Some triple-dyed idiot let his lighter catch on my lovely new drapes and they went up in banners of flame.' He stopped, overcome by the vision of his memory.

Tom felt the brush of panic somewhere under his ribs. 'Was this the night of the Courtney exhibition, ten days ago?'

'I was just telling you, dear boy. Such a loss it would have been. But my quick action and that of some other people saved us. We tore down the shreds and threw them outside before the sensors could start the sprinkler system. Nothing was lost. But I've had the most dreadful time replacing the fabric. I give you my word, I've scoured London and Paris, and only yesterday – '

'Never mind your rubbishy curtains. Was anyone hurt? You said something about her being so young.'

Theo's cheeks reddened. Then he looked hard at Tom and grinned. 'Well, well. Interested in our Miss Courtney, are we?'

'She has a fantastic talent,' said Tom, coldly. 'Are you going to answer me?'

'Karen came over all peculiar when she saw the flames. She let out a screech and ran for the door. I could see she wasn't herself and sent some of the lads after her. They chased halfway across the city before coming up with her. She'd cut her feet a bit – a few bruises and other lacerations. Nothing much.'

Tom relaxed. He took a sip of his drink, saying casually, 'So, she's at home now? I wonder if I could have her address from you, Theo.'

'It won't do you any good. She's in University College Hospital in a coma and doesn't even look like rousing.'

Tom's drink went over on the carpet. Only the frail stem remained in his hand. 'Goddam you, Theo! You said she was all right.'

'She was, after the fire. It was the next night that a car ran her down – some place in Devonshire called Ashbourne St Mary. Fellow came haring up a dark driveway in the middle of a storm and there she was standing in his path. He never had a chance of missing her, I hear.'

Even Tom, shocked as he was, could appreciate the real misery in Theo's voice. He cared about Karen.

'I'm sorry I spoke like that.' Mechanically Tom replaced the bit of crystal on the table and went down on his knees with his handkerchief to try and mop up the drink.

'Leave it. I'll have it attended to.' Theo stood aside and watched Tom wander out the door into the gallery. Several of Karen's paintings hung right beside him. He looked through them, seeing only the long, sensitive face with the dark hair swinging at the shoulders, the wide-mouth smiling at his clumsiness, and behind the spectacles the amber-gold eyes alight but with a shadow in their depths.

The famed University College Hospital was only ten minutes away in a taxi. It seemed like hours to Tom, huddled on the back seat in a fog of unhappines he couldn't explain. Karen Courtney was practically a stranger to him. Yet the idea of her being close to death dismayed him. What a terrible waste of youth and talent it would be . . .

When he finally stood outside the door of her private ward clutching a bunch of violets, he wondered whether he was making a mistake. What could he do for her? Why upset himself? He walked in.

A nurse was just drawing back the bed curtains and preparing to leave with her medical paraphernalia. Another woman stood by the window staring into the rain-washed street. Tom smiled at the nurse, then coughed politely.

The woman at the window turned bleak blue eyes on him. 'Who are you?'

'Tom Levy, a friend. I . . . met Karen at Theo's gallery.'

'I am Karen's aunt, Wilhelmina Carnot.' She thrust a thin blue-veined hand at him and he took it briefly in his.

He saw a small, stylish woman of about fifty with an indefinable air about her. Seeking some trace of likeness to Karen he could only think of small breeds of dog, like poodles or whippets. She was too well-bred, too finished. He turned to the bed.

Karen looked like a marble effigy, her only touch of colour the swatch of straight black hair lying each side of her face, and the curve of eyelashes on her cheeks. The sheet was drawn up to her chin. He could not believe that she breathed.

Billie said harshly, 'There's been no change. She's just as she was when they brought her in.'

Tom couldn't speak. His throat seemed to have closed over and it hurt like hell. He had to wait until he could relax the muscles.

'What's the prognosis? Who's looking after her?'

'Professor Townshend. He's a fine neurosurgeon. He says . . . he says . . .' Billie stopped.

Tom looked up at her. 'Well? He says . . . ?'

'That it is a good sign that she breathes for herself. She can swallow and her bodily functions are also maintaining themselves well. But she could go on like this for a long time. He . . . she . . . The longer she remains in coma, the less likely it is that she will recover.' Billie turned back to the window, her narrow shoulders bowed.

Tom would not have believed that mere words could hurt so much. It was as if a very dear friend had had the death sentence pronounced upon her. His eyes went to the pale face on the pillow.

'There must be something . . .'

Billie sighed and walked over to her side of the bed. She too looked down at her niece. 'That is what everyone says in a crisis. There must be something. But there is nothing we have not done. The outcome is with God.' She added in a venomous undertone, 'A cruel God who takes and takes and never gives back in return.'

His gaze flicked at her, then back to Karen. He put out his hand and with one finger gently brushed back a strand of hair over her forehead.

'Do you mind if I come again, just to sit with her?'

'Why not? It cannot hurt. I will leave word with the desk sister.'

'Thank you.' Tom gave one of his ungainly little bows and left. He was halfway across Hyde Park before he registered his surroundings.

Moodily he stood watching children running with a kite, realising that the rain had stopped and there was a fair breeze. His coat flapped about his knees. He felt cold with the kind of deathly chill that usually heralded 'flu. But he knew he wasn't physically ill, just sick at heart.

Nothing seemed to make sense any more. He was failing with the patient who most needed his help, while his carefully cultivated non-faith was in tatters, with nothing of any substance to put in its place except a few wisps of mysticism and a dash of witchcraft! And now there was the brutally unfair accident to a young woman whose future had held such promise – someone he liked and respected and who could die at any minute.

He drew a coin from his pocket and tossed it into the air. Heads, he'd get roaring drunk, tails . . .

Catching the coin he looked at its upward face and shrugged. Then he called to a passing taxi.

'The nearest synagogue.'

CHAPTER 14

CHARLES HAD JUST come in from a pleasantly convivial evening spent at a tavern. He planned to retire immediately to sleep off his potations. Long ago he had acknowledged an addiction to ale, which was scarcely a gentleman's tipple, and to the company he found in taverns. Neither was the Red Cock to be mentioned in the same breath as Whites or Brooks. But then, as he told himself, who was he to aspire to such heights?

It was only when under the influence of drink that he permitted such bitter thoughts to rise. At all other times he had himself well under control. Long inured to years of slights and put-downs from persons who did not bother to consider the feelings of others less fortunate than themselves, he felt he had succeeded in carving a satisfactory niche in the world. He knew he deserved the respect commanded by diligence and a loyal devotion to the family he served, and chose to ignore any failure on the part of others to render that respect. Besides, his sense of self-worth did not permit a response to the sort of barb he was in no position to return – such as Basil Frensham's snide comments upon his lack of ancestry, or Lady Oriel's really atrocious rudeness.

The one chink in his armour was his predilection for taverns and the life to be found there. He enjoyed the smoky atmosphere and the relaxed talk of men who had no position to uphold and therefore could be completely natural in the way they revealed themselves to their fellows. He envied that freedom, even while holding himself apart.

Of course he had visited the gentlemen's clubs in company with Antony, and he was aware that the members were equally at home in the company of their peers. An insecure man might pose and anxiously try for an impression, but Charles did not see himself as insecure. Nevertheless, he still felt far more comfortable as an anonymous observer in a taproom, although he would have died in agony rather than admit it.

The scream drilled through his head, halting him by the library doors. It was followed by a confused wailing sound, both tormented and wildly angry. He took the stairs in a series of strides, arriving at the landing as Karen appeared, lamp in hand, her dressing gown trailing as she pulled it about her shoulders.

'What is it?' Charles half covered his mouth to disguise the liquor on his breath. He noticed that his hand was not quite steady.

'I'm not sure.' Her expression hinted at suppressed laughter, but he decided that could not be.

Down the corridor something exploded with a tremendous smash. Both Charles and Karen began to run. Arriving first at Sybilla's door Charles knocked at the panel.

'Is something amiss? Miss Frensham, are you there?'

With her gown caught up in one hand and the lamp wobbling dangerously in the other, Karen joined him. 'Let us in, Sybilla.'

A shriek of rage answered them and a missile thudded against the door.

'Here, take this.' Karen thrust the lamp at Charles and opened the door and marched in. He followed unwillingly at her heels.

The room had a sombre magnificence, hung in crimson damask with black and silver trim, but he would not have cared to sleep amid such splendour. Its atmosphere struck him as curiously heavy, almost repellent, and his nostrils wrinkled at the smell of sandalwood burning, and something else with it, pungent and heavily aromatic. There was too much reflective glass, too many candles, and far too much heavily carved furniture. He began to sweat.

Sybilla crouched in the middle of the floor, her long black hair in a wild tangle about her. She saw Karen and flew at her, nails crooked, spitting like a cat.

'You did this! You! What do you know of the houngan's ways? Who taught you the magic?' Her clawing fingers clutched at empty air as Karen ducked aside, and Sybilla's own impetus carried her forward to hit the edge of the door. This time she screamed with pain and reeled back, holding a hand to her forehead.

Charles struggled with his ale-dimmed wits. Could Sybilla Frensham really be attacking Caro in some sort of hysterical fit? And was Caro actually almost helpless with laughter? Bewildered, he set down the lamp with care and turned to her. 'What is happening here?'

'Ask our little household sorceress,' she spluttered, and pointed to the shards of mirror lying before the fireplace. Remnants hung from the frame above the mantel, reflecting crazy patterns of red silk and candlelight and pieces of broken Meissen.

So that was the crash he'd heard. But why had Sybilla thrown an ornament at her glass? What *was* going on?

Then he saw the doll, a manikin figure of some soft substance like wax, sprawled on the hearth, its barely formed limbs twisted in impossible positions.

He trod carefully through the mess and picked it up. 'What is this? A child's puppet?' Then he looked more closely, and felt a shudder of distaste. 'It has a thorn pressed into its throat, and . . . it looks like a smear of blood.'

'It is blood.'

He looked at Karen with amazement, and some disapproval. There had been such satisfaction in her voice. He saw her examining a place on her forearm which had been bandaged.

'Do not tell me that it is your blood!'

A hiss from Sybilla drew his attention. She'd drawn away from Karen and now huddled on the end of her bed, her dark eyes the only part of her that seemed to be alive. They were bright as a raven's, and malevolent.

Karen drew down her sleeve and looked at her steadily. 'You were right to name me witchwoman. And you are brave to cast your spells on le loup-garou.'

'Loup-garou,' croaked Sybilla, and closed her eyes. A shiver ran through her.

'Yes. You would do well to take back the magic before it turns against you, tenfold.'

'Le loup-garou,' moaned Sybilla, rocking herself in her own arms. She had clearly retreated from the present into some world of her own.

Charles regarded her doubtfully, and decided there was little he could or would do for her. He swayed on his feet. He was very tired.

Karen picked up the lamp and went to the door. 'Come, Charles. I think Sybilla wishes to rest.'

He followed her out into the corridor and along the landing to her own door. 'I am quite at a loss. What has happened to Sybilla? What meaning is attached to the puppet?'

Karen chuckled. 'She's been trying her hand at a little black magic, and I simply turned the tables on her.'

'Your pardon?' He wished she would make herself clearer. There were still times when Caro spoke like a person who did not know her own language very well. It would account for that very peculiar statement about magic.

Karen sighed. 'Sybilla has been ill-wishing me, using a silly little figure dressed up to resemble me. She even pushed a dagger through the heart, which presumably means death in a painful manner.'

Charles frowned. 'She must be unbalanced. I never heard of such a thing.'

'Oh, it's quite well-known in the West Indies as a method of dealing with an enemy. It's a part of the voodoo cult.' She grinned. In the soft lamplight she looked to him like a mischievous urchin with that flaming hair tied back and eyes alight. 'It's her misfortune that I've read a bit about it – just enough to scare her.'

'You certainly succeeded in your aim.' He thought of the horrific scream that had first alerted him to trouble, and felt a twinge of sympathy for Sybilla. He added disapprovingly, 'What is so frightening about the doll, and the words "le loup-garou"?'

'I redressed the doll to resemble her and drove a thorn into its throat so that she would believe I had ill-wished her in return. Then I told her she was tangling with a genuine bloodsucking witch who could turn into a werewolf. That should put an end to her nonsense.' She smiled kindly at him. 'You look weary, Charles. Go to bed.'

'I . . . Yes, but . . .' The words would not form themselves on his tongue. He felt that he should say something, should at the least remonstrate with her. He was sure Antony would not approve the situation. But his wits were fuddled and, there was something about Caro now, an air of authority, a self-possession. He decided to say no more.

'Goodnight, Charles.' She gave him her hand and watched with amusement as he sketched a very clumsy bow.

'Sleep well, Caro.'

He was not surprised to find Sybilla absent from the breakfast table. She seldom left her chamber before noon. But Caro's sunny greeting dispelled any lingering concern over his behaviour the previous night. She had failed to detect any oddness in his manner, after all.

'Good morning, Charles. I'm pleased that you are joining us.'

Us? He turned swiftly and saw Amanda standing by the window admiring the garden. He thought her the personification of spring, all in daffodil yellow. Her dimpled smile did something to his heart. Bowing over her hand he fought the desire to press it to his mouth and cover it with feverish kisses.

Perhaps she sensed this, for a delicate colour rose in her cheeks and she moved away to join Karen at the small gate-leg table set in the window. The meal was so informal as to be practically al fresco. They served themselves and watched the birds in the garden. At least, the two ladies did so while Charles watched Amanda and tried to press upon her the more delicate tidbits of ham and fruit. He even prepared a pear for her with his own hands, and watched her eat it with every evidence of relish.

Any restraint there might have been was soon dispelled. Karen gave her friend a lively description of last night's proceedings, and despite his disapproval, Charles found himself joining in their amusement at the confounding of Sybilla's plans.

With a piece of bread and strawberry jam poised halfway to her lips, Amanda listened to the tale of Karen's tit-for-tat stratagem, and giggled.

'How clever of you, dear Caro. I would almost give my pearls to have seen her face.' Then she sobered. 'All the same, I do not like this turn of events. It seems you may have discovered your hidden enemy, only to have her openly attack. You must have a care in future.'

Charles was struck by the fact that he had missed this point. Had his wits been impaired after all?

'You believe that Sybilla was responsible for the accidents that have plagued Caro?'

'It seems likely.' Amanda looked from one to the other, questioningly. 'We are all of the same mind, I conclude – that these were no "accidents".'

Charles felt troubled. He had always disliked Sybilla, but it violated his most strongly entrenched beliefs to cast any lady in the role of a would be murderess. Ladies did not behave in such a manner. They were delicate creatures, of inferior intellect, to be nurtured and guided by the dominant male.

To be sure, his adored Amanda at times exhibited an alarming propensity to take control, but this was to be expected in such a superior example of the female sex. It must gall her to know herself to be of finer metal than most. She no doubt felt driven to exert her capabilities by reason of the stupidity and ineptness of her peers.

Which returned him to Sybilla and her machinations.

'I find it difficult to believe that any lady would be capable of such evil.'

Amanda cut him off. 'Sybilla is not a lady. She may have been born to that estate, but her appalling behaviour is the outward evidence of a degenerate mind. It is my belief that she is one of those souls incarnate with a propensity toward evil. I have seen no evidence of a desire to control her urges. If, as you say, Caro, she has been under the influence of a black magician since early childhood, there is little hope that she can be brought to see the error of her ways. She is doomed to follow her crooked path.'

Charles looked away. He did not like to see her so condemning. She might have been the Lord Chief Justice himself pronouncing judgment on a malefactor.

Karen said hesitantly, 'There is something I feel I should tell you. I don't know whether it's my imagination, but . . . She has displayed such animosity towards Antony's first wife, Jenny.' She looked enquiringly at Charles, inviting his opinion.

He shook his head, uncomfortable. 'I do not know. She always gave the appearance of friendship. I think she liked her. And yet . . .'

'And yet?' Karen encouraged.

'You are right. Her cozing ways were false. She was ever praising and offering her services, ever admiring of the child. Yet she lacked genuine feeling. I felt it like the change in texture under the fingertips when one touches first silk, then rough-milled cotton, but I did not recognise my feeling. Sybilla did not like her cousin.'

Karen nodded, her gaze caught by Amanda's. Charles saw them exchange meaningful looks.

Then Karen said slowly, 'It was more than dislike. I have wondered . . . I have thought . . .'

'What have you thought, Caro?'

'I have wondered whether that fire was an accident.'

Charles gasped. 'Good God! I cannot believe – '

'I can.' Amanda had once again cut him off. 'Yours is an intuitive spirit, Caro. I believe you may be in the right of it. For a person familiar with the Manor and the ways of its occupants, it would have been a simple enough matter to arrange.'

To Charles it seemed as if Caro's blue eyes had clouded into stormy grey. Her voice trembled as she said, 'Do not tell Antony. It would do no good, and might even cause much harm.'

'But, if she is responsible for this frightful thing, she should not go unpunished . . .' began Charles. Once accepted, the notion could not be left to rest. If she could be proven guilty, the evil-doer must be made to pay for her crime. That was justice, as well as the law.

Karen flashed back at him. 'No! There's no proof. And he has suffered so much aleady. We mustn't rake over the dead past and bring it to life again without excellent reason.'

He thought they had a very excellent reason and was about to say so when he glanced at Amanda's face, and decided to let well alone. The room had begun to feel unpleasantly warm to him. Or was his discomfort caused by the currents of emotion swirling about him? He liked a peaceful breakfast to start the day.

Karen said, 'I have told you this because I believe someone should know what Sybilla is capable of. If anything should happen to me, I want Chloe protected. She is Jenny's child, and I will not have her at that woman's mercy.'

'I hardly think that she will dare attack you again, now that we know her for what she is.' Charles was able to feel comfortably superior once more. Females could enjoy these occasional flashes of intuitive knowledge, but their thought processes were not designed to follow through in an orderly manner.

Karen suddenly smiled and seemed to put off her sombre thoughts. 'No doubt you are right. Let us talk of other matters. Have you had word from Antony upon his journeyings?'

He said repressively, 'I regret that I have not. His Lordship does not normally communicate with me unless there is an urgent matter requiring my attention.'

'What humbug, Charles,' Amanda chided. 'A wife is naturally concerned with her husband's welfare when he is abroad from his home.'

Karen looked at her sharply. 'He is not abroad. He has gone north on business.'

'That is what I said, my dear.' Amanda's face cleared. 'Oh, I see. "Abroad" simply means "away" or "absent". You must have forgot.'

Charles was surprised at how shaken Caro looked, even as she agreed that she had made a simple slip. Surely . . . No, there was no way she could know. He alone enjoyed Antony's confidence – just he and one other man in an office so exalted there could be no doubting his integrity. Nevertheless, he would be glad when Antony returned. Matters were bad indeed on the Continent, and he had been slipping back and forth often enough for someone to have perhaps noted his movements. There could come a time when he would be in the wrong place at the right moment for his enemies – and Charles would find himself secretary to Basil, the new Viscount Marchmont. Heaven forbid!

He excused himself soon after, secure in the knowledge that the two ladies would be spending the morning in Caro's studio, with Amanda as her sitter, and returning to the house to lunch at three.

He dealt with the waiting correspondence and untangled a minor domestic crisis, then took a turn in the garden, his thoughts dwelling pleasantly on his beloved.

He had not seen Sybilla that day, and it came as an unwelcome surprise to hear her voice close by. He stopped and looked about him.

A screen of bushes separated him from the stone seat where Antony had disclosed his private worries. He realised he had wandered from the path, and could not be seen. Only for a moment did he hesitate. A gentleman did not spy. Today he would not be a gentleman.

It soon became clear that Sybilla was talking to her brother, and she spoke low and hurriedly, as if she feared being overheard.

'I can wait no longer. Your stupid scheme to have her committed as a madwoman could never have come to anything. I have discovered there is no divorce permitted between husband and wife if one party is thrown into Bedlam. Of what use would that be to me?'

Basil seemed amused. It raised Charles' hackles just to hear his sneering tone.

'It might have done little for your purpose, dear sister. But it would greatly have enhanced my chances of inheriting our cousin's consequence. 'Tis inconceivable that he would again essay matrimony, should his wife die while incarcerated in an institution for the insane – which is something that could be easily arranged, I warrant.'

Charles' response surprised him. Normally slow to anger, and cynical enough about human nature, he found he was shaking with passion. He longed for a horsewhip, or better, a sword. Restraining himself he listened further.

Sybilla was shrill with throttled rage. 'That is so like you, to think only of your own needs. Well, you have not been so clever after all. Caroline has recovered her wits well enough, and walks very carefully upon the stairs. She also locks her chamber door at night. We must hit upon another scheme, with all speed. When Antony returns he must find his wife gone, and in such a manner that it appears she has run away from him to another man. That will finish her with him.'

'Jack Thornton, her old lover.'

'Why not? 'Twould be the very thing. I can write a note for Antony in a fair copy of her hand. Such a cruel blow to his pride would banish any desire to go in her pursuit.' Her voice curled lovingly about the words.

Charles had the fancy that he was listening to a snake, the venom dripping over its forked tongue to give each syllable a deadly coating.

'Would you kill her, sister?' Basil seemed surprised at the strength of her hatred. 'This is not our dear Antony, whom we so love. We speak of his wife only. And you are aware that there is a vast difference between pushing her down stairs, or leaving her exposed in the winter night, and what must be inevitably revealed as murder, should the plan fail. It would be highly dangerous.'

'I am not such a fool as to run my head into a noose. The plan will not fail, if you will do as I bid you. And Caro, sweet, *beautiful* Caro will not die. But she might wish for death before long.' She lingered over the words, relishing them, then went on. 'You will take her by surprise in that place she calls a studio. There will be no one there to help her. Knock her senseless and have her carried away to the docks. I know of a man there who procures for me the herbs and other matters I need from Jamaica. He will keep her hid until she can be smuggled aboard ship and sold abroad into slavery – a very particular form of slavery that I do not think she will find to her liking.'

Basil began to laugh. 'You know of a man . . .'. My dear sister, you are without price.'

'And you, brother, are without hair or wit. This is no laughing matter. She knows I am her enemy and will take precautions; and the very minute Antony sets foot within the door she will tell him. This is our final chance. Do you not agree? Or do you lack the stomach for such enterprise?'

He must have hesitated. ''Tis dangerous. If Antony discovers our conspiracy he will have our necks stretched for us. But, the reward is great. Very well. I agree. Our cousin will be napped and stowed before the week is out. I too "know a man".'

'I do not doubt it. But make haste. Antony may return at any moment.' She paused. 'There is a small matter: Jack Thornton. 'Twould be useless to make it known that Caro has run off with him, then have him seen about town and in his clubs.'

'Why do you think I suggested his name? He is on the point of sailing to Val Pareiso in South America – some matter of an estate left by a relative. Do not fear. There will be no loose ties to this package. But . . . what is my reward to be?'

She seemed surprised. 'Why, what it always was – to inherit all upon Antony's demise.'

'And when will that be, sister?'

'Ah. I see. Well, brother, you have no choice but to possess your soul in patience. If anything of a fatal nature were to occur to my beloved I should know how to act. He is mine, and no hand shall touch him but mine. You understand me?'

Never had Charles heard less lover-like tones. He shuddered. Even his unimaginative nature could envisage the kind of future Sybilla had in mind for her 'beloved' Antony. How could he have been so deceived in her?'

'And, Basil, there is the fact that with Caroline gone, there will be no brat in her image to stand in your way.'

Charles strained his ears in the silence that followed. But nothing more was said. Both brother and sister understood each other too well. He drew further into the bushes and waited until their footsteps had retreated along the path to the house. Then he took in a deep breath and wiped his forehead with his kerchief.

He had seldom been privileged to overhear such villainy, and he scarce knew what to do with the knowledge. Antony should be told, but he was not available; and Charles himself was not in such a position of authority that he could accuse the plotters and have them held without proof.

He hestitated to warn Caro. She was of such a volatile nature he could not guess what her reaction would be, perhaps to tax the two, who would then quite possibly attempt to silence her forever. What to do?

Lord Edward! No, he was too old and too far away. In the circumstances, the Honourable George could safely be dismissed. Should he hire men to watch over Caro? Whom could he trust? Unlike Basil and Sybilla, he did not number hired villains amongst his acquaintance.

He took his problem with him into his workroom.

In her studio, Karen mixed paints and thought about the composition she had sketched. The canvas had been stretched and placed on the easel, and a wash background applied. Now she was ready to begin the portrait.

Glancing up at her model she paused, and said in a mock stern voice that masked uneasiness, 'Amanda, I want to bring up something which may embarrass you. I hope you will let me say it all without interruption.'

Amanda dropped the rose she was holding poised above a vase and turned her head. She looked mischievous.

'You terrify me, my dear. Have you uncovered my sordid past? There was a music master at my school whom I hero-worshipped for a whole six months. I even took up study of the violin for his sake, much to my father's distress. However, my youthful passion could not survive the vision of poor Mr Hasluck falling into a horsetrough, his wig floating away from a pate as pink and shining as a strawberry milk pudding.' She crowed at her remembered disillusionment.

'You really are the most awful chatterbox!' Karen threw down her palette and advanced on her friend.

Amanda still rocked with mirth. 'I beg your pardon. It was the sight of his wig, so brown, so exquisitely curled, floating in the hay and scum like a water rat which had lost its way.'

Grinning, Karen took Amanda's face between her palms, returning her to her pose. This morning her dress was unusually subdued, apricot muslin over an underdress of cream, with small flat bows running from neck to hemline. She had protested to Karen unavailingly. The favourite red velvet driving dress had been pronounced unsuitable, and that was that.

Returning to her canvas Karen picked up the brush and started work. 'Listen, and rest your tongue. I simply wish to tell you how much I value you as a friend. I never before had a close companion. When I was growing up I seemed always to be moving about so much. It was easier to be a loner.'

Brown eyes softening, Amanda said, 'I have seen the loneliness of your soul. 'Tis written in your face for those who care to look. You were torn from your companions once too often, I collect – and to protect yourself from pain you abjured all intimacy.'

'You're right, as always. Where do you get your insight, Amanda? Never mind. Just lift the rose a little, will you? That's perfect. I was in a state of shock for some months after my parents died. The people at the home were good to me, I suppose. I don't really remember. And my first fostering family were kind enough. Then Mr Yeats lost his job and had to travel about looking for work. I was enrolled in five schools before I turned ten. Eventually the Yeats were forced to send me back, and I lived with a cottage family before being taken by the Martins. She was a discontented shrew with a faithless husband. They fought so much that my hardening opinion of all relationships ended up setting like cement.'

'Cement?'

'A form of liquid building material that hardens in the air.'

'I comprehend perfectly. The joys of friendship were outweighed by the pain of inevitable parting; and your child's view of married bliss was a jaundiced one. Pray continue.'

'By the time I entered my teens I'd grown the toughest shell . . . Blast it! I'm talking to you in modern cliches! I must be more upset than I thought.' The brush slipped from her hand and she bent to pick it up, wiping it carefully on her rag. She had wanted to say 'thank you' without emotionalism, but it was harder than she'd realised.

Abandoning her pose altogether, Amanda rushed up and put an arm around Karen's waist and led her to a seat.

'There is more than friendship between us, there is love. You should not try to thank me for something that has come about naturally. Have you not seen how you attract others to you with the energies you display? Look at Chloe, so hostile at first, so withdrawn before you came. She is a different child, and she dotes upon you unashamedly.'

Karen's pinched look began to fade as she absorbed the words. 'You have a lot of common sense under that mop of hair. It's true that Chloe is like my own daughter. And I have noticed lately I seem to be meeting more congenial people. I don't mean the folk at the dispensary. While some of them are fearful rogues, others could give a bishop points for honesty. I'm talking about the ton. You know, I once thought polite society consisted entirely of the vain and empty-headed. Sport and lechery, clothes and the pairing off of partners were the only interests. But you've shown me a different world. Your entertainments in your home, the circle of friends who follow the arts – why, you're a British Madame Recamier!

'And this is without your charitable interests. I know you do far more than anyone could guess to help the less fortunate, and I love and respect you for that. I also like your friends, and they appear to like me.' She grinned. 'Of course, I'm not everyone's choice of dessert. There is Sybilla.'

Amanda's shrug expressed her opinion of Sybilla. 'That woman is incapable of giving or receiving affection. She is centred upon herself.'

'Her genes tell against her.'

'Your pardon?'

'I don't think I'll try and explain that one.' Karen sighed. 'I give you my pledge that before I leave here today I will take myself in hand and revert to being a lady of the times.'

Amanda nodded. ''Tis best to live always in the present, for how else shall we order the future? Having been given free will to choose our path we should do so, and not be continually looking behind.'

'You're right. Why look back?' Karen kissed her cheek and stood up. 'Now, if I could trouble my model to take up the position once more?'

As she worked she thought over the conversation. It dawned on her that she was beginning to fit into her new world remarkably well. She had a circle of almost friends – people with similar interests who accepted her as she was. She had her painting and her charitable work, and Chloe and Amanda. Why wasn't that enough?

She hastily changed her line of thought. Charles and Amanda. That situation would bear looking into. Continuing to work, she said casually, 'You're in love with Charles, aren't you?'

When the silence lengthened uncomfortably, she looked up at Amanda, who sat with suspiciously bright eyes and stiffened posture. 'I'm sorry, Amanda. I have no right to pry.'

'I do not regard your question as prying. However, I am unable to answer.' She checked herself, pressing her lips tightly together.

Karen added a touch of carmine to the lips and stood back, all her interest apparently centred on the painting. She waited.

Amanda's voice shook. 'Love is not a greatly valued commodity in our world. One should not wed to please oneself alone.'

'I don't quite understand. Are you saying that your mother would object to the match? I know that Charles is poor, but he does have prospects.'

'My mother knows nothing of the matter, and I beg you will not enlighten her.'

Karen faced her friend and openly examined her face, but learned little from that wooden expression. 'I have offended you. Amanda, believe me, nothing was further from my intention. I love you. You are the sister I never had. All I want is your happiness. Please, don't shut me out of your confidence.'

Amanda hid her face in her hands. A second later she was in Karen's arms being comforted. 'You are one of the golden people, Amanda. You give to others, constantly and unstintingly. You deserve some happiness yourself.'

Amanda shook her head against Karen's shoulder. Karen continued to hug her. 'All right. I won't say any more. It's your affair, and I'll leave it to you. But, please, if and when you need to talk to someone, come to me. Will you promise that?'

Amanda sat up. She had not been weeping, although she looked sad. 'I find it difficult to talk of my own affairs. I do not intend to close you out, my dear friend.' She sighed. 'I should tell you that I have received the addresses of another gentleman who is both eligible and kind. I . . . have not rebuffed him.'

Karen swallowed before asking, 'Will you tell Charles?'

'Not yet. I do not know my own heart, as yet. I must consider.'

Yes, consider everyone else but herself, thought Karen, and end up marrying the man who can look after her mother, breaking her own heart and Charles' into the bargain. But Karen had promised to drop the subject.

She turned back to the easel. 'I need just a few minutes more. Do you feel you can sit a little longer?'

'Of course. My emotions may be in some disorder, but not my limbs. Let us return to work.'

Fifteen minutes later Karen laid down her brush. Amanda abandoned her pose and came to stare at the wet canvas, all the while massaging cramped muscles.

Karen grinned. 'Well?'

'I shall not administer to your vanity. You must be well enough aware of your talent.' Amanda dropped the prim tone. 'Caro, I have something to say to you.'

Karen's eyes flew to her. 'Charles?'

'No, not Charles. Pierre Marnie. He is coming to London. Not only is he intrigued by your problem, but he holds out some hope of a solution.' She clasped Karen's hands in hers and squeezed them. 'My dear, I am so happy, and so sad. I do not want to lose you.'

'Nor I you. But, Amanda . . . Adele. To be my old self . . . Oh, I'm so confused.' Joy and grief warred in her, clogging her voice. Her constant hopes, her frequent bouts of despair, her secret desires, all combined in a melange of emotion that forbade any kind of clear thinking.

'I know.' Amanda's smile was a poor effort.

'There's so much to think about – so much at stake. I had begun to lose hope. Amanda . . .'

'Don't say any more, my dear. There is nothing to say. We shall simply have to wait with what patience we can until we hear the man has arrived safely. He has undertaken a dangerous journey. We should not be too sanguine.'

Charles still hadn't solved his dilemma when the ladies returned home. To tell, or not to tell? Antony's absence had placed a heavy burden of responsibility on him, and for once he didn't feel equal to the weight.

Amanda gave him no chance to speak, even had he not decided to let the matter rest, at least until they had eaten their luncheon.

'My dear Charles, you will be in raptures when you view my picture. I vow 'tis the cleverest thing. Caro has even managed to show my dimples, without making much of my more than ample proportions.'

She put out a hand to her friend, who said in a robust tone, 'I hope I have shown your nature, Amanda, and that's more to the point. Anyone who looks at the finished portrait will know you for what you are, a good, kind woman who cares about her fellow creatures.'

For once Amanda was left with nothing to say, so Charles said it for her. 'Thank you, Caro. You have the gift of discernment. I fancy your own nature leaves little to be desired or Amanda would not have taken you so much to her heart.'

Karen looked pleased. 'If we are throwing bouquets, what about one for a loyal and trusted friend who keeps our lives running as smoothly as he can?'

Amanda clapped delightedly, and only ceased when Bates trod into the room to announce that all was in readiness for her ladyship to partake of her meal. Clearly he didn't approve their levity, and it was with twinkling eyes that both ladies took Charles' arm.

He did wonder what it was that had put them in such high spirits.

The painting alone scarcely seemed enough cause. But the light in his love's eyes should not be dimmed if he could prevent it. He kept his worries to himself, promising his conscience that he would deal with them before nightfall.

Chloe came down to visit in the small parlour and the three ladies spent a pleasant hour playing at spillikins, at home to nobody. Charles kept an appointment with an acquaintance and came home to find the party in the library, showing Chloe the exact point she occupied on the globe, and vaguely looking over some of the tomes that had stood undisturbed for decades. They did not appear to have found much of interest.

Most of the books had been purchased as a job-lot to furnish the shelves (by a Frensham with absolutely no literary pretensions whatever). There was little to the taste of Antony or Charles, and even less to please a lady. Chloe, however, discovered a folder of sketches on a lower shelf, squeezed between volumes of religious dissertations, and apparently long ago relegated to this position of unimportance to moulder.

Blowing off a coating of dust, she staggered to the desk with the heavily bound folder. 'Look, Mama. Here is a picture of our house.' Her shy smile was intercepted by Charles, who took great interest in the new relationship between stepdaughter and stepmother.

Karen looked up. 'Show me, darling.'

The bundle was thick, but the sketches lay loose in their binding. She leafed idly through, then stopped. The quality of her stillness attracted the others' attention.

'What have you found, Caro?' Amanda came forward, her eyes suddenly anxious.

Charles, too, felt uneasy, and could not think why. He thought Caro had grown pale, and she was rigid as a statue.

She didn't speak. Her hands lay on the desk top, pinning the sketch there. She looked not at it, but through it, seeing something visible only to her.

Charles peered over her shoulder. ''Tis merely a sketch of Ashbourne Manor – a very good likeness indeed. I wonder who was responsible for it?'

Karen continued to stare into space.

He looked curiously at her, while Amanda took both her hands and shook her gently. 'Caro! What is it? Why do you look so?'

Karen gave a shudder and her eyes refocused back on the sketch.

'Did you say . . . Ashbourne Manor?'

Charles nodded. 'Yes, where Lord Edward resides. I believe I did say that Antony will not go there. 'Tis a pity. You would find it a lovely place.'

'I have been there.'

'I fear you are mistaken. You must be thinking of another of Antony's houses, perhaps the one in Wales – '

'No. I know this place. I know that garden, and the ruined tower . . .' Her voice trailed away. She moved decisively, closing the folder on the other sketches and retaining the one of the Manor. Then she turned to Amanda. 'My dear, will you excuse me? I cannot explain to you at this precise time, but I know you will understand and forgive me if I leave you.'

'Of course. But, may I not know your plans?'

'I am going down to Devon.'

'Caro!'

'I must. Charles, you will see to Chloe in my absence?' She dropped down on her knees and looked into the child's eyes. 'And my little Chloe will be a good girl while I am gone, and not give nurse any trouble.'

Chloe nodded solemnly and kissed her.

'But, Caro, what would Antony say?' Charles pulled at his lip and prepared to be stubborn. 'You can't go posting down to Devon like this, without adequate preparation.'

'I can, you know. Although I shall not go post, of course.' She looked at him steadily. Even on her knees her air of authority was not diminished. 'Kindly make the necessary arrangements. My own preparations will be simple and I expect to leave within the hour.'

Charles helped her to her feet and pulled the bell cord. When a servant entered he gave orders for the light travelling carriage to be brought around with the greys poled up, and a pair of outriders to make ready.

'Charles, there is no need for an escort.'

'My dear Caro, Antony would have my head if you were to travel out of town unaccompanied. In fact, I am not at all sure that I should not accompany you myself.'

'No thank you. I wish to go alone. I must tell Lucy to pack a bag.' She swept out of the library, leaving the three to stare after her whirlwind passage.

'What do you suppose has set her in such a flutter?' Charles was ruffled. He could not accustom himself to Caro's new decisiveness that took no note of his advice, nor even asked for it. In Antony's absence he felt it was his place to give counsel. His sense of fitness was chafed.

Amanda patted his arm reassuringly. 'I would not hazard a guess. Nor would I try to stop her. Whatever drives her to this start is important to her, and we do not have the right to interfere.'

He put a hand over hers, pressing it to his arm. 'My dear . . .'

'Hush. Not now, with the child present.' She indicated Chloe's neat brown head bent over the sketches.

He felt a moody desire to send the child to perdition. Why was there always another present on the few occasions when Amanda was within reach? He saw her socially, but never with an opportunity for more than the most casual exchanges.

'She is not aware. Amanda, I must speak with you privately. Will you drive out with me tomorrow to Richmond? I have an errand there, and we could take a picnic luncheon.' He openly pleaded with voice and eyes, and was satisfied to see her weakening.

'I had thought to spend the day with my aunt, who has an indisposition which confines her to the house, but – '

'I too am lonely. I pine for the sunlight of your presence. I am wan and listless in the shade of your absence. I need to say what cannot be said in the company of others.'

She gave great attention to her gloves, smoothing them on with precise little tugs and pats. 'I should be delighted to drive out with you in the morning. Shall we say at ten o'clock?'

He bowed, letting her see his elation. His arm trembled a little as she laid her hand on it and moved with him to the door. He had forgotten Chloe. So, apparently, had Amanda.

The child came after them with a rush. 'Are you leaving, Aunt Amanda? You did not bid me farewell.' She clutched at Amanda's skirt and raised her cheek for a kiss.

Amanda bent down to her, then abruptly straightened and took her leave, barely allowing Bates time to reach the main door ahead of her.

Charles stood where she had left him, a slight smile on his usually stern mouth. She had not rebuffed him. She would hear him out. And he'd be damned if he couldn't wear down that soft heart of hers and have her return his regard. What mattered their different estates? He knew that would not weigh with her. As for his lack of fortune – he would ask Antony to help him to preferment of some kind. Perhaps some sinecure in the Defence Ministry, one that he could fill while remaining on as comptroller of the Roth estates. There were ways.

He took Chloe by the hand and led her upstairs to her nursery.

CHAPTER 15

IT TOOK KAREN more than thirty hours to cover the distance between London and the village of Ashbourne St Mary, just over the Dorsetshire border into Devon. She changed horses every ten miles or so, but on that first night never paused for longer than it took to pole up a new team, or for an extra few minutes to take a coffee and roll, before urging her coachman on. She was in the grip of something stronger than reason, and it urged her to hasten towards the discovery that lay ahead.

The sketch of the Manor lay in the pocket of her travelling coat, and at intervals she brought it out and studied it by the light of the full moon, trying to elicit some hidden meaning. There had to be more to it, far more than the fact that the Manor was familiar to her.

The ruined tower was particularly intriguing. No, more than that. It disturbed her. Not just a melancholy reminder of destruction and decay, it held a message for her, and a threat. 'Keep off', 'Danger lurks here!' Had the stone walls been hung with hazard lights and a skull and crossbones, the warning could not have been more explicit.

The nerves along her spine crept like a thousand caterpillars right up into her hairline. She was afraid to go on, but the urge to do so was greater than her fear.

And all the while she fended off that other matter claiming her attention, the small matter of a possible return to her own time.

There came a moment when she couldn't ignore it any longer. Deliberately taking down the mental barrier, she let the message flood in on a massive tide of mixed feelings, swamping everything, even the urgency of her flight. The rhythm of the horses' hooves beat out a phrase in her mind – 'going home, going home'. At last, after all the tears, the refusal to accept what looked like the inevitable, the months of gradually dying hope – at last she saw the possibility within her grasp. It devastated her. She couldn't cope with the irony. Just when she'd come to a point of reconciliation with her strange new life, the pendulum had been thrust back again.

Struggling to maintain her balance, she drew on her memories. With a feeling of shock she groped for Adele and found her a pale and wavering ghost, the chubby baby features now overlaid in her mind with a piquant, elfin grin, blonde curls turned to a smooth dark cap of hair moulded to Chloe's head. And behind her stood another shadowy figure that she would not, dare not acknowledge.

Guiltily she strove to recapture something she'd thought she would never forget. The love for her daughter was still there, and the pain at separation, but it had faded a little, overlaid by present needs. Her life's focus had shifted without her noticing it.

The realisation hurt. A terrible lump had risen in her throat and she sobbed dryly. No relieving tears for such an unworthy mother, she told herself, administering a mental whipping for disloyalty. How could she have forgotten? Adele remained in the hands of a sometimes brutal, always insensitive father, cared for by strangers, needing Karen. But she hadn't really forgotten. Distance and hopelessness had simply worn away the sharp edge of sorrow, blunting it to make it bearable.

Of course Chloe, too, needed love; but she did have Antony. His performance didn't fool Karen any more. She'd discovered the real Antony – a loving man who had been hurt badly enough to guard himself, yet remained vulnerable. Now that Chloe was no longer afraid to show her own loving little ways, she and her father were rediscovering each other. It was one of Karen's principal joys, watching this happen.

And what of your own needs, said a small interior voice? She was stern with it. Her long-made decision hardened – no involvement. She might have fallen in love against her will, but she had managed to keep the fact hidden, more or less. Charles and Amanda might suspect, but they would never violate her privacy; Sybilla discounted her as a rival, and Antony himself gave no indication of anything more than a pleasant attraction. He was still heartwhole with his Jenny, and always would be.

Having decided all that satisfactorily, she then found she could enjoy the relief of tears, and sobbed for a good three miles before pulling herself together.

The carriage rolled into Ashbourne St Mary at ten o'clock on a beautiful summer's evening. Karen felt tempted to order the coach on to the Manor, but remembered the weary driver and outriders. The horses, too, were hanging their heads. She'd been on the road for nine hours since lunch, and felt exhausted herself. At The Bull, a somewhat basic hostelry but the only one available, she took a room and private parlour, leaving a message at the stables for the morning.

Although acclimatised to luxury during the past few months, she was too keyed-up to care about small, stuffy rooms and unaired beds. Lucy had been left in London and so Karen accepted the willing services of the one chambermaid to unhook her gown, and sponge and press it against the next day's use. Then, for the better part of the night she sat at the window in her wrapper and thought about her life back in twentieth-century London.

She thought about Theo and his kindness to an unknown artist, about Billie's revelations and her strange, ambivalent attitudes. She considered her own ill-starred marriage and its result, Adele. She searched for a plan, something that would make sense of it all. After a while her recollections started drifting further back. Time gathered speed, unravelling like a dropped ball of wool down a staircase. She saw herself running backwards, running away from things, from people, from the many challenges that could have taught her so much, had she taken them up.

At the beginning of the strand was her birth, and the five cosseted years with Mama and Papa. Then came the huge tangled knot of the accident, the cutting of the strand, and herself a loose end blown in every breeze. Figuratively fingering the frayed ends of fibres she relived the awful desolation of that time. Now she understood the reactions of the child she'd been then – the periods of hiding alternating with wild demands for affection. Love at any price, from any source, an impossible and ultimately disastrous burden on the people responsible for her well-being.

What a waste. What an appalling waste. If she had the time over she'd use it very differently. For one thing, she would hopefully grow up and start taking responsibility, instead of letting life just happen to her. If she did get back to her own time she'd make sure she lived every minute to the full, extracting the essence of each moment and sharing it with others around her. Never again would she travel alone. The lessons of the past were not to be ignored. Too much of the world suffered hurt and loneliness, and Karen Courtney must not add one more featherweight of pain.

She'd try again with Billie – sealed off in her hard little shell. She'd support Theo's efforts to promote her and her work, instead of trying to hide away from the cruel, unfeeling world she'd believed in; and she would try to deal fairly with Humphrey, to see his point of view, and maybe win him over to seeing her own. She smiled wryly at that. Yet, miracles had happened, and they were by their nature totally unexpected and unlikely.

The moon set and small night creatures came out and moved about the darkened fields at the back of the inn. The delicate scent of wisteria blossom came in on the breeze, reminiscent of the vine twined about her bedroom balcony at Rothmoor House. She sighed and stretched and went to lie on the bed for the brief hour left before dawn. Time enough to make promises if she ever found a way back again. The French seer, this Pierre Marnie, had first to make it safely to London, and then, hopefully, come up with a means of sending her back through time. It was asking a lot. It might prove to be impossible. Meanwhile, she had this urgent need to explore the subject of the sketch, Antony's boyhood home, which had such a feeling of familiarity to her – and such a feeling of foreboding, too.

The sun had risen only a few degrees above the horizon when the carriage stopped a good hundred yards before the gates of Ashbourne Manor. Climbing down to the road Karen dismissed the coachman and walked the remaining distance. To avoid bringing out the gatekeeper she slipped through a gap between post and park rail, and started up the long oak-lined drive. She wanted to arrive unheralded, to see the Manor before it saw her. She struck out purposefully in her sturdy boots.

The day had begun with a low-lying fog, and she could see no more than three paces ahead. Warm moist air was sucked into her lungs. It clung to her clothes in fine drops, dampening her hair until it flew into wild ringlets. The oaks closed in around her, an eerie guard of honour advancing and retreating with the movement of the fog. There was no sound but the crunch of her boots on the gravel.

Something called from amongst the trees. She turned swiftly to face it, her heart pounding uncomfortably. It came out of the fog, swooping across her face for a brief, shocking instant, and was gone. An owl, a bat? Something with teeth and claws? Best not to think about it.

Her breathing became laboured. The ground was rising and the fog began to thin. She tried to analyse her feelings, to rationalise them so they could be put aside as unimportant, external to her purpose. Was she afraid? It seemed like it. She felt jumpy, and the difficulty with breathing wasn't caused entirely by her exertions.

Why was she scared? Being alone in a fog was not a good reason. Perhaps she feared what lay ahead. Perhaps some part of her brain withheld a dreadful memory. What secret did the Manor hold, and how could it pull at her so strongly that not even a squadron of bats would cause her to turn back?

The last two oaks stood like sentinels on either side as she emerged from the fog onto a wide grassed area. To left and right the drive curved away. Across the lawn, a distance of at least two hundred yards, a stone-flagged terrace rose, and above it the walls of a perfect Palladian house, its pillared portico lined with stone urns, its balustrades running the length of two side wings, set back from the main building. One of these wings, the eastern, was much older. It had been built of mellow Tudor brick, then later cleverly incorporated into the new design, with the continuing terrace and shrubberies balancing the whole.

How restrained and beautiful, she thought. Just like the sketch. Only one thing marred it – the tower. She could just glimpse it away to the right at the end of the Tudor wing, its blackened stones bulging like an excrescence on a work of art. It must have been part of an even older original building. But why, having suffered partial destruction, had it been left to fall into greater disrepair until positively dangerous, by the look of it?

So many questions, and no answers. Abruptly she set off along the right-hand fork, skirting the lawn and main house and following the line of the terrace. The tower drew her. It exuded a horrid fascination that she couldn't begin to account for.

The sun had cleared the tree tops and reflected in the windows of the Manor, so that the house seemed to peer from behind frosted lenses. Karen felt overlooked. Her nerves on edge, she forced herself to go on – on toward the tower.

It loomed much larger than it first appeared, a broken, crumbling thing, but powerful still. It had walls three feet thick at the base, the stones cracked and soot-blackened, the narrow window slits naked to the wind. The roof had gone, and most of the upper storey, leaving just a finger of stone, a calcified bone pointing to the sky. A part of the stairs still clung like broken piecrust to the curved inner wall. But where the damage was greatest, it had fallen away to reveal great heaps of rubble, weed-choked broken blocks like the fallen headstones of giants. Karen felt she was looking at a tomb.

A cloud must have passed over the sun. She shivered, and felt a chill run through her. Then she began to shake. No effort of will could control the rigours that gripped her body. Sweat broke out on her forehead and ran down her face. Her stomach heaved with nausea. Then, worst of all, a hidden door in her mind swung open. She looked through. She saw the flames, heard the ravening howl of the monster as it stampeded up the stairwell after her.

'Chloe! Antony! Nooooo . . .!' Her scream faded as she collapsed on the scarred turf, her head inches from the doorsill where Antony had fought to save his Jenny, and lost.

'I'll tell you, she would not heed me. She was determined on the journey and I had no power to restrain her.'

Charles faced an Antony he had not seen in years, a man whose icy intensity of rage could quell a mob uprising, and actually had done so when a rabble of unemployed weavers smashed the mill machinery of a friend before going on to attack the owner's house. Having witnessed their rout Charles could swear to its truth, without quite knowing how it had been achieved.

Now Antony had that same look, controlled, but with a set jaw revealing how rigidly his control was exercised.

'You could have found a way – the carriage disabled, the coachman drunk . . . Something of a like nature should have occurred to you. But to permit her to set off alone on such a journey . . . to that place!'

Ah! There was the root of the trouble, thought Charles. It was not so much Caro's absence as the knowledge of where she had gone. Antony ceased to be rational where the Manor was concerned. It loomed in his mind as a place of horror and destruction which could not be allowed to touch anything or anyone he valued. The fact that his father chose to live there was beside the point. He had no jurisdiction over the old Earl, frail and arthritic but determined not to quit the home he liked best. Antony could not move him.

But Caro, his wife, for whom he cared more than he knew, had chosen to go to that place he feared and hated.

Charles understood that his friend had to find a whipping boy, but could not resist saying in a deliberately aggrieved tone, 'I did send outriders.'

'One would hope so!' retorted Antony, unappeased. He strode over to the library window and stood with hands clasped behind his back, his shoulders set like rock. He had done no more than remove his travelling coat before asking Charles to make his report.

Charles wished he'd had better news. He could not even give a satisfactory reason for Caro's sudden flight. To say she had seen a sketch and was seized with a sudden desire to view the original would scarcely find acceptance with the angry man before him.

Antony whipped around. 'When did she leave?'

'No earlier than five o'clock.'

''Tis light until ten, and then a full moon. She may not stop.'

'The road is bad beyond Richmond, and she is unused to travelling such distances. She will surely spend two nights resting. Antony – '

'Have Lightning saddled and brought around immediately. I must change.'

'But, you have not supped nor slept, after the journey you have had . . .' Charles put out a hand as Antony brushed past him.

He paused in the doorway and looked back. 'I ate and slept on the crossing. Do as I bid you, Charles. You will forward the papers in that packet on the desk to Lord Liverpool, and inform him that I shall do myself the honour of reporting in person before the week's end.' His look of strain lightened and he added with an attempted smile, 'Never fear, Charles. I am aware that you could not curb my lady's starts once she had the bit in her teeth. But I must go after her. I cannot endure the thought of her in that hellish place. It once caused me to lose the treasure of my life, and I will not risk another such loss.'

Charles was thoughtful as he put his orders in train. He had been in the right of it. Antony cared very much for the welfare of his Caro. It was a far cry from his attitude of a few months ago – an intriguing reversal.

Only after Antony had left the house did it occur to Charles that he had not spoken of the matter of Sybilla and her brother's plottings. Of course, with Karen away, there would be no immediate danger to her. Yet he could not be at ease. Who would credit such perfidy within the actual heart of the family? He pondered on this for a time, concluding that there must be a strain of madness somewhere in Lady Oriel's august lineage.

Then another thought came to him, of an even more horrifying nature. His assignation with Amanda would have to be postponed. It would take him some time to gain access to the Foreign Minister, and the precious documents could be entrusted to no one else. He swore a long and comprehensive oath before sitting down to pen a note to his love, and looked up to see Bates' shocked gaze upon him.

Antony rode throughout the night. His horse all but floundered under him, although he had been careful to give it periods of ease, and he was forced to stop by mid-morning. In the yard of a roadside hostelry somewhere on the Salisbury Plain he reeled from the saddle, flung an order at an ostler, and downed a tankard of ale before throwing himself on a hastily prepared bed. A boy pulled off his boots and coat and took them away to be cleaned, and he slept like a man bludgeoned into unconsciousness. Six hours later he was on the road again.

His third horse went lame not thirteen miles from Ashbourne St Mary, and neither cajolery, threats nor bribes could find another that night. Through necessity, he spent several hours chafing at the delay, unable to rest and trying, without success, to put a rein on his runaway imagination.

Reason said that Caro would be in no danger at the Manor. The only persons in residence were his father and a small staff to serve him and maintain the property. Aware that he could not justify his apprehension, Antony felt it growing, feeding on the delay like some monstrous serpent that swelled and coiled itself around his heart.

Wide awake, and oppressed by the walls of the inn, he paced the courtyard cobbles through the early hours, greatly disturbing his fellow travellers and suffering the tortures that can only be inflicted by an imaginative and emotionally engaged mind.

He knew now that he loved his wife, and had done for weeks past. As far back as the first evening when she appeared in public after her accident and was approached by Jack Thornton – even then, he'd known. Seized with fury, he'd wanted to attack and throttle the man in Lady Wharton's drawing room.

Of course he could not admit to common jealousy. That would be too confronting altogether. What? He, in love with a woman whose activities had fed the gossips so well for a twelvemonth – a woman who had smirched his name and laughed as she did so!

But that was not the Caro he now knew. How greatly she had changed, softening in some ways and growing firm and strong in others. It was like seeing a reverse image in a looking glass, the same yet not the same. Some alchemy had transformed her most unlovable characteristics. Where she had so often shown the world an expression of churlish boredom, or other evidence of self-interest, now there was grace and a gracious attention and care for the feelings of others. There was also a guardedness, with an underlying sadness that provoked his most deeply felt urge to protect. She seemed haunted by an inner vision he could not share, and he was even jealous of that.

He welcomed such hungry pain as an indication that he *could* react. For too long he had let life flow over him, with little more response than a dead man; but now the vacuum in his heart had filled with warmth and feeling. He loved again, and his world had gone from grey to all the rainbow hues. His hearing, long deaf to all but the call of duty, was now attuned to the many songs of happiness this world held. But . . . she had gone to the Manor.

The sluggish nag eventually provided for his use would not be hurried by any means he could devise; yet he turned the wretch's head into the drive of Ashbourne Manor an hour after sunrise.

At his hail, the gatekeeper hurried from his cottage, fumbling his work in the fog.

'How goes it, Crimmins?'

'Yarely, my lord. I thank 'ee.'

'Has there been another caller in the past day – a lady?'

Crimmins swung the gate and stood back. 'No, my lord.' He sounded surprised.

Antony paused, then urged his horse forward. He might as well go on and warn his father and the household to expect company. As well, a solid breakfast would render him more fit to organise the search.

Fog swirled over his boot-tops, surrounding him in a milky sea. If it had not been for the oaks as markers he soon would have strayed off the track. Crimmins' report had not been reassuring. Caro was still somewhere on the road, without his protection. Anything might have happened to her. His mind churning with visions of coach accidents, highwaymen and worse, he found himself hovering at an agonising pitch of anxiety. He wanted to cram his mount to a gallop, to release the unbearable tension. But he retained sufficient sense to know this could bring disaster on them both. To go crashing through fog amongst trees invited broken knees for the horse and a broken neck for himself; and who then would care for Caro?

For Antony, minutes, hours and years were the same until he finally emerged from fog and trees onto the freshly scythed grass before the house. Ashbourne Manor. At last he saw it again, this scene of halcyon contentment and the blackest, most bitter despair. Long repressed emotions swept over him. He sat trembling, and the tears that he would not permit himself before ran down his cheeks as he mourned his past lost love. It was a cleansing, and he felt the better for it. But it was not finished yet. Before he could go to Caro with a free heart he must face that last, most dreaded symbol of his despair, the tower. He nudged the horse on towards the eastern wing.

Blinded by reflection from the windows, all he saw was a grey and blackened blur, a jagged stump of stone that might have been anything. Then, rounding the terrace he came to the heaped-up ruins. The doorway with its massive lintel still stood, and at its step lay a huddle of blue cloth.

Dread hit him over the heart with a physical pain. He bowed over in the saddle, a silent litany of curses and prayers weighing him down. This was not happening. It could not be.

Clutching the pommel, he willed himself to retain his senses. When his breath returned he slid to the ground and flung himself on his knees beside the still figure. Gently he lifted her and turned her over.

Her eyes were closed. Her lovely face was scratched and smeared with soil. But the bosom of her gown rose and fell evenly.

Thank God! Thank God! Holding her to him, he buried his face in the bright springing hair and sobbed, a man reprieved from damnation.

Once again she woke in a strange room, and with a feeling of disorientation. She'd been in the middle of a strange dream and it lingered, mixing with waking reality so that she was unsure of where she was, or even who she was.

Light poured through windows to illuminate the pretty floral walls and hangings of a bedchamber. She looked about her, still confused, then centred on the man slumped in a chair beside her, holding her hand as he slept. He had not shaved, his stock beneath his chin was creased and grubby. He looked exhausted.

Antony. Her eyes roved lovingly over the dishevelled figure. She wanted to smooth back the thick dark hair falling over his forehead, and erase the lines of exhaustion that added years to his face.

Her fingers must have tightened on his, because he was suddenly awake and looking into her unguarded eyes. What he saw there struck an answering spark in his own.

He moved to gather her in his arms. 'Caro, my dearest girl.'

'Dear love, what is it? Why do you name me so?'

His grip tightened convulsively. She stifled an exclamation. From a distance of inches his gaze had an intensity that almost frightened her. 'What did you call me?'

'Dear love. 'Tis my name for you.'

His voice seemed to rasp in his throat. 'And what is my name for you?'

With his fingers biting into her shoulders, she said on a gasp, 'My . . . my lady sweet. It came from the love poems we read together, do you recall? Why do you ask?'

His grip slackened and she fell back against the pillow. Sinking into the chair, he stared ahead of him. Colour seeped from his face while she watched, leaving it waxen. His expression had an edge of horror.

'Antony!' She sat up and put out a hand, but he drew back as if from something repulsive.

'How could you know? How could you do this?'

She said anxiously, 'My dear, you are not well. I shall send at once for Dr Styles. Or, better, I shall go down to my stillroom for a decoction of dandelion flowers and a root that I know of . . .'

'Great God! What is this?' He was on his feet, trembling like a tree buffeted in a storm. His face was so terrible that she cried out and sprang from the bed to hold him to her.

'Antony, you must sit down.' She gave him a push, and as if all power had left him, he collapsed back into the chair. Kneeling, she took his hands in hers and chafed them. Her eyes searched for signs of what really ailed him.

His own eyes closed in denial, he reasoned to himself, 'There was Feathers' reaction. He knew her. Then the way she used her maid, refusing to let her sit up late to wait on her. Her changed manner, her sweetened temper. Then Chloe. The child now dotes on her. Why did she come here? She has never cared to live in the country. She knows Styles. And now . . . this.'

'My dear, will you not let me help you?'

His hands turned in her grip, and now she was held fast, imprisoned in a relentless hold. His eyes were beams of concentrated energy. 'Tell me, who are you. What is your name?'

'Are you funning, Antony? This is no time for games . . .'

'Tell me!'

'Antony! You are hurting me. You know I am your wife, Jenny.'

The silence stretched, time stretched. It seemed they had sat there, eyes-fast, forever.

Suddenly he was on his feet, dragging her to the looking glass that stood in a corner of the room. Pulling her hard against the length of his body, her back to him, he faced her in reflection.

'Then tell me, Jenny . . . who is this?'

She stood and stared. The beautiful woman in the glass looked back at her with bemused eyes.

'Well?'

When she continued to stare dumbly he gave her a little shake. 'Tell me about this glorious creature with her termagant locks, and the face and figure that set half London afire in her first season. Tell me how she could be my little brown Jenny, my lovely, sweet Jenny? Can you explain that?'

Still she stared. She'd heard him speak but the words passed by her like wind over a lake, scarcely rippling more than the surface. She'd gone down to a place where he could not reach her, and in those depths she could see herself in two distinct facets – as Jenny, as Karen. She heard Amanda saying, 'Give credence to the possibility of a soul being reborn in another body, in another time,' and she knew without any possibility of doubt that this had happened to her.

Once she'd inhabited the frail limping body of Jenny Marchmont. The many-faceted spirit that was the intrinsic She, the personality that could never fade or die, had chosen to pursue that particular lifetime. It had also chosen the role of Karen. She was a composite of both, and of many more men and women in countless lifetimes. She was a soul caught between time frames yet bound to the karmic wheel that decided her fate.

With a sigh she released herself from Antony's slackened hold. It seemed he could no longer bear to look at her. Like a blind man, he stumbled across to the chimneypiece and stood there, his fisted hands resting on the shelf, his head bowed. She didn't fear the jealous rage he'd once shown her. He was beyond that. She could feel his immeasurable hurt in her own heart, and went to him, saying softly,

'Antony, question me. Ask me what you will and I shall answer truly.'

She waited, then went on. 'Do you remember me telling you months ago that I had come from another time in the future? It was the truth, my dear. My name is Karen Courtney, and in my own life I have been married and born a child. For my birthday I was given a miniature of a gentleman of the Regency. It fascinated me. I knew that face. I had seen its original. And yet, I knew that couldn't possibly be so. In tracing its origin I was led to a country house in Devon, a house called Ashbourne Manor – a house with a ruined tower.' Her voice faltered.

Antony's shoulders moved, then he was still.

Karen continued. 'Something happened to me at that place. A thing buried deep in the most forgotten part of my mind was triggered by the sight of that tower. I felt overwhelmed with panic, stunned by it. I couldn't think or see. It was awful. I never want to experience such terror again.'

This time she paused because her voice had dried up. She swallowed, and when he didn't respond, eventually went on. 'I don't know what happened after that. Amanda seems to think I must have fallen and injured myself, and that my spirit was shocked out of my unconscious body. What I do know is that I came to my senses in another time and place, and in the body of a stranger.

'Amanda believes that Caroline died from that fall downstairs. She thinks my roaming spirit entered the vacant body before it ceased to function. That explains my strange behaviour as Caro – because I was not Caro at all. I have had to *learn* how to behave like a woman of her times. It hasn't been easy. I've never ceased to long for my own place and time, and for the little daughter I was forced to leave when she needed me.' A sob broke off her narrative. She couldn't go on.

Then Antony moved. Slowly he turned to her and she saw his ravaged face. He brought his fists down to his sides. His voice was weary, as if he had difficulty in forcing it out.

'Let us suppose that I credit this farrago. What possible connection does it have with my Jenny? If you are as you aver, this woman from a future time, you cannot be Jenny as well.'

'I am both,' she said calmly. Meeting his gaze was possibly the hardest thing she had ever done. His torment was her own, and she could do nothing to help if he refused to believe her. 'Do you know anything about reincarnation?'

'I am told it is a mystical eastern belief in the recurrent birth of the soul – ' He broke off. 'No! I am no simpleton to be taken in by such claptrap! If that is the sort of explanation I am to receive . . .' Shaking his head he turned away and moved towards the door.

'Antony!' The urgency of the cry stopped him. 'Dear love, do you recall our last day spent together in the tower? You were to ride out to meet with some of your tenants. It had been a hot summer and there were crop losses, and much discontent over them. We played with our baby girl and talked a little and loved a little, and then, I shared with you a secret that no one else held.'

Arrested with his hand on the latch, he stood immobile, waiting, as if her next words would mean life or death to him. Very slowly he turned his head and looked at her.

'Oh, Antony. We were so happy. We were to have another child.'

Their eyes locked, building a bridge between them, so tenuous and frail, yet quivering with unspoken hopes. Karen felt as though she had run a great race and collapsed on the finishing line. The bones of her spine and legs softened and melted, letting her slide down to the floor in a billow of silk. But yet her eyes held his, sending him a message that had transcended time.

His whisper had the clarity of a shout. 'No one else knew. Only we two.'

'Only we two,' she echoed.

'I cannot, yet I must believe it. You are Jenny?' It seemed he could not take it in. His hand still clutched the doorknob with whitened fingers. He looked at her dazedly, seeming rather to look through her at his own thoughts and visions.

She bowed her head and let the tears come. She could do no more.

He had crossed the room in three strides and gathered her to him, pressing her wet face to his chest so that he could feel the sobs racking her.

'Love, do not weep. I cannot bear to see you unhappy.'

'You always said that,' came the muffled voice from his shirt front. 'Even when I wept with happiness, you were distressed.'

Gently he lifted her chin with his fingers and she saw the tears standing in his own eyes. 'God has been good to me. He has sent you back to heal the wound that has drained my heart's blood for four years. I am a whole man again.' His lips came down to meet hers, blotting out all misunderstanding, all need to explain.

CHAPTER 16

'TELL ME MORE about your own time. I want to know the circumstances that shaped you. I have this need to understand everything about the woman who has me in her toils.' Antony looked down at Karen with such a laughing, tender light in his eyes, she felt tears spring into her own.

Her new emotionalism frightened her a little. It was so foreign to her. Ever since the day she'd finally acknowledged her Mama and Papa were never coming back to her, that the string of carers and foster parents would never feel the same way about her as her own parents had, she'd closed off one side of her nature. If love couldn't be coaxed or brought or stolen, then she'd learn to live without it, which meant denying all the softer, more vulnerable feelings that went with love. It was too easy to have them trodden on and mangled. Better not to let them out at all. Better to be a stoic.

She'd made the right decision. Just look what happened to her when she let Humphrey draw all those feelings out of cold storage. Yet, now she was allowing it to happen all over again. Was it wise? Was it safe? Was it possible that she'd been wrong, after all?

The early summer morning had begun to wake around them. The air thrummed with birdcalls and was heavy with the rich scent of roses – hundreds of them – creating a private bower for lovers to stroll in. Karen now knew a great deal about the Manor, although the memory of her life there as Jenny still remained fuzzy and out of focus. Her own latent homemaking instincts had been boosted by the recent discovery of a lady's memoirs in the bookroom, and in these a detailed account of the laying-out of the garden by Antony's grandmother, in an age when formality was the rage. The Lady Hermione, disdaining to be one of the herd, had gone ahead with her own notions of how a garden should look. The Elizabethan herb plots were added to, and the espaliered fruit trees, their limbs as thick as a man's arm, continued to roam over the red brick walls. Above all, the roses had been encouraged, grafted and added to, even given new red brick walls of their own to enclose and trap the sun's heat, creating an arbour more intimate and equally as lovely as that of Hampton Court Palace.

Karen paused to sniff at a particulary choice pink bloom, which her husband promptly picked and tucked into the bosom of her gown. The sight of long brown fingers gently moving among the lace frills made her feel weak at the knees. Nothing had prepared her for the night she'd spent with Antony renewing their knowledge of one another, nor the many nights that followed.

While able to recall her life as Jenny, over the last few days the memories had faded. Now it was much like rereading a loved story – a dream of the past, to be treasured and kept green in the memory. But it wasn't real. The emotion that powered all experience had seeped away from her recollection. It was the difference between a rose long pressed between the pages of a book, faded and frail and dry, a mere redolence of what a rose really was, and the vibrant perfumed reality, richly velvet, sequined with dew, its golden heart wide open to the world.

Thus, Antony's lovemaking had come as a shock. She still remained, in most ways, a woman of the twentieth century – mentally emancipated, emotionally prepared, but hoping not to be used. Romantic yet cynical at the same time. Used to going it alone, she'd longed for a soul mate – and got Humphrey, who taught her what it meant to be really used.

Now there was Antony, a gentle man in the best sense, a strong man who used his strength to protect, not violate. In his hands she experienced for the first time the selflessness that made two into one, and emancipation sank without trace. Totally bewitched, she gave herself up to the new experience, half fearful that she'd wake one morning and find she'd dreamed of being loved. Knowing what she was inviting in the way of guilty suffering, she made her choice. Whatever opportunity might come in the future, she'd stay with him.

'You have not heard me, little featherhead. What are you thinking?' The teasing voice recalled her.

She flushed a little, but answered honestly, 'I was thinking about love, married love. Our love. I am still overwhelmed by it. I never dreamed that two people could be so close, nor so full of trust for each other. We even seem to have the same thoughts, simultaneously.'

He smiled wickedly. 'And what are my thoughts at present, do you suppose?'

Laughter bubbled up and out. 'The usual ones, I imagine. And yes, they are my thoughts, too. Oh, Antony, I'm frightened at such happiness.'

His arms came around her and the rose was crushed irretrievably between them. Karen felt she might lose her senses, caught in the powerful turbine of passion this man could arouse in her. No one had told her such feelings existed. She wouldn't have believed them. Who could relate the power of command with tenderness, the wildness of riding the stormy winds like a Valkyrie, and the peace when cradled in the valley of a man's cupped hands? No poet she ever heard of could find the rhythm and metre to describe two madly pulsing hearts in the moment of revelation. No song ever written, no painting, no creation of the hand and mind of man could do justice to these things. They must be experienced.

When they drew apart she brushed her fingers across the bruised sweetness of the rose, and said in a shaken voice, 'I do love you so much. I've never said that before to anyone. I didn't know I *could* say it.'

Antony turned her face up to his. He searched each feature, examining, seemingly memorising, as if she were a map and he must learn his way so that it would never be forgotten.

'My Caro. Do you recall the particular sonnet that compares a woman with a summer's day? "'Thou are more lovely and more temperate. Rough winds do shake the darling buds of May, and summer's lease hath all too short a date. But thy eternal summer shall not fade." You will always be my Jenny, a part of me... and my Caro, and the sum of all the lovely parts of you scattered through time. I am the most fortunate of men to be granted a second chance at heaven on earth.'

'We are both fortunate. I... my life in my real time was not happy. It was largely my own fault. My marriage was such a disappointment that I rejected love, or rather, denied that it even existed. But for you, I might never have known what it was like to give until the giving came back a thousandfold. With you I feel empowered. It's like a gift of wings so that I may take flight. It's... beyond any words.'

Keeping an arm about her he stroked her springing hair back from her forehead and dropped a kiss there. 'You had no one at all?'

'There was Adele. I have told you about her.' She couldn't keep the sadness out of her voice.

'My love, there is no way for you to return to your little daughter. Can you not be happy with me, and with Chloe, who is also your child?'

'I can't help being torn. It's useless to long for what I cannot have, yet if offered the choice, I couldn't bear to give you up. I love you and I love Chloe, but, God help me, I want more.'

He held her close, comforting. She felt the steady beat of his heart beneath her cheek, and knew how fortunate she was to have his support in every way. Telling herself to stop crying for the moon, she gave herself up to the enjoyment of what she had.

They took a picnic lunch into the park and spread it beneath the shade of a massive chestnut tree. Antony's semi-crippled father, the Earl of Roth, kept to his own apartments for most of the day, although in deference to Karen's presence he struggled into evening clothes and dined with them. Karen felt that he was wary of her, which made her sad. She thought him a fine old man whose intellect and will allowed him to rise above his physical disabilities. He led a disciplined and rather spartan life in his suite in the western, modern wing, only emerging upon occasion in a wheeled chair to take the air on the terrace. With the help of a secretary, he worked each morning on the compilation of a history of his line, but he never discussed this. His conversational skills eased their meetings, but she felt she was kept at a distance. He was an enigma to her, and one she'd have liked to solve.

Karen fed her man and was filled with the contentment that this brings. Inspecting the remains of the chicken and pasties, the orange peel, the near empty wine bottle, she remarked, 'I should like to show you a modern picnic. It would startle you.'

'I am not easily startled.'

'Well then, you would be nonplussed. I defy you to describe the taste of salami and cream cheese bagels, passionfruit pavlova, coca-cola, hot dogs, chilled fruit cocktail . . .' She stopped and laughed at his expression. 'That wasn't fair. I'm sorry. I come from a world where anything portable can be whisked from any place on earth to halfway around the equator in a matter of hours. Pineapples and bananas from the tropics can be put with strawberries from our own gardens and crushed ice from the nearest fridge . . . Oh, I haven't described a fridge . . .'

'If it can be carried on a picnic then I should very much like to have one. Crushed ice could be used to cool the wine.'

'It can't be carried. It's too big. And you would need electric power. No, that's stupid. We take a cooler on a picnic . . .'

Antony grinned. 'You are becoming confused, my love. But I will admit to an enormous curiosity concerning the hot dogs. What is their purpose?'

Karen stared at him. What a Pandora's box she'd opened. Where to begin to explain? How?

Antony's grin widened. 'Now I fear it is you who are nonplussed.' Then his amusement faded. 'Caro, you must have a care when speaking of such matters. 'Tis an uneasy thing to know the future, and those who can are seldom understood by others.'

She nodded. 'I will guard my tongue.'

'But not with me.'

'No, not with you.'

Later, his manner turned solemn once more. As they gathered together the remains of the meal and placed it in the basket provided, he said, 'There is a thing I need to know. Caro, can you tell me, will England succeed in crushing the French tyrant?'

She could understand his anxiety. Matters stood badly at present, with England desperately alone against a totally subjugated Europe. The news-sheets cried it all over London. Cartoonists showed the Tsar in his vast frozen eyrie vacillating like a weather cock. The Crown Prince Bernadotte walked a tightrope between him and the predatory French eagle, while the new-freed American Colonies still made warlike noises.

She carefully folded a napkin and laid it in the basket. 'Napoleon will fall. The beginning will be his hollow victory in Moscow next year.'

'Moscow! So, his Imperial Highness will align with us after all. But – a French victory, you say?'

'Napoleon's army cannot yet be defeated by force, only by attrition. He will have no choice but to retreat, and the Russian winter will bring him down.'

Antony seized her and pulled her erect, dancing her about the grass in a mad mazurka. 'A victory! The tyrant will fall!'

Laughing and capering he danced her around the basket and back to the foot of the tree where they collapsed together on the picnic cushions.

Breathless, Karen warned, 'It will not end next year, my dear.

Not until 1815 will the western world be able to finally lay down arms against the French. Wellington will be the hero of the hour, and Blucher, the Prussian commander.'

Antony sobered. 'So long. So many lives to be lost. He will have a heavy accounting to be made, the little Corsican.'

'He will. But we both know that it will be paid in full measure. There is no escaping the universal law.'

'You really believe that? I find the mysticism of the east sits not well in my practical mind. Yet, you are the living proof of reincarnation.' The deep tones caressed her more sweetly than any physical touch. 'I adored you as Jenny. You were the music of nature personified – a nymph of the woodland, a darling of the gods made mortal. Now I am struck dumb by the new Caroline, the wayward flame who has slipped into my heart and holds it prisoner.' He placed her hand over his heart, then raised it to his lips.

'And more, I find I have wed a woman of the future, a fine, intelligent creature who speaks her mind and does not hesitate to champion the unfortunate, no matter who opposes. I was proud of you at that dinner, so many months ago. You told those time servers you saw through their equivocations. You knew what should be done, and so did they.'

She shook her head. 'They were guests at our table. I should not have embarrassed them'

'Embarrassed!' Antony threw back his head and laughed. 'They know not the meaning of the word. You caused but a momentary pause in their step, I assure you. Still, it was well done. Few women would care enough for the cause, and too much for the possible social consequence of plain speaking. I fear you will not be popular with many of your peers.'

'I don't give tuppence for them. Do you, Antony?'

'By no means.' He let go her hand and sat back, resting comfortably against the tree trunk. 'In fact, I should prefer to leave them all to their paltry little lives and take up permanent residence with you here at the Manor. What say you, my lady sweet?'

She could have hugged herself for joy. But she answered carefully, 'Is that what you really want?'

'It is indeed. You will not long for the delights of town?'

'Never! As Amanda would say, "'tis a famous notion, my lord". Just you and Chloe, and life in the country. What heaven.' She hesitated, and he waited for the thing she found difficult to put into words. 'There is something, one of several matters we have not yet discussed.'

His parody of comical dismay drew only a brief smile from her. 'It's serious, Antony. It concerns your . . . your secret work.'

His expression didn't alter and she gave him full marks for performance. Perhaps he'd learned to school his features to save his life.

'What do you know of a secret work?'

'I overheard you one day speaking to Charles. The library door was ajar and I heard enough to know that your so-called journeys into the country are actually across the Channel on business for the government. Oh, my dear, I have worried about you.'

'I see. I have been criminally careless.' He seemed more vexed with himself than her. 'Have you told anyone about this?'

'Of course not! I'd never endanger you. Your life is too precious to risk. Must you continue with this work?'

He leaned forward and cupped her face. 'Can you really ask that of me? With our country assailed from every quarter?'

'No. Of course not. You must do what is right for you.' She attempted a smile. 'Just remember that it's my life too, as well as yours. You have relinquished it into my care.'

'I will remember.' His lips sought hers, and they lay embraced in the moving shadows of the chestnut leaves, outside of the world and time.

Hoofbeats on the ride coming from the east wing disturbed them. Karen looked up to see a lone horseman following the freshly scythed avenue between the trees. He sat wearily and his mount could be roused to little more than a plodding walk.

Antony came to his feet, drawing her with him. "Tis Charles. I know that awkward mare. Why he will not let me mount him decently . . .'

'He is proud.' Karen studied the approaching silhouette against the harsh afternoon light. It was almost too bright. There was a storm in the wings. 'Do you suppose he has urgent news?' Her throat tightened. 'Dear God! Not another journey so soon!'

He squeezed her waist then released her and went to meet Charles. 'What brings you from town? Has Boney sailed up the Thames and taken the Tower?' He grasped Charles' shoulder as he slid to the turf and swayed. 'By thunder, you must have ridden hard, man! What's to do?'

Charles slapped dust from his coat and tried to speak and could not for the dryness of his tongue.

Karen came running with the last of the wine. 'Did you not stop at the house, Charles?'

He drained the bottle gratefully, then nodded. 'Aye. They told me where you would be found. I did not tarry. I have letters for you, Antony, and . . . a word in your ear, if you please.' He glanced significantly at his employer.

'You are asleep on your feet. Take that breakdown of yours to the stable and we shall meet in the library within twenty minutes.'

Too weary to react to the slight upon his mare, Charles hauled himself back into the saddle and trotted off.

Karen watched him go, frowning. 'He is worried, Antony. Do you suppose it really is bad news of the war?' She saw that he was lost in thought.

'We shall know soon enough. Come, love. Leave these things for the servants. My curiosity is as large as Charles' thirst.'

In the library Karen would not be dismissed. Charles, fortified with a glass or two of madeira, stood just inside the door, an uneasy spectactor of a battle of wills. Karen's chin was up. She had no doubt she looked about as impressive as a terrier bearding a mountain lion, but it didn't move her.

'I have a right to know if you are going into danger. Antony, it is far worse to have to fall back on the imagination. Can't you understand?' Now she had him by the lapels of his coat, emphasising each sentence with a tug.

Half-laughing, he pulled her hands away and held them in his clasp. 'Would you strip me, woman? Have done. You know I dare not share these secret matters, my dear. They are not mine to divulge.'

'What rubbish! I dare say I could tell you more about what's going to happen than you and all your informants and master planners together.' She released herself and sat down in the nearest chair, saying more calmly, 'The problem is that although you have accepted intellectually the fact that I do indeed have knowledge of future events, you cannot believe it in your heart.'

Charles made a sound, something between a gulp and a snort. She rounded on him.

'Yes, it's true. Whether you want to think so makes no difference. I *do* come from the future and if you will only bend your minds – you too, Antony – to the possibilities, you will see that I can be a help to you. I know roughly the sequence of events, the major battles, for instance, that will take place in Europe within the next four years. What's more, *I know who wins!*'

There was silence in the room. Outside the day had darkened as clouds scudded up from the south, bayed by the gusty voice of the storm. Karen felt a drop in temperature as the heavy floor-length curtains lifted and fell, ushering in the wind. Papers rose off the desk. A set of Chinese bells on the chimneypiece chimed sweetly. An eddy of cool air brushed her bare arms and she clutched them to her. The door opened slightly and a servant slid in, crossed to the window and latched it closed, then departed like a phantom.

Antony finally spoke. 'There is much in what you say. Truth to tell, I had not quite absorbed the fullness of it, being more taken up with other matters at the time.' He smiled at Karen, then turned to his secretary. 'You must agree, Charles, there is little point in shutting Caro out of our deliberations now that the truth is plain to her.'

'How did she discover it?'

'I did not tell her, if that is what you infer. She overheard us talking carelessly one night. Is that not so, my dear? As to the matter of her spying into the future for us, it would be difficult to overestimate the value of such information.'

Charles looked as if he'd very much prefer to do without this form of assistance, but he nodded obediently, and Antony went on, 'Caro has proved to me beyond doubt that she has existed in another time. No matter that you do not understand how. Please be assured that I am not mistaken in this. Now, I should be glad to see those letters.' He held out his hand for them, and seated himself at the desk.

Karen rose. 'I will send for candles. It is growing quite dark in here.' Having won her point she was prepared to give Charles the chance for private speech with Antony, as he clearly wanted this. She would give him ten minutes, and then come back to hear what plans were being made.

Also, with an extra person at table she wanted to make some changes to the dinner menu. Somehow, neither she nor Antony had managed to pay much attention to meals in the past week, while her father-in-law ate sparingly and never made comment upon the food. It was time she took up her role as mistress of the Manor if she intended to live here.

Having spoken to the housekeeper and conferred with the cook, she returned to the library in the wake of a footman carrying tinderbox and taper. She was thinking of Chloe, and how much better it would be for the child living in the country. A good governess could be lured down with the promise of high wages, while Karen herself wanted to spend so much time with the child, giving her all the love and attention she expected from her Mama.

And there were so many other things to do, like learning to ride and muddling in the garden. She could transfer her studio to an unused part of the house, and interest herself in the needs of the rural poor. Did the local borough provide a clinic, she wondered. Or was the poorhouse the only alternative for the sick and needy? Perhaps Amanda could be induced to pay an extended visit. She would join in her plans.

Her head buzzing with ideas, she re-entered the room and stopped, aware of an atmosphere that acted like a physical barrier.

A swift glance at Antony showed her a face smoothly masked against enquiry. Charles looked uncomfortable. She waited until the candles were burning, and the fire kindled against the sudden chill. When the door closed behind the servant she spoke.

'I can see something has happened. Are you going away again, Antony? Or is it something else.'

Charles edged towards the door. 'I believe I have one or two matters – '

'Stay, Charles.' The words were rapped out in an iron voice that Karen had not heard before. Charles stood still. Karen didn't blame him. She looked uncertainly at her husband's face and wondered whether she knew him after all. She realised that the mask was a covering for some strong emotion, but couldn't guess which.

'Caro, it seems that I must return to London within the hour, and alone. Charles will remain to bear you company. And my father, of course.'

The last words were such an obvious afterthought that Karen picked up immediately on the real message . . . 'you need Charles to look after you'.

'Do you think it fair to leave me like that without telling me what is going on? I thought you had more respect for my intelligence.' She faced the mask and figuratively tore at it. She wanted no falsity between the two of them, no hiding, even if he thought it was for her own sake.

Charles said abruptly, 'He is going on another mission.' He faced Antony's fierce look. 'She should know, Antony.'

'I see.' She felt the blood draining from her face, but forced her wits to work. 'You will be needing Charles. He oversees all your journeys, I know. There must be a hundred ways in which he can help. I can come back to Rothmoor House until you return.'

'No!' thundered both men in unison.

'Well, well. There's more to this than I thought. You had best tell me, my dear. Are you afraid for me?'

The mask shifted, and for an instant she saw intense anguish looking out of his eyes. Then he recovered.

'I beg that you will cease this probing, Caro. I do not intend to tell you any more. If you wish to spare me further worry you will obey my wishes and stay here at the Manor with Charles. I shall send Chloe and her nurse, and Bates and some others of the staff also, to see to your comfort.'

'Why not a regiment of troops and a cannon?' she flashed angrily. 'It seems I can't be trusted to look after myself in London.' It was her bitter disappointment speaking. They'd had just one week together, and now their lovely idyll was shattered. Antony had reverted to the man he used to be. While he might speak of worry for her, his abruptness, his withdrawal into concerns barred to her, told another tale. Had she been a mere interlude, after all?

His hand came out to her, then dropped. 'My dear, you do not understand.'

'No, and whose fault is that?' She knew she was behaving badly, but felt too upset to care. She ran to the door and opened it, keeping her face averted. 'Since you will not trust me, I have nothing more to say. I shall not come down to dinner tonight.'

Before either man could move she'd whisked herself out and closed the door on them. Racing upstairs to her room she locked that door against intrusion and gave herself up to an explosion of grief and disappointment.

Outside the storm dashed itself against the walls of the Manor, building to a crescendo for the next hour then gradually losing strength. Exhausted by her inner tempest Karen fell asleep to the sound of water gurgling in the leads and the retreating mutter of thunder in the hills.

She slept through the dinner hour and most of the night, awakening to find Antony had already left with first light.

CHAPTER 17

Breakfast with Charles began awkwardly, but Karen's reassurances that she was not going to act out an emotional scene clearly came as a relief to him.

She had long ago realised that Charles lived most of his life vicariously. Denied the usual outlets of a gentleman of money and birth, he enjoyed nothing more than a little gossip, cornering the inside knowledge that made him appear a man of the world and intimately acquainted with momentous affairs. His connection with Antony's exploits could be shared with no one – except Karen herself.

Soon she knew all about the exchange of clandestine correspondence between the Crown Prince of Sweden and the Tsar, and Antony's part in the secret negotiations between the powers. When she reciprocated with details of imminent British victories under Wellington in Spain, and Napoleon's first major defeat in Russia, Charles could scarcely contain himself.

However, they came close to argument over his insistence on guarding Karen. When she found him immovable, she resorted to cajolery. 'Come, Charles. Are we not friends? Surely, whatever the danger, I should be safer knowing where it lies.' She could hardly credit her own coaxing tone. Six months earlier she'd have despised the use of feminine wiles, yet now they came easily enough. She was amused at the thought.

Charles crumbled. 'Very well, I shall tell you, because I believe you should be warned.' He paused impressively. 'There is a plot against your life!'

'Is that all? Stale news, Charles.'

'You could not know, for I overheard the villains plotting the very day you left London!' His nettled manner gave her even more amusement, but she hid this, sparing his fragile self image.

'Two villains. I wonder ... Sybilla and, yes ... Basil. Am I right? I see that I am. Well, we have known for some time about Sybilla, and Basil is an obvious choice if only because he's a nasty specimen of humanity. What were they planning for me?'

'Kidnap and slavery in the West Indies.' He could be terse, too.

The bald statement had more effect than any florid descriptions of what was entailed in such a fate. Karen felt her skin come up in goosebumps, and her near-empty stomach turned nauseous, threatening to reject the cup of tea she had just finished.

'How . . . unpleasant!'

He nodded, seemingly unaware of how shaken she was. Of course, she realised that to a man of his times such a plot was not particularly unusual, nor even reprehensible, had it not threatened a friend.

She did her best to copy his sangfroid. 'So, that is why Antony hastened back to town.'

'You will understand that he was most anxious to confront the two and warn them that their villainy is known to him. It is scarcely conceivable that they will attempt to harm you in his absence, but the possibility exists. Hence, you are to be guarded.'

'No wonder he was in such a fury. He was worried about leaving me . . . and I let him go without healing the breach.' Karen turned away, speaking to herself, rather than Charles. At that moment she hated herself, and knew that her punishment would be not to know for weeks whether Antony was safe or lying in some prison cell in Europe – or worse, in an unknown grave.

Concealing her self-inflicted wound, Karen went off to find useful and time-consuming occupation.

It had helped to discover a letter and a rose sitting on the chimney-piece of her bedchamber, overlooked in her hurry that morning.

The letter was a quotation she had never come across, and was not attributed. It read:

'Love is many things and all things. It can be a weapon or a tool – an article of usefulness, a grip, a plug, a rope to save a drowning man.

Love is used by us all. From day to day, by simply being, it enhances life. It has many aspects, and even in the passive form love can accomplish much.

Love is a force. Truth is its basis, honesty its crown. What or who are we without it? Lower than the animals, less worthy by far because we have chosen to throw away this priceless gift.

Rejoice in love. Spend it and use it and accept it. Let life be love and live it to the full, and know that it can never die.'

It was signed, simply, 'Antony.'

Karen puzzled over the meaning of the words. Were they meant to chide her for her hasty rejection, or as a reminder that love was impervious to such minor human vagaries. It didn't matter. At least Antony had not gone off to London angry with her.

Her next move was towards a better understanding with her father-in-law. While she waited for Chloe and her entourage to arrive, she decided to approach the Earl in his suite and ask if there was some service she could perform for him, such as reading aloud. Dressed in a becoming jonquil crepe gown, her magnificent hair bound in a matching scarf, and carrying a bouquet of roses she walked to the west wing and knocked at the entrance doors.

They were opened by a surprised servant, dressed in the Earl's livery of grey and burgundy.

'Please enquire of his lordship whether this is a convenient time for him to receive me.' She looked about her at the old-fashioned shabbiness of the furnishings, the books and papers lying in untidy heaps on every available surface, a chess table with a half-finished game, a wine glass with dregs staining the leather desktop, and decided that the old man was either very badly served or had a penchant for living in a mess.

While the manservant hesitated, a large ragged-looking dog rose from beside a wingbacked chair facing the window and came to inspect her. His rheumy eyes revealed his age, but she noted that he was well cared for, despite his peculiar rough coat.

'Hello, boy. You're an odd-looking one. Where's your master?'

He whined and turned his head to the chair. A voice she knew, aged yet with a lifetime of authority in it, said quietly, 'He is here. Pray enter, madame. Wilkins, a chair for her ladyship.'

Karen handed the roses to the manservant and took the seat placed for her, with a smile. In his mid-sixties, his lordship looked his age and more, the telltale twisted knuckles resting on the chair-arms showed why. His voice had the same timbre as his son's. Although she had no memory of him from her life as Jenny, at their first meeting she'd been struck by the likeness to Antony in the grey-green eyes under frowning brows and in the set of the chin. His magnificent mane of hair was white as the immaculate linen he wore, and there was nothing old-fashioned about the cut of his plain black coat. Well-kept hands displayed several rings, but he wore no other jewels.

'To what do I owe this honour, Lady Caroline?' There was no welcome in the words.

Karen kept her smile in place. 'I beg your pardon if this seems like an intrusion, but I wished to know you better. We have met only at dinner and you normally retire before we have an opportunity to talk.'

The heavy-lidded eyes surveyed her, and she continued quickly, 'I had thought you might appreciate someone to read aloud to you, or carry out other small tasks...'

'Thank you. I have servants to perform any errands, and I do not have a large correspondence.' He raised two fingers and the waiting servant stepped forward.

'A glass of ratafia for her ladyship, Wilkins.' When the man had gone he continued to stare at Karen, but she would not be put out of countenance. Calmly she looked back at him.

'Why did you come?' he said abruptly. 'Curiosity? Or is there something you want of me?'

'I have told you, I want to know you. You do not like me, I fear; but then, you do not know me. I should like a chance to remedy that. Antony and I plan to live here at the Manor and I would be on good terms with other members of the family.'

'How admirable, and how pragmatic.' He seemed cynically amused. 'And what if I have no desire to improve our acquaintance?'

'That is your privilege, my lord, and your loss, may I say? My aim is to make Antony happy, and any friction, or even lack of understanding between you and me will mar that happiness.' She leaned forward a little. Sunlight slanted in through coloured panes, casting rainbow patterns on her gown.

'Lord Edward, there has been too much hurt in Antony's life. Please, I beg of you, help me to cover over the scars and start afresh – for his sake.'

His knotted fingers tightened on the chair arm, then relaxed. He said slowly, 'It is inconceivable that you are the same woman as married my son. You could not have changed so much.'

'I have changed. Believe me, there is nothing of the old Caro left. I love Antony and will do anything to prove it.'

'Astonishing!' He paused as Wilkins returned and offered a tray with a glass to Karen.

She took this with murmured thanks and set it down on a table beside her. The dog came over and lay on her feet, panting gently and looking up into her face.

'Rufford has made his assessment, I see. Well, madame, it appears that we should indeed know one another better. You may begin by explaining this sudden decision to reside at the Manor. As far as I know, my son holds the place in abhorrence.'

Waiting until Wilkins had retired again, she began to weave a tale of rediscovered love between herself and her husband, his recovery from the horror of Jenny's death, the need for Chloe to experience a quiet country life. It all came together quite well, she thought, watching some of the lines go from Lord Edward's face. He must have worried about his son and fretted at his inability to help him. All he could do was to load further responsibility on his shoulders as the arthritis took stronger hold.

She left after half-an-hour, feeling her time had been well spent. They were to lunch together on the terrace that day and make plans for the entertainment and teaching of Chloe when she arrived. The child seemed to be much in his mind, and although there was no hint given, Karen could feel the unspoken hope for further grandchildren in the future. Her pulse quickened at the thought. Only let Antony return to her safe and whole and she would do her part.

Charles' presence was explained by the need to transfer estate matters to this new venue. He took over a small room at the end of the east wing and began transforming it into an office, happily co-opting furnishings and the services of maids, carpenters and men to act as couriers between the Manor and Rothmoor House. Watching in amusement, Karen noted that he had put aside his role of bodyguard in the enjoyment of his new circumstances.

His distinctly upbeat attitude was explained by the arrival within the week of not just Chloe, Nanny, Feathers et al, but also a travelling coach from which erupted an ebullient and outlandishly clad Amanda to tumble into her friend's welcoming arms.

'Dear, dear, Caro. You do not mind? I wanted to surprise you, and Mama can spare me for a few days since her sister has come to bear her company. And, what do you think? I have brought a trunkful of the latest country modes. You will be ravished, I swear. What think you of this?' She pirouetted so that the skirts of her orange twill travelling gown swirled out in a froth of petticoats.

Karen blinked. So harsh a colour against the fair skin could be just tolerated, but not with yellow and brown bands of braid criss-crossing from neck to hem, and a jacket, bodice and sleeves trimmed with huge gilt buttons that caught the sun and made her look like some kind of circus ballerina ready to perform in the ring.

'I am stunned, Amanda. I don't know what to say.'

Fortunately Charles bounded down the steps to take Amanda's little kid-gloved hands in his own, blind to everything but the fact that she had arrived.

'Miss Crayle! Amanda!'

'Dear Charles.' Her eyes were soft on him, Karen noted as she turned to receive Chloe's welcoming rush. Somehow Feathers became mixed up in the greetings, and it was a lively few moments before everyone was sorted out sufficiently to move inside.

While Nanny and her charge inspected the nursery, Karen took Amanda upstairs to wash her hands and remove her monstrous orange turban equipped with three brown feathers.

Her hair neat once more, Amanda plumped down on the settee and said, 'I am quite distracted with unanswered questions. Pray, tell me all that has transpired since you left London.'

'Where shall I begin?' Karen motioned away the maid who had been about the unpack the first of Amanda's trunks. 'You know you are welcome to stay until the last trump, but do you really need to travel with all those clothes?'

'Pooh! The veriest necessities, I assure you. Do not be so aggravating. Tell me what happened. Did you see something at the Manor to explain your strange urge to come here? Was there a clue to your translation from the future?'

Karen took a deep breath. 'Hang onto your wig, Amanda.'

'My wig? My wig? Oh, you wicked thing. You are funning me. And why have you reverted to that very odd manner of speech? I do beseech you, Caro, do not fall into the habit of forgetting all your training.'

'Sorry . . . I mean, I crave your pardon, Amanda. What I should have said is that you will be knocked off your . . . Dammit! Must I always descend to modern idiom? You will be greatly surprised by what I have to tell you.'

'Just tell me, you infuriating creature.' Amanda sprang to her feet and shook her friend, half in earnest.

'I must go back to the journey, first. It was while I waited overnight at the inn that I came to an important conclusion. I realised that Antony's happiness means more to me than my own. Yet, I also made a vow that, if possible, I would return to my own time and put my life to rights. I wanted to do all the things I should have done long before, to express the love hidden inside of me, be the person I was meant to be.'

Amanda looked disturbed. 'I cannot conceive how you could retain both ideals. They are quite incompatible.'

'I realise that. I had to make a choice.' The words came out jerkily, as if Karen's vocal machinery had begun to run down. 'I came to the Manor in the early morning. It rose out of the mist like an enchanted house. I walked down past the east wing just as if I knew my way, and I saw it – the tower. I saw it as it was four years ago, filled with fire. The flames came bursting through the shattered windows to lick the outer walls. I saw myself crouched under the roof, trapped. Chloe was screaming in my arms. I heard Antony calling, and my own desperate cry as I thrust my child out into space. I felt the skin begin to scorch from my bones. I saw my own death, Amanda.'

'Jenny! You were Jenny! Good God above! 'Tis past belief. Did . . . does Antony know? Can he credit such a thing?'

Karen smiled slightly. Her face was pale but composed as she took her seat opposite her friend on the settee. 'He had no choice. I revealed to him knowledge that only he and Jenny shared.'

Amanda was lost for words. Then her face crumpled and she leaned over to take Karen in her arms.

'What a dreadful experience for you. To relive such a death!' She sat back, still holding Karen's shoulders. Tears glistened on her plump cheeks, but she could smile. 'Do you know what you have done? You have proven the deathlessness of love, that the bond between man and woman continues unbroken as they go on to evolve spiritually from life to life. I always knew it, but you and Antony, together . . .' She sniffed and released Karen to search for her handkerchief.

Karen felt a weight of loneliness rolling off her. To share her experience with someone who truly understood was an immeasurable relief. Antony still had to come to grips with the theory of reincarnation, but Amanda *knew*.

'Is it always so, do you think? What of those who lose love, who separate and find other mates?'

'Do we not often lose our way? If it happens as you say, then the partners must wait to be reunited in another existence. But still the bond does not part. They are tied to one another, predestined to eventually meet and reconcile their differences before they may continue to grow.'

Karen looked thoughtful. 'You see my dilemma now, Amanda?'

'Indeed! If we find a way to return you to your own time, you must choose between present love and the possible loneliness of failing to meet in that particular future. There is no guarantee that you would meet in your life as Karen Courtney, is there?'

'Exactly. How can I possibly give up the greatest joy a human being can have? You do not know how happy we are, Antony and I. It's as though a whole lifetime of bliss has been released in essence all over us. We drown in it. It is almost too much.'

Amanda looked grave. 'Then enjoy it to the full while you may. For there are storms ahead, my dear. You know that I am able to foresee some events, or rather, sense the energies that surround them; and for some time now I have been aware of dark forces about you. There will be a struggle. You will face terrible choices. But the suffering will also bring great joy. I see the storms melting away in the heat of the sun, and that always symbolises to me the love of the Creator. So, take hold of your joy and experience it to the full, but be prepared for trouble.'

Karen was shaken. 'Did Charles speak to you about a plot against my life?'

'No. He mentioned nothing of it. Is it Sybilla?'

'And Basil. Antony has gone to deal with them. He will be away for some time.' Her voice cracked. 'Amanda, I was angry with him because he would not tell me. He was trying to spare me, and I let him go without so much as a God speed.'

'He will return soon enough and you may make your peace with him. Remember the storms to come, and do not waste your time of happiness.' Amanda looked so sad that Karen's thoughts were diverted from her own problems.

'Forgive me for prying, but, are you and Charles in difficulty?'

Amanda shook her head. She didn't meet Karen's eyes. 'Our affairs do not prosper. There are barriers.'

'You are referring to his lack of birth, perhaps? I did not think that would weigh with you.'

'It does not. I care nothing for an accident that should not be laid at Charles' door. He is as much a gentleman as any born to power and consequence, in fact, more so.' She sprang up in agitation and began to pace the room. 'How could you imagine that I would be swayed by such considerations?'

'I did not, and I truly beg your pardon. But, what then is the barrier?'

''Tis partly money.' It was said in a whisper.

'Money? You, Amanda?'

'Oh, you do not know what it is to be poor, to struggle to keep oneself looking decent, to appear beforehand with the world. But that is not the worst. Since my father's death, my mother has been unwell, as you know. She requires the best of treatment, a special invalid diet of expensive items, constant visits to Sir Henry Elsom, the specialist in diseases of the blood. He recommends that she should leave London and live in the fresh coastal air, but we do not have the money.'

'Why on earth did you keep this from me? I thought, I understood, looking at your wardrobe . . .'

'I make all my own clothes. The fabrics come from the Pantheon bazaar, as do my shoe buckles, my gloves, my stockings. I hire a carriage when I must have one, and walk whenever possible. My mother's small annuity from my father's estate pays our rent and buys a little food. We have just the one servant. I do much of the work myself. That is why I am considered over-particular in the matter of social engagements. I have not the time to attend most.'

'And you took on so much with me, shepherding me about, teaching, endlessly explaining. You must have had no time at all for yourself.'

'Hush. I do not regret one second of it, my dear.' Amanda smiled and held up her hand. 'I know what you will say. Your generous nature will require you to offer pecuniary assistance. Please do not do so. I should be forced to reject such an offer, and this could damage our excellent understanding.'

Karen sat back, the offer on the tip of her tongue stillborn. Her own sensitivity allowed her to feel Amanda's pride. She couldn't take that from her.

'What will you do? Does Charles have any hope of advancement? Could Antony help him?'

'I have no doubt that he will do so.' Amanda hesitated. 'I hope that Charles will find happiness with someone, some kind and loving girl who will come to him unburdened, and love him as he deserves to be loved. Caro . . . I do not think that my feeling for Charles is passionate love. He is more a friend.'

'There's someone else – that other eligible man you spoke of!' Karen knew she was right, and her heart ached for Charles.

Amanda nodded. 'Oliver Stamford. You have met him in my company several times.'

'Rumour has it that he is wealthy. Do you love him, Amanda? Are you sure you would not be sacrificing yourself for an idea of duty?'

'He is gentle and thoughtful, the most complete man of honour. He shares my tastes. He understands and supports me.' Amanda's eyes revealed her depth of feeling. 'You do not know how much that means. All my life I have cared for others, willingly. But always I have been the strong one. Oliver has a strength, a rootedness that is rare. He may give the surface appearance of mildness. You might perhaps think him a little inept socially; but few know him as well as I do. I know if I give my heart into his keeping he will cherish it.'

Two nights later Karen stole out into the garden long after the house slept. She had lain awake for hours worrying about Antony, and eventually put on her gown and outdoor shoes and crept down the back stairs to a little garden entrance she often used.

The moon-silvered lawns and trees beckoned her into an enchanted world. Dew-covered leaves on the rhododendrons glittered with a frosting of starlight, and down beyond them in a hollow of sable lay the lake, a molten mystery drawing her on. In her white gown she was a part of the landscape. She stood with her face turned up to bathe it in moonlight, and saw a flicker of movement over near the foot of the tower. When she really looked, she saw a shadow gliding past the fallen masonry and up onto the terrace of the east wing.

She blinked, and it had gone. Not just imagination, she thought. There had been someone, and the only possible place for him to have gone was through one of the long terrace windows. Without pausing to consider she hitched up her gown and ran back towards the house.

Arriving panting on the east terrace, she slowed down and crept more cautiously towards the end. The second window from the tower was open a crack, the window to Charles' office. A thief? What was there to burgle from an estate office except dull journals filled with details of husbandry? Or did the intruder intend to venture further within the house? With a cautious finger she edged the glass outward and stepped into the recess made by long velvet drapes. An arm snaked between them, jerking her forward into the room.

The cry surprised out of her was half-stifled as she recognised Charles standing by his desk. The man who held her was a stranger, a rougher type than the usual visitor to the Manor. She tried, unsuccessfully, to tug her arm free and said with all the hauteur she could manage, 'Will you kindly release me, and explain this secretive rendezvous in my house?'

Charles looked harried – his usual expression whenever he found himself explaining matters to her. 'Caro, Your Ladyship, allow me to present Monsieur Lafitte. He is . . . a sea captain with whom I have some dealings.'

Lafitte released her arm and stepping backwards, made her a bow. She saw a man of slight build, his brown hair clubbed and drawn back in an old-fashioned style over his ears. Plainly dressed, he lacked both coat and hat. His features were not memorable, but a pair of merry brown eyes disposed her to like him on sight.

'Lafitte? Not, Jean Lafitte, by any chance?'

'The same, madame.' Again he bowed. The brown eyes positively danced.

'Jean Lafitte, monsieur, is at present pirating his way around Central America. Have you stolen his name, or do you merely covet his reputation?' Secretly amused, she made her face stern, as befitted her position. Poor Charles, she thought. He looked so helpless.

The stranger was unruffled. 'Madame, you have penetrated my *nom de guerre*. I will admit to having adopted the name of that bold adventurer.' He swept forward a chair and assisted her into it. 'I am desolated to have so rudely attacked a lady. I took you for a spy, alas!'

Charles made an abrupt movement, then was still.

She looked at him impatiently. 'Do stop dithering and wondering what story to concoct for me. It's quite plain that Monsieur Lafitte is connected with Antony's activities and is here on business. I won't interrupt, nor even demand an explanation. But please, don't take me for a fool.'

Lafitte looked startled, Charles, resigned.

She turned to the visitor. 'Are you employed by my husband? Do you know where he is?'

'Madame...'

Charles broke in. "Tis useless to dissemble. Her ladyship is in Lord Antony's confidence.'

The brown eyes, which had lost their merry glow, turned on her. 'I regret, madame, that I do not know the whereabouts of Lord Antony.'

'Thank you. I will not question you any further. And I'll leave you to your meeting. But I really have to ask – are you a pirate?'

He laughed. '*Non, madame.* I am a sailor of fortune, a restless spirit that will not be tied down; but I do not prey upon others.'

'I have it! You are a smuggler. You bring contraband across from France, and no doubt carry people back and forth.'

An ugly look wiped the good humor from his face, and he took a step forward. Suddenly he was no longer the Gallic ruffler, but a formidable man.

Charles said sharply, 'Lafitte! Remember your place. Her Ladyship will not betray you. She knows how to hold her tongue.'

'I sincerely trust that you are right.' There was no doubting the menace in his tone.

Karen judged it prudent for her to retire. 'Goodnight, gentlemen. I shall see you at breakfast, Charles.'

It was difficult to sleep after her small adventure, but finally she did. In the morning, as far as she could recall, there had been no frightening dreams of Antony in danger, or worse.

Amanda had brought with her the entire contents of the Chelsea Studio, and Karen set up her work in a well-lit second floor room at the end of the east wing. Beyond the far wall lay the ruined tower.

She had mixed feelings about this, but decided that she should be sensible and put aside the past. Her memory of life as Karen Courtney grew more shadowy in contrast with the rich fulfilment of the present. Chloe was in every way her own child. She felt the bond between them strengthening daily, as the little girl blossomed in the aura of contentment permeating the Manor.

Lord Edward doted on his grandchild, and it soon became evident that Caro and he had found common ground. Delighted to be asked to sit for her, he had himself wheeled to the studio every morning. On the rare occasion when the light was not good enough he stayed to chat, often enough on the subject most dear to them both, Antony.

Amanda left for London a few days later, and two days afterward Antony returned.

Persuaded by Karen, he took his father into his confidence, and dinner that night was a lively affair as the two men rapidly renewed their old ties. Lord Edward, clearly delighted with his son's new-found happiness, swelled with pride in his exploits. Karen watched them indulgently, encouraging the old man to lead the conversation. The wine glasses were filled and refilled.

Antony smiled at Karen. 'You would like Sweden. The people may appear stiff and cold, like their buildings in the heart of winter, but they are actually very hospitable. They have such a wilderness of forests, lakes and streams; and in the summertime the fields of flowers should be seen.

'Perhaps one day I shall accompany you there, when the war is ended.'

'I fear that day will be long coming.' Lord Edward took up his glass and sipped the port that, despite Karen's presence, had begun to circulate around the table as soon as the final course had been cleared. It would appear that tonight she had been granted honorary membership of the male sex, she thought with some amusement.

As Lord Edward spoke, she looked over at Antony and shook her head slightly. Any explanation of her very odd circumstances to a man like his father would be unwise. He was a pragmatist, a dealer in real values, someone who believed in what he could touch and see. He'd never credit her story; and she would not risk losing his regard.

Charles said with elaborate casualness, ''Tis my belief that another four or five years may pass before Bonaparte meets his fate. Wellesley is an able man. Perhaps we shall live to be grateful to him.'

'Wellesley? I knew him before he was Viceroy in India. Is he not occupying the post of Foreign Secretary?' Lord Edward brought out his snuff box and laid it on the table. 'He is known to be an excellent administrator, but as for defeating Bonaparte, he'll never do it through the channels of diplomacy.' He offered the pretty gold-trellised box to Charles, who seemed overcome at the honour.

Gingerly taking a pinch between finger and thumb he laid it on the side of his other hand and carried it to his nostrils. He paused before sniffing.

'I was referring to the Marquess' brother, Viscount Wellington, leading our army in the Peninsula.'

'Ah, yes. The hero of Talavera. He does not impress me. The man is forever withdrawing instead of carrying the war to the enemy.' He frowned as Charles gave a gargantuan sneeze into his handkerchief.

Karen opened her mouth, then closed it on the hasty words that would have revealed foreknowledge of events. But she could not let the great commander go undefended.

'Wellington drove the French out of Portugal; and Massena's troops outnumbered him almost four to one. He has never yet been defeated.'

Her father-in-law's eyebrows rose. 'You are well informed, my dear.'

'I am interested enough to follow the war bulletins, particularly now that Antony is so involved.' She turned to her husband. 'Can you tell us about your latest mission, or must it remain a secret?'

He lifted his shoulders. 'I must not speak of some matters, but I can say that Bernadotte appears to be giving ear to Britain's blandishments. He actually fell into a fury and dismissed the French Ambassador last week. And it is a fact that he has for some time been intriguing with certain traitorous French ministers. I am hopeful of the outcome of our negotiations.'

Charles sounded mournful. 'He is still ruler of a small and not particularly important country – strategically important, I grant you – but without influence. After all, the Tsar is technically in alliance with Bonaparte, and he is the powerful one.'

'Alexander grows weary of his French ally, and wary of him. He is in communication with Bernadotte. In fact, I myself have a finger in that pie.' He paused to look at his father, whose fingers had slipped from the stem of his wine glass. 'Sir, I fear we have wearied you.'

With an effort, Lord Edward held himself erect. 'By no means. I have enjoyed the discussion. Yet I confess that I am unused to such late hours.' He turned to Karen. 'If you will excuse me, my dear, I will bid you goodnight.'

'Of course.' On an impulse, Karen rose and went to him, bending to kiss the wrinkled forehead. 'Goodnight, sir.'

Wilkins was summoned, and the Earl was escorted to the door by Antony.

Karen felt that Charles' attempts at conversation tonight lacked his usual aplomb. He seemed dismal, and she wondered whether Amanda had given him his dismissal before she left for London. Yet, surely she'd have said something to Karen. Lost in her worry over Amanda's affairs, she was alerted to a change in topic when Lafitte's name came up. Soon Charles was relating her adventure in the estate office when a smuggler came to call.

Fortunately, Antony seemed amused. 'Lafitte need not concern you, my love. He is totally loyal to me, although not necessarily to any particular nation. Money might be his god, but his word is his bond.'

'I'm glad of that. I was afraid I had done some harm. Does he help you leave the country secretly?'

'He does. His ship berths in various hidden coves along the coast, but our contact is his sister, who lives out near Seven Rock Point.' He grinned. 'You may trust Lafitte with your life, but not with your honour, you understand?'

'I shall keep it in mind, my lord.' They both laughed.

CHAPTER 18

Antony ordered champagne brought to Karen's boudoir, an elegant chamber, its walls washed in palest blue and ivory, and furnished with restraint. The Chinese rug was a particular favourite with her, as were the pale-wooded chests and the cream brocade chaise beneath the window. As a setting for the vivid Caroline it could not be bettered, although she'd had no hand in decorating any part of the Manor. Jenny was mistress here, the last woman to be chatelaine.

The thought made Karen uncomfortable. Or maybe it was a new shyness in her husband's presence. The week spent with him before he'd gone away should have made him familiar. In some ways it had. But their argument, bitter and devastating to her, and his perilous absence, had changed him. There were many facets to this man, and so far she'd discovered only a few.

Then there was the embarrassment of her own new-found sensuality. She'd never suspected its existence. If she could be so abysmally ignorant of her own nature, what hope was there of understanding Antony? She had no doubt she loved him, but she hadn't yet come to terms with the effect he had on her. And she was afraid to give herself wholly, to surrender her cherished independence, for fear of being let down again.

Antony had removed his evening clothes and donned a magnificent padded dressing gown, frogged and quilted in gold thread upon green. He looked very much at home in her room, lying back on her chaise longue and watching her through lazy-lidded eyes.

Her own gown was a chaste satin, enclosing her from neck to toe, and yet she felt exposed. She moved to the table and poured two glasses of champagne, saying with bravado, 'A toast to your safe homecoming, Antony.' She drained the goblet and poured another.

Antony rose and took up his own glass. It seemed to her that he towered over her more than usual, and certainly she distrusted his expression that seemed to hide secret laughter.

It annoyed her. What did he have to be amused about? She remembered the patronising way he had treated her enquiries, how he had ridden off without explanation, and said abruptly, 'What did you do with Sybilla and Basil?'

'I bundled Sybilla out the door and informed them both that their days of sponging were over. They may apply to their parents for assistance if they wish, but I will not continue to support persons who plot to injure my wife.'

'Is that all you did?' She was suspicious of such a mild reaction. There had been murder in his eyes when Charles told him of the plot.

He drank his wine and replaced the glass on the table, watching her move in agitation from one part of the room to the other. She could not seem to stand still. Gently he took her arm as she passed by and led her to the chaise, seating himself beside her.

'Did you think that I might call Basil out? Or even arrange for the two of them to suffer the fate they planned for you?' The teasing note left his voice and it hardened. 'They deserve far heavier punishment, but I cannot risk the scandal. Your name will not be bandied about while I have the power to prevent it.'

'I see.' The name again. Always he was concerned with the name, with preserving his precious heritage.

She looked away from his searching gaze and thought that she had never felt less amorous. She loved him, yes, but she didn't want him to touch her while every inch of her skin felt bristly with disappointment. All the difficulties and sadness she had suffered in the past months rose up to choke her. She felt she'd had enough to bear. And now the man she loved seemed remote, no longer the kindred soul whose loving empathy had reconciled her to her lot.

'What are you thinking, Caro?' He waited while she struggled to steady her voice. 'Well, my love?'

'I . . . You'll think I'm a fool.'

'I could never think such a thing. Look at me, Caro.' He turned her gently, forcing her to meet his eyes. 'What is troubling you, my heart?'

'You! It's you troubling me. I'm in love with a man I know and don't know. You and Jenny had this wonderful relationship which you remember and tack on to me, expecting me to feel the same. I mean . . . I know I was Jenny, but I don't remember what it was like. I don't feel it, here.' She hit her chest with a fist. The desperately inadequate words couldn't begin to describe how she felt. How could she expect him to understand? Tears of frustration swam in her eyes, blurring his face. The old terrible feeling of aloneness swept through her. What was she doing here? She'd been mad to think she'd ever fit into this strange way of life with a stranger who could make her heart turn over but hadn't the smallest understanding of the woman, Karen Courtney.

'I understand more than you might think.' His eyes held hers, but he did not touch her. His smile had gone, and something in his face made her wonder whether he had ever been young and carefree. 'We are two of a kind, Caro, both lonely creatures in search of someone to care about us. I believed my search had ended when I found Jenny, only to lose her. As you say, I see many of her lovely attributes in you, and I cannot help but revere them. But 'tis you I love, not a past memory – you, Caro, with your vital beauty, your intelligence and courage, your empathy with those in misfortune. Everything about you is precious to me, including the occasional prickliness and temper. I see many things that are not, and never could be Jenny. But Jenny belongs to the past. You are the present. You have given me back a reason to love life. You *are* my life.'

She sat very still, her hands clasped tightly in her lap, feeling his emotional outpouring as a tingle of awareness through her body. Something that had lain sleeping for a lifetime stirred – something so foreign to her that she had no terms of reference to describe it. It had sweetness and a poignancy that hurt her. It had no name.

In his striving to make her understand, Antony gripped her shoulders with hands that trembled, drawing her close. When he kissed her, her rigidity collapsed. She slumped against him, glad to be held and supported. His mouth was kind and undemanding, giving her the opportunity to draw back. When she did so, he sighed and picked up her hands, looking down at them as he made his plea.

'I know very well what your life has been these past months. I have seen you grapple with the unfamiliar, the distasteful. Your pain has so often been mine. You have been victimised by the restraints of our society, forced to play a role you dislike, burdened with fears and misunderstandings and grief. I wonder that you have retained your balance under such a load. And 'tis my everlasting regret that you were left to combat these things alone for so long. I did not realise . . . I could not believe that what I felt for you was indeed love. I resisted. I fought my own desires, hourly and daily, telling myself that you were the old Caroline, that you were false and devious and would trample my poor battered heart, if given the opportunity. But I could not withstand you.' His composure cracked. 'In the name of God, Caro, do not turn from me now. I could not bear it. You are all that I want in a life companion. I need you, so much.' Dragging her hands to his mouth he covered them with kisses, burning with the despair he didn't attempt to hide.

'You *need* me?' She couldn't keep the doubt from her voice. No one had ever needed her, save Adele. No man had ever said she was so necessary to his happiness. Could she believe him?

He raised his face, and she almost cried out. 'Don't! I can't bear you to look like that. I love you, truly and deeply, my darling. Oh, Antony.' Wrenching her hands free, she flung herself at him, burying her face in his neck so that she wouldn't have to see his naked craving. No man should have to live with such a hunger in his heart.

The urge to comfort him gave her the words she needed. She said unsteadily, 'It's been hard for both of us. Maybe we needed to tell each other how we felt. Our reunion has been too sudden for complete understanding between us. If, as you say, you don't see me as Jenny, then we're really two strangers, powerfully attracted and thrown into intimacy almost against our will.' His pulse quickened under her cheek and she felt his arms tighten in response. She looked up. 'Forgive me, Antony. I was thinking only of myself.'

He gave her a little shake, then slid his hands beneath her hair to cup her head inches from his own. 'I, to forgive *you*!. Oh, my dear one.'

'Then we'll forgive each other. We start afresh from this moment.'

His lips were on hers, this time demanding a response. Then the satin robe fell from her shoulders and she stood revealed in her sheer bedgown, her glorious hair cascading down in a river of amber. She welcomed his gaze, glad that he found her lovely, wanting him to claim her. For a heartbeat they faced one another on the brink of their great commitment, the rare moment stretching out to bridge the gulf of time and experience that had divided them.

Then she was held fast against him, feeling the leap of passion as it speared through her body, melting it to a flux that blended and bonded with his. He lifted and carried her into the bedroom. She would not release her hold, even when he threw off his clothes and hers, tumbling with her into the depths of down mattress. Mindless with her need she closed her eyes and rode the waves of sensation that billowed and rose ever higher, until reaching a final crescendo of exquisite pain. She heard his shout at the moment of her own release, then together they dropped back into a gentle trough of exhaustion, limbs entwined, their breath mingling – unable to bear any kind of separation.

Sated, drifting, Karen felt her mind blaze with sudden understanding. Up until this minute her whole life had been subject to her great weakness, the need for love. The desperate search that had led her into so much unhappiness, was over; and in the revealing light she saw what she might have been, far more clearly than in the night of revelation at the village inn. That had been a vague groping, an almost grasping of possibilities. Now she knew it all. The giving and receiving of genuine soul-deep love had made her whole.

She heard, but shut out, a small voice that warned of humankind's deepest superstition – the jealousy of the gods, the need to pay for happiness in equal measure. It was a myth, after all. Things would be perfect from now on.

Turning her lips to Antony's ear she whispered, ' "Love is many things. From day to day, by simply being, it enhances life." Now I know what it means – that love is not merely sensation, no matter how enchanting. It's as prosaic as a master's tool of trade, and just as important.' She sat up, so that she could look into his face. 'That's it, isn't it? Love is a part of everything we say or do. It makes noble the dullest task when performed in a loving way, blessing the one who performs it and the one who benefits. Where did you find those words, Antony?'

His face had changed. Looking down on him, relaxed against the pillow, she saw that lines of strain had been smoothed away as if by a hand brushed across sand. She saw a youthful eagerness and impetuosity in eyes that had for too long been weary with the weight of memory. The mouth that had so recently seemed shaped especially for her pleasure now smiled in delight.

'I wrote them, for you.'

'You?'

'Once I created a *Sonnet to a Pair of Brown Eyes*.'

'I remember.' And she did. The box which contained all the treasured words written by him to Jenny had perished with her in the fire, but the phrases themselves . . . they were returning like leaves blown along a pathway towards her. She caught one here and there, isolated, fragmentary – a crimson leaf of passion, a fresh green memory of spring, the sere yellow that spoke of life's mellow pleasures. 'I remember,' she said again, and felt the tears rise, overflowing to drop in warm splashes on his neck and chest. She didn't know whether they were for herself now or as Jenny, or for the man who had been forced to watch her torment.

'My dear love, I beg you not to cry.' Tenderly he cupped her face and brought it down to his, kissing the wet cheeks and eyelids, smoothing back the wild tangle of hair.

'I don't usually,' she sniffed, moved to fresh tears by the intensity of her feelings. 'I'm making up for all the years of not crying.' How could one man embody so much tenderness with strength, such delicacy and sureness of understanding? She wanted to give him something precious in return. 'I wish I could say to you what I feel, but I don't have your gift with words.'

Drawing her down into his arms he buried his mouth in her hair. 'I have no need of words. I have you. You are all my life, my soul, my salvation. Never leave me. Never.'

'I promise you, my darling. I promise that if ever we are parted, we shall surely find one another. Death itself could not destroy the bond. You will never be alone again.'

CHAPTER 19

11 December, Tuesday

Tom came awake shouting. He'd been waving his fist under Phil's nose, ready to make his point in a physical way, if need be.

He shook his head, trying to drive away the remnants of the dream. Why had he been bullying poor Phil? It wasn't his way of winning an argument, however upsetting. On the whole he was rather glad he couldn't remember the point at issue. Probably something ridiculous, as it was a dream.

He'd been sleeping badly, lately. His troubles had begun soon after the regression sessions with Valerie. She was a difficult patient, moody and inclined to throw her weight around when she didn't get her own way – all of which could be handled. But the past-life stuff. That was getting to him. He didn't know how he stood with it.

And then there was Karen. She was so sweet, so defenceless, lying there in her hospital bed, barely making a crease in the coverlet. His heart felt wrung every time he thought of her. And that, too, was getting to him. He couldn't understand why he felt so strongly about a woman he barely knew.

All in all, it wasn't much wonder he slept badly.

Shuffling from bed to bathroom he turned on the shower and looked at himself in the mirror. He shuddered.

Twenty minutes later, fresher and beardless, he sat in his window seat nursing a mug of coffee and vying with Habbakuk for the doubtful warmth of the early sunlight. It was time for a complete recap of the situation.

Valerie's difficulties could wait. She was in no immediate danger, and in fact, was enjoying her experiences under hypnosis. Instead, he projected his mind back to Sunday afternoon in a hospital room. His nostrils filled with a mix of antiseptic and the perfume worn by that odd little woman – what was her name? Carnot. Wilhelmina

Carnot. He saw the late sunlight slanting through cloud and between the wet branches of a tree just outside the window, striking the glass in a dazzle of colour. He heard footsteps in the corridor and voices, people answering bells, people rushing trolleys about. He felt the crispness of the sheet drawn up under Karen's chin. All his senses had come alive with the memories of that room, as keenly as if he were right there, although at the time nothing much had registered.

He'd felt so numb. Karen's appearance had shocked him more than he could say. Living death! The phrase kept on hammering at him. It was unclinical. It went against his training. But seeing her lie so cold and still, he just knew her vital spirit had left her body. The essential Karen had gone away – he was as sure of it as he was of his own name. And there was something else. Absurd as it seemed, he felt that somehow he was linked with her in that twilight place where she now dwelt – that he could make contact if only he knew how, and call her back.

He pictured the faces of medical staff, and the aunt, if he asked to sit with Karen and try to do just that. It wasn't an unheard-of technique. The sense of hearing was the last to go and the first to return, and recovered coma patients had been known to report whole conversations they'd overheard whilst apparently deeply unconscious. However, Tom was neither Karen's medical adviser nor a member of her family. He felt it was hardly the prerogative of a stranger to walk in and offer his services. He couldn't even kid himself that Karen would remember his voice if she heard it. If she had any memory of him at all it was likely to be as an opinionated clown!

But someone had to try and reach out to her, perhaps her aunt. Maybe she'd already tried, and failed. He needed to talk further to her, to discover what specifically had been done and would be done in the future to speed her niece's recovery.

Karen had to recover. She was too young, she had so much to offer the world. She was not going to die.

The Tuesday night session brought a change. Valerie's head had barely hit the cushion of the recliner before she'd gone, wafting down through the subterranean passages of her personal labyrinth at incredible speed. Tom watched her with the concentration of a cat at a mousehole, and he knew Phil did, too. She didn't speak for a long time, but when she did, it shocked him.

'Release him from the tranquillity chair. He struggles too much. We shall have him cracking his head open once more.'

Tom heard Phil's breath hiss in his ear. 'By God, she's a man this time. Look at her face!'

Tom noticed the now familiar shift in light, the subtle change that announced a different personality in the same body. Valerie's features had rounded and coarsened. She seemed to have developed a bulging forehead and a shadow covered her chin so that she appeared to be bearded, and yet was not. But her voice was the greatest change. It had gone both deep and nasal, with a strong North American intonation, and it was undoubtedly male.

The thickened lips parted and the new personality appeared to be whistling soundlessly, the eyes beneath closed lids darting like fish in a pond, back and forth, watching something closely.

'Careful now. I don't want him hurting himself before the next treatment. Dr Rush is explicit on the matter. That's it. Tie him tightly so his head is supported at the edge of the table. Now stand back. I will set the mechanism in motion.' He leaned forward, hand cupped around an imaginary lever.

Phil whispered again. 'What do you suppose she – he's doing? Is it a hospital?'

Tom held up a finger for silence. He leaned forward, his face almost touching his patient's arm, listening.

'Pay close attention, if you please,' said the voice that might and might not be Valerie. 'With the illness known as torpid madness, which as you know is caused by too small a flow of blood to the brain, Dr Rush's favoured method of treatment is the gyrator. We have here a patient who has failed to respond to the other more common methods of cold baths and ducking. He has also been subjected to sudden severe frights, and periodic starvation, to no avail. It is therefore a last hope for this patient. I have determined to give him five minutes at maximum revolutions of the table. The blood will be driven to his brain by centrifugal force, and will bathe the cells with the necessary nourishment. Pay no attention if he screams. He will be silenced soon enough.'

Valerie's hand pulled the imaginary lever.

Looking at the small, cruel smile almost hidden in the chin shadow, Tom felt his flesh creep. She was enjoying the 'treatment' being meted out to the unfortunate victim. She revelled in her power, and didn't bother to hide the fact.

Phil nudged him. 'She's become a monster. Look at her tongue sitting in the corner of her mouth while she pushes that damned lever even harder.'

'Hmm. But someone's interfering. She's frowning. She's pulling back, although reluctantly.'

They waited and presently heard a petulant sigh. 'Oh, very well. But I resent your words, sir. You have absolutely no right to address me in such terms, and I shall take up the matter with the board of the institute.' Blood welled up in the plump cheeks. 'What? You dare accuse me . . .'

There was silence for what seemed like a very long time. Tom waited patiently, but Phil seemed restless. 'It's damned frustrating only hearing his side of the conversation. I wonder what's being said to the little prick?'

Tom smiled slightly and went along with the change of gender. He, too, found it hard not to believe they were watching a man. 'Whatever it is, he's not liking it. But I get the impression that time is passing. Look at the blankness of the face. Perhaps he's asleep.'

'Oh, great! We could be here all night.'

'No, time seems to be relative in this other place. I'm betting we'll have the next scene quite soon. Look! He's waking up.'

The thick lips yawned, showing Valerie's perfect caps which managed to look unaccountably yellow and decayed in spots. The man muttered to himself and seemed to be searching in a cupboard or drawer. At last he appeared satisfied, making the motions of taking up a pen and writing.

Phil almost danced with frustration, but Tom shushed him as the man was about to speak.

'I'll finish my notes, and then I'll go down and finish him.'

The calm malevolence of those few words took Tom by the throat. He could scarcely breathe. It was like being in the theatre, watching and understanding the person's actions, yet powerless to prevent them, knowing they were outside reality, yet feeling the echo of past horror ringing down the years to maul his senses.

The imaginary pen moved for a few minutes, then the man sat back with a grunt. 'I'll order him whipped. After all he's been through he will not survive that. And it is a perfectly legitimate treatment. Rush used it for years and advocated it for the most stubborn cases.'

The small private laugh was worse than anything Tom had yet heard. He jerked back, as if afraid of contamination. But the concentrated frown between his eyes had lightened. 'I think I'm beginning to get the hang of all this. The way this bastard is abusing his power . . . that's the key.'

'Well, you see more than I do,' growled his friend. 'If I had one wish I'd take the Starship Enterprise back through a time warp and put such a crimp in this character's style!'

'Look! It's over. She's coming back.'

They watched, fascinated by the metamorphosis from one personality to another. Features appeared to move, the change barely visible to the eye. Then Valerie was there, and Tom was greeting her and guiding her back up the labyrinth into daylight.

She seemed shaken and confused, as before. Not quite aware of her surroundings.

'Are you all right?' Tom and Phil spoke in unison.

She shivered and blinked a few times. 'Yes. I think so.' She looked from one concerned face to the other, her expression changing to exhilaration. 'Boy, what a workout. But it was worth it. At last we've discovered what's going on.'

Tom sat back and looked at her. 'You're talking about karma, aren't you? The pay-back system.'

'If that's what you want to call it. I see it more as the redressing of an imbalance.'

'And what form do you see your imbalance taking, Valerie?'

'That's easy to see. I've been guilty of abusing power.'

Phil had to break in. 'You mean, as a medicine woman you actually tried to practise witchcraft?'

Her smile was enigmatic. 'I don't know. Where's the fine line between natural medicine and occult practice?' She returned to Tom. 'What do you think?'

'Maybe you did abuse your gifts in that life, but not to kill people, as you apparently planned to do in the latest session.' His eyes met hers and held until she looked away.

'You picked it up. I thought you might.'

'Picked up what?' said Phil plaintively. He looked dishevelled with tie loose, hair thrust up by excited hands.

Tom was aware that the sessions were having as much outward effect on his friend as on the patient herself. It seemed Phil had invested heavily in the outcome. Very likely he now felt vindicated in his beliefs and wanted Tom to admit unequivocal belief himself. But he wasn't ready for that yet, not by any means. Besides, what was true for Phil might not necessarily be Valerie's truth. It was still possible that she was inventing the episodes, subconsciously. Her up-front reactions were too natural to be an act, yet she could be deceiving herself.

'What did you pick up?' Phil persisted.

'That the victim in the first life had become the persecutor in another.'

'It's beautiful, isn't it?' Valerie looked flushed and excited. 'What's dealt out in one life is balanced in the next.'

Tom shook his head. 'I see a problem with that. Two wrongs don't make a right in any philosophy, and I can't see your downward progression from healer to tormentor (and possible murderer) as an improvement. In fact, to extend your own statement, you'd be taking on a further karmic load yourself.'

'Of course I should. I probably did. Don't you see, I've been going from life to life failing to recognise what I've been doing? Each time the emotions and events that were not dealt with have been presented, I've continued to sidestep the opportunity to resolve them. Now – here and now in this life – is my big chance to put matters right, because now I'm uncovering the problem. Each time I regress I learn more. When we finally put it all together I'll have the answer. I can redress the balance.'

Tom looked dubious. He welcomed enthusiasm provided it was based on reality. But if matters didn't turn out the way she expected, Valerie was in for a heavy disappointment, perhaps a devastating one. And yet . . . and yet. There was something quite alluring in the idea of such perfect balance. What a magnificent philosophy. If it could only be true.

Phil's change of tack made a welcome diversion.

'This fellow Rush. Have you heard of him, Tom?'

'As it happens, I was reading about his work only recently. He seems to have been something of an entrepreneur back in the late eighteenth and early nineteenth centuries. As Physician General of the Continental Army and Treasurer of the United States he was well positioned to indulge his charitable social conscience. He did a lot of good for the poor in many ways. It's a pity he had such odd notions on treatment of the insane.'

'The gyrator?'

'Amongst other things. Evidently Valerie's alter ego was a disciple of his procedures.'

'So, where do we go now?' Phil looked at the other two, and Valerie said immediately, 'To the next session. I want to find out if I'm a murderer as well as a suicide.'

'It sounds a bit morbid.'

'Not at all. I'm quite detached about it. And I'm eager to find out all I can. It's all so fascinating, I can hardly wait.' She turned to Tom eagerly. 'How about it, Tom? Can we have another session straight away? Is there any reason why we shouldn't?'

While he hesitated, Phil added his weight to Valerie's plea, the longing in his face like that of a child begging for a toy.

Tom took a turn about the room, ending up in front of his painting. He felt uneasy. There was too much pressure from two people who might not know what they were doing. His faith in Phil had suffered since his friend had allowed himself to become emotionally involved in the proceedings. Tom had himself felt the fascination, to the extent of participating in Valerie's scenario in his own dreams. It simply wouldn't do to have both therapists overly engrossed. Someone had to maintain a detached viewpoint. And Valerie was still an unknown quantity.

Tom stopped trying to sell himself. He knew how badly he wanted to go on – now – immediately.

'Tom? Hey, where are you, pal?'

He blinked, and Phil's distant voice was suddenly loud in his ear. Once again he had been looking down the misty gorges, snared into a meditative trance. The painting was no help at all in maintaining a proper therapeutic separation!

Turning his back on its siren song he made his decision.

'Okay. We'll try once more, but with the proviso that Valerie is tied into the chair. I don't want another suicide attempt. We might not be so lucky again.'

'Agreed.' Valerie smiled nervously.

While Phil went off to fetch some climbing rope from Tom's flat close by, Tom tried to warn Valerie not to expect too much of the experience. She wouldn't listen.

'Tom, this is the most exciting, the most meaningful thing that's ever happened to me. I feel a sense of purpose. I'm finally going somewhere. Can you imagine what that means to an emotional drifter like me?'

Tom understood well enough. He felt a strange diffidence in presenting his own view.

'Look, I'm not trying to be a wet blanket, truly. I guess I'm scared. You're taking a risk, pinning everything on the outcome of these sessions. I'm afraid of what a disappointment might do to you. Life isn't tied up in neat little bundles, Valerie, but you're expecting just that.'

She smiled across the gap in their understanding, undisturbed.

Tom floundered. How to get through to her? He feared that she'd missed the point. Reincarnation, if proven, meant a monumental change in personal philosophy. The moral and spiritual issues must affect the believer to an extent that was hard for him to comprehend. He hoped he was wrong, but something about Valerie's attitude didn't ring true to him. She seemed eager to 'redress the balance', yet the words sounded to him like cant, lip service paid to disguise another purpose. Perhaps, to her, it was merely a thrilling departure from the mundane, a sensational episode for the personal enjoyment of Valerie Winterhouse, and a measure of her new importance.

It wasn't that he wanted her to believe so much as he needed the reassurance that she would not grow dependent on continual regressions for 'kicks'. Valerie could do with a strong personal philosophy. She didn't need to play games with her psyche and end up disappointed, and worse off than before she began.

For a moment he grasped an inward vision of what his own life could be, if it were all real. A chance to do things over again, to make good the mistakes – and the knowledge that everything he thought and said and did affected his own future lives. It'd certainly make him raise his game! And if everyone else 'knew' about karma, the pay-back system, they'd certainly lead better lives. People's attitudes would be revolutionised overnight. The world could enter an era of tranquillity previously undreamed of. It could be an age of miracles!

Valerie moved impatiently and, with a sigh, he relinquished the dream, and came back to reality.

Ten minutes later, with her body tightly bound to the recliner, Valerie had returned to the past.

The man huddled over his rigidly clasped hands, sobbing bitterly. His shoulders heaved and he was trying to speak, but the words came out oddly broken and disjointed.

'I did not mean . . . I could not . . . Oh, God above, hear me! I must have been mad . . .' Again he broke off into an unintelligible mumble. Then a terrible groan came from him. Raising his puffy face he appeared to stare in horror at some visitation only he could see.

'Forgive me! I tried to fight it, but the compulsion was too strong. I was driven by fury. I was not responsible. I *could* not stop myself.' He cringed back, protecting his ravaged face with his hands.

It could have been a caricature of terror, but to the two watchers the scene conveyed a disturbing reality. The man had been reduced to a wreck, a cowering creature filled with remorse and fear of the consequences of his behaviour.

'Looks as if he killed the other one,' muttered Phil.

Tom only nodded. How could Valerie possibly put over an act like this, so quickly, so convincingly? Foam flecked her lips and her skin had taken on a greyish tone.

'There is no redemption,' moaned the tormented being now thrashing about in the recliner, held only by the knotted rope. 'They will come for me and confine me in one of my own cells. I deserve no better. But I cannot bear the thought. Death would be preferable.'

Oh, oh, thought Tom. Here we go again.

With a feeling of inevitability he watched the man dive into a pocket and produce an imaginary something, holding it to his head. His eyes, beneath closed lids, seemed ready to come right out of their sockets as he faced some monster of his own creation.

'We shall meet in hell!' he screamed, and slumped down in his bonds.

Tom knew it was very late, probably close to dawn. Too exhausted to bother raising his wrist he was content to take a guess. The fire had burned down to embers, although it was still warm in the flat, and he'd sunk so far into his chair that he looked like a hibernating bear, wrapped in his warmest pullover and fleecy-lined boots.

Phil slumped in the opposite seat, half asleep. Having seen Valerie home they'd returned to Tom's flat for supper. Since then they'd been at it for hours, arguing, cajoling, pleading for each other's understanding. And where had it got them, Tom wondered? He yawned and pulled himself up to a sitting position.

'Let's close down, Phil. I'm too whacked to think any more. Do you want to spend what's left of the night on the couch?'

'Thanks.' Phil, too, yawned. 'That bloody animal won't try to get in with me, will he?'

'He wouldn't lower himself.'

Habbakuk, curled tight like an overgrown snail on the hearthrug, opened a golden eye and stared contemptuously at Phil.

Tom laughed. 'My familiar. I'll bet he's more psychically aware than any of us. Do you suppose animals and humans are karmically linked?'

'I haven't thought about it, but I don't see why not. Seriously, Tom, this pattern that's emerging shows an alarming tendency on Valerie's part. When life gets too difficult to handle she simply opts out.' He looked at Tom from the corners of his eyes. 'Now, since you appear to be a part of the cycle . . .'

'Oh, for crying out loud! We've been over this so many times, and I still say you're basing your conclusions on too little evidence and a whole lot of wishful thinking. My dreams are my own, not Valerie's. I involved myself.' Tom pulled himself up, aware that he was becoming far too impassioned. 'The suicide pattern can scarcely be called a pattern after just two lifetimes.'

'What about the Friday dawn episode?'

'We're not even sure that it was a genuine attempt.'

Phil snorted. 'Valerie was reacting to the pressure you were bringing on her. She might have told you she wanted this, but at a deeper level she didn't mean it. You were making her dig into forbidden areas – that is, areas she had made forbidden. Her fear was so great she simply decided to opt out rather than face it.'

'That's entirely possible. I had thought of it, and it's why I insisted that Valerie herself should make the decision whether to go on. Unlike you, I believe she wants and needs to do this, both consciously and at every other level.'

'Well, there you are. You have the suicide sequences. We could go on having Valerie regress through any number of lives, and I'm betting, in the great majority, she'd follow the same pattern.'

Tom appeared to be sunk in thought. He'd been listening with a part of his attention; but the remainder was occupied with an astonishing realisation. Without any thunderclap, no roll of drums or heavenly choir, he'd come to a truly momentous point in his life. Emotionally he had just stepped across a line, or a better description would be that he'd passed through a curtain he'd never realised was there. One moment he was the old Tom Levy, bristling with prejudices and fears, most of which he'd carried as so much extra baggage since childhood; then, with the one step, he'd left his old self behind and entered a new phase.

Tom wanted to know that he had lived before. His mind seemed to be crowded with voices from the past, all begging for a hearing. He wanted the promise inherent in the law of balance. He wanted to know that life and death were momentary passages in a continuum, that he was as important to the rhythm of the universe as any and every other part of it. With every particle of the mind and body and soul and intellect that was Tom Levy he wanted to believe. Great Lord of Moses and all the Prophets, he wanted it to be so!

He felt tears come to his eyes. The intensity of his longing was a pain in his chest, spreading and filling the cavity, pressing on his lungs so that he found it hard to breathe. His muscles tensed, and he felt as if he was straining against the confines of his body. A part of him soared above the pain and constriction, freewheeling like a bird released from a cage, delighting in the sunshine it had never thought to see again.

Then, as suddenly as it came, the exaltation and the pain faded. The longing stayed with him. But the wave of passionate feeling had slowed and brought him back to his own familiar shore. It didn't dump him, just deposited him gently on the beach, and receded. Tom felt groggy.

When he finally focused back on his friend, his expression must have shown that he'd missed something vital.

Phil threw up his hands. 'Christ, you're a stubborn bastard! I might as well talk to your wretched cat. I get about as much response.' He hauled himself out of his chair and picked up his coat.

Tom shot up after him, detaining him with both hands on his shoulders. He said in a voice that shook with intensity, 'Phil, relax. I'm not rubbishing you or your theories. In fact, I'm far more impressed by them than I've let you see. No doubt it's been my stupid pride getting in the way.'

Phil didn't answer.

Tom's smile was rueful. 'Please, try to understand. If I take on this credo, it means challenging all my previous notions of how the universe is structured. If I put those aside, I put aside everything I've ever believed in. I need time.'

Phil wouldn't give way. His expression was equally rueful. 'It's not me you have to ask for time. I don't know why, but I have a feeling it's running out fast, for all of us.'

CHAPTER 20

Antony left the stables and took a roundabout route to the House, through the herb gardens and his grandmother's prized wilderness of barely tended shrubs, emerging at the eastern-most end of the Manor. He stood and contemplated the tower. A wind blew up from the coast, shredding itself against the bits of fallen masonry, tugging at the weeds that grew in the cracks where mortar had fallen out. It was a scene of utter desolation, grey sky, grey light, grey world. Depression settled on him more firmly.

Christmas had gone by with dancing and festivity, and a house full of guests. He had enjoyed it all, but always in the background was his worry over the political situation. Bonaparte bestrode Europe, as invincible as ever. His occupying armies spread across the map like the tentacles of a sea-monster. It seemed to Antony there was but one way to break its grip, to cut off its head.

He and Caro were badly at odds with one another. Why could she not understand? He did not believe her to be unmoved by her country's plight, and yet she refused to discuss a means of despatching the greatest tyrant the world had seen since the Roman Emperors. Time was running out for England. Unless she could find some allies, the noose that Bonaparte was drawing about her would end in strangling her commerce, and without trade she would die. Bernadotte still struggled to withstand pressure from France, but his little kingdom could so easily be trodden under. And the Tsar, that wily fox, would not commit himself. He waited to see which choice would be more advantageous – and meanwhile England starved.

If Bonaparte were dead, his empire would crumble. There was no one to take his place. Of course it would not be easy to reach him, but Caro's special knowledge could help so much. Why, why would she not help? It was nonsense to speak of historical integrity, to insist that events must not be tampered with. What was that to him? England stood in desperate need, and she quibbled about 'history'.

His mouth tight with frustration, he turned away from the dismal ruin and looked out over the acres of field and wood, the soft hills and distant rugged line of coast that he loved so much. To him it represented all that was best in his country. It was to be fought for and preserved for his children and his children's children, as was England herself. He had to make Caro see that it all stood in jeopardy.

He stood braced against the wind, angry enough to wring Caro's neck – figuratively. Then, without warning, he was hit with a notion that blew his anger into oblivion. He felt stunned with the enormity of it. But, however reluctantly, he let it take hold. What if Caro was not Karen Courtney, a woman from the future? What if her tale was one huge, unwitting fraud?

Well enough for her to say quite definitely that Bonaparte would be defeated in a certain year. Possibly he would. Who, at this point in time, could refute it? Of course, Caro believed implicitly that everything she said was truth. She was no conscious deceiver. But where was her proof? Her forecasts, unfortunately, still lay in the future. And the more he considered her personal concept of natural universal law, the less comfortable he was with it. He wanted to believe, God knew how much! To know that death was but a doorway into life – that he was a minute part of a continuum, along with every other living thing – a dot in the Creator's pattern, and integral to that pattern. But there was this vein of scepticism in him that would not let him wholeheartedly embrace such a theory. Karma, reincarnation, future lives. No, he could not.

He was tired. Looking about he found a riven block of stone to lean on. His thoughts turned inward, and he no longer saw the vista unrolled before him. Although brief, the inward battle was the cruellest he had ever fought, and it was unfairly weighted on one side by fatigue and worry, and an extreme sense of responsibility that was too much a part of his nature to be put aside.

Finally he straightened up, his decision made. He'd managed to pigeonhole the Jenny/Caro situation as some kind of convenient one-time miracle. Put simply, he had lost his love and found her again. Miracles were not open to interpretation. He could accept that. But as for Caro's 'future' existence, it had to be a delusion. He adored her, mad or sane, and would protect her with his life; but the more he pondered her story of time travel and her startling predictions, the more unlikely they appeared to be.

His first joyous acceptance of all she claimed and believed, having once begun to wane, now formed itself into a small, hard, unresiliant core of common sense. Theory and fantasy had no part in the present desperate struggle for survival. Sadly, he put aside the part of him that wanted his wife to be what she said she was, accepting that she would not help him because she could not.

He re-entered the house through the window of his bookroom just as Karen burst in, looking quite distraught.

'Antony, you must help Charles. I think he is on the brink of breaking down.' She held out her hands and he took them in his, drawing her close and saying in a comforting tone, 'Tell me, and I will do what I can'.

The tale came tumbling out, at first haphazardly and then with more coherence as Karen regained her poise. It appeared that Amanda had finally told Charles she could not marry him, and he'd taken it very badly indeed.

'So she has given him his congé. I am sorry for it.' He truly meant it. Charles' bleak personal life had always troubled him, and although he'd done what he could for his friend, some situations could never be overcome. He admired Charles for continuing to support his widowed mother and the clutch of stepbrothers and sisters still too young to go out into the world; he appreciated him as a hard-working secretary, and he trusted and liked him as a man. But none of these things worked in Charles' favour when it came to taking a wife.

Karen shook her head at him. He wanted to kiss her worried expression away and reassure her, but she wouldn't let him.

'You don't understand, do you? He's really desperate. He loves Amanda with such intensity. I don't think he believed her when she told him months ago that it was hopeless. She tried to warn him, but he stopped up his ears and went on dreaming. Now, he's had to face the truth. She has told him she loves Oliver Stamford and will marry him. Charles is almost demented.'

He drew Karen over to the sofa and made her sit down with him. 'Let me understand this. Amanda maintained the connection, knowing Charles' feeling for her?'

'She is my friend. She couldn't help meeting him in our house when she came to visit me. Besides, she is very fond of Charles. If Amanda has a fault, it is her inability to hurt people. She's only done it now because there is no other way.'

'This is a sorry tale.' His concern grew as he contemplated the effect of this crushing blow on a nature such as Charles'. 'Where is he now?'

'He's disappeared. I saw him rush out of the house towards the stables. Amanda is in her room, packing to go back to London. I couldn't persuade her to stay. Oh, Antony, I am so unhappy for them both.'

His immediate response was to gather her to him, resting her head on his shoulder and stroking the fiery hair he loved to touch. 'I will seek out Charles and see what may be done.' He thought for a moment, then added, 'Amanda is aware of Charles' coming preferment, is she not?'

'Of course. But money isn't the real issue. She truly loves Oliver Stamford, and is merely fond of Charles.' Karen detached herself from his hold and got up. 'I should go back to Amanda. She's heartbroken at the damage she's done. Do find Charles and see what you can do to comfort him.'

Gloom settled over the Manor, muffling the senses so that it seemed to Antony everyone spoke more softly and guarded their expressions. Caro, upset for Charles, and rebuffed by him, spent hours locked in her studio, using her painting as an outlet.

Charles had no way of discharging the molten fury that ate at him. For he was angry, Antony could see that. All his hurt had been transformed into bitterness against the fate that had come upon him through no fault of his own. Nothing served to cheer him, not even Chloe's wholehearted attempts to drag him into her games.

Declining escort, Amanda had left that same morning of the upset. A week later both Antony and Charles followed to London, ostensibly on business matters. In fact, Antony had promised his Caro to deliver her warning to Spencer Percival on his coming assassination in the Houses of Parliament that May. Although Antony no longer placed any credence in her forecasts, he could not tell her so; also, it suited him to remove Charles' blighting presence from the Manor. Perhaps a few days in town would improve his mood. He was unlikely to meet with Amanda as they did not normally move in the same circles, and their stricken relationship was not common knowledge.

Antony's own mood was not improved by a visit from Sybilla. She came to Rothmoor House alone and at night, and took him unawares as he was finishing his dinner. Angrily he surveyed her charming figure outlined in the doorway, and wondered where she had the money from to array herself in such splendour. Her dress was wine-coloured satin, extremely décolleté, and the neckline and sleeves sewn with garnets. Her very white skin glowed in the candlelight, and her mouth was an inviting curve as she accepted his curt invitation to the bookroom.

'Pray be seated, Sybilla.'

She laughed at his chilliness and took her time choosing a chair before subsiding gracefully into it with a swirl of satin skirts.

'I fear you are not pleased to see me, dear Antony,' she began in a honeyed voice.

Antony forced back the words he'd have liked to utter and said instead, 'I have no liking for your games, Sybilla. Be plain, I beg you.'

'Why, I play no game. 'Tis simply that I wished to see you again, to explain what you were too angry to hear the last time we met.'

'The last time we met, you and that hell-born brother of yours were engaged in a plot to deliver my wife into a life of degradation.' He spoke without emphasis, but no one could have mistaken the emotion behind the words.

She lowered her eyelids and said softly, 'I will admit my error. It was a mistake, born of my great passion for you, my dear one. I was outside myself with jealousy.'

'Spare me talk of your passions, Sybilla. They are merely the unbridled lusts of a nature that has never known any restraint. Why did you really come here? Did you hope for money?'

The mask had not shifted. Her beautiful face serene, she fixed her black eyes on his and smiled bewitchingly. 'Antony, why can you not believe me? I have loved you since we first met. My heart cracked when you wed your Jenny, and totally crumbled into small pieces when Caro took her place beside you. I will admit that I was driven almost to madness, knowing I had lost you. In my dementia, I gave ear to Basil. 'Tis he who plots against your wife. He covets your position, and cannot bear to think that a child of yours might deprive him of his hopes. Thus he schemed to remove Caro, and in my great pain and need, I agreed to help him. 'Twas monstrous. I do not know how I could contemplate such a foul deed. Oh, forgive me, Antony, my love.'

In a movement full of grace and drama, she went on her knees before him, her gown flowing about her in a wine-coloured pool, her white arms uplifted in a pleading gesture, her bosom rising and falling noticeably with each breath. She had never looked more beautiful, nor more dangerously sensuous.

He surveyed her, unmoved. In an implacable voice he said, 'There can never be any talk of your kind of love between us. I neither like nor respect you, and I can never forgive what you have done to Caro.'

The eyelids snapped wide open, and naked fury blazed at him. She scrambled to her feet. 'Pah! Then I spit on your forgiveness! What milksop fluid runs in your veins in exchange for red blood? Are you, in fact, a man at all?'

It was his turn to smile. Her efforts at seduction had foundered so quickly on the rocks of her own insecurities. He could almost feel sorry for her. But he knew her for a calculating schemer and a bitter enemy. At the thought of Caro's probable fate if Sybilla had her way, his brief amusement turned to an ice-cold rage.

'Leave this house, and do not return. If I ever find you here, or anywhere near me and mine, I shall stamp you out of existence.' He took a pace forward, and Sybilla cowered back. For the first time in his experience he saw fear of him in a woman's face. Disliking himself for it, nevertheless he grasped her ungently by the shoulders and forced her towards the door. 'I mean what I have said, Sybilla. If you are wise you will take Basil and leave this country altogether.'

Her whitened face filled with blood. She pursed her lips and spat at him. Then wrenching free she stalked into the entrance hall, snatching her cloak from the footman deputising for the absent Bates.

At the main door she turned. Injecting her voice with all the venom that boiled in her she said, 'You have not heard the last of this. Believe me, you will regret the things you have said to me this night.'

With popping eyes, the footman ushered her out into the night, and closed the door behind her. Antony had no doubt he would fly to the servants' hall with this titbit of news, but he didn't care. He was sickened by the horror of the unclean spirit that possessed Sybilla. Outwardly a normal, lovely young woman, on the inside she was hopelessly flawed, incapable of giving or receiving real affection. It was tragic.

He didn't for an instant believe in her threats. There was nothing she could do to injure him personally, and he would take good care that his family was protected. Sybilla had neither money nor influence to purchase the instruments of revenge. Her challenge had no substance. But the sadness he felt had to do with a young girl who once had admired and looked up to her older male cousin – a girl whose mind was even then unsound, whose future was ruined before it began to unfold.

Two days later London was electrified with the news of Bonaparte's invasion of Pomerania – Swedish Pomerania.

A message came from the War Office, via Charles Hastings. Antony should prepare to leave immediately for urgent talks between Bernadotte and a very high representative of Tsar Alexander. The meeting would be most secret and its importance could not be exaggerated. This was England's chance to gain the allies she needed. Bonaparte just might have overstepped himself at last.

Antony couldn't contain his elation. 'Charles, this is beyond what I had hoped for. They say Davout has behaved with such severity towards the Swedish troops and officials, there will be no holding back now for Bernadotte. He must avenge his new countrymen or stand branded as a weakling, unfit to rule.'

'Then you must take advantage of the situation, and leave immediately. I will make the arrangements.' Charles spoke heavily, as though he found it difficult to be really interested.

Recognising this, Antony left him to his work, the planning and preparation of permits and letters of introduction under various names and nationalities, bank drafts, cash, maps, appropriate clothing – the organisation of the journey to the coast, and from thereon. He knew that Charles would be thorough, whatever his personal unhappiness. There was no danger of him falling into French hands through any negligence on the part of his secretary.

Attending an undercover meeting with Lord Liverpool, he learned that this time he would carry with him the power of the Prince Regent himself, and his Ministers of the Crown. He was to represent his country and somehow, anyhow, draw into his net the two rulers who had so far escaped Bonaparte's iron grip.

The War Minister himself escorted Antony to the unobtrusive exit from a house not known to be his own. He appeared to be searching for the right words.

'Marchmont, a very great deal hangs on this conference. Perhaps the freedom of the world as we know it. It will be the turning point in Swedish policy, since the Crown Prince now knows exactly where he stands with Bonaparte. If Sweden goes with Russia, which I believe she will, given that the Tsar is offering the inducement of Norway as a prize, then Britain must form a triumvirate with the two. If nothing else, that will serve to encourage other waverers.'

Antony nodded. 'Austria and Prussia grow restive. If we can prove a strong alliance against France they could find the courage to rise against her once more. I believe that Napoleon Bonaparte will one day recognise this move on the chessboard as his first great tactical error.'

Down in Devon, Karen had the news as quickly as Antony's courier could cover the distance. She felt as if she'd been winded, and had to sit down, disguising as well as she could the sudden onslaught of an entirely unreasonable panic. Why should this trip be any different to the others? Why should she be suddenly hit with a barrage of groundless fears? Antony could look after himself, he'd proved it often enough. So, what was it about this trip that drained the blood out of her heart, leaving her faint and sick?

She went to Lord Edward for comfort, and listening to his calm, common sense analysis of the situation, she felt a little better.

'He is not going into France, my child. He will be safe in Stockholm. The Swedes may have been well disposed towards the French, but this error will alter their attitude.'

'Still, we are at war with Sweden. Antony could be as much in danger there as he would be in France.' In deference to Lord Edward she controlled her urge to pace the floor and sat rigidly opposite his great wing chair, looking out over the winter bare gardens. The scene was as bleak as her own inner view.

'Technically we are at war. In fact, we are trading as heavily as ever. Until this invasion, the Swedes had no interest in firing shots, or taking prisoners. The Emperor miscalculated badly. He has lost himself an ally and Count Bernadotte must be rubbing his hands in glee.'

'Why? He is a Frenchman, after all.' She kept the conversational ball rolling, but all she really wanted was reassurance. It seemed to her that Napoleon's 'miscalculation' was simply going to lead to more fighting, and in an area where her husband might be found.

Lord Edward smiled and patted her hand. 'Child, do not distress yourself. Antony is safe, I swear it. Bernadotte has not long been elevated to his high position and his people will be watching for him to prove his worthiness. He will ally himself with the only countries capable of helping him avoid the French yoke – Britain and Russia.'

'I know you are right, but I cannot help viewing these momentous events from Antony's position. He is all that matters to me.'

'My dear, he is all that matters to both of us. And I do not fear for him.' He leaned forward, taking her hands in his and kissing her on the forehead. Holding her eyes with his he repeated his reassurance, and only released her when he saw the beginning of hope in her expression.

'Where is that minx, that grandchild of mine, this morning? She has not paid her usual visit to the old bear.'

Amanda posted down to Devon as soon as she had the news, and Karen received her with joy tempered by her worry over Amanda and Charles. Her concern for Antony had to be hidden from her dear friend, or so she thought.

Amanda soon disabused her of this idea. 'Caro, you must try to stop Antony. This latest journey could be very dangerous for him.' Her normally rosy cheeks were pale, and she appeared to have lost weight recently.

Staggered, Karen simply looked at her. 'Is nothing at all hidden from you? How did you know about Antony's trips?'

'That is unimportant. You must listen to me. Antony must not go on this mission. It will be disastrous for you both.' Amanda's fingers pulled at the stitching of her fur muff, systematically taking it to pieces. She hadn't even paused to take off her hat before plunging into her speech. Fortunately, Bates had retired to supervise the removal of her baggage from the coach – an astonishing single portmanteau.

Karen grasped her friend's elbow and dragged her unceremoniously into the bookroom, shutting the door behind her with a kick. 'Sit down, Amanda, and tell me just what you know.'

Amanda flopped into a chair and burst into tears. 'I cannot tell you,' she sobbed. 'I have not seen anything, but I have felt it, right through to my bones. There is danger and betrayal in the air. It hangs over this house like a miasma. Oh, Caro, I am afraid for you both.'

Karen sent for her maid. She would not be lured into discussion until the fresh-faced country girl who served her so willingly had arrived and been sent to make a soothing posset. Amanda was relieved of hat and coat and ensconced near the fire. She began visibly to relax.

'You must have left in a devil of a hurry to bring only one bag.

Of course, I am delighted to be honoured with your presence so soon after our Christmas festivities . . .'

'Pray, do not tease me, Caro. I am in a torment of worry. Only for you would I leave my mother ill, and attended by a simple maidservant.'

'Of course I won't tease, darling. I am so very sorry about your mother. Ah, here is Lily with your posset.' She waited until Amanda had drunk every drop, then dismissed Lily and said, 'Right. I want the whole story, my friend. Start talking.'

Amanda talked.

Afterwards, upon reflection, Karen realised she'd been expecting trouble. She'd been uneasy for some time, in a vague way. Intuition? Psychic sensitivity? Whatever. Amanda was merely confirming these feelings.

She'd long known about Amanda's premonitions. This strange extra-sensory awareness had proved itself too often for either of them to doubt the strong message that had brought her friend rushing down to Devon.

Amanda hunched foward in her chair. 'I felt an indescribable fear. It came to me like a black rushing wind and enveloped me, choking the breath from my body. It was horrible.' If possible, she grew even paler. 'I knew it meant danger for you and Antony. That is why I have come. I had to give you a warning, however nebulous. Oh, how I wish I could be more explicit, but I cannot.'

Karen stared at her, already infected by Amanda's fear. 'Do you know what Antony does, Amanda?'

'I know that he will travel abroad and into danger for the sake of his country.'

'Then he must have betrayed himself in some way. Do you think others may know of his secret work?'

Amanda shook her head. 'Have no fear. I have made a study of your husband since realising his importance to you. Not many learn to rely upon their intuitive sense as I do. Then it was a simple matter to extract confirmation from Charles. Poor darling. Naturally, he does not know that he has told me. He would rather be shot than endanger Antony.'

Karen leaned back in her chair and sighed. She felt exhausted. It must be the result of her inner tension.

Her friend looked at her commiseratingly. 'Caro, you must use every means at your disposal to persuade Antony to remain here in safety. If he leaves England he will meet treachery. And you, too are terribly at risk.'

'How can that possibly be? I can't go with Antony.'

Amanda shook her head. 'The betrayal I sense will involve you both. You are both objects of hatred and envy.'

Karen hit the table with her fist. 'Why can't you tell me more? Why? Why? If you're so gifted with clairvoyance, why can't you help?' Immediately she regretted her outburst.

But Amanda was not offended, only pitying. 'I would give anything to spare you – '

'Save your sorrow for when I'm dead, Amanda. Right now I'm in a mood to fight for my happiness. Will you speak to Antony? Do you think you could convince him of the danger?'

'I shall do what I can, but I do not count upon our success. 'Twill challenge Antony's notion of his highest duty.'

'What else can we do?' Grateful to Amanda for her help Karen tried to show this by making her friend as comfortable as possible for her one night's visit. Her own rest was fitful and she was woken early by the arrival of another messenger.

Standing by the window in the cold light she read Antony's tender note of farewell. While Amanda was still on the road to Devon he had left for his secret place of embarkation, and sailed upon the next high tide.

CHAPTER 21

13 December, Thursday

VISITING HOURS HAD ended when Tom drew into the near empty parking area. He had permission to see Karen late, since his own commitments prevented him coming during the day. He had kept scrupulously to routine, despite the upset of Valerie's special needs, and his own desire to help the sleeping beauty of University College Hospital. Many people depended on him, and he couldn't just cut them off because he felt weary, in fact, almost overwhelmed by the events and insights of the past fortnight.

Not for the first time, he asked himself why he was so eager to help a stranger. Often enough, he'd given up precious personal time for others, when it was the only time available, but then it had been for the usual reasons. The patient had been disabled or otherwise disadvantaged, and unable to come to his office or clinic; their problem had been of specific interest, falling within Tom's field of expertise; he'd been asked, as a favour by a friend, to take on extra work. The reasons were many, but they were valid. He had no good answer when he looked for a reason to sit by the bedside of a young woman in a coma, knowing intellectually that there was little he could do for her, yet prepared to wait for inspiration to visit him.

He could tell himself that he cared about the waste of talent, perhaps genius. His feelings about his new painting couldn't be put into words, although he knew that it had enriched his life. He could recall Karen Courtney's haunted look that night at the gallery, a look that he'd helped to erase for a time, and admit that he'd been attracted to a woman of unusual style. Neither of these explanations was good enough. He simply didn't have one that was.

As he entered the lift with a couple of whispering nurses he had a job to prevent himself sagging against the wall for support. His hand went out to the buttons, hitting several, not just the floor he wanted. One nurse stared at him and asked if he felt all right.

'Just lack of sleep. I'm okay.' He managed a lopsided smile.

When he stumbled leaving the lift he heard a giggle behind him as the doors closed. Probably he did look more drunk than dog-tired.

The antiseptic corridors were hushed at this hour, and the lights dimmed. He pushed open the door to Karen's room and looked in.

She lay almost motionless beneath the soft blue coverlet, her hair spread across her pillow like dark silk, her breast rising and falling almost imperceptibly. Billie sat on the far side of the bed watching the still features. She reminded Tom of a small temple cat sitting guard on the holy treasure. Because she was unaware of being watched her face had a vulnerability he wouldn't have expected. A lot of pain showed there, as well as grief and strain, and the kind of accepting patience that a terminally ill patient will often display. Tom felt like an intruder.

'May I come in?'

Instantly Billie's mask was in place. She looked up sharply then seeing Tom, relaxed.

'It's you. You may as well. There has been no change.'

Tom pulled up a chair opposite Billie and looked at Karen. 'She's not here, is she? I wonder where she's gone?'

Billie frowned. 'What an extraordinary thing to say.' She picked up Karen's limp hand and held it gently cradled in her own. The blunt-ended nails had grown and been shaped by someone else. The traces of ingrained paint had almost disappeared. Billie carefully redeposited it on the coverlet. 'Of course, you are right. I worry that she might be suffering in that place, wherever it is. I fear she may not come back to us.'

'Has anyone tried to reach her on a regular basis? Is there a program?'

She shook her head. He noted that her hair, while neat, was displaying silver grey at the roots with pink tips that had grown out. Surprised at this telltale lack of grooming, he realised that Karen's aunt was far more upset than she would like the world to know.

'Attempts have been made. Professor Townshend brought in a psychiatrist. I was not permitted to be present, and I do not know what methods he used. They were not successful.'

'Have you tried calling her back yourself?'

'Of course I have,' she snapped. 'I could not count the hours that I have spent questioning and cajoling, and trying to find the key to the gate that was closed on her. There has been no response whatever.' She sounded angry with Karen, but now Tom knew better.

'There may not be a key,' he said gently. 'Then again, you may not have found the right one. Would you be willing for me to try?'

She turned her pale eyes on him and used them like searchlights. He felt as if the most secret fears and desires of his heart had been pulled out, examined and judged by the time she gave a little nod, and withdrew that uncomfortable gaze back to Karen's still face. 'You have my permission.'

'Thank you.'

They sat in silence for a time. Traffic noises were distant and muted through the double-glazed windows, and the coming darkness seemed to press around the softly-lit room, creating a well of intimacy, a cocoon for three souls connected by the strands of loving concern. Then Billie began to talk.

At first the words came slowly, almost unwillingly, then they increased in pace as she was caught in the rush of a cathartic release.

'She is all I have. The war took most of them. There is no one left but Karen.' Her tone did not ask for pity. She was speaking to herself, Tom realised, and allowing him to listen in if he wanted to.

He settled back and waited.

'I do not deserve to keep her, I know. Once I threw away my chance to earn her love, then tried to buy it back, too late.' She sighed, leaning forward to smooth the sheet under the sleeping girl's chin. 'My sister was very beautiful, but the man she married was not. He gave their child her straight dark hair with straight dark brows that frown. He also gave her quickness of mind. They both bequeathed their creativity to that grave little scrap of a thing. I do not know where she found her eyes. They are magnificent – amber, like a tiger's eyes. Also, she has the proud temperament of just such a jungle creature. I have discovered it, to my cost.'

She looked up at Tom. 'Have you ever done something you so regret that you would give all you possessed to recall the act, knowing that nothing can ease your guilt?' Her voice remained steady, yet Tom recognised a question loaded with deep-core emotion.

'Yes, I have. I imagine we all have at some time done something we have to bear with us all our lives. We can only admit it and then go on.'

Billie laughed harshly. 'How profound! Do all human beings talk in platitudes?'

Tom shrugged. He knew she was nowhere near finished.

Billie relapsed into silence for awhile, then resumed her monologue. 'Her father occupied the Chair of History at one of your great universities. He was supposedly of good family, but they had died out. I could not see why my sister should love him. I did not believe she would leave me to marry him and set up house in some drab little English town, and become a drab little *menagere*. I kept myself apart. I would not even answer her letters. And then . . . then she died. My lovely gifted Fleur, so young, so *vivante*.'

Her voice broke at last. She could not continue for a time. 'I could not take the child. I was too desolate. And there were other reasons. No matter. When I finally came to look for her, ten years later, she was a young woman formed. She did not easily forget the barren years without family; and how she longed for love! Like a dried out sponge, she thirsted for it. Her nature was meant to be tender. It is a surface thing, this brittleness she has fashioned for her protection. She wanted to give me her trust, even when I had failed her before so badly. But, *helas*, I have not the way of expressing the emotions easily. When that pig she married dragged her through hell, I could not show what I felt. It is my cross that I must bear.'

Tom stamped on the little inward spark of anger that had flared. Here was another self-absorbed woman, just like Valerie. How much hurt they inflicted on others.

'What happened to her father? Surely he didn't abandon his child.'

She said indifferently, 'Oh, he died, too, in the caravan fire.'

'Fire! Was Karen burned?'

'No. The first blast threw her aside. She was badly shocked, how badly we did not realise at the time.'

'She was traumatised by fire,' Tom said slowly, recalling Theo Sampson's version of her flight from the gallery. 'Then flung into a strange world amongst strangers. Poor mite.'

A faint colour stained Billie's cheeks. She looked away.

'Karen is going to be a great artist one of these days,' Tom said, with emphasis. 'Whatever life has done to her it has formed a spiritual basis for her creativity that is very powerful. I believe she will grow into one of the most profound exponents of artistic expression this country has seen.'

'You really think so?' Billie's interest quickened. 'I, too, have thought it possible. That is why I asked Theo Sampson to give her a showing.' The light died out of her face. 'But no. It is too much to hope.' She gestured despairingly at the pillow. 'Look at her face. It has been wiped clean of all living.'

'You are not to give up on her, do you hear!' Tom spoke sharply, with all his authority. 'Her greatest need is for people who believe in her, who will fight for her day and night, hour by hour.'

She looked at him. 'Show me how, and I will fight. How I will fight!'

'You could start by not being so hard on yourself. Negativity is catching. We need to create a positive atmosphere in this room, and carry it into everything that concerns Karen. When you touch her, speak to her as though she was listening to you. Brush her hair and tell her how much you love her. Massage the muscles of her hands and talk about the work those hands will soon be doing. She will be having plenty of physiotherapy, I know. Why not combine it with a . . . a cornucopia of verbal reassurance, pouring out all over her. Is there anyone she particularly cares about – someone whose presence might penetrate through to her consciousness?'

'Adele! *Mon Dieu*, why did I not think of that?'

'Who is Adele?'

'Her child.'

'It might be traumatic for a child to see her mother in such a condition. But if all else fails . . . What about her husband? Is he really as bad as all that?'

Billie's teeth snapped together viciously. '*Cette espece de cochon*! To call him a pig is to flatter him. If he came it would be to gloat.'

Tom paled. 'What kind of a bastard is he?'

'The worst kind. I cannot begin to tell you the things he made my niece suffer. When she thought she had escaped he tied her to him with a cord about the neck, her own baby. It is an exquisite torment he has devised. Adele is dangled before her eyes and withdrawn. He makes a promise and revokes it at the last moment. How she suffers.'

Tom felt it was fortunate he'd had so much practice in keeping his emotions in check. He said quite mildly, 'No court would keep a mother from her child unless she was unfit, and I refuse to believe that anyone could say such a thing about Karen.'

'You have not met Humphrey. He is unique. Yet Karen has learned to fight. There was to be a big court case soon after Christmas. She had a very good chance of gaining custody. You see, during the divorce she was too upset, and still very ill. Overwork and malnutrition are poor preparation for giving birth. She gave a bad impression, and Humphrey Doran capitalised on this. He is also extremely wealthy, and could hire the most skilled counsel. We were not well advised, and she lost her right to bring up her own baby. The court gave Adele to that pig.'

'I see. And if Karen cannot appear the case will go by default. What rotten luck.' Inwardly he jeered at himself. What a time in life to discover the instincts of a knight errant. All the same, he felt Karen needed a champion. There'd been few enough in her life.

Billie was studying him. 'Who are you, Tom Levy?'

He understood what she meant. 'I am a psychotherapist. I practise in London, mainly in the East End, although I have rooms near my flat in Camden Town. I also see patients at clinics, and if necessary, in hospital.'

'Karen did not . . .'

'No, she didn't seek my help. I attended the opening of her exhibition at Theo Sampson's gallery and met her there.'

'Then you have known her . . . Tiens! You have met only the one time.'

'Yes.'

'You spoke of her work with feeling. Do you have something of hers?'

'I bought a mystical painting that has had a very strange effect on me. It's had an effect on nearly every person who has seen it. There is meaning and truth in it, and a passionate belief in the beauty of existence. That's why I say she has a future in the art world. She's going to set it alight.'

He looked down at the sleeping girl. 'You will do it, I swear you'll have the chance.'

He turned back to Billie. 'I must go. Think about what I've said – about positive thoughts and actions around her all the time. Pass it on to the relevant staff. I'm sure there will be no opposition. If you do meet it, insist that the staff member be replaced.' He smiled. 'I do not suggest you apply this rule to Professor Townshend himself. In any case, he's one of the most positive men I've met. Goodbye, Miss Carnot.'

She took his hand. 'You are an original, but I like you. You may call me Billie.'

'Thank you.' He gave his odd little bow, a heritage of his courteous

289

European-born father. 'I'll begin my own program of positive action tomorrow evening. Please, if you can, arrange to keep other visitors away.'

She nodded. '*Au revoir*, Tom Levy. Sleep well tonight.'

From the start, Tom refused to treat Karen as a patient. Not for her the detachment and strict protocol of the therapist–patient relationship. Whenever he sat down at her bedside he told her how lovely she looked, and how happy he was to be there with her. He talked about himself and his interests, about rock scrambling in Wales and hiking in the Cotswolds, about his books, his music, his cat. Billie Carnot listened for the first session, then gave her tacit approval by not appearing for the next and following ones. He felt she had understood that his interest was personal, although platonic, and she was prepared to use any means of reaching through to her niece.

With Karen's limp hand in his Tom sat by the bed and talked into the night hours, injecting his deep voice with humour and the love of life that formed his character. He read to her from his favourite novels and short stories, and played music from his collection on a tape recorder he brought with him. He also went in for storytelling. The stories had to have meaning for him, to convey genuine feeling. He really believed that. It was a strong emotion that would forge the key to Karen's gate and open the way to whatever land she now lived in.

First he painted for her a word picture of his growing up, a Jewish child in a background of semi-poverty, but totally unaware that he was deprived. He told of his mother's gentle strength and his father's code of moral teachings, lived daily as an example to his children. His sisters, Rosa and Rachel, were children again, little mothers tyrannising their baby brother, Tom himself. His grandparents, bewildered, uprooted by the war, their hearts left behind in Lithuanian soil, but slaving into old age to give their children a foothold in the new land.

Karen lay unresponsive. But Tom was ready for a long siege.

The next night he asked her questions about her painting, and supplied the answers himself. He discussed the techniques she used and the subjects she chose, being deliberately provocative. On Theo and his ambitions he waxed positively libellous.

Adele was a fruitful topic. He reminded Karen of her love for her child, and her responsibility to see that she grew up in a caring atmosphere. Shamelessly he played on this theme, although with great delicacy. The snapshot Billie had brought in from Karen's flat gave him the cherubic likeness on which to embroider. Then he told of his own love for children, how he helped them professionally and hoped one day to have some of his own.

It all flowed over Karen without leaving a trace.

Billie came the next evening and he cut short his visit, acknowledging her prior rights. He thought she looked very tired. It didn't make her any happier to hear there had been no progress made.

'Dr Levy, I have been making enquiries about you. It seems you are well thought of by your peers, but I do question your expertise in the case of my niece.'

'I claim no such expertise,' he said mildly, noting his swift demotion to the distancing 'Doctor'. 'But I do believe in constant stimulation of the coma patient. I work with words, Miss Carnot, and with emotions. To each his own tools and methods. If we are to penetrate beyond the barrier to Karen's present reality I believe it will be done with those tools.'

Was she going to forbid him to see Karen? She was capable of it, and within her rights. He held his breath.

Billie smiled. Her face was transformed. Cold grey eyes became limpid and sparkling. An entirely natural but well banked-down charm was allowed to pour forth like a warming flood to bathe his stunned senses.

'It is still 'Billie", Tom Levy. Do not look so surprised. I have my own methods of testing people. It is my business to do so. Now, you will sit down and tell me something of yourself.'

Amused yet annoyed at her tactics, Tom decided his own interests would be best served if he let himself be charmed. All the same he would tailor his life-story, or whatever it was she wanted, to suit her volatile temperament.

'What would you like to know?'

She eyed him speculatively. 'Tell me about your failed marriage.'

He didn't gasp, nor retort that it was none of her business, but looked steadily back at her. 'Of course, it was doomed from the start, as any marriage must be when husband and wife had a basic ignorance of each other's needs. Our little illusion of compatibility soon shattered when I found that I needed freedom, and had tied myself to a strangler vine. Poor Cherry. She couldn't help being the over-indulged only child of a social-climbing Papa. There is no one so jealous of his status as the self-made man, let me tell you. Papa Bell of Bell's Better Biscuits just about fell down in a foaming fit when the daughter of his bosom went out slumming with a Jew-boy and ended up marrying him.' He could laugh now, but at the time he'd been furiously hurt.

Billie put her finger right on the point. 'You must have been wilful children with your eyes only half-open.'

Tom spread his hands in acknowledgement. 'We rushed into rebellion against our respective backgrounds, and we paid the price. Cherry hadn't a thought in her head beyond dancing and clothes, and having a good time. I, as a partner and fellow party-goer, turned out to be an A-grade flop. All I wanted was a fire, a cat and a corner with a good book, plus several hours' sleep to keep me going at work. The whole thing now seems so cliched and inevitable. But I was sorry to hurt my parents.'

He sat in silence for a time, remembering. Absently, he lifted a piece of black silk from the pillow and wound it around his finger, stroking the smooth strands.

'I turned against my too rigid religion, then I married a gentile and renounced my faith altogether. The divorce was one blow too many. I could see in my mother's eyes that she blamed me for Grandpapa's death. That made me more angry and guilty.' He sighed. 'And that, too is a cliche. This is a boring story, Billie. I think that tomorrow I shall bring some poetry and read to our Sleeping Beauty.' He got up and leaned over the still figure in the bed.

'Goodnight, Karen.'

Karen made no answer.

Valerie came daily to Tom's rooms for what he could only describe as her peformance before witnesses. Phil came along, too. Clearly, he was enthralled by his busman's holiday, and it would take radical surgery to detach him.

In one way Tom welcomed the presence of another observer. An additional trained mind on the job, not to mention a strong restraining physical presence, gave him comfort. He'd got over his guilt at his inability to control and thereby help his patient when she regressed. There was nothing he could do about it. She slipped away of her own accord. Surely it was better for her to do so under supervision. He had to accept this as the price they paid for continuing investigation.

Lately, however, he'd begun to doubt the value of their reward. Nothing much had changed since the first startling episodes. A lot had come to light in the way of historical footnotes, especially as they concerned Valerie. More importantly, Tom felt they had glimpsed a part of a grand design in the universe, something like a blueprint for all living matter. It had sneaked up on Tom and changed his thinking forever. Yet now it seemed they'd stuck – as if they were being told to stop going over the same ground and get on with the rest of it themselves.

But Valerie was adamant. They must go on. So Tom shelved his private nightmare, of her slipping into regression in front of a semi-trailer. He tried not to think about her failing to return from the past and becoming trapped between two worlds. Again, there was nothing he could do. Valerie sat in the driver's seat. He just went along for the ride.

Her obvious enjoyment baffled him. One morning before Phil arrived, Tom allowed his lack of enthusiasm for the approaching session to peak and overflow.

'Valerie, how can you want to go on? The first two lives were, admittedly, the worst so far. But you know that at the very least you're likely to experience a violent death at the end of each incarnation, and often the life itself is pretty unpleasant. Why keep putting yourself through it?' He thought her composure assumed, the studied way she arranged herself against the desk, elegantly relaxed, white hands disposed to display her rings. Light trembled and flashed. Had the fingers twitched?

'I've been giving it thought, and part of the answer is plain curiosity. I can't bear to miss anything. It's all so fascinating, learning about different facets of myself, especially as a male. I hadn't realised how much there is of both sexes in each of us. It isn't so very different, after all, being in a man's skin.'

'To a degree, that's so. Men and women do view the world from different standpoints, but social pressures create some of the differences. We're taught to repress a large portion of our psyche in favour of boosting another. It's crippling and unnatural.'

Valerie didn't give much attention to this profound utterance. Her attention was on her own experiences. She smiled coyly. 'You must admit I haven't always been a monster.'

'Certainly not.' Tom thought with amusement of a particularly risque sortie into seventeenth-century Vienna, and the total contrast of a Buddhist monastery somewhere in French Indo-China. 'Since the satisfaction of curiosity is only part of your answer, what's the remainder – or need I ask? You want to put things right this time around, isn't that it?'

'Yes. I've already explained. I want to redress the karmic balance.'

'Then, what are you doing about it?'

She looked confused. 'Doing?'

'How are you going to achieve this result? What changes are you making in your attitudes and habits? How can you know what you must do to alter the karmic pattern?'

'I'm working on it.'

Her face had closed and he sensed quite a lot of hostility in her. Debating whether to continue pushing, he decided he must. He'd do it on her ground – on the premise that her regressions were true experiences relived.

'Valerie, you're wasting time, yours and mine. I have other patients with urgent needs, and while I'm quite prepared to keep on working with you, you must co-operate. It's not progressing to keep on discovering and reliving past lives. The pattern has become clear. You know what it is that has pursued you through life after life, and it would be very dangerous for you to go on alone.'

She'd turned her back to him. He thought from her withdrawn attitude that she wasn't going to take up his challenge. Then she said, 'You're reneging on our agreement. You promised to help me.'

'I have helped you. Phil has helped you. We've given hours of our free time, resuscitated you, supported you in every way we can think of. Now it's your turn. We can't do any more.'

'I don't want to discuss it just now.'

'When, then? It can't be put off much longer.' Tom let impatience colour his voice. He'd made his decision and he would stand on it.

He now appreciated the mind set of a person accustomed to receiving unquestioning obedience. For forty years Valerie's whims had been paramount to her. Armoured in privilege, like the beautifully scaled sea-serpent she had swished across the surface of life, leaving nothing but a few ripples behind her. He didn't believe she knew the depths. Because she was unable to form strong attachments her failed marriages had damaged her pride more than her heart.

All the same, she knew loneliness and the lack of real direction. These things had driven her to him. Already she'd admitted her need to change her lifestyle, but would she do it?

Tom suspected she was hovering on the edge of decision right now. A part of her needed to deny the meaning behind all the happenings of the past few weeks, wanted to bury it and continue along her hedonistic path. But buried secrets had a habit of finding alternative routes to the surface. There would be pain whichever way she went. If she'd only understand what great rewards could come from change. He wanted to see what Valerie could become. He wanted her to make the intelligent decision.

He put a hand on her shoulder and turned her to face him. Understanding and empathy had replaced the impatience. 'Valerie, you've come a long way, and learned a lot about yourself. As you've said, the pattern has been shown to you. Now, you can choose to go on as you are, and pay the price of continually meeting the challenge in different and more taxing forms, slipping down the ladder of progress a little further each lifetime. Or you can take a hold on things, use your free will to alter the shape, structure and perspective of your personal blueprint – to make it *what you want*. That's the opportunity within your grasp. For myself, I refuse to believe that a person of your courage and ability will let it slide. Grasp it, Valerie! Make life work for *you*!'

'Do you really think I'm courageous?' She seemed startled, her aggressive edge turned by the small compliment. 'No one has ever said that about me.'

Tom blessed whatever guidance had put that word in his mouth. She looked like a child savouring a new idea, pleased yet not wholly believing.

His smile that had warmed and comforted so many, underlined the genuineness of his words. 'It will take all you have to make the change, but you can do it. There is a talent in you for loving and caring. It just needs to be released and put to use.'

'I hope so.' She spoke humbly. 'Tom, would you help me just a little more? Have dinner with me tonight at my place, and talk to me about how I tackle this thing. Please, Tom.'

He wavered. It meant cutting short his time with Karen. But he did owe it to Valerie to finish the job, and that meant seeing her feet set on the new road. She had to be weaned away from the habit of regression, and this new compliant mood should be reinforced and used. Hiding his regrets, he agreed.

When told that the session had been postponed indefinitely, Phil reacted with disappointment. 'We're nowhere near finished, yet. What's the idea?'

'I feel Valerie's gone as far as she's able. Now she should put to use what she's learned. It's time for a change of direction, Phil.'

'Not in my book.' Phil rounded on Valerie. 'What made you decide to stop? I thought you were fascinated. You loved trying out all those different roles. Was it your idea, or Tom's to wind up the sessions?'

'Mine,' Tom interjected. 'Stop bullying, Phil, and let me explain.'

'I don't want to hear your explanations. You've been against this right from the start, haven't you? And now you're running scared. You're afraid of what you might discover if you go on. You're thinking of the publicity and the fact that you might have to admit your change of values to a community still bound up in Victorian hide. Valerie's the greatest thing that's happened in this line since Guirdham's investigations of the seventies, but you don't want to let anyone else in on her.'

'His work was discredited in the end,' Tom interjected. He'd read the English psychiatrist's publication, *The Cathars and Reincarnation*, and been impressed by the detail and complexity of the work. Giurdham's subject had seemed perfectly genuine, and uncannily correct in her reportage of her life as a Cathar in thirteenth-century France, and her horrifying death in the massacre of these people at Montsegur. But for Tom the whole analysis was nullified by a later claim that Guirdham himself had been a Cathar involved with his subject at that very time. This seemed an obvious development of the usual patient fixation on her therapist. He'd thrown the book down in disgust.

Phil ground his teeth. 'Don't you see? You idiot! With Valerie you've got the chance to go one better, with lifetime after lifetime through the eyes of one person. You've only got to go on long enough and there'll be a whole book of life experiences we can check – dates, places, names. But no, not you, with your feet in cold water and your mind set firmly in scientific cement. Well, keep your precious privacy, and your fears. I'm through with it all. Carla and I can move on. There are plenty of places we want to visit before going home.' He flung out of the room, then hung in the doorway to vent his sarcasm. 'It's been a great experience, pal. I've learned a lot.'

Tom stood stunned. None of this was true, except perhaps his early unwillingness to continue with the regressions. But that had changed. His interest had been every bit as strong as Phil's, with the added incentive of a longing to believe. He was so close to grasping it. So close. Yet he knew the final step had to come from pressure within – not from watching Valerie's gyrations through her personal past.

Sadly, he started to lock up for the night. Valerie had slipped away, he noted. Just as well. He really felt too tired to cope with anything more.

CHAPTER 22

Karen saw Amanda off in the early morning. Frost had turned the ground iron hard, and the horses' hooves rang like hammers on an anvil. Snorting steam, they shivered and pranced, causing the coach to sway uncomfortably as Amanda mounted the step.

Leaning from the window she kissed Karen and whispered, 'See what may be done. I shall pray for your safety, and his. Whatever course you take, it must be with the greatest care.'

She drew back. From the portico Karen waved as rugs were twitched from the horses' backs and the postilions sprang up. The coach rocked forward, and they were away. Shivering with more than cold, Karen went inside.

She shut herself in the library and thought what action she could take to warn Antony. Charles would be back from London very soon. He would know how to send a message by the shortest route. Meanwhile, she must show a calm face before Lord Edward and Chloe, burying her own need to be doing something, anything at all but waiting in growing fear for justification of Amanda's warnings.

Alone in her studio that evening, Karen had a visitor. Hearing the faint click of the door-latch she looked up to see Sybilla standing watching her.

Something within her lurched, as though she'd missed her footing on the stairs. She put a hand on her work table to steady herself.

'What are you doing here?'

Sybilla smiled, and Karen wished she hadn't. There was a quality to her expression that she couldn't quite define, a suggestion of anticipation, like the cat's stillness as it listens at a mousehole.

'I am paying a long overdue call, Caro. I have a debt I owe, and this is settling day.'

'What do you mean?' The words were mechanical, a holding off while her brain leapt ahead, conning possibilities.

'Exactly what you think I mean, sweet coz. You have proved uncommonly difficult to kill, but now your measure is run. You may give my greetings to Antony when you meet.'

Karen felt the blood draining away from her head. She leaned over the table, clutching the edge, willing her mind to clear. Sybilla waited. Clearly she was savouring every triumphant second of this meeting, happy for it to be prolonged.

Karen raised her face and said simply, 'What have you done?' She'd never before seen anyone actually wet her lips in expectation of a delicacy to come.

'He is in deadly peril, your beloved Antony. Even now he is being stalked by his enemies. Very soon they will kill him. I have arranged it.' Her smugness dissolved and she added with more irritability than venom, 'He should not have repulsed me. 'Tis his own fault that this fate has come upon him.'

'You've betrayed him! I thought you loved him.'

'I hate him! He should have been mine. It was promised. As my husband, he should have suffered the most unique torments, until I tired of the game. But it has gone awry.' Sybilla's voice had risen as her emotions began to push through the assumed calmness of manner. 'First he wed that puling Jenny. Then you, with your gaudy beauty. The man has no discernment.' She was working up a fresh load of anger to vent on her victim.

Karen faced her with dignity, hiding her grief. 'Tell me something, Sybilla. You were behind Jenny's death, weren't you? You set the fire and trapped her in the tower?'

She'd succeeded in arresting the tirade. Sybilla's expression was her answer – a mingling of cunning and shock.

'How did you know that?'

'Because I am Jenny. My spirit re-entered the body of Caroline Marchmont when she died at the foot of the stairs – your work also. I know what you have done, and you will pay a terrible price in the end, Sybilla.'

Sybilla reared back, but she recovered quickly. 'What is this nonsense? Do you take me for a fool?' The black eyes that had widened in an instant's terror, now narrowed in concentration. 'You seek to turn me from my purpose, but I am not so easily cozened. Had you been that mealy-mouthed mouse you would have exposed me long ago; and Antony would have killed me with his own hands.'

'I didn't tell him. He has enough to bear. But I will tell you . . . On that hot summer's afternoon I was playing with Chloe in the nursery. Feathers became disturbed and I let him out. He must have gone downstairs and found you, and for that you bludgeoned him almost to death. He has been simple ever since, but he knows his enemy, doesn't he?

'When I discovered the fire I carried Chloe up the tower stairs to the roof. It was a journey of torment, Sybilla. I died many times on those stairs, and I will not forget, ever.'

Sybilla stood immobile, arrested by Karen's chilling lack of emotion. The calm voice went on.

'When you killed me, you killed my unborn baby, too. For that alone, you are damned. Chloe was saved, and I've known the great joy of being reunited with my child and my husband – but now you want to destroy me once again. You are too evil to live, Sybilla. There's a strain of twisted ugliness in you that can't bear to see the happiness of others. What will become of you?'

Sybilla laughed. The raucous sound split the air and assaulted the ears, finally dying away. Watching, Karen saw the personality shift, the turning inside-out to reveal something not quite human in place of the woman she knew.

'Tittle-tattle. Any number of persons could have told you that tale.'

Karen's voice dropped to a whisper. She felt too drained to argue further. 'How many, do you suppose, knew of the letter you sent – the vicious outpourings of a mind brimming with hatred and lust? I found the letter that afternoon, slipped under the nursery door. I told no one about it, not even Antony. Only you and I knew of its existence. And, of course, it was destroyed in the fire.'

Sybilla was quiet, now, musing. 'It must be fate. To think that I rid myself of you once, and in killing another rival I brought you back to life. How strange. How very ridiculous. Well, no matter. If I cannot become a Countess I can be the sister of an Earl. Basil will be the heir within days, and Earl of Roth soon enough. And you . . . you will have a noble headstone, my dear.' She took a step forward and Karen saw the tiny pistol in her fist. It looked like a toy, winking silver in the lamplight.

She stared at it stupidly. Her mind seemed to be working very slowly, like machinery clogged in oil. The situation was too unreal. She didn't quite believe in her own danger. The remembrance of Antony's peril swamped her, and with it a terrible feeling of impotence. She was going to die, and so would he. They would lose each other again, with no guarantee of a time or place to meet in the future.

Sybilla pulled back the hammer. Karen reacted automatically and instantly. Her hand swept the table top, grasped the turpentine bottle full of brushes, and flung it at Sybilla.

With a scream, she dropped the pistol to claw at her face. But she'd warded off the bottle, and only a little of the contents had splashed her eyes . . . just enough to fuel her madness. The pistol had spun away towards the door. Even as Karen leapt for it Sybilla had it in her grasp. They both crouched like animals ready to spring.

Karen had come to her senses, too late.

Sybilla wiped her inflamed eyes on her sleeve. 'Bitch! Now you are sped.' She took careful aim at Karen's head, just as the door opened and struck her in the back, flinging her aside.

'Good God! What is happening here?' Charles took in the scene, his gaze finally resting on Sybilla. She was an unlovely sight, her hair down about her shoulders, dripping with turpentine, her face mottled with temper, her pistol once more directed at Karen.

'You can see what's happening.' Karen's voice creaked – an aftermath of shock, she supposed. 'Sybilla came to taunt me with the knowledge that Antony is going to die – and to kill me.' She wanted to move. Her muscles ached with the strain of remaining utterly still. But the pistol was held steady. Sybilla's attention had not altered a fraction.

Charles stiffened. 'This must be arrant nonsense. Give me that pistol. I can scarcely credit that any woman . . .' He took a step forward, then stopped, seeing the pistol lined up on his own heart.

'Do not move!' snapped Sybilla. 'Be damned to you for a chicken-hearted ninny, Charles Hastings.' She glanced swiftly at Karen. 'Here is your betrayer. He is the one so mad for money to wed his inamorata that he would sell his friend and benefactor. Regard him! Judas Iscariot himself!'

He winced under her contemptuous tongue, but all his attention was concentrated on Karen.

Her tightened muscles had gone limp, the adrenalin-induced energy evaporated as she stared at him, seeing a complete stranger. 'Charles? You?'

With an obvious effort he held her gaze. 'Wait. I will tell you all, but first, what did you mean, "Antony will die"? Did Sybilla tell you that?'

When Karen nodded, he said with some force, 'He is to be taken prisoner, yes. But I have been assured that he will come to no harm. It is an express condition – '

Sybilla snorted. 'Bah! 'Tis easily seen you are not cut out for intrigue. I altered the message, of course, promising the Frenchmen greater prizes if they followed Antony and disposed of all their enemies in one blow. He will lead them to his fellow conspirators and they will all die. And the cream of it is, should any person incur censure 'twill be you, alone.'

The room had grown quiet. Karen felt detached from the scene she'd witnessed. She might have been watching a play for all the involvement she felt. Charles' face, slack and grey, looked like a lump of badly moulded china clay; his shoulders sagged. But his suffering failed to move her. He was a lay figure, a representation of that standard character in drama, the betrayer revealed.

Sybilla she saw as the classic archetype, the bringer of destruction. And she, herself, was the watcher on the sidelines, aware but apart.

Then, with the impact of a bomb burst, the static scene blew apart. Charles let out a groan of agony. 'Witch! I was mad to throw in my lot with you and your brother. But I have come to my senses.'

He turned to Karen. 'I have this minute arrived from London. Lafitte's ship lies off the coast nearby, and I intend to follow Antony to warn him. I do not ask you to pardon the unpardonable. But you may believe that I shall suffer for my treachery all the rest of my life. I know now that Amanda was not meant for me, and I have forfeited Antony's friendship, and yours . . .'

Sybilla pulled the trigger.

The explosion echoed in the room, and a puff of acrid smoke caught in Karen's throat. She saw Charles stagger back. He looked down at the crimson flower blooming on his shirt-front, such a small flower with a black hole at its centre. Then he looked at Sybilla. 'Why? . . .'

'You would have warned him.' She watched dispassionately as his knees slowly buckled and he fell to the floor.

Karen flung herself down beside him, already tearing at her petticoat. 'Don't move, Charles. I'll put a pressure bandage on to stop the bleeding. You'll be all right.' Her fingers flew, fashioning pad and bandage as she spoke. 'Tell me how to reach him, Charles.' Her voice shook with the effort of remaining calm. She could see his eyes glazing over. He would be unconscious at any minute. She wanted to shake him. 'For God's sake, Charles! Tell me!'

He stared over her shoulder, his eyes widening into a look of sick horror. Karen turned.

Sybilla advanced upon her, half-crouched, her lips drawn back in a wild-cat snarl. The wet tangle of hair added to her look of savagery, and her eyes were half-closed in concentration. She placed each foot carefully, stepping with feline grace, in her hand Karen's own palette knife, its blade glinting in the lamplight.

Karen sprang up, tripping on her torn petticoat, then righting herself. She started to back away. Sybilla followed, stalking her prey.

Silence. The slurring sound of slippers on boards. The quickened breathing of hunter and hunted. A moan from the injured man as Sybilla stepped on his hand. An indrawn breath as Karen slipped in a puddle of turpentine, and as quickly recovered. A hiss as Sybilla came forward in a rush and met the cushion flung at her. But the gap was slowly closing.

Karen had backed up to the end wall where her unused canvases were stacked. She picked up one of the smaller ones and threw it. Sybilla easily ducked aside. Then Karen was struck with an idea. Clutching several thicknesses of stretched canvas across her chest, she flung herself forward, seeking to catch the knife and entangle it. Sybilla gave way angrily.

If she could just drive her into a corner, Karen prayed. If she could put that knife out of action, then she could disable Sybilla easily. It was months since she'd practised, but she hadn't forgotten how. It was a matter of balance and speed, not brawn, and Sybilla's greater height and strength would not matter.

Sybilla changed tactics. Whirling about she raced for the other end of the room, picked up the model's chair and toppled it in Karen's path. She went over it as if chopped off at the knees, crashing into the canvases and ripping them from their frames. Whimpering from the pain in her shins, she looked up to see Sybilla coming at her, the knife angled to drive straight down. In her mind she already felt it plunge into her body, the soft skin and muscle tearing away, the blood pouring out in a sticky red tide, taking her life with it.

Paralysed by the vision, she left her move almost too late. Sybilla herself supplied the motivating force to get her back up on her knees, then to her feet, shaky, but still erect. Sybilla, who could not resist the last chance to taunt her victim.

Sure of her victory, she stopped when only a few feet away, waiting, enjoying Karen's panic. 'There is no escape. You will die very soon.' She panted the words, and Karen realised she was waiting to get her breath back, as well as torment her. 'How does it feel to be the rabbit trapped at the end of the burrow? Does your heart shake in your breast? Do your limbs tremble, and your mind refuse to obey your will? Tell me, little rabbit.'

'I'd rather be a rabbit than a stoat.' Karen stumbled, rather than ran for the door, feeling as unco-ordinated as a newborn foal. Her ankle turned under her and she fell, rolling swiftly aside and landing up against the table leg. She dragged herself up and behind its feeble barrier. Sybilla came in a rush, her skirts flying behind her, a fury bent on revenge.

Karen swept frantic hands over the table top, seeking a weapon. Paints, brushes, water jar. She picked up the jar and threw it, and missed. Sybilla came on. She was very close now. Behind Karen was the window and a sheer drop to the terrace. Before her the knife hovered, only inches away.

Remember your training. Remember how it was. Karen flashed back to the hot, stuffy room, with its canvas mats and smell of sweat, the pain of aching muscles and the satisfying 'thud' as an opponent fell. She remembered why she'd spent so many hours learning self defence. It was to pull herself out of the 'victim' class in society, to give her back the self-esteem eroded by Humphrey and others. It was for precisely such an occasion as this.

Clutching her head, she leaned sideways, sagging, about to fall. The knife flashed up. In a blur of speed, Karen's arm shot out, striking Sybilla's wrist with terrific impact, sending the blade arcing through the air and half-way across the room. Sybilla screeched and gave way. Karen lunged and grabbed her skirt, twisting it about her legs. Trapped, Sybilla grasped two handfuls of her opponent's hair, leaving her own body exposed. Karen drove her fist hard into the solar plexus, at the same time tripping Sybilla's feet from under her.

Sybilla's grip slackened. Her mouth opened wide as the breath was driven from her body. Bent double, she fell backwards, slamming into the table, bringing it down with her. Paints, brushes, paraphernalia of all kinds scattered everywhere. The easel fell with a crash, gouging splinters in the floor. Glass shattered and flew like barbed arrows, to lie embedded in the wrecked canvas. Crystal shards from the broken lamp layered Sybilla's skirts, and burning oil ignited her turpentine-soaked hair. She flared like a torch.

Sybilla screamed horribly. Her face ringed in flame, she staggered to her feet, beating at her head with hands already blistered from the heat.

Horror-stricken, Karen saw only the fire she dreaded so much. Thrust instantly back into the burning tower, she was once again hunted up the spiral stairs, through air thick with smoke, on feet that bled – falling, struggling erect, the skin torn from arms and elbows, her lungs aching for the blessed relief of cool fresh air – agonised with the knowledge that she and her baby were doomed.

'Help me! In the name of God . . . !' Sybilla's voice strangled in a throat raw with screaming. Her clothes wrapped her in a flaming shroud as she fell forward at Karen's feet.

Karen could not see her. She had come to the top of the tower and thrown Chloe to safety. Now she heard the voice of the fire as it reached out for her, it's dragon's breath enveloping her, sucking the flesh from her bones. The terrible screaming in her head was the echo of her own voice as she fell into the inferno. Or was it Sybilla?

Caught up in Jenny's agony of the past, she scarcely heard the horrified exclamations as servants crowded through the open door. She looked with unseeing eyes at the mound of blackened flesh and scorched cloth at her feet, her mind an echoing chamber scoured empty by remembered pain.

CHAPTER 23

She huddled under the piled furs, not even the tip of her nose showing, and wondered whether she'd ever be warm again. Siberia couldn't possibly be worse than this frozen landscape. She didn't know which she liked least, the silent, enclosing forests, with only the hiss of the sled runners and the occasional crack of a bough giving way under the weight of snow, or the equally silent open spaces, humped with great boulders of granite, like gigantic snowballs.

It was worse when the silence of the tingling frosty air was broken by the howl of wolves. She'd never heard a more frightening sound. It ran up the nerves of her spine like an electric shock, leaving her shivering in the most abject terror. She'd thought she could face anything for Antony. Anything at all. But wolves! The sturdy little horses that pulled her lifted their heads to listen, but the driver kept them going. It would be fatal to be caught by darkness before reaching the next staging post.

Karen felt she'd been travelling for weeks, although it was just ten days since she'd left the Manor in haste, clutching a valise, a bag of golden guineas, a pistol and Charles' intaglio ring. Poor Charles. If he did recover, and at the time of her leaving this was still in doubt, he'd never be the same. Diminished in his own eyes, as well as those of the people he had betrayed, something had gone out of him.

He had done his best to prepare her for what lay ahead, and her own cautious enquiries at the little cottage at Seven Rock Point had brought her to Jean Lafitte. He'd been willing enough to help, at sight of the money and the ring – a duplicate of the one Antony wore on his journeys as an introduction to those who would help an Englishman. It was quite a network, so she was assured, and after the past few days' experience she had to agree.

Lafitte's ship, a small brigantine with the odd name, *Initiative*, was an instance. She carried flags of many nations, any one of which could be run up at a moment's notice. Lafitte also possessed an astonishing array of ship's papers, allowing him to change allegiance as often as he wished, including a pass which requested any British vessel to render him assistance upon request. Since he also held a duplicate, suitably amended, in French, and signed by Napoleon's own Minister of War, the smuggler found no trouble at all in negotiating the waters of the Channel.

Except for the winds. These he could not control. Fortunately for Karen's purpose, they had blown in the right direction, from the west until off Calais, and then more from the south-west. But they were gales, harrying the little ship so that she bucketed up and down the great crests, her decks constantly swept by sheets of foaming grey water. Karen, closeted below for safety, had been sick enough to want to die.

When they finally battled into Leith, sheltered by the calmer waters of the Firth of Forth, she'd staggered ashore more than half dead. Had her journey not been so important she doubted whether she could have returned to the ship. However, Lafitte's cure for seasickness (after the event), several glasses of brisk bottled porter, worked surprisingly well. She had little memory of going aboard and setting sail under the protection of a British gunboat escorting a fleet of small vessels through the North Sea and past a hostile Denmark to Gothenburg.

The temperature dropped hourly. She'd found she couldn't stay on deck for more than a few minutes at a time, with the air so frosty on any exposed skin, and chilling her lungs with each breath. Not even her heavy fur-lined cloak could keep her warm on those ice-filmed decks. She could have cursed her bulky skirts, wishing she might dress like a man, or as a woman of the twentieth century.

The crossing remained uneventful until ice floes southbound from the Arctic began to thicken, bumping the sides of the vessel with increasing force. She noted that Lafitte kept his ship well within the cluster of the little fleet, letting the iron-hulled gun-boat lead the way; and she saw why when at last Gothenburg rose on the horizon, a white city against a white sky on a white sea. Up ahead, the water had turned to a sheet of ice, a mass of floes melded together by fallen snow and instantly frozen solid.

Standing at the bowrail, shivering inside her furs, Karen stared across the impenetrable ice and wondered if they dared try to break through.

Lafitte appeared at her side, smiling at her expression. 'There is a way, madame. We have not come such a distance only to be defeated by nature.' He pointed to a rowing boat moving in the distance. 'Those are men out there with crowbars breaking up the floes, keeping the channel free for us.'

'But, how can they possibly break through? It must be inches thick, at least.'

'Not in the channel. They do it every day, so that the ice does not have a chance to gain a firm hold. But when a great storm comes and they cannot do the work, then the channel will be closed.'

As they watched the gun-boat moved ahead, using its strengthened bows to crash a path through the weakened ice, working its way towards the toiling men. Lafitte excused himself to see to the delicate operation of threading his ship's passage. But Karen stayed at the rail to watch, her discomfort forgotten in the spectacle presented by the fleet, following each other like ducks through the slushy sea that already threatened to enclose them.

When they had docked and it was time to leave the *Initiative*, and Lafitte, she could with honesty thank him for his care for her.

His freebooter's smile had a cynical edge. 'You did not trust me to bring you safely to Sweden. But I have proved myself, I believe.'

Karen admitted it. 'I was wrong. You have been a wonderful escort, and I thank you from the bottom of my heart. Antony will be grateful to you.' Never once during the journey had she allowed herself any doubts. She would reach Antony in time to warn him. She had to. The messenger Lord Edward sent to London would warn the Government that their plans were in jeopardy, but not in time to help her husband. Her journey had been necessary. However, she couldn't deny her suspicions that Lafitte could be trusted only so far as it suited him, and he'd been shrewd enough to see this.

''Tis an honour to serve Milord Antony. He has risked his own life for mine, and I would do no less for him, and his. Once, when we were boarded by renegade Frenchmen who took us for mere freebooters, he cut down one who would have taken me from behind. And there have been other times.' He shrugged. 'I do not think that he will be far ahead. The winds would not have favoured him when he set sail. But you must leave Gothenburg at dawn. At this time of the year there are not above six hours of daylight, and 'tis not safe to travel after dark.'

'The roads are poor?'

'The roads are buried under two feet of frost. Whatever your destination, you will have to go by sled. MacGregor will arrange that. Horses are available at staging posts every ten miles, but they must be ordered in advance so that they can be fetched in by the peasants. MacGregor will also exchange your money for rix-dollars.' He cocked his head to one side and added slyly, 'There are other dangers for night travellers who lose their way – wolves, even bears.'

Karen shuddered. 'Don't worry. I'll follow your advice.'

Carrying her valise, Lafitte accompanied her through the icy streets to the house of a merchant, Ian MacGregor, just one more link in Antony's chain of British supporters.

Plodding through ankle-deep snow, Karen's cursory inspection showed a town that could be pretty, in summer. Just now, Gothenburg seemed to be built of ice bricks. All the buildings had been white plastered so that they merged into the landscape. There wasn't even a broken skyline because the rooves were flat and concealed. Silent, unreal, everything about the city seemed to have frozen solid, including the canal. Karen quickly lost interest in her surroundings as she felt ice water trickling in her boots. Her breath came out in cloudy puffs, like steam from a little locomotive, and the ground chill seemed to strike up beneath her skirts through her very inadequate underwear. All she wanted was to get indoors to a fire.

As soon as he'd seen her inside MacGregor's house, Lafitte returned to extract his ship from the ice and head for home. Karen felt a little forlorn, standing in the hall, rubbing her chilled fingers and waiting for her host. She wished Lafitte had waited to introduce her. But the ring was her pass-key, and the Scotsman, a somewhat dour merchant of grandfatherly years, seemed friendly enough. He took her to the drawing room and introduced her to his plump, motherly little wife, provided her with a cup of very weak tea, a huge dinner in the company of his noisy extended family, and later, in the privacy of his bookroom, news of Antony and his ultimate destination.

It seemed that he'd passed through the city no more than twenty-four hours earlier on the way to his rendezvous outside of Orebro, about twenty-four miles distant.

'Only twenty-four miles!'

MacGregor's jaw quivered in what might have been a grin. 'The Swedish mile is verra long, ma'am. 'Tis more than six times the length of the English measurement. Ye should make the journey within three to four days, if the Lord sends good weather. I ha' procured a passport from the Provincial Governor, without which ye canna travel, nor so much as hire staging horses; and since there are no public vehicles such as in England, I shall provide one for ye.'

He wouldn't let her express her gratitude. However, his carefully correct manner loosened a little, and she began to see him not just as the plain dealing merchant he was, but also the schoolboy yearning to be involved in adventure and high romance. As he spoke it became clear that to him, helping Antony was a way of satisfying that yearning.

When questioned regarding any pursuit, he grew thoughtful. Nae, he had not come upon any damned Frenchies daring to show their faces in his city. Mind, there had been a party of somewhat inquisitive Englishmen at the inn where he had dined this past day. They also had been going north, to Stockholm on government matters.

Of what like were these men? Well now, their spokesman appeared a gentleman of address, well versed in the ties between his country and Sweden. He had actually claimed kinship with the Earl of Roth, and let fall the information that his lordship's son was visiting the Swedish Court as a representative of the British Crown.

Karen's strangled cry brought him up short.

'Why, ma'am, 'tis no great matter. I dinna blather his lordship's affairs about with every comer. This man had no real knowledge of your husband's plans. Nor did he offer to show the credentials that every member of our band must carry.' From the fob at his waist he detached a small flat locket of gold, opening it to display a wax seal imprinted with the mark of the intaglio ring, the head of a man.

Karen looked down at the ring she wore on her thumb. A perfect match. The fine ruby was carved with the head of Perseus, one of a pair once owned by the great Lorenzo de Medici, a noted connoisseur of such artworks.

She said slowly, 'Apart from Lord Liverpool and myself, very few people know that Antony has left England. His plans were betrayed by his enemies, and these "Englishmen" you speak of are the French assassins set on his trail.' Desperation shook her voice. 'They are only a few hours behind.'

He said pityingly, 'I am nae sae green that I cannot see the nose on my face. My grandson left for the place of meeting not an hour after I returned from my dinner. Your husband will be warned in time to take precautions.'

The stresses of the past few days had begun to catch up with

Karen. Without warning her head started to swim, and she felt herself falling forward in the chair.

MacGregor sprang to her assistance, calling for his wife and servants. Patting Karen's hand, he assured her Antony knew very well how to take care of himself. She should not be overly concerned. He was skilled at disguising himself and sinking into the background. And so on and on, all the way upstairs to her freshly prepared bedchamber. She must enjoy a good night's rest and then they would make further plans.

Tucked up in bed with a hot bottle at her toes, she found she couldn't sleep. She felt peculiar, at once tense and yet curiously deflated. After all her struggles, and with the end of the difficult journey in sight, suddenly the danger had ceased to be immediate. A sense of anti-climax hung over her. Now that it was no longer imperative for her to reach Antony, she'd fallen into a strange mood. In a startling reversal, she actually found it difficult to believe in plots and betrayals and important secret political meetings.

She realised she was deathly tired. Too much had happened to her in little more than a year, and she was suffering from overload. Just when she'd managed to conform to her life in Regency London there'd been the revelation of her previous existence as Jenny. That had taken some adjustment. Then she and Antony had fallen in love all over again and begun to restructure their relationship. There'd been the trauma of weighing all her lives in the balance, and through necessity and desire, choosing the present, along with the guilt and pain of that choice. And finally, when she'd thought it was safe to relax, without warning, that precious new life had been thrown into jeopardy, and Antony gone without even time to say goodbye.

Hard on this abrupt severance came Amanda and her fearful revelations of danger. Karen, herself, under attack from her bitterest enemy, had barely escaped being killed; then immediately she'd thrown all her energies into the race for her husband's life, battling to contain her fears and stay alert for emergencies.

Now it had all finished. The race was over, and she'd been dropped into this icy limbo, without purpose or direction. All her efforts seemed futile.

The present and the immediate past started slipping away to the back of her mind, replaced by other, long buried memories. She let them come, welcoming them – people and places from another existence – Adele and Billie and Theo – the gallery, her little flat in St John's Wood. Brash and busy modern London itself. It shook her to find how real they were to her. The people and events of the past fourteen months had faded to a distant memory.

Trying to focus on someone like Amanda, a close and dear friend, she saw her through a haze. Familiar features blurred and slipped away before she could grasp them. Even Antony's image seemed to have retreated, to a tiny figure at the wrong end of a telescope, beloved, but so far off.

Frightened, she sat up in bed, deliberately allowing the down-filled coverlet to slip away, exposing her to the cold. This was the reality, this chilly room filled with strange shadow shapes – a round porcelain stove squatting in the corner like a crouched bear, the icily gleaming floor reflecting back moonlight from a world of snow outside the window. She wondered if her brain had been affected by the cold. She'd come all this way with a mission to perform, and until she held Antony safely in her arms, she had not finished her job.

She began to make plans. Should she stay here with the MacGregors until she had further word, or go on? Might she cause further problems by going on and perhaps arriving at an inopportune moment? Antony might wish to abandon the meeting, or persuade the others to move to a safer venue. She must keep in mind the importance of the meeting. Russia and Sweden *had* to combine against Napoleon. It would be Bernadotte's experience in military strategy that would persuade Alexander to fall back before the French invaders next summer, thus luring them to their destruction. Had she impressed this on Antony? Certainly he understood the importance of a Swedish–Russian alliance to help Britain, but was he aware of its absolute necessity to keep the course of history true?

She couldn't bear to contemplate her more personal worry. Knowing Antony, he might decide to see his illustrious co-conspirators off to safety and wait to deal with the Frenchmen himself. Being aware of danger didn't make him safe. What should she do for the best?

Strained and exhausted, she finally fell asleep on the decision to continue her journey and see Antony herself. She wakened to a world still in darkness and a commotion going on downstairs. Voices were raised and she heard a woman scream. The moon had set. She put on her borrowed dressing gown and felt her way through the pitch black to the door. A lamp burned on a table in the corridor. She picked it up and hurried to the head of the stairs.

Below, most of the family seemed to be gathered in the hall, their attention on a giant of a man whose clothes dripped melting snow on the polished floor. He hadn't even waited to take off his coat in the vestibule – an essential airlock between the heated rooms and the bitter temperatures beyond the front door. Then she saw that MacGregor had his arms about his wife, and distress showed in every face.

'What's happened?' But she knew. Disaster clogged the air, dragging at her lungs, making her breathing laboured as if she'd been running. With a trembling hand, she put down the lamp and descended the stairs, placing each foot as carefully as a woman in the last months of pregnancy.

The dripping stranger looked up at her and said something in Swedish. MacGregor passed his weeping wife into the arms of her son and turned to Karen. His face was impassive, but she had the impression that he struggled for composure.

'My grandson has been found in an alley, dead. His body bears the scars of torture upon it. We must assume he has told his attackers the place of your husband's rendezvous . . . before he succumbed.'

Karen found that her voice wouldn't work. She fought to speak, anything to break the dreadful silence following MacGregor's announcement. All she could think was, they will stop at nothing. They've murdered a young boy, after putting him through hideous suffering. What might they do to Antony? MacGregor's face made her want to cry. She wanted to say something to this grieving family, but only banal and useless phrases occurred to her.

He looked away from her and spoke to the man who had brought the news. They exchanged a few sentences, the man's eyes moving to Karen and studying her. Finally he gave a nod.

'This man is named Erik Rike. He will take you to your husband. Pray God you will be in time.'

As the weak sun rose over Gothenburg's rooftops the Scotsman stood on his snow-covered doorstep and watched her leave. The little sled moved swiftly over the packed snow, although nothing could have been fast enough to suit her mood of quivering apprehension. For the first time in months she found herself longing for the convenience and speed of the internal combustion engine. The days were so short in these latitudes. At least it had stopped snowing, although the sky remained a sullen grey-white, like dirty washing. It would be possible to make good time.

Once out of the city, scattered wooden huts and farmlets did little to change the monotony of the countryside. Occasional high stone ridges broke the skyline and sometimes there were deep and narrow valleys, scarred with frozen streams. Karen looked in vain for villages. The country folk seemed to like to live in isolation. Even the mansions of the very rich seldom had more than one farm attached.

Overnight stops in very basic inns were best not recalled. At least she'd been warm enough sleeping in beds fashioned like deep chests; and she'd no doubt grow accustomed to salt herring, in time. But these small things had no importance, and were eclipsed by her desperate haste. A hollow feeling inside her warned that she was losing the race. For all their speed and the clement weather, they couldn't beat the light.

Each afternoon as the sun began to decline she started to fret. All too soon they reached the final post house for the day, and she faced long hours of inactivity, chafed almost to bleeding point by her helplessness. She knew she had no hope of persuading her sled-driver to continue into the night – but she'd have braved its dangers if she could. Erik did speak a little English, although it seemed he'd rather not speak at all if he could help it. She tried only the once to cajole, then bribe him into breaking the immutable rule of daylight travel, and had been shamed by his contemptuous refusal. Just the set of his massive head and shoulders said as clearly as possible that she was an ignorant woman, out of her milieu and her depth.

At least the weather still held. Grey skies had changed to a pale rinsed-out blue, bare of cloud; and the air was so clear, almost brittle to the touch. Every tiny detail of trees and rocks stood out with the clarity of a pen and ink drawing. Even preoccupied with her anxieties, Karen could not help being aware. Her artist's eye noted and appreciated the pristine beauty of her surroundings, and comforted her a little.

On the morning of the third day the weather changed. Under a dark and lowering sky, heavy with its burden of unshed snow, they set off for the next staging post. Where before the icy air had turned ears and nose-tips red and blue then white, now there was a heaviness, almost a warmth, as big, lazy, feathery snowflakes came swirling down. The little horses did their best, floundering along while the snow fell thicker and faster and drifts grew deeper; but by early afternoon they were struggling and almost spent.

Through the opaque curtain before her eyes Karen strained to see the roof of the staging post. She knew they had to reach shelter soon. In a world blanketed in silence, the sensory deprivation was amazing, she thought, emerging from under the mound of skins at Erik's relieved shout. He pointed ahead with his whip, and urged the horses on until an almost buried fencepost appeared, marking their refuge. He climbed down from his seat and disappeared into the falling curtain of flakes, but soon came back again. He stood beside the sled, thigh deep in snow, a yeti or Big Foot, even to the ice-crusted beard and a voice that sounded more like a growl than human speech.

'No further. Horses cannot.'

'How far have we to go, Erik?'

He shrugged. 'Not far. But horses cannot.'

Karen looked about, desperately. Apart from the wooden building in front of them there was nothing, absolutely nothing to be seen. They might have been in the frozen wastes of the Arctic tundra. The world had turned totally white and featureless, except for the treacherous caress of falling snowflakes on her upturned face.

'The French – they'll be stopped, also. Or, maybe not. Maybe they are already there, ahead of the snowfall.' She spoke more to herself, trying to work something out.

Erik's grunting voice interrupted. 'Tired horses in stable. Perhaps Frenchmen here. I go to look.'

'No! They mustn't see us.'

Gently he detached her clinging hands and turned away. 'You stay. I go to look.'

The waiting time stretched until she knew Erik, her only lifeline to Antony, was lying dead in the staging hut. The French had been suspicious and they'd killed him. When he loomed up out of the snow she could have hugged his huge frame.

'Are they there?'

He nodded. 'They wait. Fire is good. They drink brandy, wait for snow to stop. We go.'

This relatively long speech didn't comfort her much.

'But how? You said yourself that the horses couldn't go on.'

He made no answer. Instead he climbed into the sled and started digging under the covers along its length. He seemed to be unearthing two great lengths of paling, about fourteen feet long and a few inches wide. Only now did she realise that they had not been a part of the sled sticking out like shafts on either side of the horses. Erik dropped the timbers onto the snow. Then he picked up something she did recognise, a pair of ski stocks.

In a kind of appalled wonder she said, 'If those things are skis, I couldn't possibly use them!' She thought of her long skirts, the gigantic length of the skis – and the fact that she'd never been on a pair in her life.

Erik looked at her stolidly. 'I wear. I carry you on my back. See, here.' He held up what looked like a huge satchel.

Karen realised she was meant to step into this and crouch like an Indian baby. Without a word, she got up, gathering her skirts around her, and climbed in. Erik tucked her hood about her head then threaded the flaps of the satchel closed until only her nose and eyes showed. She felt his muscles strain, and the grunting breath as he wriggled the straps onto his shoulders, and she gave thanks that her borrowed body was so slight, and the Swede so heavily built.

She felt him bend, and assumed that he was fastening the skis, and then began the rhythmic rolling bump as he worked his leg muscles back and forth in the stride of the cross country skier. It must be killing labour, she thought. The weight of the skis alone would be hard. She wondered how he found his direction in the white waste around them, praying that he knew what he was doing. Her utter dependence frightened her. With so much at stake, she could do nothing but place her trust in others – an unusual situation for the independent Karen Courtney, but an increasingly common one for Caro Marchmont. It seemed as though she did nothing but face hard facts about herself and learn lessons in this new lifetime.

She tried to shift her cramped up legs, worried that they might collapse when she needed them; but complaints were the last thing on her mind. They were so close to their destination. Would the Frenchmen stay long by their comfortable fire? She doubted it. Men who followed their calling, either from a sense of patriotism or for simple gain, would find a way to press on. Maybe they believed they had plenty of time to spare. But no, the poor murdered boy would have told them the time of the meeting, and the date.

The more she considered this, the more panic rose in her. Erik's long steady strides could not satisfy her. If only she could get through the snow under her own power. If she could only use the gigantic Swedish skis. If she could just fly!

Erik stopped. With frozen hands she made a bigger gap for her face and peered out. Snow whipped across her eyes, driven by a rising wind. Almost all the light had gone.

'What is it? Why did you stop?'

Erik turned a little so that she was facing at a ninety degree angle from the way they'd come. His arm was a signpost pointing down and back. She cupped her hands like binoculars about her eyes and peered until they watered.

'I can't see . . . Yes, I can! Something dark moving down there in the snow. But it can't be the French. They had no skis . . .'

She thought Erik couldn't have heard her, but then his growling voice reached her over his shoulder. 'Not skidor – skates. River goes to Lake Hielmare, Orebro. Frenchmen use river.'

Karen drew in her breath, and choked on a mouthful of snowflakes. 'Will they . . . can they get there ahead of us?'

He made a sound deep in his chest, and suddenly it burst out as a roar. 'No! We will win!'

They must have been poised on the brink of a valley. Without warning Erik went into a crouch, dug in his stocks, and sent them crashing into an avalanche downhill. Karen knew the sensation of being trapped in a runaway elevator. The sheer breathlessness of the drop left no time for fear. All her insides seemed to rise up to the top of her chest, and the air was like a solid wall on either side of her, a tunnel of darkness tearing away into the distance as she and her steed bolted into oblivion.

They couldn't make it. It was nearly night, and there were trees and rocks. Any minute there'd be a disastrous collision, and they'd both go hurtling to their deaths. Karen hung on to the edge of her satchel and compressed her lips so that her insides couldn't escape. She waited for the inevitable crash.

It didn't come. Miraculously they began to slow as the land beneath them flowed into a gentler slope. And then, at the last possible moment, Erik's left ski hit something hidden beneath the surface of the new snow. She heard the ski snap. Her involuntary scream cut off as she felt them rise up in a crazy cartwheel into the sky. They hung there for one long moment, snowflakes whirling about them in a mad dance, then crashed back to earth.

Erik had landed on his face. Karen came down heavily on top of him, every bit of air knocked out of her. For a few seconds the wind dropped and snow sifted down like a layer of powder over her face. Quiet enveloped them.

CHAPTER 24

The room was dark and dank and smelled of disuse. Two braziers brought in to warm it made little enough impression on the cold, and added quite imaginatively to the grim aura of the place. Antony grinned to himself, picturing his companions' consternation should an occupant of one of the coffins suddenly sit up and demand to know why he was being disturbed. He admitted he'd be a trifle surprised himself.

Of course, the bell tower being used as a mortuary worked strongly in his favour. No one was likely to disturb the dead before tomorrow's service and interment. The Swedish habit of building the wooden bell tower separate from the main body of the church meant even greater privacy. In fact, the only drawback was the difficulty in heating an unlined building.

The smile left his face as he felt again that indefinable itch between the shoulder blades that usually warned of trouble. He felt uneasy. His journey to this desolate place had not been comfortable, but neither had it been dangerous. He'd taken all precautions against being followed, and he knew his companions, also, had been discreet. He had no reason to suppose that any ill-disposed person knew of their rendezvous. Yet, something was wrong.

Sentries paced the entrances to the church a few yards away, making their rounds in utter darkness. The horses and sleds were hidden in a nearby barn, leaving no indication that the church was not completely empty. Since the holy day began on Saturday evening, the conspirators had timed their arrival to coincide with the short evening service, masquerading as members of the congregation coming late. After the bells had rung and the service begun, one by one they slipped into the tower, the two princes and their equerries and, lastly, Antony himself. It had all gone smoothly. Too smoothly, perhaps. He laughed at superstition. Yet, there was that warning itch telling him the meeting should end and all of them quickly disperse into the darkness.

Crown Prince Carl Johan of Sweden looked up from studying a chart by the light of a lantern hooked to the wall. It was hooded, as were the braziers, and a false ceiling of pitch-coated canvas stretched overhead. No light could possibly escape to the opening forty feet above where the two bells hung. From his position by the door Antony studied the strong profile outlined against the shadowy wall, the mouth taut above a firm chin, the tall, narrow frame dressed severely, even to the black satin stock about his throat. He looked a forbidding figure, a man of force. Dark eyes stared back questioningly at Antony.

'I crave your pardon, sir. You addressed me?'

'No, Lord Marchmont. I was observing you. What is it that brings such a wary expression to a man well used to running into danger?'

Antony hesitated. 'I . . . am not certain. But I should be pleased if your Highnesses would bring your final deliberations to an end. We have, I believe, covered every eventuality that can be foreseen, and we are in accord?'

Prince Grigoriy Malenski Romanov, representing his most Imperial Majesty, the Tsar of all the Russias, shifted on his uncomfortable stool and scowled. His expression was echoed by his aide-de-camp, a gigantic bearded Cossack, standing close behind. Antony had know as soon as he saw him that the Russian prince would be a man conscious of his rank and dignity. Richly dressed, despite the need for anonymity, he strutted with the gait of a portly pigeon and thrust his heavy jaw out. However, he had demonstrated no mean ability as a negotiator, and this, together with his knowledge of European politics made him a worthy viceroy of the Tsar.

The man Antony always thought of as Bernadotte, the Swedish Crown Prince, raised a hand. 'I have the greatest respect for the sixth sense of a man who lives much of his life in peril. We will, I think, adjourn this meeting within ten minutes, if your Highness is in agreement?' He spoke with perfect courtesy, but his eyes were hard. His own aide, General Count Carl Lowenhjelm, stood with a hand resting lightly upon his sabre, thoughtfully watching the Cossack.

Antony drew in his breath, aware of the antagonism between Swedes and Russians, although their spokesmen had achieved unanimity in their negotiations with speed and surface amicability. The Tsar had been willing to promise Norway to his new confederate, even to send a Russian corps to help persuade the unfortunate Norwegians in the event of resistance. In return, Bernadotte relinquished all Swedish pretensions to Denmark, and both rulers mutually guaranteed each other's existing possessions. They also undertook to launch a diversion against the German coasts should Bonaparte advance upon Russia.

Bernadotte's fury at the invasion of Pomerania and the treatment of his people underlay the whole meeting. It pulsed like the heart of a volcano, not yet ready to erupt. He had willingly revealed to his new allies the weaknesses of the French Army, the bickering and jealousy between the marshals that ate away at discipline amongst the common soldiers. His reward had been a delicate hint that, should he care to divorce his wife, the Tsar would not be averse to a union with one of his own sisters.

Bernadotte would be inhuman if he were not flattered by such an offer, thought Antony. A former member of the bourgeoisie who even now ruled over a mere five thousand subjects (nominally ruled, since the king had relinquished all pretence to policy making) – a Gascon soldier who had fought his way up through the ranks – this man was now on an equal footing with the most powerful ruler in the western world, barring only Bonaparte himself. What an achievement! But shrewd as he was, he'd best have a care when supping with the half-oriental and exceedingly devious Tsar.

He watched the two princes carefully inscribe their names on three copies of the same document, the article of agreement between the two countries. Britain, too, had made offers and concessions, mainly regarding trade; she had also, pending ratification by cabinet, entered into a secret military alliance with Sweden and Russia. Hopefully, when this triple agreement became generally known, supporters would rally – the European nations who were only waiting for an opportunity to rise against Bonaparte. It would work. It had to work, or there was no hope for the world.

The Russian Prince looked up at him. 'Naturally this document will be affirmed as soon as possible by a person of status, a prince of the blood royal at the least. Your title is comparatively minor, is it not?'

Antony had had enough. For the past hour, in subtle ways, this arrogant prince had missed no opportunity to gibe at him and his country, and he'd grown heartily tired of it. This had also been a subtle thrust at Bernadotte, whose plebeian background stuck in the Russian's throat. No doubt he felt free to give rein to his prejudices, now that the alliance was a fact.

Taking his copy of the signed document, Antony placed it carefully in his coat pocket and said, 'Even a mere Viscount may represent the British Crown, when so empowered, your Highness. In this case, it happens that I also speak for the British Government, and therefore the people of my land. I am proud to say that they are given a voice in their country's deliberations, and not used merely as pawns and slaves.'

The Cossack aide sprang forward, his sword half out of its scabbard. Bernadotte's voice stopped him.

'Hold! Your Highness, please order your man to put up his weapon. We have no time to indulge in petty arguments.' He glanced at Antony. 'Lord Marchmont, your comment was uncalled for. An apology would be in order, I believe.'

Antony bowed stiffly and faced the Russian Prince. 'Sir, I withdraw my remarks.' Scarcely an apology, he knew, but as far as he was prepared to go. He turned back to Bernadotte. 'I believe we should now disperse. It is snowing heavily, and even the short distance to Orebro will be difficult enough for the horses.'

At a nod from his master, Count Lowenhjelm left the tower, his exit carefully masked by a blanket hung over the door. The Cossack stayed, a looming menace overshadowing the room. When Prince Malenski eventually stood up to leave, he attached himself like a grim shadow.

Without warning the door crashed back and the Count appeared in the opening, his face concerned.

'Your Highness, a woman has been found nearby. The guards stationed at the barn brought her in. She was on foot, struggling through the drifts, and appears to be half out of her senses. I can make nothing of her words, but she speaks in English.'

'English!' Antony stepped forward. 'I do not like this development. It would be wiser for this woman to be kept in ignorance of your identities. Will you give me leave to deal with the matter, when you have departed?'

Prince Malenski looked impatient and waved a dismissing hand.

Bernadotte said thoughtfully, 'I shall leave at once. I am giving a state dinner tonight for the members of my Diet, and as far as anyone knows I am now on my way from Stockholm. Please deal with the matter as you see fit.' He turned to the Russian. 'Prince Malenski, your escort to Vasteras awaits you.' He bowed and deferred to his guest, who snatched up his hat and hurried outside, attended by his shadow.

Antony followed, anxious to see this 'English' woman and discover how much she knew. He grew more uneasy by the minute.

As soon as the sleds had drawn away he beckoned to the two men supporting a bedraggled, snow-covered figure against the church porch.

'Bring her to the tower, where there is warmth and light. Then return to your posts. And keep a sharp lookout. She may not have been alone.' He spoke in Swedish, and the woman did not look up. It was impossible to make out any features in the dark. When the men dragged her forward she collapsed in the snow.

'Carry her,' snapped Antony, leading the way.

In the eerie atmosphere of the tower, flanked by coffins, Antony and the woman faced each other. She had slumped down on a camp stool, against the wall. Her wet hair straggled from beneath her hood, and in the relative warmth from the braziers her clothes had begun to drip.

Antony reached forward and pulled back her hood.

Blue eyes glazed with enormous fatigue looked up at him from a face so pinched it was almost bloodless.

'Caro!' For a moment he stood frozen, off balance, his arm still raised. Then the moment passed and he had swept her up into his arms, dripping cloak and all. 'Caro, my darling. My dearest girl. How come you here?'

Her chilled mouth was unresponsive to his kiss, but he felt the movement of her throat muscles as she tried to speak. Swiftly he deposited her back on the stool and dug in his coat pocket for his flask, holding it to her lips while he supported her. She swallowed a little brandy and choked. Recapping the flask, he brought a brazier closer, removing her wet gloves to chafe her hands, and watching anxiously as the blue shade about her mouth gradually faded.

When he saw awareness in her eyes, he felt the tension go out of him. 'Allow me to remove your cloak, my love. Now, tell me what has induced you to undertake such a journey.' He knew it had to be bad news. Nothing else could have brought her such a distance under such circumstances.

'Erik!' she croaked.

'What of this Erik?'

'Mr MacGregor's man. Out there in the snow, injured.' She struggled to her feet, swaying.

He sprang forward to hold her. 'Rest there, my love. I will send out a search party.'

'No! We must leave this place.' She grasped his coat lapels and pulled feebly. 'You were betrayed. The French are coming to kill you, and the others.' She looked about her as if wondering where the others had got to.

Antony felt her words hit him like a blow to the chest. Betrayal. Who? And why?

Karen's voice rose frantically, when he failed to respond. 'They're only minutes away, if that. Don't you understand?'

'Wait. Let me think.' With an effort he controlled his instinctive reaction, to run, to take Caro to safety. He thought about the two princes, speeding away in widely different directions. By now they should certainly be beyond range of an attack. The French would have to divide their forces and give chase – an uncertain and risky procedure. Perhaps they believed the meeting still to be in session. If so, he could lure them into a trap.

'Caro, did they know the exact time that we would hold our secret conclave?'

'I . . . yes, I believe so. They captured Mr MacGregor's grandson and made him tell. Then they killed him.'

Antony stifled a groan. The poor young lad; and what a desperate blow to MacGregor. ''Tis possible that he gave them a false time. My illustrious co-conspirators have already gone, the alliance signed and in their pockets.'

'Thank heaven for that. We must go, too.' She tried to drag him towards the door, but clearly her legs were no longer capable of holding her. If he hadn't supported her, she'd have fallen.

'Caro . . .'

The bombs, thrown simultaneously, crashed through the church roof and exploded, one beneath the loft above the door, the other before the altar. Everything blew apart into little pieces, shot out into space, and fell back again in a storm of dark hail. Bits of scorched timber flew like blades, shearing away branches in the nearby forest. Glass shards embedded themselves in the trunks. The acrid smell of gunpowder hung in the air. Trees around the churchyard were flattened by the blast, and inches of frost scoured away to expose the iron hard ground. Church and belltower had disappeared. When the lethal hail stopped, there was nothing but rubble and silence – dead silence.

Snow fell softly on the wreckage. It began to hiss and steam, a sibilant prelude to the sound of flames taking hold somewhere deep within the pile.

Men came out of the night like wolves and looked upon the destruction. They waited, and when nothing moved, they melted away back into the night, as silently as they had come.

Behind them the fire spread slowly, but inexorably, through the rubble towards the ruins of the tower.

CHAPTER 25

20 December, Thursday

Tom stood at the door of Valerie's apartment and pressed the bell. For the past hour he'd been preoccupied with the problem he faced – how to set his patient on the new path opening before her. He had no doubt she was capable of change. She had the strength and intelligence, but perhaps she hadn't the will. Her lifetime attitude of 'me first' had to be turned around before she could even look at the possibilities opening up.

He wanted to help her. She needed support and guidance, and there didn't seem to be anyone else but him offering. Yet he wanted to bow out. He found Valerie's temperament too abrasive, and her basic attitudes completely foreign; the line between therapist and patient had been erased and he was becoming entangled against his will. Damn Phil! If he'd only stayed in America. If Valerie had been just another patient. If, if, if . . .

A full minute had passed, so he pressed the bell again, juggling the bottle of claret and a single spray of Thai orchids – gorgeous matt-white blooms with throats that matched the wine. Valerie's personality seemed to call for something more exotic than roses.

Valerie opened the door. Tom gasped, and just stopped himself stepping backwards, the bottle slipping in his fingers.

'Hello, Tom. I'm sorry you had to wait. I was fixing you a cocktail.' Her smile dazzled him. He'd never seen her in full battle array, with her face superbly made up, hair like lacquered gold, and a gown that did astonishing things for her figure. Warning bells and signals would have been superfluous.

She stepped aside and he edged gingerly past. In the pastel peach livingroom he looked about him with dislike at the spongy chairs coming up out of the rug like an abundance of fungus. He'd begun to feel thoroughly uncomfortable.

'I'm sorry I'm late.' He presented her with the wine and orchids and added slyly, 'I hadn't realised we were dressing for dinner.' If she says, 'what, this old thing?' I'll probably burst out laughing, he thought.

He should have credited her with a little more finesse. 'Thank you for the gifts. The spray is beautiful. I'm pleased you noticed my dress. It's one of my favourites.' She pirouetted, making the folds of flame-coloured sheer fly about a good pair of legs. Her smile had a small edge of malice. 'I wore it to honour my guest.'

Tom blinked. For one fraction of a second he'd thought he'd seen . . . No. He had Valerie's witchwoman on the brain.

She gestured towards the drinks trolley where a jug of iced martinis waited beside chilled glasses. Tom obediently trotted over and picked up the jug. He hated martinis, but resolved not to say so. Valerie was up to something, and until he was sure of her motives, he wasn't about to give away points. Modesty had never been his strongest attribute, but surely she wasn't planning a seduction. Once the usual patient–therapist fixation had been dissolved, there'd been nothing loverlike in her attitude during their past weeks together – no warning at all that tonight he might have walked into a perfumed trap.

'Will you excuse me for a few minutes, Tom? I'll put these in water and check things in the kitchen.' Valerie cradled the orchids against her cheek for a second, then left the room.

The electric logs glowed pleasantly in the fireplace; polished brass fire-irons, unnecessary, but decorative, shone in the glow of a Chinese porcelain lamp. Tom sank back in cushioned comfort and sighed. Wouldn't Phil just love to see him in this situation? How he'd roar.

Thinking of this morning's episode made him sad. Phil's attitude had been a shock – childish, really, with overtones of 'If you won't let me play, I'll take my bat and go home'. He wondered whether he could have handled things better, been less abrupt in announcing the end of the past life sessions. Phil had looked really upset. Perhaps he should try again to phone him.

He'd almost managed to struggle out of the chair when Valerie came back and sat down close beside him. She raised her glass in a silent toast, and he did the same. They both drank, Tom repressing a shudder as the gin hit his tastebuds and curled them like salted snails.

She leaned gracefully back against the curve of the seat. 'I thought we'd leave our discussion until after dinner, if that's okay with you?'

Tom smiled. 'Well, I had hoped to make it a fairly short evening.

I've been visiting a friend in hospital each night this week, and starting work early. You can probably see the results in my haggard face.'

She leaned forward and stared at him with disconcerting intensity. 'You poor thing. I can see you've been overdoing it. And I've been so demanding, haven't I? Of course you must see your friend. I'll serve dinner at once.' Her eyes had darkened and had a hooded look. Her smile seemed to be painted on, a disguise for a very different expression.

Thoroughly uncomfortable, Tom put down his glass and heaved himself out of the chair. 'I'd like to make a phone call, if you don't mind.' He wanted to get away for a few minutes. He had to reassess the situation and his own sudden wariness. Valerie wasn't bent on seduction, and there was nothing humorous about the atmosphere she'd managed to create.

'Make your call later, Tom. You wouldn't want the meal to spoil, would you? Let me freshen your drink?'

He watched as she crossed to the drink trolley, following her movements carefully. What on earth was he watching for, he asked himself? Did he suspect her of trying to poison him, for God's sake? Was the great ruby she wore on her left hand a Borgia ring? Disgusted with himself, Tom deliberately sank back into the lounge. When the fresh glass was handed to him he took a large gulp. Valerie's smile looked completely normal.

'Finish your drink while I pour the soup. I hope you're partial to French onion?' Nothing could have been more normal than her tone of voice.

'It's my favourite.' Tom was determined to be pleased. Valerie had gone to some trouble on his behalf; the least he could do was put a stopper on a too-vivid imagination for the evening.

As he raised his glass to drain it, the doorbell rang. It kept on ringing, persistently.

When Valerie failed to appear, he called, 'Shall I answer it?'

'Let it go. I'm not at home to anyone else this evening.' Maybe the distance and closed door to the kitchen had muffled her voice, giving it that strained sound.

The bell kept on ringing, drilling into his brain. Tom hesitated. Finally his need to respond got him out of the chair. He went to the door and opened it.

'Phil!'

'Hi, pal. You're looking a mite chewed 'round the edges. Isn't it a bit early to be hung over?'

Phil's grinning face had never looked so good to Tom. 'What are you doing here? I thought you'd be at home packing your bags.'

Phil looked shamefaced. 'As it happens, I came to apologise to you and Valerie for my unprofessional behaviour this morning – my unfriendly behaviour, as well. Once I'd calmed down I realised what a louse I'd been. I'm really sorry.'

'Nonsense! There's nothing to apologise for. We all got a bit excited, and your disappointment was perfectly natural.' Tom closed the door and drew him into the living room.

Valerie emerged from the kitchen, her face tightly unwelcoming. But Tom ignored that. 'Look who's here. Do we have a martini to spare for a penitent therapist who wants to rejoin our circle?'

Valerie filled another glass and silently handed it to Phil, who accepted it and the rather rigid smile that went with it, then sank into the nearest lounge chair. He took a long swallow and sighed.

'Sit down folks, and listen to my little dissertation. It won't take long.' He looked at Tom. 'You know, I've been thinking along the lines of your involvement with Valerie, and while I know you reject this, I want you to hear what I've got to say. I think you're both in a very dangerous position.'

Valerie moved to the edge of her seat, her attention fixed on Phil. Tom rolled his eyes to heaven.

Phil grunted, as if to say just what I expected. 'Look here. Are you going to give me my five minutes or are you going to sit there like a stuffed monkey with your ears blocked up, and that thing you call a mind tuned right out? Don't I deserve a fair hearing?'

'Okay, okay, I'm listening.'

'Let's go back to Valerie's first life as a supposed witch or wise woman, where you were the prosecuting priest. I know it was only in a dream that you took on the role, but look how it fitted in. You really feared her powers. You reacted like a superstition-ridden man of those times. Let's say that you *were* Valerie's opponent in that lifetime.

'Next, the life where she deliberately killed a man, and found she couldn't live with the knowledge. He was someone she hated and feared, just as in the previous existence. He was her opponent. If we analyse every life sequence she's been through where she came to an untimely end herself – and note that there are many more of these than there are uneventful lifetimes – in every case she's been battling an opponent who either brings about her death, or is killed by Valerie, prior to her own suicide. It's a pattern that we've all recognised.

'Now, you haven't exactly said so, but I think you are ready to admit that these experiences are genuine, that Valerie really has lived them before. Tom, if this is so, then you also have to admit to a belief in the immortality of the soul. If Valerie has reincarnated all these times, so have you, and I, and every other person now existing on this planet. It's commonly held that we return in mortal guise in the company of other souls close to us, perhaps in different roles, but still in near relationships. Together, we work out our patterns, sometimes quickly, sometimes gradually, over a number of lifetimes; but always and inevitably we are forced to deal with them.

'Valerie has been avoiding dealing with a major problem, and so, I think, have you. I believe you two are karmically linked in a very strong pattern. I think you are Valerie's opponent. If you don't both break the pattern here and now, it will be repeated and you'll destroy each other once again.'

The silence in the room seemed to echo Phil's words, resonating long after he'd finished speaking. Valerie's quick drawn-in breath cut across it like a shout. Tom had stiffened, but he held Phil's gaze for a time before looking away, down at his own tightly clasped hands. He knew sincerity when he heard it. It was pointless to mock a man's honest reading of a situation. He no longer wanted to.

'No comments?' Phil watched him closely.

'What is there to say? Obviously you believe in this karmic link-up . . .'

'So do I.' Valerie, too, stared at him, her eyes so wide that he could see the whites all around the iris. 'I've felt the strongest pull between us, right from the beginning. And yet, I wondered whether I really liked you.' There was hostility in her tone, its edge blurred with fear. She'd drawn herself back in the chair, away from Tom. He could practically see the aura of rejection she put out.

He turned to Phil. 'There's no way to prove or disprove your theory, except by waiting to see if violence flares between Valerie and me.' His lips twisted, but he couldn't have said whether he derided himself or his friend.

'You're wrong. There is a way. I could regress you.'

Tom felt the jolt from heel to crown. For a crazy moment he

thought his spine had actually telescoped into half its length. 'You're not serious.'

Phil looked at him.

Tom licked his lips. 'How do you know you can do it?'

'I won't know until I try. Will you co-operate?'

It was then that Tom really astonished himself. 'Yes,' he said.

'You will remember everything you see, everything that happens to you. You will have total recall. You are now descending the steps, one by one. You are counting each step down from twenty . . . nineteen . . . eighteen . . . seventeen . . .'

Tom could hear Phil's voice counting, but only distantly. He felt the steps beneath his feet. They were solid, real. He knew he was about to enter another place, but already he had forgotten where he'd come from. He was in a limbo, an inbetween world, moving slowy downward.

He became intensely aware of himself in a new way. Nerve endings prickled and tightened, his ears sang on a high sweet note. A peculiar upsurge of energy from his toes and fingertips through to the crown of his head left him feeling lighter than a cloud, yet in some way more real and dense – a million atoms whizzing about their appointed paths to create the body pattern that was Tom Levy – but with a further dimension. He knew who he was, yet he also knew he was more. He took another step down.

'What is this place? So hot. Can't breathe. Must get out.' He was lying on his back, pinned down. He let out a muffled cry. 'Damn! My leg! The cursed thing must be broken. Now there's the devil to pay.'

Dust filled his throat and lungs, and every time he coughed something tore in his chest. He strained his eyes, but couldn't see anything.

'What is this place? So hot. Can't breathe. Must get out.' Antony let out a muffled cry. 'Damn! My leg! The cursed thing must be broken. Now there's the devil to pay.' He clenched his teeth and twisted experimentally to one side, then lay back, sick and sweating. He couldn't think what had happened. He couldn't remember. With a dreadful feeling of having taken a step into space, he realised that he didn't know who he was.

Out of the darkness a hand came into his, a soft small hand, and with it a voice he knew and loved. 'Antony, are you all right?'

He jerked half upright, unable to suppress a groan.

'What's wrong? Are you hurt? Antony, tell me, for the love of God!' The hand travelled frantically up his arm to his face, pausing at his neck pulse.

Antony? He strangled the cough and tried to breathe shallowly so that he could speak. 'Caro? Is it really you? The blank space in his mind took on shadowy shape. He knew Caro. In a moment he'd remember his own name. 'There is something lying across my legs. I cannot move, my love. Can you come to me?'

He heard her rustling movements and felt a warm body nestling beside him. Her lips were gritty against his cheek. A great wave of protective love flowed over him, reaching out to his unseen companion.

'What happened, Caro?'

'I don't know. I think it must have been a bomb.'

A bomb! Now he remembered! The appalling, head-splitting sound of air under tremendous pressure, the explosion of gases vaporising, the concussion in his head. He suddenly knew where he was and who he was – Antony Marchmont, heir to the Earldom of Roth, representative of the British Crown on a mission of the utmost urgency – and husband to Caroline. And they were both buried in the ruins of a church tower somewhere close to the middle of Sweden, almost certainly victims of a plot by Napoleonic supporters.

Bernadotte! The Tsar's kinsman. Both safe. The last missing fragments had returned, along with a feeling of tremendous relief.

'Thank God you are alive.' He felt a teardrop on his face and said in sudden alarm, 'You are unhurt?'

'Not a scratch,' she assured him shakily. 'I'm covered in dust and my boots are gone, but that's all. Antony, can you try to shift whatever is trapping you if I help?'

Before answering he felt about him, around and above, his hands pausing briefly overhead. 'It would not be advisable. Listen.' In the silence he heard again the ominous creaking of settling rubble, and a sifting, slithering sound, too, like a thousand tiny feet running.

'What is it? Rats?'

'Grit and minute particles. The wreckage is shifting under its own weight. We must not disturb it.' He drew her close with one arm in a futile attempt at protection. 'It must have been a large bomb, perhaps more than one. Your Frenchmen were close indeed. 'Tis God's mercy they were just too late to trap Bernadotte and the Russian.' He felt her quiver.

'But not too late to trap you. Antony, we must try and dig our way out. You're hurt, I know it. You need help.'

He shook his head, then realised that she couldn't see him. 'Caro, the obstruction across my legs is the beam that carries the bells. I have felt the shape of a bell above me. If we disturb it, it may drop and crush us completely. We should wait. The explosion will have been heard for miles. Help will come.'

She seemed to relax and fit herself more comfortably beside him. Relieved, he distracted her further with questions.

'Tell me how you found me. Who was the betrayer?'

'I'm so sorry to be the one to tell you, but it was Charles.'

'Charles.' He breathed the name, incredulously.

Her hand gripped his more tightly. 'I've given this a lot of thought lately, and I believe that poor Charles was not in his right mind when he agreed to do it. You know how upset he's been over Amanda. I don't think we realised how desperate he felt when she told him she was marrying someone else. He had some idea that if he could only get his hands on a lot of money she'd agree to marry him – a mad idea, but I think he was a little mad. He'd reached his lowest point when Sybilla approached him, whispering her poisonous suggestions, telling him he could make enough money to have his Amanda, and that you would merely be imprisoned for a time. He never meant you to be killed, you know.'

The pain that had stabbed him when she said Charles' name receded a little. He still found it hard to believe such a thing of his friend, but Caro would not lie. Of course, anything was possible with Sybilla.

He hardened his voice against the pain. 'How did you learn of his perfidy?'

'Sybilla came to the Manor to gloat, and to kill me. She had gone completely over the edge. I could see that.'

'Has she recovered her senses?'

'She's dead. I killed her.' Her words were hardy enough, but he felt her shiver through the length of his own body. 'I can't talk about it. It was so horrible, Antony.' She began to shake uncontrollably.

He crushed her to him, kissing her tear-wet face, whispering comforting words. Finally, when her sobs ceased, he said, 'Regrets are useless. Sybilla was doomed from the cradle, and I think we all had realised that, even her parents. If I had only understood how dangerous she was, you might have been spared the horror of her death. You might have lived a full life as Jenny. We might never have come to this pass.' He forced down his anger. Caro didn't need to be reminded of all she had suffered through Sybilla. 'But that Charles should turn against me! I find it inconceivable that he would reveal my affairs to her in the first place. Yet she must have known, long before he became vulnerable through his disappointment. Otherwise, how could she have plotted her approach to a man who ostensibly disliked her? Was it all false play acting?'

'He hated her. You may believe that. And he was always your friend. At the end, he couldn't go through with it. Only, his distress over the loss of Amanda blinded him; just as her own love blinded her intuition in his case. She picked up on the danger, but failed to recognise its true source. Antony, did you keep any details of your work in that secret compartment at the head of your bed?'

His hold on her tightened. 'Is there nothing hidden from you, my witch? Yes, often I left papers and plans, and other valuables in that place. Are you saying that Sybilla knew of it?'

'I'm afraid so. She showed it to me, trying to upset me with tales of Jenny.'

'Then that explains her knowledge.' He sighed. 'What a nest of conspirators in my own household. It would seem females are devilish hard to deceive.'

'Sybilla has paid heavily for her treachery, my dear.'

'Indeed. What of Charles? You say he regretted his part at the end.'

'When he heard that Sybilla had plotted your death, he seemed to wake up and really understand what he'd done. He was appalled. She taunted him, letting him know she'd arranged for the French to follow you and kill whatever important person you planned to meet. He said he'd go after you and warn you – and she shot him.' She shuddered again. 'Then she turned on me.'

'My poor Caro. You have suffered so much, my brave girl. And poor confused Charles. Will he live, do you think?'

'I don't know. Lord Edward is seeing to his care. So much depends on the will to survive, doesn't it?'

They lay quiet for a time, resting in each other's arms, each feeling the reassuring heartbeat of the other.

Later, he asked about her journey. She described it briefly, ending with her concern for Erik, lying injured in the snow.

'How could I have forgotten? He will die of exposure if we don't get help.'

'Hush. There is nothing we can do at present. Tell me what occurred after the accident.'

'Why, nothing. I waited until I'd got my breath back, then set off on foot.'

'You walked through the snow?'

'It seemed like miles, and I dreaded I might be going in circles. But it wasn't so far. Erik very nearly made it the whole way.'

Antony pictured her struggling through the drifts, lost, alone, and probably desperately afraid of so many things, from wolves to French assassins, but never giving up. She'd almost died of exposure and exhaustion, yet she had finished the long journey magnificently. What man could have done more?

His voice was soft with love. 'Caro. I have tried to demonstrate all that you mean to me. You will always be my life's joy. But now I revere you. Your little body has the heart of an Alexander, a Boadicea. You are magnificent.'

The rubble shifted, and the bell above his head clanged and fell a few inches. Dust spattered his face. He tried to thrust Karen away, but she clung to him. He peered up into the darkness and waited, but nothing happened. His pulse slowed, then quickened again.

'Caro, I have changed my mind. I should like you to try and make your way out of this wreckage and go for help. It may be that people are already on their way. Even one of the sentries might have survived the blast.'

'No. I can't leave you here, trapped.'

'You will not help me by remaining. You could do more good by – '

'No. My movements might bring down the bell on top of you. Oh, my dear, I know that you're thinking of my safety, but I will not leave you alone. If you die, I die with you.'

'Caro, I could never allow you to forfeit your life so needlessly.'

'You have no choice, my dear.' She chuckled, and wormed her way even closer. 'At least we are warm underneath all this wood.'

Despair coloured his voice as he gathered all his strength of will to use against her. 'Caro. You are warm because the wreckage is afire. I have heard the flames for some time without realising what they were. Listen.'

She listened to the crackle and snap of wood exploding. A vision of searing heat and pain filled her mind. He could feel her dread, almost taste the metallic bite of it.

'Fire! Antony, we've got to get out!' She crouched down at his feet and began tugging uselessly at the beam pinning them.

Tormented by his helplessness and fearful for her, he said harshly, 'Leave it. Get out, Caro, now!'

She ignored him. He heard her grunt and strain. Something moved overhead, and the bell muttered. Orange and red light flickered in amongst the fallen timbers. Firelight.

'Caro!' It was a cry of desperation. He felt her turn and knew she'd seen the flicker, too. The rubble overhead shifted again. More dust fell.

He heard her begin to sob. 'I can't move it. I can't move it.'

'Will you go? I do not want you here.' Painfully he struggled into a half-sitting position, thrusting her away from his feet, driving her off with hands and words.

She avoided both, ducking beneath his arms to attack the beam with more vigour. Smoke had drifted into their small space and he could clearly hear the crackle of burning wood. He realised there was a soft red glow about Caro. He could see her outline.

With a loud crack, the beam across his ankles shifted and gave way. Karen was thrown backwards, her started cry cut off, as she disappeared into the blackness.

'Caro! Caro!'

She heard him, but she couldn't answer. Her mouth was full of dust and her head spinning from hitting the ground with force. Something seemed to be holding her down. She felt numb from her waist to her feet. When she opened her eyes she could see the fireglow, still some distance away, but growing brighter.

As her head cleared she realised that she herself had been trapped. She could move only her upper body and arms. The rest of her was pinned down in some way. Antony's frantic voice came to her more loudly and urgently, and she cleared her throat and answered, 'I'm here. I'm all right. Just give me a minute to pick myself up.'

She knew he would have come to her if he could, which meant his legs must be badly hurt. She didn't want him trying to drag himself to her through the rubble, damaging himself further.

She called as steadily as she could, 'Don't worry, my love, and please don't move. That bell is still unsafe. I will be with you as quickly as possible.'

The terror that had driven her to such a stupendous effort of shifting the beam now hovered perilously close. Its wings fluttered at the doors of her mind, seeking entry. She knew if she gave in to it, she was totally lost. She had to think. What could she do?

Sitting up carefully, she felt the waistband of her dress rip as she pulled against whatever held her. Fearfully she ran her hands down her body – and broke into wild laughter.

'Caro, what is it?' Antony's anxiety pierced her near hysteria, bringing her back to her senses.

'It's nothing. It's only . . . I'm not trapped at all. A post has pinned down my skirts, pulling them around me tightly, like a shroud. If I tear them off I'll be free.' She began to work at the fabric, tugging at the tough weave with fingers that felt stiff and awkward. She noted with detachment that they were torn and bleeding in several places.

While she worked, she came to a decision. Antony must get out of this trap, whatever else happened. He was too important to so many people – Chloe, Lord Edward, his own countrymen – and she knew she couldn't watch him die and stay sane herself. If there was any chance at all, he must take it. And if he couldn't be got out, then she'd stay, too. Life, on any terms, would be quite unbearable without him.

The word 'sacrifice' didn't cross her mind. There had been so many barren years without love. Now she'd had the best; and while life remained in her she'd fight for that love. Perhaps she would have to carry on alone in other lifetimes. There were no guarantees. She had no choice but to take the risk. Death was a doorway to the future, and she'd step through it gladly to wait for Antony on the other side. The promise would be redeemed, the karmic cycle would eventually bring them together again. The energy of love would survive the destruction of the body, and go on to its many appointed rendezvous in endless time.

Her skirt ripped and gave way, leaving her free, if in tatters. She crawled and scrambled across the jagged pieces of timber, back to Antony.

He was on his elbows, straining to drag himself forward. She went down on her knees beside him, as a voice overhead bellowed, 'Hola! English lady, you are there?'

'Down here,' shouted Antony. 'Go carefully, or you will crush us. And for the love of God, make haste.' He dragged Karen up into his arms and held her there, fiercely.

Her voice cracked. 'Erik! It's Erik! He's all right.'

'Certainly he has a thick Swedish accent. I believe it is your friend. Now pay attention, Caro, and do not argue with me. When he reaches us you will allow him to lift you out to safety. Then he can return to help me.'

She shook her head, knowing he could see her clearly in the glow of the approaching fire. Sweat ran down her back, and she felt slippery in his hold.

'I come, Englishman,' roared Erik. The wreckage shifted violently almost above their heads.

Karen took her husband's face between her hands and looked deeply into his eyes. 'I've already said I will not leave you. I don't want to go on living without you.'

'Do you think I could watch *you* die – again? A man cannot exist when his heart has been split in two for the second time. No one should be asked to bear such agony. I beg you, my dearest – '

'Antony, don't let us waste these moments arguing. Just remember that if we are parted now, it will not be forever. To the universe our lives are just a blink in time, and tomorrow, or the day after, we'll be together again.'

She saw the anguish in his face, and heard it in his voice. 'If I could but believe it! But I fear that you delude yourself, and me. How can I bear to risk what we have now for a future that might not exist?' He gripped her fiercely, hurting her. They both gasped for breath as smoke curled around their faces and was drawn into their lungs.

The voice of the fire had risen to a dull roar, filling the space where they lay – a savage reminder of what was to come.

'We may not have the choice, my love. I'm sorry that you still haven't accepted this truth, but I believe, and I can look on death more easily than I did.' Tears began to flow down her cheeks, but her eyes held his, bright and steady. 'Kiss me, Antony. It may be for the last time in this life.'

As he kissed her deeply, she shut her mind to all else, twining her arms desperately around him as if she could somehow imprint the feel of him there forever.

'My lady sweet. Remember those words when I come to you again. If this is farewell . . .'

With thunderous force, a pile of timber exploded into a million sparks, leaving a sulphurous, gaping hole in the rubble. The fire came rushing through. A forked dragon's tongue of flame licked out and brushed Karen's foot. She screamed.

As Antony thrust her across his body, Erik's great hands appeared in an opening overhead. He wrenched at the wreckage. The bell swung. With the strength of terror, Karen twisted aside, dragging Antony with her. The bell crashed down where his face had been seconds before, giving one last iron knell as it cut deep into the earth, dragging Karen's foot with it.

She didn't faint. After that one moment of agony, she felt nothing. Antony lay half on top of her. She watched as Erik took a grip under his armpits and started to drag him upwards through the gap. His head lolled, and she saw he was almost senseless with the pain of being moved. Cold air fell on her face, and a few flakes of snow. The fire had almost reached her.

So, this was the reality, the fulfilment of Amanda's prophecy, the consummation of her life's plan. Had it been inevitable, after all? Was all her struggle a vain pitting of the small self against the grand plan of another?

It was neat, no doubt about that. Immolation as Jenny, and again as Caro. However, this time around there was a difference. She knew why it was happening. She'd put herself in this position voluntarily – or, rather, made her decision at a deep level where choice didn't exist. The truth she'd come so far to learn was too much a part of her to be ignored, even in the face of death.

Love – genuine, selfless, empathetic, the passionate touchstone of existence – was all that had ever mattered. Whatever name men gave it, love, in all its forms, powered the material world and raised it closer to the eternal planes. For it she would give all she had.

Watching Antony being drawn to safety, she silently said her goodbye.

He opened his eyes. He looked down at her and began to struggle in Erik's hold. 'Let me go to her. Do not leave her. My God . . . my God . . . Caro!'

Erik heaved mightily, and they both fell backward out of sight.

With the crash of field guns firing, the wreckage of the tower collapsed completely. The hole in the rubble had disappeared.

Valerie was on her feet, her voice a barely recognisable screech. 'You bastard! You shall not escape. That is not the way I planned it. The bitch has gone, and you shall follow her to the devil!'

'What in hell . . .?' Phil barely had time to voice his bewilderment before she'd passed him in a whirlwind of fury, brandishing the brass poker like a sword.

Tom had started up, only half aware. 'Sybilla! How can you be here? Caro said you had died.'

'You shall never say that name again,' panted Valerie, and swung the poker down on him with all the power at her command.

His upflung arm took the blow. He heard it crack as he fell. Through a haze of shock he heard Phil's voice as he struggled with the demented woman.

'No you don't. Give me that.'

A shriek, the sound of a body hitting the floor, and wild sobbing. Phil's hands gently feeling his arm, his breathless cursing. Then total, blessed silence.

CHAPTER 26

21 December, Friday

Tom's flat was cosy and firelit. Habbakuk sat on the hearth, washing himself meticulously. Tom occupied his favourite chair, slouched with his chin on his chest, as usual, his broken right arm supported in a sling. Phil had hung up his dripping raincoat in the vestibule and now he squatted by the fire, rubbing his hands. Outside the drainpipes filled and gushed over. Christmas hovered, four days away.

'You don't have to worry about Valerie. She's in a nursing home, under sedation for the present; but with the treatment program she'll be undergoing, she'll come out of it okay. I've promised to stick with her until she's fully recovered.'

'Good. Thanks for taking care of everything, Phil.' For the first time in his working life, a patient's interests came secondary to Tom's own. He simply had no space to accommodate anything other than the astounding experience of last night.

Astounding was too mild a word. Earth-shattering? No. For he didn't feel in the least shattered. He felt enlarged. The time journey had expanded his understanding to galactic proportions. He had actually experienced his own immortality.

'How does it feel, having been another man in another time? Pretty chaotic at first, I suspect . . . Tom?'

'Sorry. I guess I won't be making much sense at the moment. Can we talk later? Do you mind?'

'Hell, Tom! I went through it with you, and only heard one half of what was going on. Have a heart. At least tell me who this Sybilla woman is.'

Tom's whole arm was a nagging ache, and he was in a fever to return to the hospital, and Karen. Still, he felt he owed Phil an explanation. It must be frustrating to be the only one excluded from such an extraordinary episode.

'I've ordered a taxi, and when it comes, I go. Agreed?'
'Agreed!'
'Right. Here goes. Sybilla was a nasty piece of work who killed off my first wife in the lifetime I regressed to.'
'Which century?'
'Nineteenth. Jenny died in 1806. Sybilla was her cousin and mine. I remarried in 1809, Caroline, an enchanting archwife of the highest order . . .'
'A what?'
'Regency talk for bitch. Sybilla pushed Caro downstairs and – here's the hard part – when she died, the spirit of another woman entered her vacated body. This other woman came from the future, from our present. We had just fourteen months together, and I learned to adore her more than my life.' His voice broke. The memory of Caro's death would always tear him apart, whether or not they recognised each other and loved again. Nothing could erase such a recollection. The girl lying in a coma might die tomorrow, or she might awaken and know him. Whatever came, he could never experience greater suffering than he had in his life as Antony Marchmont.

As was the case with Valerie's episode as a witchwoman, he recalled the whole of that past experience. He'd believed Caro's tale of being from the future to be a delusion, and lost all hope of finding her again. The miracle that returned his Jenny to him as Caro could never be repeated. His last words to her, about encountering one another in some different dimension of time, were more a desperate prayer than a belief; and he'd been lost in despair for months afterward, until shown by Amanda that he was destroying two lives, his and Chloe's. For his child's sake he'd put on a semblance of normal living, but when an inflammation of the lungs finally carried him off ten years later, he'd been more than glad to go.

Phil coughed and looked distressed. He'd been in on that final scene in the ruins of the church tower, Tom remembered. He'd know what an appalling loss he, Tom, had suffered.

'You'll probably have to think about that for a while, Phil, but it will make sense, eventually. Cases of possession by a wandering spirit are not unknown. The next hurdle is the fact that Caro, my beloved wife, had lived before – as Jenny.'

'I don't believe it! I mean . . . If you say so. But, Jesus . . . Guirdham and his Cathars have nothing on you. Holy shit. What a story!'

Tom grinned wryly. 'Don't get too excited. I'll bet you anything you like no one believes it outside of you, me, Valerie . . . and Karen.'

'Karen! There's another one?'

'I told you she came from our present. Karen/Caro/Jenny, my wife, is at this moment lying in University College Hospital in a deep coma. For all I know her soul is wandering between lives, searching for me. She may even be reliving the past as another woman entirely. I don't know. What I do know is that she means everything to me, and I'll never give up on her. I'm going to her now. There's the taxi, Phil. Hang out the window and tell him I'm on my way, will you?'

Phil followed him down the stairs and helped him into the taxi, talking all the time. 'So Valerie was Sybilla, and you were her opponent in that life, also. What a build-up of karmic debt between the two of you. I suppose the stress of her immense unresolved hatred, and seeing you relive your love for your Caro, jerked her back into the past; and as Sybilla she tried to kill you.'

'What's that?' said the cabbie, sticking his head through the slide window.

'A bedtime story I'm writing for my kids,' snapped Phil, closing the door. 'I'll be on your doorstep tomorrow, Tom, and you'd better be ready to talk. Give her my love.' He grinned and waved as the taxi moved off.

Tom sat back and tried to sort out his feelings. Excitement, trepidation. He could never have described the joyful anticipation filling him to bursting point. He was going to see his Caro. Yet, he was afraid, too – terribly afraid that she might slip through his hands again. The thread holding her to the earthly plane seemed so tenuous, just a thin silver cord connecting her with the wandering soul somewhere out there in the cosmos.

How could he bring her back? He'd tried so many times, even before he knew how dear she was to him. Strange. He should have known that first night at the gallery when he felt so drawn to her, and attributed the feeling to fascination with her work. Karen, herself, had been the lodestar – Karen/Jenny, whom he'd known as Caro, his wife and love over who knew how many aeons?

Dashing through the hospital entrance he met Theo, a vision in striped lime green slacks and an ochre-coloured sweater from Gianni. Like some exotic insect, escaped from its Amazonian habitat, he looked totally out of place in the clinical atmosphere.

'Tom Levy. You look as if you've gone ten rounds with Mohammed Ali. What've you done to yourself?'

Tom glanced down at his sling. 'This? A blonde attacked me with a poker. Have you been up to see Karen?'

'I have. She's much the same. I thought I'd bring in her *Bella Donna* portrait to hang on her wall, just in case she opens her eyes – so she'll see something familiar.'

'A nice thought, Theo.' Tom looked across at the bank of lifts and felt a tightening along the muscles of his spine. So much depended on the next few minutes. All at once he wanted to back off, to keep Theo there talking, or take him out for a drink – anything to avoid going upstairs and plunging into his future.

Theo had already turned away. 'Here's my car. I'll say goodnight, and good luck with our little lady up there. You know, I have a lot of time for her. She's made of the right stuff.' Looking a bit pink about the ears, he made a dash through the rain into his chauffeured Bentley.

At least he doesn't expect his man to hold an umbrella over him, thought Tom. Some people would. He moved over to the lifts and pressed the call button.

Billie met him at the door of the dimly-lit room, her face masked by shadows, but clearly near exhaustion. She was gradually deflating, like a child's balloon left out in the weather.

'*Mon Dieu*! What has happened?'

'My arm? It's a long story, and it'll keep. But I'm assured the break will heal without trouble. You look all in. Why don't you go home to bed? I'll stay with Karen.'

He felt like a pistol on a hair trigger. It wouldn't take much to set him off. Gunpowder in the pan, ready for the touch light, that's me, he thought, surprised by the outdated analogy. Go, Billie. Go home, now.

'I shall go. But not before I tell you something of importance.' She drew in a deep breath. 'I have decided to fight Humphrey for Adele, for the sake of her mother. There will be no expense spared at the next hearing.'

Tom touched her hand in swift compassion. 'You're trying to make amends for the lost years, is that it? Billie, keep faith. We're going to win through, all of us.' He held her eyes with his, projecting a certainty that had come to him from nowhere, filling him with power. He *knew* their future was assured. There was no room left for doubt.

She startled him by rising on her toes to kiss his cheek. 'Thank you, my dear. You, yourself, are so worn. Promise me you will stay for a short time only.'

'I promise. Goodnight, Billie.' He kissed her quickly and almost pushed her out the door. He turned to Karen.

Past and present blended. His gaze blurred. The face on the pillow was a long oval, pale, the mouth wide, with a slight sad droop, the hair a frame of dark silk strands. For a split second he felt cheated. Then another face superimposed over the original – a gamine expression, small, bird-like features, brown skinned, topped with a knot of curls. Great brown eyes looked up at him, projecting the loving nature that had been Jenny.

Tom's own eyes filled with tears. His heart seemed to move within his chest. But as her image shifted and dissolved he said goodbye. He knew it was time to give her up, as he should have done long since.

It was no surprise when Caro's charming porcelain features made their appearance. The cloud of glorious red hair seemed to vibrate with a life of its own. Slumbrous blue eyes held an invitation he remembered too well. He choked on the emotion that clogged his throat, threatening to cut off his breathing. She'd been so lovely, and so loving. How could he bear to give up the memory of her? Yet he knew he had no choice. Life wasn't for looking back. It was to be lived in the here and now. All the joys and tragedies, the beauty and the ugliness, comprised an ongoing experience for the learning soul. He had recognised and finally accepted this truth. He had to move on.

'Goodbye, my darling,' he whispered, as the image that was Caro shimmered and faded, leaving the still, pale face of Karen to emerge once more.

He sat down on the bed, gazing at the woman who meant everything to him. 'Karen,' he whispered.

Her breast continued to rise and fall evenly. He knew there was no one to hear him.

The image of those last moments together in the rubble of the church tower, filled his mind. They had each made a vow, to meet somewhere, sometime in the future. Now the moment of fulfilment had come.

'Caro. I'm here, my lady sweet. I've kept my promise. Come back to me, Caro. It's Antony.'

The room waited with him. He felt the shrouded silence cutting them off from the rest of the world. In the soft glow of the night light he studied her features with an intensity he'd never given to any other matter. His whole life balanced between heaven and hell as he waited on his destiny.

Dark lashes moved and trembled. A sound like a sigh came from between parted lips. Karen opened her eyes.

A curtain of haze shifted between her and the world. She felt strangely muffled, as if swathed in layers of gauzy mist, cut off from sight and sound. Yet, surely she'd heard Antony calling her.

The mist drifted and thinned, until her straining eyes found a light, a dim glow whose source was concealed, but enough to show her the bed she lay in, and four walls – and a man's shape in silhouette beside her.

She flinched against the pillow as he moved. 'Who is it?' Her voice felt and sounded rusty. What was wrong?

'Don't you know me, darling? Look closely. See with the eyes of the soul.'

He brought his face down to hers, only inches away. She stared into features that were only vaguely familiar.

This has happened before, she thought. I have wakened in a strange room with strangers around me. I know this feeling of disorientation. Who am I? Caro. My name is Caro. For a brief instant a scene flashed into her mind, of a cramped place, dark and hot, with danger all around. Feelings flooded over her, terror mixed with elation, then a bitter-sweet sadness. Finally came peace. She closed her eyes and shivered. Tears seeped from beneath the lids and crept down her cheeks.

A hand gently brushed them away, and a voice that was both deep and tender said, 'Don't be afraid. You are loved and cherished. This is your rightful place. It will all be clear to you in time.'

She forced herself to look at him. Through her tears the outline of his features blurred. For a moment she thought she saw . . . 'Antony!'

'Yes, I'm Antony.'

'But . . .'

'I said that when we met again you would know me by these

words – 'my lady sweet'. Oh, Caro, can't you see past this face and into my heart?'

'It can't be! You're nothing like . . .'

He leaned across to the bedside table, and picked up a hand mirror. Holding it face down he said softly, 'We are no longer in the same bodies as Caro and Antony. We have moved on, my dear. Look, and you will believe me.'

She took the mirror, supported by his hand, and looked at her reflection.

Her first reaction was disbelief, and almost at once, the same deja vu feeling, of having had this experience before. Her mind felt unsteady. She wanted to put up her hands and hold it in place. She raised imploring eyes, seeking reassurance, and hesitated. Moving on . . . another time, another life . . . crossing time . . . She felt her wavering mind split into several sectors, each part running through a series of scenes like movie reels. There was no sequence, no past or present or future. They all ran simultaneously and the people portrayed were all familiar. She saw herself as Jenny and Caro and Karen, and a host of others, men and women. She saw Antony as himself – and as Tom Levy.

Recognition was instantaneous. From nowhere came a rush of feeling like a wind lifting her, carrying her up out of the fear and bewilderment into a new day. She raised a face radiant with love and held out her arms, and Tom came into them.